THE CRUCIBLE OF EMPIRE

THE CRUCIBLE OF EMPIRE

ERIC FLINT
K.D. WENTWORTH

THE CRUCIBLE OF EMPIRE

A Baen Books Original

Baen Publishing Enterprises
P.O. Box 1403
Riverdale, NY 10471
www.baen.com

ISBN: 978-1-4391-3338-5

Cover art by Bob Eggleton

First printing, March 2010

Distributed by Simon & Schuster
1230 Avenue of the Americas
New York, NY 10020

Library of Congress Cataloging-in-Publication Data

Flint, Eric.
   The crucible of empire / Eric Flint and K.D. Wentworth.
      p. cm.
   "A Baen Books original"—T.p. verso.
   ISBN 978-1-4391-3338-5 (hardcover)
  1. Human-alien encounters—Fiction. 2. Space warfare—Fiction. I. Wentworth, K. D.
II. Title.
   PS3556.L548C78 2010
   813'.54—dc22
                                                          2009050667

10   9   8   7   6   5   4   3   2   1

Pages by Joy Freeman (www.pagesbyjoy.com)
Printed in the United States of America

This book is dedicated to the memory of Jim Baen,

who started Eric's career as an author

and had faith in Kathy's career

when she most needed it.

CONTENTS

Cast of Characters   ix

The Crucible of Empire   1

Glossary   417

Appendix A: The Ekhat   421

Appendix B: Interstellar Travel   427

CAST OF CHARACTERS

Humans

Rafe (Raphael) Aguilera: Former tank commander, Third Construction Supervisor for the *Lexington*

Andrew Allport: jinau sergeant in Baker Company

Dr. Eleanor Ames: chief Jao physician (medician) on the *Lexington*

Michael Bast: doctor on the *Lexington*

John Bringmann: jinau in Baker Company

Melonie Brown: Bridge Engineering Officer on the *Lexington*

Nancy Burgeson: jinau in Baker Company

David Church: Tully's batman, half Cherokee, from Oklahoma

Scott Cupp: jinau in Baker Company, private

Kristal Dalgetty: jinau in Baker Company, pilot

Charles Duquette: Lead-Pilot on the *Lexington*

Debra Fligor: jinau in Baker Company, sergeant

Dennis Greer: jinau in Baker Company, corporal

Thomas Kelly: jinau in Baker Company, corporal

Dr. Jonathan Kinsey: Professor of History, specialist on the Jao

Caitlin Alana Stockwell Kralik: daughter of the President of the Jao's native government of North America, a member of Aille's service, Ed's wife

Ed Kralik: Jinau commander of Earth forces, Major General, Caitlin's husband

Samuel Lim: jinau in Baker Company

Caewithe Miller: Lieutenant from Atlanta, jinau in Baker Company

Wallace Murphy: jinau in Baker Company
Willa Sawyer: head of Human Resistance in Rocky Mountains camp
Benjamin Wilson Stockwell: President of North America,
     Caitlin's father
Gabe (Gabriel) Tully: former Resistance fighter, now a member
     of Aille's service, ranking as a major, and commander
     of Baker Company, a jinau unit
Rob Wiley: Former U.S. Army lieutenant and military
     commander of the North American Resistance, now an
     officer in the jinau
Gary Young: jinau in Baker Company

Lleix

Alln: Eldest of Ekhatlore
Branko: Eldest of Weaponsmakers
Finat: older unassigned male of the *dochaya*
Grijo: Eldest of all and leader of the Han, also Eldest of the
     Dwellingconstructors
Hadata: Starwarders pilot
Hakt: Eldest of Shipservicers
Jihan: originally of the Starsifters, founds Jaolore
Kajin: youth released from Ekhatlore to help with Jaolore
Kash: Starsifters, senior to Jihan
Lim: unassigned female of the *dochaya*
Lliant: Ekhatlore
Mahnt: Eldest of the Childtenders
Pyr: formerly unassigned youth accepted by Jaolore
Sayr: Eldest of the Starsifters
Segga: Starwarder

Jao

Aille krinnu ava Terra: Jao governor of Terra (was Aille krinnu
     ava Pluthrak)
Amnst krinnu ava Krant: current Krant kochanau
Braltan krinnu ava Krant: young male terniary-tech on his first
     voyage

Breen: Subcommandant who, two thousand years ago, refused the Lleix's offers to help the Jao free themselves from the Ekhat

Brel krinnu ava Terra: Subcommander equal in rank to Rob Wiley

Chul krinnu ava Monat: terniary-adjunct who was in charge of the submersibles refit two years ago, expert in adapting Earth tech to work with Jao

Dannet krinnu ava Terra: Captain of the *Lexington*, born of Narvo

Kaln krinnu ava Krant: Senior-Tech on her destroyed ship

Jalta krinnu ava Krant: pool-sib to Mallu, ranked Terniary-Commander on the destroyed ship

Mallu krinnu ava Krant: Krant-Captain, pool-sib to Jalta

Mant krinnu ava Terra: jinau in Baker Company

Naddo krinnu ava Krant: Krant crew member

Nam krinnu ava Terra: jinau in Baker company

Nath krinnu ava Terra: Floor-Supervisor of the Pascagoula Refit Facility, Aille's first-mate, mother to his son and daughter

Otta krinnu ava Terra: Pleniary-Commander, second in command of the *Lexington*, born of Nimmat

Sten krinnu ava Terra: navigator on the *Lexington*, formerly of Binnat

Urta krinnu ava Krant: Krant crewmember

Wrot krinnu ava Terra: formerly retired veteran of the Conquest, born of Hemm, now an elder in Terra's new Jao taif

Yaut krinnu ava Terra: Aille's fraghta, born of Jithra, an elder in Terra Taif

PART I:
Terra

CHAPTER
1

Gabe Tully was on detached duty in the Rocky Mountains Resistance camps when his Jao-issued com buzzed in his shirt pocket. A breeze rustled through the coin-shaped aspen leaves overhead as he silenced it quickly, hoping no one working nearby had heard. Even though Earth's Resistance was cooperating with the Jao invaders to fight the Ekhat—for now—many of his former comrades still resented him for apparently "selling out" by taking service under the Jao governor, Aille krinnu ava Pluthrak.

That hadn't exactly been his choice in the beginning, but there was no way to explain the situation to men and women who had never been exposed to Jao culture. They didn't understand that joining a Jao's service was more like taking an oath in a brotherhood. His loyalty was to this one particular Jao who didn't seem as bad as most.

And, of course, he wasn't going to point out to these rugged freedom fighters that, for all intents and purposes, they were enrolled in Earth's new human taif whether they liked it or not. The way he saw it, membership was a plus, guaranteeing them rights the Jao had previously denied, but until his Resistance brethren had seen the things Tully had seen and fought the battles he'd fought, there was no way they were going to understand.

Tully understood the old ways were forever altered. There was no going back. Mankind was living in a much more dangerous universe than any of them had ever credited. After the video record

had come in from China two years ago—the smoking remnants
of towns, forests blasted into cinders and mountains into slag—it
was clear exactly what the Ekhat intended to do to Earth. If this
alliance with the Jao could protect their world from another such
attack, it deserved their allegiance, however grudging.

In order to talk privately, he slipped away from the hodgepodge
of ramshackle cabins and tents that sheltered a good portion of
what was left of America's free fighting force, then settled under-
neath a stone ledge. Bright morning light streamed in from the
east. He braced his back against the sun-warmed rock and keyed
the com's channel open. "Tully."

"Tully, Ed Kralik here."

Tully scowled. There had never been any love lost between the
two of them, for all that they'd watched each other's back during that "unpleasantness" two years ago when the Ekhat attacked
Earth. And of course, Kralik, as head of the Jao's jinau troops,
outranked him, always a sore point. "Yeah, I'm kinda busy."

"Aille wants you in Pascagoula on the double."

"I'm in the middle of negotiations with Willa Sawyer," Tully
said, watching an eagle soar above the pass. "Can't this wait a few
more days? If I hot-foot it back to Mississippi now, I'll have to
start all over when I return, and these folks are not crazy about
the whole idea of working with us in the first place."

"This is big," Kralik's deep voice said. He hesitated. "Real big, to
judge by all the excitement it's stirred up. The Jao are scurrying about
like ants who've had their hill kicked apart. Aille understands how
important your work is, and he still wants you back on base—now."

Wind shifted through a stand of pines higher up on the mountainside, filling the air with their cool pungence. With fall just
around the corner, change was in the air. The seasons turned
early at this elevation and the steep pass up into the mountains
would probably be snowed in before he could return, isolating
the settlement for the winter.

Tully sighed, then massaged the bridge of his nose. Goddammit.
Four weeks of talks shot all to hell, just when that old she-badger
Sawyer seemed on the brink of saying yes. But there was no
wiggle room with the Jao. If one who outranked you said "jump,"
you didn't even get to ask "how far?" You just closed your eyes
and leaped. They would tell you where you landed later—if and
when it suited them.

He stared at the plastic com as though this were all its fault, then ran fingers through his wind-blown blond hair. "It's not the Ekhat, is it?" he asked with a stab of dread.

"Not allowed to say," Kralik said. "In fact, Aille hasn't even told me yet, but there's plenty of speculation around here. Everyone agrees that something big is brewing. Just pack up and head out. I'm sending a small courier ship to pick you up down by that old airport in Aspen."

"You mean what's *left* of Aspen," Tully said. Most of the former millionaires' playground was now in ruins, abandoned by its former owners and then plundered by the desperate Resistance. "It'll take me a whole day to get down into the valley on horseback unless I can persuade Sawyer to waste some of her precious gas to send me in a truck." He shook his head. "And even then what's left of those roads will shake your teeth out if you drive too fast."

"Sooner would be better," Kralik said. "Make the best time you can. Your ride will be waiting."

Yaut poked his head into Aille's office and the younger Jao, current governor of Earth, looked up from the flimsies he was studying. Aille's golden-brown nap was still damp from a morning swim as his ears settled into *polite-inquiry*.

"Tully is on his way," Yaut said. His fraghta's ugly face was creased in thought. He had that classic bullnecked solidity that his birth-kochan, Jithra, prided itself upon breeding. His *vai camiti*, or facial striping pattern, was pure Jithra, strong and unabashed. "He is the last."

"But in some ways, the most important," Aille said. He shoved the flimsies aside and stretched to work the kinks out of his back. "Surprising, I know, but true."

"You always understood that one better than I did," Yaut said grudgingly. He sank onto a soft pile of traditional *dehabia* blankets along the wall. The room was suitably dim as Jao eyes preferred, mimicking the less brash stars of their homeworlds, both very far away.

"I just felt from the first moment I came across him that he had a quality I wished to understand, and that understanding it would lead me to comprehend something important about his entire species," Aille said. "I am not certain, even now, that it could be put into Jao words. It is so uniquely—human."

"He was certainly difficult to train," Yaut said, "but in the end exceeded my expectations." He stared moodily into the air, his angles signifying *contemplation* in the no-nonsense Jithra body-style. "You should order him to stay out of those mountains, though. Lately, he's been increasingly obsessed with negotiating with the Resistance, even though his efforts in that direction are obviously hopeless. Those of their number who can see reason, already have, like Rob Wiley. I doubt that the rest of them will ever accept the inevitable and willingly make themselves of use under your rule. They will just have to die out."

Aille considered, his ears pitched forward in *careful-thought*. "I think you misjudge the situation, which admittedly is full of variables. As for Tully, he possesses a great deal of fierce energy, too much to be down here, drilling his new unit all the time. Before he fell into our hands, he was always on the move, infiltrating the next military base or unit. He never stayed in one place very long."

"A human would say—'he can't sit still for two seconds,'" Yaut put in.

Aille's ears signaled a sketchy *amusement*. He was classically trained in postures, of course, like all highly ranked Jao, but he and Yaut were old companions who had no reason to impress one another with the elegance of their movements. "That energy is directed now, put to work in our favor. What he has been doing is critical, though we can no longer spare him. After this situation is resolved, though, I intend to use him to recruit members of the Resistance to staff several official positions in our new human taif so that the group edges toward full association with the Terra's Jao taif."

Yaut sniffed dismissively. "Tully is one thing, but what is left of the Resistance up there will never be that civilized. We cannot afford the time to intensively train them, one by one, through *wrem-fa* as we did him. Those still skulking up in the mountains are hard-core ferals who have not been held to account by any authority since the Jao took this world. In fact, I doubt even their own government, before the Conquest, could have made use of them."

"The secret is—they are in agreement with us already," Aille said, "only they do not yet realize it."

"By the time they do," Yaut said, his whiskers bristling with *doubt*, "this reckless world will be a glowing cinder."

Memories of the Ekhat attack surged back over Aille. Two orbital periods ago, a fiery plasma ball launched by the Ekhat had broken through combined Jao-Terran forces to incinerate the southern area of China, resulting in at least three million dead, perhaps more. The human authorities of that area had never been able to make a full accounting.

Aille rose and prowled the length of the room, restless with memory. Just the thought of that spectacular failure made it difficult to sit still. And there was something else, too, waiting out there to make itself known. Faraway, but significant. Lately, he could feel the flow of the nascent situation increasing bit by bit. Something, somewhere, that concerned them all was about to come together. "We can never let the Ekhat get that close again."

Yaut's green-black eyes gazed steadily at him. "Then you will have to make everyone on this world of the fullest use, including the rebels. They will have to be driven out of their mountain strongholds and then forced to understand where their best interests lie," the old fraghta said, "and right now I do not feel that flow ever completing itself."

"Let us hope you are wrong," Aille said.

Caitlin Kralik and her husband, Lieutenant General Ed Kralik, reported to the office of the governor of Earth, as requested. Even though she was a member of Aille's personal service, Caitlin had not seen the young Jao in several months. She'd been traveling the east coast with her father, who was still the President of North America, overseeing the repair of the last of the infrastructure devastated in the original Jao conquest of Earth. Virginia in particular had been shamefully neglected, but at last that was being put to rights.

Even after two years of Aille's supervision, people were still wary, still did not want to believe that things had changed. Most did not understand this new partnership with their former rulers. She often had trouble believing how much things had changed herself. The absence of her abusive former Jao guard, the unlamented Banle, did more to reassure her than anything else.

"Once more into the breach," Ed murmured, as they paused before the shimmering green door-field of Aille's office.

"You aren't expecting trouble, are you?" she said, one hand resting on his broad shoulder. "Matters have been going so well, I even gave Tamt leave for the next month and she's gone down to the Mexican coast to swim. I don't think the poor thing has had a day off since she was born, but I can recall her if you think I'm going to need a bodyguard again."

"I don't think that will be necessary," Ed said, taking her hand in his and squeezing it. "I'm not really expecting a blow-up, but you never know with the Jao. No matter how smoothly things have gone lately, they are aliens. Their priorities will never be ours and we won't always understand where they're coming from."

"The directions taken by the new taif are interesting," she said as the door-field winked off, allowing them entrance. She could make out Aille's familiar *vai camiti* within. "They've finally selected a designation. They're calling it 'Terra,' so now everyone can apply their new surname, if they like."

"Makes sense," he said, "but I still don't see you taking part in official taif activities."

"That's because my father has a cow every time he thinks about how we were all just inducted, willing or not," she said and stepped into the cool dimness of the spacious office beyond.

"Your sire has acquired a bovine?" Aille said, rising from his desk.

"Um, no," she said. She was struck anew, every time they met, how tall this Pluthrak scion was, even for a Jao, with powerful limbs and that impressive classic Pluthrak *vai camiti* in the form of a solid black band across his eyes. As always, he carried himself like a prince.

"If it would please him, we could have one sent over," Aille said, his angles settled into *polite-inquisitiveness*, "though I was not aware that such creatures were highly prized in urban households."

Caitlin fought to keep a grin off her face, letting her body assume instead the Jao posture signifying *appreciation-of-intended-favor*. "That is very thoughtful," she said, "but 'having a cow' is just another of our expressions. It means—" She thought fast, trying to be circumspect. "It means he does not approve."

Aille flicked an ear at her, indicating his understanding. Benjamin Wilson Stockwell, her father, had lost two sons to the Jao, one killed in the original conquest and the other murdered on no more than a vicious whim by the former governor of Earth, Oppuk krinnu ava Narvo.

"Father does want to know when elections for the human government of North America can be held," she said, noting that the wily fraghta, Yaut, was curled up in a pile of *dehabia* blankets and studying her. "He's eager to step down and restore the democratic process."

"Not yet," Aille said, "though it feels that the moment will be soon."

She nodded, then sank into a visitor's chair. The famous Jao timesense had spoken and there was no arguing with that. Jao claimed they always knew when something would happen, not a form of prescience exactly, but something else even more mystifying, an inexplicable sense of time that was right far more than it was wrong. They had no need to depend on anything as primitive as a clock. She wondered if the devilish Ekhat had bred that into them, too, back when the aliens uplifted their species into sapience, along with their physical strength and indomitable wills.

"So why have you called us here?" Ed positioned himself behind her chair and rested his hands possessively on her shoulders. "I know it must be important to take us away from our current projects."

"One of our ships has discovered something intriguing in a distant nebula, one which bears the designation NGC 7293 for human astronomers," Aille said. "Its crew, or at least the survivors of the crew, have been sent here for questioning and Bond analysis of the situation."

"Survivors?" Caitlin glanced up at Ed.

"Yes," Yaut said, rising. The stolid fraghta was all *repressed-excitement* to her experienced eye. "I will notify Preceptor Ronz that you are here."

The door-field winked off as Yaut approached and then Gabe Tully entered, looking rumpled and out of sorts. His hands were shoved into his pockets, his cheeks wind-chapped, and his blond hair disarrayed. "This had better be good," he muttered. "I almost had Sawyer argued down!"

Yaut ducked out, then Rafe Aguilera followed in on Tully's heels, still limping from an old war wound, but head held high. He too had embraced the opportunities provided by the new taif and now was a superintendent in the construction of Earth's newest spaceship being built here at the Pascagoula facility.

Ed held out his hand. "Rafe! I had no idea you were coming."

The two men grasped hands. Aguilera shook his head. A few more threads of silver were apparent, but otherwise Caitlin thought he looked good. "Something big is cooking," the older man said. "I can't wait to find out."

The door-field crackled and Caitlin looked over in time to

see Yaut return with Preceptor Ronz, along with the old Jao veteran, Wrot, a tall Jao female with classic Narvo *vai camiti* facial
striping, and three unfamiliar Jao clad in maroon trousers and
harness. Though most Jao had brown nap that could vary from
gold to a reddish cast, these three were surprisingly dark with
nap that might have been called bay, if they'd been horses. Their
black *vai camiti* were almost invisible against such a deep brown
background, which she thought might be perceived as a mark of
homeliness by other Jao. A distinctive facial pattern was prized
above all other physical attributes.

To anyone trained in the subtleties of Jao body language, their
postures were blunt and unashamedly singular. The first individual
radiated *disapproval*, the second, *unease*, and the third, glaring at
all of them as though in challenge, had allowed her every line
and angle to settle into unadulterated *rage*.

The situation was difficult to understand, Mallu krinnu ava Krant
told himself, as the elderly Preceptor herded them into the room.
As though it weren't traumatic enough to lose their ship, he and
those of his crew who had survived had been dispatched all the way
across the galaxy to this backward planet. True, Krant was a small
kochan, isolated and little regarded by such luminaries as Narvo and
Pluthrak, but even a backwater like Krant deserved consideration.

The rest of his crew had been sequestered in adequate hous-
ing, but he and his top two officers, Jalta, terniary-commander,
and Kaln, senior-tech, had been summoned to this meeting. The
room, though comfortably dim, was infested with *humans*, as the
natives of this misbegotten world were called. He'd heard about
them in scattered conversations during the voyage here on a Dano
ship, troublemakers and savages by all accounts, not worth the
firepower it had taken to subdue them.

They were, he thought, even uglier in person than the ship's
vids had led him to believe, their skin mostly naked, their faces
flat, ears tiny and immobile, with not a single whisker to be seen.
Their bodies were chaotic, angles completely random.

Another human entered the now crowded room behind them,
followed by several more Jao. He heard the names "Chul," "Dannet," and "Nath," which were at least Jao, along with "Kinsey," a
slippery mouthful of sounds which had to be human.

A tall golden-napped Jao approached, his body subtly sliding from one welcoming posture to the next, then doubling signifiers without effort, the result, no doubt, of intensive tutoring by a classically trained movement master. Krant, of course, had no resources for such niceties. "I am Aille krinnu ava Terra," he said, ears pitched at a friendly angle. The free and easy presentation of his name was in keeping with his high rank. "Welcome."

"Terra?" Mallu's own ears wavered. He glanced at his fellows. They looked baffled as well. "I thought that was the name of this world. How can it also be a kochan?"

"We are officially two taifs under a single designation, one human and one Jao, named after this planet, newly established and sponsored by the Bond of Ebezon itself," Aille said. "Though we hope to achieve full kochan status one day. We are unique because our membership includes both humans and Jao."

"You allow natives taif status?" Mallu felt his angles go to *surprise*. A taif was a kochan-in-formation, which one day might take its place beside the other Jao kochan of the galaxy, an unheard-of honor for a conquered species. Beside him, Kaln and Jalta froze in mirrored *shock*.

"We 'allow' them nothing. Humans have earned the right to belong," Aille said, his body stiff with *determination-to-be-courteous*. "When you know them and their world better, you will understand. They are like no other species the Jao have ever encountered."

Kaln stiffened, her lines *disbelieving*. "We will not be here long enough to acquire such understanding," his senior-tech blurted, as though the disrespectful words simply could not be contained. She pushed fretfully at a battered ear which still would not stand, despite medical treatment.

Embarrassed by her bad manners, Mallu stared his female officer into silence. This was the *Bond*, not to mention a highly ranked individual born of fabled Pluthrak, whatever he was calling himself these days. They could not shame themselves with poor behavior here, of all places. "Do this one the courtesy of not listening," he said, trying not to breathe too deeply. His ribs ached, broken in the fierce battle that disabled their ship. "She took a blow to the head during the fight and has not fully recovered. Also, we witnessed the destruction of two Krant ships and the death of half of the crew of a third, a heavy loss our kochan can ill afford."

Aille regarded them with flickering green-black eyes. "I have heard the reports. You are fortunate to be alive."

"Encounters with the Ekhat rarely go well," Mallu said. "Just surviving can be counted an achievement."

"I thought this had nothing to do with the Ekhat," a human said, speaking in passable but accented Jao. Though its skin was hideously pink and naked, it did have a thatch of silver nap upon its skull.

"Ekhat were involved," Preceptor Ronz said, seating himself before a large table off to one side. "But our Krant comrades destroyed the Melody ship they encountered, which was exceptionally well done, by the way. Therefore, the Ekhat are not what is of importance here."

"Then what is?" the human demanded.

The creature's posture was bold, even self-assured, Mallu thought. This individual was obviously of high status among its own kind.

"There is evidence in the readings recorded by your ship's sensors of something possibly very interesting concealed in that nebula," Ronz said. His eyes studied Mallu, then Jalta and Kaln, as though weighing the worth of each. "I wish to send a ship back to investigate."

"We have no ship," Mallu said stiffly. "Ours was too badly damaged for repair and Krant will not be able to assign us another." That reality was the worst of all, that he and his subordinates would be remanded to other ships upon their return, demoted and disgraced for having lost their own craft, however valiant their victory had been.

"The Bond will provide a transport, one that will be listed as under the control of the taif of Terra." The Preceptor gazed at the three survivors, his posture an enigma. Mallu had heard the Bond were always so, completely neutral in affect so that dealing with them was inevitably off-putting. "You and the rest of your command will be assigned as part of its crew, along with selected humans and a number of Terran-based Jao."

"Humans—crewing a Jao ship?" Jalta's ears flattened with *disbelief*.

"You will study selected recordings before the ship leaves," the Preceptor said. "They document a battle against the Ekhat which took place in this system two orbital periods ago, mostly inside the star's photosphere. The ships were of human construction, the crews mixed. The results were—impressive."

Mallu fought down his unease. All Jao had to respect the Bond of Ebezon, at the very least. Unless they were a major and powerful kochan like Narvo and Pluthrak—and even they were not usually exempt—they were also required to pay heed to the Bond's wishes, in practice if not in theory. It was unfortunate that Krant scions had fallen under Bond notice, but in the end, they could do nothing but obey and attempt to render such good service that Krant would benefit.

"Very well," Mallu said, struggling to remember his long-ago lessons in deportment, scanty though they'd been. The eye of the Bond rarely fell upon those so lowly as Krant. It was an honor that one placed so high believed Krant could be of assistance. He coaxed his lines into what he hoped was a credible stance of *acceptance*. "We wish only to be of use."

"Of course," the Preceptor said.

The mood in the room shifted to anticipation.

Tully had followed most of the discussion, even though it had been conducted in Jao. His command of the language had been passable even before being drafted into Aille's personal service. It was far better now. Enforced practice, called by some "immersion," had a way of achieving that.

So the Preceptor suspected something interesting was concealed in the heart of that nebula. He shuddered to think what that might be. Some of the things that Jao found interesting could give a human nightmares.

Wrot was watching him closely from across the room. Though he didn't have much use for Jao generally, he had a grudging respect for the scarred old warrior, who years ago had retired on Earth when he could have honorably gone home to his own kochan, then had taken up active duty again as a member of Aille's service. Wrot had then resigned from Aille's service with the formation of the new Jao taif on Terra and now served as one of its elders.

"I have just the ship in mind," Preceptor Ronz was saying. "A new prototype being developed by the Bond. It is nearly ready for a voyage to fine-tune its more innovative features, what humans would call a 'shake-down cruise.'"

"And the rest of the crew?" Aille said, his ears pitched at an angle which indicated curiosity.

"I wish to send my top advisors," Ronz said, "mostly humans, but at least a few Jao. Chief among those will be Wrot, who has

proved himself not only in battle, but as an elder in Terra Taif
and in his wide understanding of human culture. The others—"
Ronz glanced around the room. "I wished of course to send
Professor Kinsey, but he is very much occupied at the moment
with important research."

Kinsey, who had to be sixty-five if he was a day and had probably been born in one of those academic jackets with the classic
suede-patch elbows, looked from Ronz to Aille.

Tully tried to imagine Kinsey out sailing the stars, traveling
the way Jao did—a form of transit that involved creating point
loci that dumped you out in the photosphere of a star. He shook
his head.

Kinsey's face crinkled unhappily. "I would go, though it would
disrupt my work."

"Your willingness is appreciated, Professor," Ronz said. "But
I have need of you here. That means Caitlin Kralik is the most
logical to go."

"No!" Ed Kralik glared at Ronz, hands gripping his wife's
shoulders.

"You can't be serious!" Professor Kinsey blurted.

Caitlin rose from her chair, her face flushed. "Hear him out,
please."

Though she was the daughter of Benjamin Stockwell, once
believed to be an infamous American collaborator with the con-
quering Jao, Tully had grown to like Caitlin. She had more nerve
than any woman he'd ever known, and that included some pretty
tough babes back in the Resistance camps. He still remembered
her amazing performance two years ago when she had testified
before the Naukra itself and helped bring into being the new
social pattern under which they all, Jao and human, now coexisted.

And, once Oppuk had been dislodged from power, the truth
about Stockwell's enforced cooperation had come out. The former
Vice President's family had been hostage to his every decision.
Caitlin had grown up a veritable in-house prisoner with a so-
called Jao "guard" dogging her every step. Neither of her brothers
had survived.

"She is the most logical choice," Ronz said. "Her command
of the Jao language is among the best on the planet, including
her sophisticated movement vocabulary, and her understanding
of Jao culture unsurpassed. In the two orbital periods since the

new taif's formation, her cultural and political advice have never once been in error."

"She's only a child," Kinsey said. His dark face had gone pale. "Her father will never agree."

"I'm twenty-five years old and a married woman," Caitlin said. "And, as much as I love him, my father has nothing to say about this."

"Don't worry, Professor," Ed said grimly. "She's damn well not going anywhere without me! I'll go too."

"It's just surveillance," Caitlin said, a hand on his arm. "A short hop there and back." She turned to the Preceptor. "No fighting, right?"

"The Ekhat ship patrolling that area was destroyed," Ronz said. "The likelihood of encountering further danger of that nature is relatively low, though I cannot promise it will not happen. But there was enough data collected by the surviving Krant ship for us to be certain that weapons had been used in that nebula which were not designed by either the Jao or the Ekhat."

"Someone else lives there, then," Caitlin said, raising an eyebrow. "Another sapient species."

Tully felt the impact of that statement ripple through the room.

Ronz gazed at each of them in turn. "This mission is classified as exploration only. It is entirely possible that the new species in question was only traveling through the area. They may not actually reside in that region."

"And you are needed here," Aille said to Kralik. "We cannot spare the commander of all of our jinau forces on Earth to accompany his mate to conduct simple surveillance."

Jao did not pair-bond emotionally in the same way as humans. Instead, they formed marriage-groups and mated only when progeny were desired. Tully knew that the Preceptor and Aille were not picking up on Kralik's very real distress. He didn't blame Kralik one bit for objecting to them dispatching his wife off to God-knows-where. Space travel was terrifying, all that fooling about inside the hellish photospheres of stars themselves, not to mention the different factions of Ekhat turning up when you least expected them, the crazy bastards. Only an idiot would want to go.

"In addition," Ronz said, "I assign Gabriel Tully."

CHAPTER
2

"Me?" To his horror, Tully's voice squeaked.

"Your expertise will likely prove invaluable," Ronz said. For a second, the old Jao's eyes glittered electric green.

"What expertise?" Tully gazed around the office, baffled. Everyone was staring at him like he should know, and there was the faintest smile on Caitlin's lips. Though he had gone on the nightmarish trip to "confer" with the Interdict faction of the Ekhat, he hadn't participated in the subsequent battle with the True Harmony in the sun. Instead, he'd been dispatched to the mountains to track down Rob Wiley, trying desperately to arrange support from that quarter.

"I refer to your negotiations with Earth's Resistance," Ronz said. Unlike the rest of the Jao present, his body was perfectly, implausibly still, in keeping with the Bond's trademark disdain of any sort of movement style. "As well as your background as a spy and current post as commander of a reconnaissance unit in the jinau. In all of these roles, you have been quite effective."

"Oh." Sweat rolled down Tully's neck and soaked into his collar. Aguilera, he could see out of the corner of his eye, in particular was enjoying this. The man's expression was sardonic and his dark eyes positively gleamed with amusement. Damnation. The two of them had never gotten along. No doubt Rafe would love to see Tully make a fool of himself in front of Jao bigwigs.

Say nothing, his inner voice cautioned him. Don't get into an argument he was sure to lose. It would only provide entertainment for all concerned. With an effort, he ducked his head and waited though his mind was whirling.

"I want to know more about the ship," one of the newcomer Jao said. He was a stubby fellow with the darkest nap Tully had ever seen. His maroon harness didn't quite fit and he kept shifting from foot to foot as though uncomfortable. "Would it not make more sense to send a model with which we are all familiar? If we encounter something unexpected, not understanding the qualities of our craft will make maneuvering more difficult."

Tully knew that Jao generally found it difficult to develop tech improvements on their own. They called innovation of any sort *ollnat*, which literally meant "the ability to make things-that-were-not," and regarded its practice as no more than the foolish occupation of the very young. Whether that Jao aversion to innovation was something genetically bred in them by the Ekhat or simply a cultural feature produced by the Jao's very conservative clan structure was not yet clear to Tully. But, either way, it was a characteristic that sharply delineated the difference between human intellect and Jao, and one of the reasons many Jao still classed humans as overly clever savages.

The Preceptor held up a tiny blue memory chip, then inserted it into Aille's reader. The image of a ship sprang into focus just above the broad oak desk, heavy and rounded, black with eight evenly spaced keels. It was hard to tell exactly how big it was, but Tully got the impression it was truly massive. Was *that* what they'd been building for the last year in the vast, cordoned off area outside the refit facility? He'd glimpsed the rounded shape above the barriers and wondered from time to time what all the fuss over that particular ship was about.

"The design has been adapted from Earth vessels originally intended to function beneath water," the Preceptor said as the roomful of Jao and humans crowded around the desk to examine the rotating 3-D representation. "It is more heavily armored than a typical Jao warship, as well as more radiation resistant. This mission will involve travel into a nebula possessing harsh radiation and thick gases. Such qualities may indeed prove useful."

The dark-colored Jao turned away. He moved with an odd abruptness that his two fellows shared, not the exquisite, carefully cultivated grace sought after by most Jao. It was his body language, Tully thought with a flash of insight. It wasn't, well,

accomplished. None of these three seemed to be continually dancing the way most Jao did. Maybe they were the Jao equivalent of
hicks, from some backwater of Jao society where such niceties
weren't followed or didn't matter.

"I will arrange for all of you to tour the new ship over the next
few solar periods," Preceptor Ronz said. "Terra-Captain Dannet,
who originally came to us from Narvo—" He gestured at a female,
standing in the back, sporting a startling Narvo *vai camiti*. "—has
been making herself of use all during the construction phase and
is highly qualified to head the new ship's first mission. Her input
has been invaluable. The rest of you should hasten to familiarize
yourselves with its features before your mission leaves."

Tully cleared his throat. His back was ramrod-straight. "And
when will that be, Preceptor?"

The Preceptor's eyes flickered again with enigmatic green fire.
"When flow has completed itself," the old Jao said as he turned
away. "You should understand that as well as anyone here by now."

Ed Kralik managed to keep a lid on his temper until he and
Caitlin were well away from Aille's office. He took her arm possessively as they clattered down the steps, then plunged outside
into the golden Mississippi fall sunshine. His chest heaved. "I
don't care—!"

"Yes, you do care," she said, putting her hand over his and
squeezing. "We all care. They wouldn't send a ship if it wasn't
important, especially not this particular ship."

"But they're hiding something," Ed said. He headed toward their
Jeep, his steps so long, he felt her hustle across the pavement
to keep up. "That devil Ronz always does this. He manipulates
everyone and never tells the whole truth!"

"But," she said, "he's always had Terra's best interests at heart."

"Jao don't have hearts!" He opened the passenger door and
gestured for her to slide in, then slammed the door. Startled
pigeons took flight a few feet away.

"Not in the same sense that we do," she called after him through
the open window, "but they do invest emotional energy in their
projects. They take pride in succeeding and in seeing us do well."

Her gray-blue eyes were thoughtful as he jerked open the
driver's door and entered on his side. He knew that look. Goddammit, she was intrigued. She *wanted* to go. "They don't care

if you die," he said, his hands clasped so hard on the steering wheel, he could feel his blood pounding, "just as long as you make yourself—and your death—of use."

"Death doesn't mean the same to them." She turned to face him and touched his cheek. "But they were right about the Ekhat, and they are most likely right that we should go and take a look at this—whatever or whoever it is. Another species! It's possible we could even make them our allies against the Ekhat. Ronz will tell us more in his own time."

"'When flow is completed,'" Ed said bitterly. "How I hate that goddammed timesense of theirs!"

"We are fumbling in the dark that way, compared to them," she said, "but I wouldn't have a Jao mind even if I could trade." She settled back against the upholstery. A car full of Jao pulled around them and drove away, headed for the beach. "They don't have imaginations, Ed. Think how dull that must be."

He hesitated, struck by that. They didn't have imaginations, *ollnat*, as they termed it, but they thought something important was out there, concealed at the heart of that nebula.

So it most likely was.

"You're going, aren't you?" He stared at his clenched hands on the steering wheel.

"And you'll stay here and do your job," she said softly. "For the first time since the conquest, humans and Jao are almost in a state of complete association. That's sacred to them. We can't blow it."

He felt like he couldn't breathe. Memories of his mother dying in an epidemic after the conquest, then father and brother slaughtered by so-called "Resistance" bandits, resurfaced. He had no one in the entire world but her. "What if you die?" he said in a strangled voice.

She touched his face again with outstretched fingers. "How about if I promise I won't?"

"Oh, *that's* comforting," he said with a rueful shake of his head, then gathered her into his embrace. She was warm and soft and smelled of blackberry-vanilla, her current favorite soap. He closed his eyes and breathed in her scent, the weight of her in his arms, trying to imprint them on his memory. There was no home for him, no comfort, no center, except where she was. His throat constricted. "I'm damn well going to hold you to it."

They remained that way, her head on his shoulder, his arms

tight around her, the Mississippi afternoon sun slanting in through the windshield and warming their faces, for a long, long time.

Mallu checked on the rest of his crew again after the unsettling meeting at the refit facility. The Krant survivors had been housed in what humans called a "barracks," which was a distressingly angular structure without flow, but had access to a common pool. Most of the injured had recovered enough to swim at this point and morale was slowly improving. Still, to the last individual, they all wanted only to go home to Krant and make themselves of use there. No one wanted to sit here on this out-of-the-way world with its skulking, flat-faced natives, brooding about their shameful failure at NGC 7293.

Then he went back to Jalta and Kaln at the somewhat better quarters to which their ranks entitled them on this sprawling installation. They had been assigned a section of blue and gold quantum crystal building, well poured, suitably dim inside and equipped with soft *dehabia* heaped along one wall, a supply of woody *tak* for scenting the room, and, best of all, a small but deep pool with its salts perfectly balanced.

Jalta was swimming with the enthusiasm of one long denied. The transport that brought them to this world had been equipped with a pool, but the three of them had rarely used it, intimidated by the presence of so many born of higher ranked Dano. Kaln, still dripping, eyes wildly green, crouched at the pool's edge, evidently just emerged from the water.

Mallu eased onto a pile of gray patterned *dehabia*. His injured ribs protested with a stab of white-hot pain as he twisted to unbuckle his harness and he braced them with one hand. The memory of that battle in the nebula assaulted him again, the frantic maneuvering, the terrible energy beams crackling over his ship as circuit after circuit fried so that even when the enemy Ekhat vessel imploded, it was all they could do to limp back to the nearest Jao base with half his crew dead and most of the rest injured. They had survived, but at such a cost!

"So we will return," he said, not meeting his officers' eyes.

"Evidently," Jalta said. He ducked beneath the roiling water and swam more vigorously as though he could wash the memory away.

Kaln's angles went to unmitigated *distress*. One of her ears had been damaged and now dangled at a permanent angle. She was sensitive about the disfigurement and had not seemed her formerly sensible self since the battle. "What is the point?" she said, her eyes flickering angrily. "Unless they do not believe us."

"I think they most definitely do believe us." With a metallic clink of the buckles, Mallu deposited his harness to one side on the gold quantum crystal floor. He would have to requisition some polish. The straps were looking positively shabby. "Else why would they want us to go back?"

"There may be more Ekhat waiting," Kaln said. She shook herself and drops of water flew through the air.

"Perhaps," Mallu said. "But even if we do come under fire again, it is still an opportunity for Krant to make itself of use to the Bond." He stared into her dark face, seeing the faint outline of her *vai camiti*, which was quite attractive, once you took the trouble to make it out. "Think of it—no one else was there, seeing what we saw, doing what we did. Not Narvo, or Binnat, not even great Pluthrak itself. Though we are small and little regarded, still it was Krant who sacrificed ships and crews, killed the confounded Ekhat, and then brought back whatever information the Preceptor sees in that data."

"Krant who lost all its ships and most of its personnel!" Kaln said with a furious flip of her single able ear.

Jalta's dark head popped out of the water. His whiskers bristled. "But what in the name of all the seas does the Preceptor see? I have examined the readings repeatedly and can find nothing more than a few unfamiliar weapon signatures. If there was another participant in that fight, they did not make themselves apparent to us—and we were there!"

"When the flow is right, Preceptor Ronz will tell us." Mallu stared moodily into the roiling water. They would go back and face their failure, even if cost their lives. That was the nature of *vithrik*, making oneself of highest use, and perhaps in the end they could at least improve Krant's ranking among the kochan.

He slipped into the pool and dove to the bottom, letting the cool liquid support him. Gradually, the ache in his ribs eased. Really, the mix of salts was quite good. One might almost think oneself landed on an altogether civilized world.

As prearranged, Wrot krinnu ava Terra met with the Preceptor down by the shore in the early-dark—early evening, as a human would have termed it. Waves lapped at the beach and starlight played across the restless water. A few white gulls landed on the sand a short distance away and watched them dispassionately with gleaming black eyes.

"So…" Preceptor Ronz was gazing at the waves as they rolled in. The tide was rising, each wave surging just a bit higher on the sand than its predecessor. "How goes the new taif? Your perspective must be far more telling than mine."

That was because Wrot had been among the first to apply for membership in the unique mixed human-Jao organization and was now an official elder. Wrot scratched his ears. "Two steps forward, one back," he said in English. His stance was *rueful-acknowledgement*. "Humans are the most astonishingly quarrelsome creatures. Many of them would argue even if you said they were always right."

"If they were not so divisive, we would never have conquered them in the first place," Ronz said. "They have been as much their own enemy as ever the Ekhat will be."

"But their minds—" Wrot shook his head, a useful scrap of human body language he had adopted long ago. "They are endlessly inventive, never at a loss for ideas, even about the most inconsequential of matters. Our new association house in Portland is simply amazing with a unique synthesis of Jao and human comforts and styles. You will have to visit it, once events are more settled."

"Yes, 'events,' as you put it." The Preceptor sighed. His ears, normally exquisitely noncommittal after the fashion of the Bond, slipped into faint *wariness*. "I called you out here where we can be utterly alone to tell you what I would not say before the others."

Wrot waited as flow brought them both to the moment of revelation. The nearby gulls screeched, then flapped away. Something out in the water jumped, scattering the starlit spray.

"I believe the data recordings from the battle indicate life on one of the worlds concealed inside the nebula," Ronz said. "Sapient life, most likely a civilization we have long thought extinct."

"Many species have been exterminated by the Ekhat," Wrot said. "They wish to be alone in the universe with their own perfection."

"And quite a number of those died at the hands of the Jao under their direction, before we freed ourselves from their bondage."

"That is a great tragedy," Wrot said, "but it was not our desire

that caused their deaths, no more than a discharged laser wishes
to kill its victim."

Ronz hesitated as the waves rolled in and in. The wind gusted,
carrying the acrid scent of seaweed and rotting fish. "I think the
signs point to the Lleix."

Wrot's mind whirled. Everyone down to the youngest Jao
crecheling knew that name. It was the stuff of legend. The Lleix
had been a powerful force in the history of the Jao. "*Them?* Are
you sure?"

"Of course not." Ronz shrugged out of his black trousers and
harness, dropping them to the sand, and stood, feet apart, letting the sea breeze buffet his scarred old body. "Why else would
the Bond fund this expedition? Idle curiosity is the province of
humans, not the Bond."

"But there is not the slightest possibility the Lleix would accept
our advances," Wrot said. "They would in fact most likely do all
in their power to destroy us. Our arrival would only sow panic
because they undoubtedly would believe that we've come to complete their extermination."

"That is why, even though you will have *oudh*, the crew should
contain a high percentage of humans," Ronz said. "Especially
ones skilled at negotiating under difficult conditions, like Caitlin
Kralik and Gabe Tully."

"You set us an impossible task." The soothing hiss and roll of
the waves was seductive. Wrot unbuckled his harness and dropped
it on the sand, itching for a swim. "Even if the humans successfully approach them first, they will learn of our close association."

"We owe the Lleix a great deal," Ronz said. "They saw the
potential for freedom in us, when we could not see it for ourselves. The Ekhat made certain that innovation was not part of our
nature. If not for the Lleix, the Jao would never have conceived
of fighting free of the Ekhat."

"At what point will we tell the rest of the crew your suspicions?" Wrot said.

"When you have reached the nebula, thoroughly evaluated the
data coming in, and they are suspicions no more."

Secrets to keep, then. Wrot was good at that and the Preceptor
knew it. Between them, the two had kept many secrets for a long
time and worked at hidden purposes for the betterment of both
Jao and humans. Now they would do it yet again.

As one, they waded into the cool dark waves, then dove into this world's wonderful wild water. Though Wrot had swum Earth's seas many times, he always found the foreign salts exotic, teasing at the senses, hinting at new discoveries yet to come.

The bay's current carried them out and they swam far into the night.

Goddamn high-handed Jao! Tully sat on a peeling vinyl-covered stool at the Foul Play, a retro bar decked out with stainless steel tables and godawful aqua chairs just outside the Pascagoula base. He stared moodily into his amber glass of locally brewed beer— execrable stuff, but effective. Any time he got to thinking maybe the Jao weren't so bad, or maybe at least *some* of them weren't, they turned around and bit him on the behind—figuratively, at least.

The bar was crowded mostly with humans, but a few Jao were scattered throughout the dimly lit room. All around him, glasses clinked. Men and women laughed. Voices beside him murmured just on the edge of comprehension. Behind the bar, popcorn was popping, and some noxious new song, more screech than melody, was playing on the jukebox. He could see his reflection in the mirror behind the bar, red-eyed and haggard from lack of sleep, and it just pissed him off even more. "What are you looking at?" he muttered to the image.

"Thought I'd find you here," a voice said from behind, then Ed Kralik, still in his blue jinau uniform, slid onto the seat next to him.

Kralik's cool assurance never failed to irritate Tully. "I didn't think your wife let you out these days without a leash." Tully scowled and traced the glass's cool rim with a finger.

"Feeling sorry for yourself?" Kralik signaled the bartender, a former jinau who still wore his regimental service insignia on his sleeve, for a beer of his own.

"I don't see your name on that freaking crew roster," Tully said, in no mood for Kralik's usual air of superiority. So what if Kralik's rank was lieutenant general and he commanded thousands of jinau troops? That didn't make him one whit better than the lowliest Resistance fighter as far as Tully was concerned.

"I wish to God it was," Kralik said, as the glass was set before him. His face was drawn, his gray eyes bleak. "I'd trade with you in a heartbeat."

Tully took a long pull of beer and let it trickle down his throat. The frosty bite was soothing. "Well, as you heard this afternoon, they don't want you—they goddamn want me." The slightest hint of satisfaction at that thought seeped through him. Someone actually thought Gabriel Dorran Tully, Resistance camp brat and former spy, would be better at something than the highly regarded commander of the jinau.

"I want you to watch Caitlin's back," Kralik said, his gaze trained on Tully's face.

"Like I wouldn't unless you asked?" Tully drained the rest of his beer and set the glass back with a rap. "That's flattering as all hell."

"She's reckless sometimes," Kralik said, drumming his fingers on the gleaming black bar. His gray eyes seemed almost colorless in the dim light. "She always thinks she understands the Jao better than anyone and that gets her in trouble."

"No one understands the Jao," Tully said. "If I've learned nothing else in the last two years, I've learned that. I'm not even sure they really understand each other, and all that fancy dancing around they do just obscures things. From what I've seen, it's entirely possible for their words to say one thing and their bodies something else."

Mercifully, the song ended, but then someone dropped more change into the jukebox. Green and yellow lights flashed as the blasted machine lurched into another popular caterwaul. Tully winced. He was a blues man, himself. Some of the world's best blues musicians lived up in the Resistance camps he'd once called home.

Even though they were sitting beside each other, Kralik had to raise his voice to make himself heard. "This mission will be a minefield." His gaze followed the bartender as he moved up and down the counter. "You've got representatives from the Bond, a Narvo ship captain, members of Aille's service, Resistance fighters, and humans from half the nations on Earth, not to mention Jao from different kochan spread across the galaxy, all locked up in one big tin can."

"And whatever's out there waiting in that nebula," Tully said sourly. "Let's not forget that."

"Aren't you the least bit curious what's got Ronz so worked up? I mean, think about it. This is the Bond. They think in such long-range terms, they don't get excited about anything that takes less than twenty years to play out."

Now that Kralik mentioned it, there was just the slightest buzz of curiosity in the back of Tully's mind, a hint of interest despite his glumness at being forced to abandon his crucial Resistance negotiations for what seemed on the surface little more than a whim. Something intriguing waited out there in the heart of that nebula and they had a damn big ship in which to go look at it. If this whatever-it-was looked back at them even halfway cross-eyed, they'd just blast the hell out of it and go home.

Of course, the Ekhat had damn big ships too, the practical part of his brain pointed out, and they were barking crazy to boot.

Kralik was staring at him expectantly. Tully sighed. "Of course, I'll keep an eye on Caitlin. Though, as I recall, she's always been more than able to take care of herself."

"That she has," Kralik said, raising his beer. "Here's to self-sufficiency."

"And big freaking guns." Tully raised his own glass and they both chugged, never taking their eyes off one another.

CHAPTER
3

Mallu rousted Jalta and Kaln out of their shared quarters at first-light. The two wanted to go down and explore the tantalizing native sea, glittering gray-green in the distance, but flow felt very insistent that it was time to inspect the new ship. Since it was an unfamiliar design, learning its strengths and weaknesses was of paramount importance if the Krants were to find a way to make themselves of any real use. They donned their worn harness, boots, and trousers, all the traditional maroon of their kochan, and headed out.

Kaln in the fore, as befit her lower rank, they walked across the sprawling base, past bizarre angular buildings that chopped up space into ugly squares and rectangles with no flow. Rain had fallen earlier and the temperature was pleasantly cool, though annoying native species of insects buzzed back and forth. Vehicles passed them, some mag-lev, but others on strange black wheels, bumping along and reeking of scorched hydrocarbons.

The sun was overbright so that they were soon all squinting against its fierceness. It would have been pleasant to swim again in untamed water, Mallu thought, as they trudged across the damp pavement. His eyes kept straying to the everpresent sea.

This inspection was pointless anyway. However splendid, this craft was not their ship and never would be. He and his crew would only be along for some inscrutable purpose of the Pre-ceptor's, not true members of the ship's company. They probably would have been better off going to the ocean instead.

"We should have summoned a transport," Kaln said finally. Despite her recent erratic behavior, she had always been a consummate tech. Her able ear swiveled as another of the odd vehicles swerved around them. "I would have liked to see how the local technology works."

"We have been shipboard for a long time, and soon we will be in space again," Mallu said, though his ribs ached just a bit more with every step. A ship captain never admitted to weakness before subordinates. "I would rather get some exercise."

An immense building loomed in the distance, the one where the meeting with the Preceptor had taken place on the previous day. They had not explored its cavernous interior at the time, but now Mallu could make out actinic flashes inside as though small bolts of lightning were striking. Screeches and the clang of metal striking metal filled the air, and it was much bigger than he remembered, since they walked and walked and it seemed to grow very little closer.

Finally, a wheeled cart with three empty seats rolled out of the building, drove across the remaining stretch of pavement, and finally stopped beside them. A well-made female with exotic russet nap and a lovely *vai camiti* regarded them with *merry-anticipation*. "Captain Mallu krinnu ava Krant?" she said.

Mallu's angles dropped into a rough approximation of *acknowledgment*, not one of his best stances, but a ship's captain had far more important things to worry about than the subtleties of his postures.

"*Vaim*," she said, indicating *we see each other*, thereby declaring herself their equal in rank, a brash move. "I am Nath krinnu ava Terra." Mallu was stunned at her lack of manners, blithely forcing her name upon them. Either living on this forsaken planet had sapped her civility, or she'd come of a low kochan that taught its progeny no better.

Her eyes flickered. She knew exactly the effect she was having, Mallu thought crossly. The reckless presentation of her name was clearly intended to provoke. They were only Krant, after all. Why bother with courtesies to such?

"I am Floor-Supervisor here at the Refit Facility." She gestured at the empty seats. "I have come to take you to tour the Bond's prototype ship."

"Krinnu ava Terra?" Kaln said. Her good ear flattened in

distaste. She massaged the damaged one distractedly. "Then you have joined the new taif?"

"I have that honor," she said as the three climbed in and wedged themselves into the inadequate seats.

"But it admits humans as well," Kaln said from one of the back seats. "I fail to understand how you—manage—such an arrangement? You do not actually—?" She broke off, her ear pitched forward in *unease.*

Nath glanced over her shoulder as she turned the vehicle back around and drove toward the building. "Mate? By the Beginning, what a strange notion!" The element of *merriness* in all her angles increased as she abandoned *anticipation* altogether.

"Then are there no marriage-groups?" Mallu asked, bracing his ribs as they careened over the bumpy pavement.

"Not containing humans!" Nath slowed as a particularly large hole wrung a grunt from Jalta in the back to his obvious chagrin. His pool-sib's body bruises were still particularly painful. Mallu clung to a support and endeavored to suffer in silence with his own healing injuries.

"Actually," she said, "we are two separate taifs, one human and one Jao. And the natives have peculiar ideas about mating. Half of them seem ready to engage in it at almost any moment with very little preparation or ritual, but only in pairs, rarely larger groups. The other half flee in the opposite direction if you do so much as make a polite inquiry about their practices."

"It does not matter how the new taifs handle such things," Mallu said, *sternness* pervading all his lines, though the effort wrung a deep stab of pain from his ribs. The discussion made him uncomfortable. The three of them had never been called back to the kochan to join a marriage-group, and after losing their ship, it was highly unlikely that they would ever be so honored.

"It matters if we are going to be shut up shipboard with them," Kaln said. Her lines looked stubborn, off-center, even *angry.* Mallu was going to have discipline her again at the first opportunity. She was not well. Perhaps, despite the Bond's plans, she should just be remanded back to Krant where her actions could not further shame them before strangers. He would endeavor to have an interview with the Preceptor at the earliest opportunity and suggest that.

"I see," Jalta said, though Mallu was quite sure his pool-sib did not. "Those assigned to this ship will not be mating on the voyage, will they?"

"They are mostly private about such matters, though not nearly as reticent as we Jao," Nath said, stopping just under the immense building's roof, then turning off the cart's engine. She slid out of the seat and looked around, as though expecting someone. The squeal of saws cutting metal assaulted Mallu's ears. "Sometimes, their *entertainment* media portrays the act, or at least, I have been told, a simulation, but I have never actually seen it performed in public."

"'*En-ter-tain-ment*?'" Jalta emerged from the cart, head cocked in *puzzlement*. "That is a Terran term, is it not?"

"It is a native form of *ollnat*, things-that-are-not," Nath said. "There is quite a lot of that here, some of it productive, but most a waste of time by our standards. Governor Narvo actually forbid it among the jinau personnel and on military installations like this one, though the troops often did not obey. Since the change in *oudh*, the present governor has found ways to use this trait to our advantage. You will find that humans set great value upon such activities, once you know them better."

"I have no wish to know them better," Kaln muttered.

Mallu resisted an impulse to cuff her into silence. He did not want to call attention to his lack of control over her behavior.

A human male limped toward them through the shadowy building, passing the security checkpoint with only a wave at the sentry. "That is regrettable," he said in heavily accented Jao, "because the crew will contain a number of them. I just wish I were going, too."

He had black "hair," as the longish head fur was termed, liberally frosted with silver. That signified something about a human's physical condition, Mallu had learned after accessing the base's information cache in their new quarters, but at the moment he could not remember exactly what.

"Rafe Aguilera krinnu ava Terra," the human said, "Third Construction Supervisor for the new ship." His body was stiff and straight, unreadable.

Was everyone on this benighted world determined to be rude? Mallu stared at the newcomer stonily.

"You are damaged?" Kaln said, glancing at the male's heart-ward leg.

"I was a *tank* commander in the Battle of Chicago, over twenty orbital cycles ago," Aguilera said. "Never healed right, not that there was much in the way of adequate medical treatment then."

Jalta glanced at Nath, *puzzlement* flattening his ears.

"Rafe refers to the Conquest, when the Jao originally came to this world," Nath said. "It is an uncomfortable subject for discussion. Even after so many orbital cycles, many humans are quite incapable of being reasonable about it. I would not bring it up, if I were you. We have—as humans say—agreed to disagree about those events."

That made no sense whatsoever. Mallu gazed at the human, but the creature did not meet his eyes. "We wish to tour the new ship," he said finally to break the silence.

They passed through the security checkpoint, Nath vouching for them. Just beyond, the enormous building held a number of vessels, each cradled in a framework of what looked to be a local variety of wood. The air was filled with its pungence, oils of some sort, no doubt, released by cutting. Saws screeched on and off. Automatic hammers chattered. Fat white sparks flew as metal was cut, shaped, then welded.

"This way," Aguilera krinnu ava Terra said and limped deeper into the vast shadowy interior with its islands of harsh illumination.

The human leading, they walked across a poured floor of some gray substance, which was stained and abraded from heavy use, past a number of long black vessels, swarmed over by mixed crews of human and Jao workers, trailing cables and showering sparks. Voices called back and forth, some in Jao, but more in the slippery native tongue. The mood was industrious and focused and oddly collegial as though the members of the two species saw no differences between them.

Mallu glimpsed a large ship in the middle which seemed to be of a different design, though it did not have the odd keels he'd seen the day before at the meeting. "Is that it?" he asked.

Aguilera made a strange chuffing noise as though he were having difficulty breathing. "No, Krant-Captain," he said in his accented Jao. "Your transport is actually just beyond the building on the other side, in a high-security, fenced-off area. It is far too large to be constructed in here."

"Too large even for this place?" Mallu was baffled.

"Yes." Aguilera turned, leading them around one more of the

long black ships, then stopped before a shimmering green door-field flanked by two human guards. He keyed it off and stood aside.

Kaln stepped through and stopped, trailed by Jalta, who did the same. Mallu followed, then stood just beyond, stunned, his field of vision filled by simply the biggest ship he'd ever seen, no doubt the biggest ever built by any kochan anywhere. Indeed, he thought it even surpassed an Ekhat ship in its dimensions and surely out-massed one.

"We have named it *Lexington*," Aguilera said.

Aguilera studied the three Jao's expressions. Their faces were still, but then Jao features were not nearly so mobile as those of humans. Their bodies, especially their ears and whiskers, betrayed them however. Even he, not very accomplished in deciphering Jao formal movement patterns, could read amazement, awe, and bewilderment.

"It is so—big!" one of them said. Aguilera thought it was the female, Kaln, made easier to identify by the droopy ear.

Nath joined them. Her eyes flickered with green fire. "Soon," she murmured.

Soon it would launch, she meant. Aguilera smiled. Even the Jao were impressed. Considering their experiences out in the universe, which included any number of encounters with other space-traveling species, that really meant something.

"What does the term lex-ing-ton indicate?" the tallest of the newcomers said. By the service bars incised on his cheek, Aguilera knew he was the captain, Mallu krinnu ava Krant. "Is it a numeric designation?"

"Humans like to name their ships," he said, having already had countless versions of this discussion with Jao, starting two years ago when the *Lexington* had been nothing more than a few lines on a blueprint. "It gives us a connection to them." Of course, the Jao entirely missed the sly reference to the first battle of the Revolutionary War when Americans had begun their struggle for freedom from a hated oppressor. He smiled. It was a quiet allusion that the humans on the project enjoyed and kept to themselves. He suspected that Wrot or Ronz might have perceived the connection, but, if so, they had quite wisely never mentioned it.

"Humans sometimes feel a form of—affection—for their machines," Nath said. "It makes no sense to us, but they must enjoy the sensation all the same, because its occurrence is frequent. Sometimes they even assign gender to them."

"Affection—for a device?" Kaln flicked her good ear in clear *dismissal*. "That is primitive and ridiculous."

"Human insistence upon naming such devices can be both a source of strength and weakness," Nath said. "Fondness for a particular ship can inspire them to be even more fanatically devoted to a mission than they might have otherwise been." She hesitated, glancing sideways at Aguilera. He nodded at her. "But it also encourages rampant factionalism, which has been, in the past, one of the species' greatest weaknesses. We do have to be careful about that."

"Have they no kochan-parents to instruct them?" Kaln said. She was the tech, the equivalent of lead engineer on her former ship, Aguilera realized, having carefully read the update released from Aille's office about the new crew members. Jao techs tended to be female, something about their brain structure having more affinity for the work than that of males. He'd had a lot of contact with Jao techs during the construction of this new ship. Disagreements between such often proved quite physical when they lost patience and resorted to *wrem-fa*, body-learning where nothing was explained. He'd incurred more than one set of bruises that way.

"Human kochan are very small," Aguilera said, "usually no more than a single mated pair and their children." He edged prudently out of reach, lest Kaln forget herself and strike him. "Humans and Jao are of course quite different in many regards, Senior-Tech Kaln," he said, "but we here on Terra have found that sometimes our mental differences allow us to work more efficiently together than apart."

"You are saying that humans know more than Jao?" Kaln's whiskers stiffened. "That is an insult!"

"No," Nath said, moving between the two, "actually it is not. Our two kinds have different strengths, neither more than the other, neither less. Combining the two disparate bodies of knowledge leads to a synthesis and increase for both sides." Her body had assumed the often seen stance of *waiting-to-be-of-use*, which even Aguilera could interpret.

"Desist," Krant-Captain Mallu said. "Such bickering is pointless. You shame Krant by behaving so. The Ekhat are our enemy, not the Terrans."

"Say that to those who died taking this world," Kaln said. "I viewed the records and have some idea what this world cost in Jao lives."

Aguilera felt his face warm. Things had been so—well—uneventful since Oppuk fell from power, he'd almost forgotten how nasty and condescending Jao could be.

"Enough!" Aille krinnu ava Terra, current governor of Earth, stepped through the door, looking magnificent with his height and regal bearing as always. "Aguilera is a member of my personal service. You will not speak to him so, nor any other human member of the *Lexington* crew."

Kaln's good ear wilted. Mallu, the dispossessed captain, stood stiffly before Aille. "Forgive her brashness, Governor," he said. "She is young and foolish, and still traumatized at both the loss of lives and of our ships."

Aille was silent, gathering the moment to himself, something at which he very much excelled. Aguilera had seen the highly ranked Jao do it over and over again during the last two years, pouring oil on troubled waters as he settled squabbles between the numerous rival kochan stationed on Terra.

"It is a great honor," Aille said finally when all eyes were focused upon him, "to be assigned to this crew in any capacity. The *Lexington* represents a tremendous stride forward for both our species."

Aille must have suspected there would be trouble from this new outfit, Aguilera realized. These Krant seemed abrupt, mulish, almost provincial, if such an adjective could be applied to Jao. It was like they didn't know things that other Jao knew, like *they* were the uncivilized ones, instead of humans.

"Take them through the ship, Aguilera," the young governor said. "That is where our focus should be, not on battles that occurred over twenty orbital cycles ago, and in which most of us *present*—" He fixed the three Krant with a flickering green gaze. "—took no part, unlike Aguilera here, who served his kind with great fortitude and now makes himself of use to our new taif."

"Yes, Governor," Mallu said, his body subdued. "We understand." He glared at the other two. "Do we not?"

The other two Jao fell into identical stances. Aguilera thought he read *assent*. They weren't graceful about it, though, like Nath or Aille would have been. Their movements were jerky, almost primitive, like football players trying to perform ballet. And their *vai camiti* were barely visible through that dark, dark nap. By all accounts, bold facial striping was one mark of Jao attractiveness. Were these three—homely?

Aille was staring at him, clearly waiting. Aguilera cleared his throat. "This way, Captain, Senior-Tech, and—?" With a jolt, he realized he'd forgotten the third Jao's rank.

The Jao glowered, and he felt his ears warm. That was a blunder, he told himself. The giving of one's name was a mark of Jao favor in social situations and this was hardly the moment to ask for that.

"This is Terniary-Commander Jalta krinnu ava Krant," Aille said without ceremony, defusing the moment.

"Terniary-Commander," Aguilera said, heading toward the immense ship. "If you will follow me." That at least he'd remembered. With Jao, the lowest ranked always went first. This was neither the time, nor the place, to argue relative status.

The *Lexington* had been constructed outside because the shipyard's main building, large as it was, had been simply inadequate. The new vessel was four thousand feet long, three thousand wide at the thickest point, shaped something like a stubby gray dirigible tapered at both ends.

Of course, no dirigible had ever possessed even one keel, much less the eight evenly spaced around this ship. The scope of those keels became more apparent as they approached. "The *Lexington* is much more heavily armored than usual," he said, "to allow it to better withstand the stresses of fighting inside a solar photosphere. Even the interior walls are thicker."

Mallu's ears waggled and he could not seem to look away. The captain appeared almost hungry. "What are those extrusions for?"

He meant the keels, Aguilera thought. "Those are the ship's weapons platforms," he said. "Half of them contain laser mounts and the other half, kinetic weapons."

"Kinetic weapons?" Kaln said. "That is rather primitive tech, is it not?"

Aille answered the question. "We experimented with a hastily converted form of this tech when we fought the Ekhat in this star's photosphere two orbital cycles ago. The weapons, pulled off pre-conquest Terran fighting vehicles, were originally rapid-fire *tank* cannons. As you can read in the reports of the battle, the innovation proved most efficacious." Aille gazed up at the ship as they walked. "And I do recommend that you make yourselves familiar with the reports, since you are going to work closely with a number of very talented humans. The information should prove—enlightening."

He stopped. "I will leave you now as I have a meeting at my *office*."

" '*Off-ice*?' " Mallu echoed the Terran word.

"It means 'working space,' " Nath said smoothly. "An adaptation of local custom. We have found it most useful to separate room functions as humans do."

Mallu looked enigmatic, but said nothing more as Aille turned back. There was definitely something going on inside that thick Jao skull. Aguilera just wasn't sure exactly what.

At any rate, the three Krant reminded him far too strongly of Earth's pre-Pluthrak dealings with the Jao, when tyrannical Governor Narvo had set the mood for human-Jao interaction. Narvo, along with the great kochan of Dano and Jak, had deemed human ideas worthless and humans fit for only the lowest grades of grunt labor.

As it turned out, Jao were very good at some things, humans at others. Braiding their talents, combined human-Jao forces had proved themselves strong enough to stand up even to the Ekhat on short notice, and, as he had good cause to know now, that was saying something. If humans and Jao went back to pitting those divergent strengths against one another, as they had for far too many years, they would all die—messily—when the Ekhat returned. A single battle with the Ekhat in this system had proved that to even the most doubting on both sides.

He would find the right words to make these Krant listen, Aguilera told himself. That would be the best use he could possibly make of himself.

The sounds of construction rose as they neared the immense ship, so that Aguilera had to raise his voice to be heard. "This way," he said, and motioned them to follow him under a tangle of temporary power cables feeding into one of the *Lexington*'s eight keels.

Speechless, the three Krant followed.

Caitlin Kralik presented herself at Preceptor Ronz's office in the Bond annex without an appointment. Jao disliked the human predilection for reserving one small bit of measured time for a particular event or activity. Instead, they relied upon their innate timesense to know when something would occur. Therefore, if Ronz didn't know she was coming, it was his own damn fault. She smiled to herself as the green door-field winked off.

"Ah, Caitlin," the old Jao said, rising from a soft pile of *dehabia* with a grace that belied his age. "*Vaist*. It felt as though someone would be here soon." He was clad in unrelieved black harness and trousers and she could see more than a few scars on his chest.

Vaist was the superior-to-inferior form of greeting, literally you-see-me. She'd heard plenty of *that* growing up. Coming from the Preceptor, though, it pretty much lost its sting. She wasn't certain how much of the current Jao-human alliance had been his design, but signs certainly pointed in his direction.

She smiled and let her body flow into the graceful curves of *willingness-to-be-of-use*. Years of observation and study had gone into her ability to use Jao body-speech. "*Vaish*," she said in return. I-see-you. Agreement between the two of them as far as rank was concerned, anyway. Of course, that wasn't difficult in this case. Ronz outranked everyone on the planet, including Aille.

"Your parents are well?" the old Jao said, and settled into one of the human-style chairs before a standard desk.

"Yes." She settled in the chair beside his and gazed down at her hands, trying to think how to diplomatically frame what she wanted to say.

"You wish to know what I think is out there," Ronz said in English, "what is worth going so far and risking our new ship, not to mention all of your lives."

"Y-yes." She met those flickering green and black eyes. Even growing up under the direct supervision of a Jao guard, she'd never learned to read Jao eyes. No doubt all that dancing green fire meant something—at least to another Jao.

"I am not going to tell you," Ronz said. His body was very still. The Bond did not hold with elaborate body styling. The whole fad was heavily influenced by fashions that varied from kochan to kochan. One trained in the Narvo style, the Dano, or the Pluthrak. If a Bond member were seen to prefer any one style over another, that would show favor, and above everything else, the Bond was neutral. Else it could not perform its primary function of coordinating the quarrelsome, often divided kochan scattered across the many Jao worlds.

"If we do not know what to expect, then how can we prepare?" Caitlin schooled her own body to neutrality too, adapting to the game they were playing.

"The very act of expectation might alter what you find or what you do, if you find it," Ronz said. "I have shared my suspicions with Wrot krinnu ava Terra. When—and if—the moment comes that the rest of you need to know, he will be the one to decide."

"Someone knows, then." She bent her head, wondering, once the *Lexington* took off, if she could worm it out of the old Jao veteran in an unguarded moment. He had "gone native" to a degree far greater than any other Jao of her acquaintance. And that was saying quite a bit these days.

Ronz leaned toward her, his eyes almost entirely green. "No," he said softly, as though she'd blurted her thoughts aloud, "for all that he comes of blunt-spoken Wathnak, I am confident Wrot will keep silent until he should not."

Caitlin's face heated as she tried to erase all vestiges of unconscious posture from her limbs. Damn body-language! How was she ever going to make it as a diplomat in the midst of a species that could read her every move like a book?

Ronz leaned back and his body almost, but not quite, implied *sly-amusement*. "Nice try," the old rascal murmured in English.

CHAPTER
4

Mallu found the interior of the great ship bewildering. They passed crew quarters, startlingly spacious, many of them intended evidently for single occupants. Blatantly wasteful. And there were what Aguilera called "recreation areas," which included spaces designated "coffee bar," "TV room," and "theater."

Coffee was a popular concoction that acted as a mild stimulant on humans, Nath explained. While it made Jao nauseated, humans often functioned better with its judicious application. Other beverages would be served there, too, including a number of favored Jao teas as well as light snacks. The TV room and theater were for displays of *ollnat* in off-duty periods.

"*Ollnat* again," Kaln said, her single ear struggling to communicate *bafflement*. "This world is obsessed with it!"

Aguilera turned back to face her, his gait ungraceful. "*Ollnat* is what saved this world when the Ekhat came," the human male said stiffly. "Our ability to come up with new ideas is one of humanity's greatest strengths."

As before, Mallu found it off-putting to gaze at that naked face. No whiskers, nap, or, worst of all, facial striping. He could not figure out how the creatures told themselves apart. Their skin coloration varied, from a pale pink to a dark brown. But their bland features all blended together and talking to one felt like conversing with a child still confined to its natal pool.

Nath gazed at the trio, her arms falling into *determined-patience*.

"Human *ollnat* bears little resemblance to our own expression of that trait," she said. "They have the most amazing ability to come up with fresh combinations of familiar elements. In time, we expect our new taif to be at the forefront of a wave of invention, and that will be of use for all Jao."

"They are only natives!" Kaln said brashly.

Her stance was veering into blatant *belligerence*. Mallu found himself alarmed.

"And conquered natives, at that," his senior-tech continued. "How can you elevate them to a rank equal with even lowly regarded Jao?"

"You will not speak of them so in my presence," Nath said, her body gone very still. "They deserve your respect!"

"The floor-supervisor is correct," Mallu said. How bad had Kaln's head injury been, anyway? Perhaps he should have her examined again. She seemed to have lost all sense of propriety. "You have not been here long enough to know what you are talking about. Keep silent!"

The five of them walked on through the busy ship then. Crew members, both human and Jao, constantly passed them, intent on their tasks. Walking just behind Aguilera, Nath was full of energy, her movements confident, her postures precise. *She* certainly did not seem lessened by her time on this world. "What kochan gave you birth?" Mallu asked.

"Tashnat," she said. "I was Nath krinnu Tashnat vau Nimmat."

Two midlevel kochan, well respected, certainly more highly regarded across the Jao polity than Krant.

Kaln's eyes flared. "Then how can you dishonor both Tashnat and Nimmat by abandoning them for a taif infested by these primitives?"

Aguilera was watching their exchange with an intensity that bordered upon fierceness. Mallu realized that Kaln had angled to present her back to the human, a subtle insult in Jao body-speak.

"What we do here is for the future of all Jao, in fact, for all sapients who face extermination from the Ekhat," Nath said, her lines gone to an elegant version of *disbelief*. "You should be honored that the Preceptor believes you can contribute on this mission. If you feel he is in error, then you should inform him immediately."

The moment reeked of potential ruin. Mallu froze. Krant was so little regarded in the great sweep of things, it was hard to believe that they had been drawn into something meaningful, a situation where their actions might actually make a difference, where they could be of use to others outside their own small sphere. This kind of chance to serve the wider *vithrik* rarely came to Krant.

Jalta and Kaln were watching him. As the highest ranking officer, he had *oudh* here, minuscule as that charge might be to outside eyes. "The Preceptor is not in error," he said. His ears flicked back and forth, his body unable to settle into anything recognizable. "We do not wish to make it seem otherwise."

He turned to Kaln and forced her to look at him. "And we will keep silent about local matters which are outside our current understanding—is that understood?"

Her whiskers quivered, but her good ear flicked *assent*.

Nath's lines flowed into a breathtaking rendition of *mollified-acceptance*. Embarrassed, Mallu turned away as though he did not see. Other kochan could spend time and resources on tutoring their offspring in such beautiful—and pointless—affected elegance, while Krant on its two inhospitable worlds struggled to merely live and produce the next generation. Sometimes he thought other Jao with their exotic seas and exquisite manners were not the same species at all.

"Now," Nath was saying, "I will let Aguilera conduct you to the weapons platforms and the command deck. His knowledge of both is unparalleled and I have other tasks which require my attention."

Aguilera gestured with his heartward hand. "This way," he said and set off.

Kaln's whiskers bristled, but then, as was proper, the three Krants followed.

Tully spent the night at the Pascagoula base in the quarters his batman, David Church, maintained for his use whenever his commander was on-site. Tully had been on detached duty for the last few weeks, but his regular post these days was commander of Baker Company, a special unit of ground troops, both human and Jao, trained mostly for reconnaissance. Jao disliked overspecialization, though, so he made sure his company was highly adaptable, good at hand-to-hand, trained on all manners of weapons, ready for whatever the situation required.

Something had changed inside him two years ago on the northwest coast, when, at a critical moment, Aille and Yaut had trusted him, despite knowing his origins and holding him prisoner for weeks at that point. He'd grown up a Resistance camp brat, fatherless at four, then motherless too, a short time later, stealing food when no one could, or would, share what little they had, sleeping out in the snow and rain huddled into the lee of boulders, learning to scavenge with the best of them. Look out for number one at all times had been his credo. That, and kill Jao, whenever and wherever possible. The Resistance was hellbent on taking back Earth whatever the cost.

Then he had been forcibly drafted into Aille krinnu ava Pluthrak's service. At the time, it had seemed a disaster, an enslavement he would have literally given his life to end, but actually, in some inexplicable way, it had been the making of him, almost as though a stern parent had taken him in hand.

Now that he had traveled with Aille, Yaut, Ed Kralik, and Caitlin out into space and actually experienced the alien insanity of the Ekhat for himself, he knew the truth. If humanity and the Jao didn't stand together against the Ekhat, whichever maniac faction came along next, they would all die, a whole lot sooner rather than later.

When he'd reached his quarters last night, his comboard indicated that not only he, but his whole unit, was assigned to the upcoming expedition on the *Lexington*. He spent the next few hours requisitioning supplies, drafting orders, and downloading background to absorb. They would help man the *Lexington*'s main guns while on the mission, so he left orders for the company to report to the ship and start qualifying on the new artillery first thing in the morning.

Fresh from a shower and shaving, Tully caught a ride over to his office, which was in the same complex as Aille's and part of the refit facility. Rain had swept through just before dawn, as it tended to do on the coast, and now the sky was blazingly clear. He'd overindulged at the bar last night, matching Kralik beer for beer, so his head was a bit tender. Inside the administration wing, the Jao preference for low lighting proved a welcome relief from the morning sun.

As luck would have it, he encountered Yaut in the hallway. The bullnecked old Jao looked mulish as ever. "*Vaish*," Tully said, halting prudently out of reach. I-see-you. He was well aware that, as far as Yaut was concerned, opportunities for further instruction never ceased. The Jao was a great believer in *wrem-fa*, "body-learning," where you simply thrashed an offender repeatedly without explanation until he figured the infraction out on his own. Whenever the weather changed, Tully could swear he still felt the bruises.

The grizzled fraghta flicked a careless ear. As always, his harness gleamed with polish, his traditional trousers, now the blue of the Terran taif, were immaculate. His nap looked well brushed. "*Vaist*," he said sourly, as though Tully's quite proper courtesy had been lacking.

Several clerks, one human and the other Jao, ducked their heads and hurried past in the dim passageway. "Have you been assigned to the *Lexington*?" Tully asked.

"The governor has too many matters which require his attention here," the old Jao said. And, of course, Yaut went nowhere that Aille didn't. A fraghta was never separated from his or her charge. Their devotion was legendary.

But Yaut wanted to go, thought Tully, analyzing the cant of the Jao's ears, the angle of his spine. He looked—*regretful*. "Too bad," he said casually. "What little the Preceptor let slip sounds interesting."

"It does not matter if the expedition is interesting." Yaut's whiskers bristled. "It is expected, above all else, that you will make yourself of use and do Terra Taif honor. As a member of Aille's service, what you do reflects upon him!"

Tully sighed. "You can't fault me for being human. We like novelty."

"I have noticed," Yaut said, his shoulders stiff. "I believe that the appropriate human expression is—'you have the attention span of an annoying small flying insect!'"

"Close enough." Tully kept even the slightest hint of a smile from reaching his face. Yaut was adept at reading human facial expression these days.

"Aille wishes to speak with you," Yaut said.

All amusement drained out of him. Tully nodded and edged around the fraghta into Aille's office. It was spacious, with a gleaming oak desk on one side. A floor-to-ceiling wall of glass looked out over the work floor on the other side. Below, workmen swarmed over the subs being refitted, as well as a number of small Jao spacecraft, the pace frantic. The Ekhat would be coming back and everyone knew it, human and Jao alike. There was no time to be spared anywhere on this world.

Aille looked up from his com. He had a bold *vai camiti* slanting across his eyes like a mask, a mark of Jao comeliness, and his nap was lustrous with frequent swims. He radiated confidence and purpose. "I wished to confer before you leave on the Bond's mission."

"Will it be that soon?" Tully stood before the desk, his body as *attentive* in Jao terms as he could manage.

"Yes," Aille said. "As a human would reckon such things, I think only a few days, perhaps even as little as two."

"I still have a lot to do then," Tully said, "and not much time in which to do it." His mind leaped ahead, calculating.

"You will listen to Wrot in all things," Aille said. "I say this, because I believe it would not be apparent to a human, but Wrot evidently has the Preceptor's confidence. He is being given *oudh* in this situation."

Wrot had the top authority? Tully's eyebrows rose. "Not the captain of the ship?"

"The captain is in charge of taking you and the rest of the crew where you need to go, as the driver of a ground vehicle might pilot you around the base," Aille said. "Wrot will decide what should be done once you arrive."

Wrot wasn't a bad sort, Tully thought, as Jao went, not nearly as stiff-necked and full of pride as your average scion of one of the great kochan. He'd even been a fellow member of Aille's service before resigning to be one of Terra Taif's first elders. "I see," he said carefully, mindful of Yaut glowering behind him.

"You are the commander of an accomplished unit," Aille said. "I was very pleased with its performance in the last maneuvers. You should know that a number of them are listed for possible advancement."

That was news. Of course, Tully hadn't seen the evaluations since before he'd taken off for the Rockies. "That's great."

"We have many more deserving humans than we can promote at the moment," Aille said. "The number of officers in both the human and Jao taifs must be balanced as much as possible, so that neither one nor the other has the advantage."

The new taif didn't mean the same to a human as it did to a Jao. To them, taif—and the kochan that it would eventually become—were tied up in a sense of personal worth. If one's kochan was not well regarded, then neither were you. Many of the Jao who had flocked to the new taif were of lowly ranked kochan, or, like Caitlin's current bodyguard, Tamt, had been all but abandoned by theirs, having in some measure not lived up to what had been expected of them.

It appealed to Tully also, feeding into his desire to belong somewhere, anywhere. He'd had no home since he was almost too young to remember. Here was a group that needed him, filled with people, both human and Jao, who thought that he, Gabriel Tully, actually had something worthwhile to offer. It was the only place he had ever really felt he belonged. And he found that commitment and regard making him a better man.

"Then we need more Jao," he said.

Green fire danced in Aille's enigmatic black gaze. " 'Easier said than done,' as the saying goes," the young governor of Earth said. "This mission may well be a way to achieve that, though. Once Jao and human are seen to work well together under difficult circumstances, to accomplish much and then return home safely, that may lure the more skeptical of my species to make the same commitment."

"Accomplish much?" Tully echoed. "So far, no one will say exactly what the hell it is that we're supposed to do besides fly into the heart of some nebula, where at least one Ekhat ship was recently destroyed, and see what, or who, is there."

"The Preceptor has his own reasons to withhold information." Aille rose and stalked around the desk, each step a different posture, his body easily flowing from one into another, as though it took no thought at all.

Tully couldn't read ordinary Jao bodyspeak very well, and hardly at all at that speed, but he knew out and out agitation when he saw it, human or Jao. He waited, shoulders back, arms straight, body at attention, communicating *respect* in the human fashion. "What do you think is out there that's worth risking the Bond's shiny new ship?"

"Not the Ekhat," Aille said. "The Preceptor has already said that much."

"Other than the Ekhat, humans, and the Jao," Tully said, "who else is there?"

"Sapience is more common than you might think," Aille said.

His gaze turned to the wall of glass and the workers busily refitting the ships below. "And, due to the mad persecution of the Ekhat, who only wish to be alone in the universe, little of it is willing to be contacted."

Even if it was the Jao who found you instead of the Ekhat, Tully thought, they came with lasers, raining death from the sky, hell-bent on ruling what was left after the fires died down. If someone was hiding in that nebula, most likely the last thing they wanted to see was a Jao ship—like the one he was scheduled to ride on.

"Then we will have to be careful," he said.

"Your unit may be of great use out there," Aille said. "I chose it because of all the jinau under my command, Baker Company has demonstrated the highest capacity for innovation in the field. See that you are prepared for all possibilities."

The new ship *overwhelmed*. Mallu could think of no other word to describe his response. The *Lexington* possessed passenger quarters for six thousand soldiers in addition to crew quarters for just over a thousand. His own ship, damaged in combat with the Ekhat back in NGC 7293, had carried no more than five hundred, when at full complement, which it seldom was. Krant was rarely able to recruit from other kochan and training of the new generations took time. "A-kee-lara," Mallu said, struggling to reproduce the alien syllables, "why is this ship so very large?"

The human blinked its unvarying brown eyes. "To fight the Ekhat," he said in passable Jao. "Is there any other reason to build a ship, either large or small?"

The creature was right, unless one mentioned the Jao practice of subjugating newly discovered sapients and exploiting their resources, and Mallu sensed that was not a subject to be discussed under these circumstances. He prowled corridor after corridor, poking his head in here and there, encountering labs equipped for scientific study, pools, exercise rooms, medical bays, food halls, even more facilities for *ollnat*, equipment storage, repair stations, weapons platforms, and of course the great engine room, which ran the entire length of the ship. Everywhere they went, the walls were thicker than he was accustomed to seeing, the bracing massive, the scale far beyond anything he'd ever thought to experience. It was unaccountably luxurious, space wasted upon the most frivolous of functions.

"Wait here. I cannot take you on the *bridge* just yet," Aguilera said finally, stopping just outside a sealed door.

The human term was unfamiliar, but the entrance was labelled like all the others they'd inspected in both Jao and alien squiggles. "You mean the command deck? You do not have the authority?" Jalta said, his ears twitching.

"No," Aguilera said, his body still, his odd angles altogether uncommunicative, "the three of you do not have clearance."

Kaln edged toward the human, dwarfing him even though Mallu had observed that their guide was taller than most of his kind. "*We* are not allowed inside the command structure, but you are?" she said.

"I am the highest ranked human here, third in charge of the entire project," Aguilera said. "So it makes sense for me to have clearance." He pulled a pocketcom out of a fold in his trousers and spoke into it.

A single breath later, a tinny voice answered in the local tongue, which had a choppy cadence, like waves out on the wind-swept ocean. Aguilera bobbed his head, then turned to the three. "All right," he said, "now you can go in."

Aille krinnu ava Terra had maneuvered them into this position for a reason, Mallu thought, as he trailed after the limping figure onto a vast command deck with stations scattered around its periphery. Whatever his affiliation now, the young governor had begun life as a Pluthrak, and that kochan was known across the galaxy, even all the way to Krant, for its cunning and subtlety.

By directing this tour be carried out in precisely this fashion and under the authority of this particular guide, the governor had clearly meant the three Krant to grasp the position of humans here. They were not merely conscripted workmen, as were other species invaded under similar circumstances. Somehow, they had achieved a place in the grand scheme of things, where their contributions were valued and their opinions counted. *They* were to be allowed to matter in the great ongoing struggle against the Ekhat.

Krant rarely mattered, with its two barren worlds and its isolation from other kochan who possessed not only better resources, but plentiful opportunities for association.

Mallu's long-simmering resentment of the great kochan intensified. Even humans, who looked like they could drown if you so much as poured a handful of water over their heads, had achieved association. But who ever came looking for Krant? Who sought *their* scions for marriage-groups, inquired of their elders for wise council, or requested their backup when facing the Ekhat? Who among the great kochan required Krant for anything?

Except now, the back of his mind whispered. They were being sought now and their input heeded. Whatever happened on this odd-ball voyage, they must make the most of this rare opportunity.

Kaln was prowling the *bridge*, as Aguilera termed it, pulling control panels open to examine the wiring, keying on screens and displays. Indicator lights blinked, many of them green, but others red and amber. Power hummed and the whole place felt oddly alive. Off to one side, Jalta was staring fixedly into a screenful of statistics as though they meant something.

Mallu settled into an unoccupied chair, while Aguilera stationed himself beside the door, waiting. It was an impressive ship, perhaps the greatest ever constructed by Jao, but it was being built by humans too, and incorporated more than a little of their technology. Those kinetic weapons certainly bordered on the primitive. Apparently, *Lexington* would carry humans to operate them as well as Jao to handle the traditional energy guns, while he and the remnants of his crew would rate only the lowly status of mere passengers.

Kaln and Jalta crossed the bridge, then came together, discussing the merits of the long-range sensing devices. Mallu glanced back at Aguilera. The human was standing in what was, for him, an awkward posture. Mallu stiffened, reading in that alien body a distorted, but recognizable, *intent-to-insult*.

Kaln turned too, saw what he saw, then launched herself across the floor. "Stub-ears!" she cried. "Lowest of the low! How could you possibly believe you had the right to insult anyone?"

"Kaln!" Mallu cried, but the tech was beyond responding. It was all crashing in upon her, he knew, the battle with the Ekhat, the loss of their ships, the death of two-thirds of their comrades, lives that Krant could ill afford to lose, the baffling summons to this backwater world by the Bond, and now brazen effrontery by a primitive.

She meant to kill it, but Earth's young governor apparently set great store on this particular savage. Blood thrummed in Mallu's head as disaster loomed. She would shame them all by her lack of control. They might even be deemed useless and sent away, losing their chance at association. His broken ribs stabbing at every deep breath, he launched himself across the room and tackled her just as she reached her goal.

CHAPTER

5

Mallu struck Kaln midbody and wrestled her to the deck, pulling her weight down on top of him. His still-healing ribs gave way with a sickening wave of brilliant white pain that stole his breath. A step beyond, Aguilera hastily flattened himself against the wall.

Voices shouted, both human and Jao, as boots pounded across the deck. "Desist!" Mallu gasped into Kaln's battered face. The command deck undulated in time with his stuttering heartbeat. Above him, the tech's undamaged ear was flattened in pure *rage*. He clung desperately as she struggled to free herself. Air wheezed in and out of his chest, each breath more difficult than the last.

Jalta leaned down to pull Kaln off. She struck at her crewmate, still thrashing to free herself. "They—they—!" she sputtered, her eyes gone to mad green fire.

"This one has done nothing!" Mallu said. The deck flooring pressed hard against his cheek. "Think!"

"Its body!" She twisted, but couldn't break his hold. "You saw!"

"This creature is an alien!" he said. "Its angles are no doubt quite different from ours. What looks like *insult* to us may indicate no more than weariness to them. Think!" He tightened his grip and waited, ribs a blaze of agony, for her to either regain control or lose it forever. If her reason were permanently broken, she would have to be put down, and, as ship-captain, he would have to be the one to do it. Krant had no resources to succor the useless.

"Krant-Captain?" a Jao voice said from the doorway.

49

He looked up, still gripping Kaln, and saw an unfamiliar *vai camiti.* "Yes?" he said stiffly. Each breath stabbed like the bite of a white-hot brand. He had not hurt so intensely since that moment in the battle when he'd been knocked across the command deck and struck his chest upon a console.

"Is there something you require?" the newcomer, a short, sturdy male, said, as though the three Krants were merely paying a courtesy call between kochan and perhaps refreshments were appropriate.

"N-no." Mallu eased his hold upon Kaln, each movement wringing fresh misery out of his tortured ribs. "Senior-Tech Kaln?"

Breathing hard, she sat up and stared at her hands as though they belonged to someone else. "I—require nothing."

"As you perhaps noted earlier," the Jao said, his body reflecting *determination-to-be-of-use*, "we have accommodations on this ship for both Jao and human. This close to launch, all services are operational. You have only to express your needs and we will endeavor to satisfy them."

"This is Terniary-Adjunct Chul krinnu ava Monat," Aguilera said, gracelessly forcing the newcomer's name upon them, yet another breach of manners, though Mallu supposed by now the creature simply knew no better. "He is a specialist in the refitting of Earth ships and adapting Earth technology to be used on Jao ships."

Kaln rose unsteadily, chest heaving, and tugged at her twisted harness. Her eyes were sane again, though, and Mallu sagged back to the deck, concentrating on just trying to breathe.

"You—have not joined the new taif, then," Jalta said in a transparent attempt to deflect attention away from Kaln's would-be attack on the human.

Aguilera edged prudently out of her reach, his unvarying human eyes wide, hands knotted into fists.

"No, though I am giving the idea serious consideration," Chul said. His angles slipped into *concern* and he bent over Mallu, who was now trying to sit up and failing. "Do you wish assistance, Krant-Captain?"

They had shamed themselves before this well-spoken stranger, Mallu thought, and, even worse, further disgraced themselves by demonstrating lack of association within their own kochan in front of a primitive. How many crew had been on the command deck to witness this humiliation?

He tried to answer Chul, but a great roaring like the seas of some wild world running high before the wind rose in his ears. His jaws gaped and he could not speak.

Chul stood again, and pulled out a pocketcom. "May I suggest we adjourn to the ship's medical facilities?"

Mallu attempted to protest that he just needed a moment to recover his composure, then ravening blackness engulfed him.

Wrot's pocketcom buzzed while he sat at an information cache in the base communications center, studying the intriguing stats from NGC 7293. He pulled the sleek black device off the waistband of his Terra-blue trousers and keyed it on, still gazing at the screen. So much information had been brought back, and so much more could be inferred. He had barely dived beneath the surface so far, but he could already see what had intrigued Ronz.

"We have trouble at the new ship," the Preceptor's voice said without preamble. "I wish you to take care of it."

"Certainly," the formerly retired Jao warrior said, rising at once. "Though I am not very close at the moment. Surely there are those in authority on-site who can see to it in a more timely manner?"

"They are already at work," the Preceptor said. "I wish you to quiet this storm. Our visitors from Krant are having difficulty finding ways to make themselves useful."

That was a diplomatic way of saying that they were more per- haps more trouble than they were worth. Wrot cleared the files from the viewer, then headed for the door at a half-run. Other Jao and humans in the center prudently cleared out of his way. He disengaged the door-field and came out into the exuberant light of this system's sun. Cool, sea-scented air rushed against his muzzle and his whiskers stirred. "Did our staff cause the problem?" he asked into the device.

"No, it was one of the Krants," the Preceptor said.

"I—see." And he did, at least to some extent. By all accounts, Krant was infamously hardheaded and self-contained. Though they were low ranked, they rarely sought association with larger, better regarded kochan, preferring their own path whatever the cost. They were so isolated that he'd never actually worked with any, despite, as a human would term it, his long years of service.

"Maneuver them into cooperation—now," the Preceptor said, "before the mission leaves, or there will be trouble later on."

"You could simply send them home," Wrot said, signaling a

passing ground vehicle headed in the right direction to pull over. Tires squealed as the driver complied. "We have their data already, and though many of them gave their lives to acquire it, I doubt the survivors understand what those readings imply."

"But they may," the Preceptor said. "So I cannot have them running loose back at Krant, spreading rumors, perhaps even generating an expedition of their own. If I am right, this is the most controversial discovery made in some time and we have but one chance to make full use of it. We must proceed most carefully." He hesitated. "And this may be a splendid opportunity to bring Krant into association, at least to some limited degree."

"That bunch?" Wrot snorted as the groundcar stopped and the passengers in the back seat, both human male jinau officers, made room for him without protest. "They are notorious for their stiff-necked solitary pride. I have a feeling they would rather die than give it up."

"It is your job to make certain that does not happen," the Preceptor said.

"You always ask the impossible," Wrot said as the groundcar lurched and then continued on its way toward the looming refit facility. It swerved to avoid a pothole and he slid into one of his companions who, obviously intimidated by his rank, apologized without being at fault, something a Jao would never do. Wrot flicked an impatient ear.

"And I always get it," Ronz said. The pocketcom clicked off.

Kaln led through the maze of ship corridors as white-coated human attendants carried Mallu's unconscious body on a stretcher. The two creatures with their disturbingly immobile ears had initially tried to take the lead, and now looked at her askance, but she could tell where they were headed by subtle hints from their bodies each time they came to an intersection. And she deserved no better than to go first. She had made herself lowest of the low and everyone should see that.

Chul followed at the rear, while Jalta paced at the stretcher's side, *misery* in his every line and angle. Kaln knew better than to speak to her crewmate. She had shamed herself, shamed all of Krant with her loss of control. There was nothing to say. When he recovered—if he recovered—Mallu would order the three service bars on her cheek obliterated and she would serve out her days as a drudge on some scow, scraping rust and cleaning pools, testing and adjusting salts for her betters until her skin cracked.

Aguilera kept pace, though prudently hanging back out of her line of sight. Mallu had been right. The creature was an alien. Its angles most likely meant nothing. She did not know what was wrong with her! She just felt so angry all the time since the disaster in the nebula.

They reached a medical bay and turned in. The room had pale green walls the color of sea foam and smelled of astringents and traditional Jao balms, bringing back painful memories of Kaln's own injuries in the battle with the Ekhat. She edged aside as the attendants hefted the stretcher onto an examination table. A human, obviously female and tall for her kind, met them, pulling white flexible gloves onto slender hands that looked far too feeble to be of any use. She had brown head-fur laced with silver, something like Aguilera's, but much longer. "I am *Dr. Ames*," she said in decent Jao and leaned over Mallu's unconscious form. "What happened to him?"

Kaln glared at Aguilera. "You brought us to a *human*? What can such know of our kind? We want a real medician!"

Aguilera just stared at her, dark-brown eyes static.

"Dr. Ames is the lead Jao medician on the *Lexington*," Chul said, smoothly stepping between the human and the Krant. His body-angles communicated *patient-instruction*. "She is quite skilled."

Kaln's whiskers bristled. "She is only a native!"

"I *said*—what happened to him?" The female's voice was coolly insistent. "We do not have time for quarreling about my status if you wish him to continue breathing."

"He damaged his ribs back in the battle with the Ekhat," Jalta said in a subdued tone. His ears and whiskers were limp with unallayed *distress*. "Though he has not complained, I do not believe they ever really healed."

"Probably punctured a lung sac." She turned to a white-coated attendant and issued a series of commands in the choppy local language. Her fingers probed Mallu's chest, eliciting a faint groan even though the captain was still unconscious. "Fortunate for you lot that you have eight to our two. A human would be in much more serious condition with this sort of injury."

She gestured at her assistants who then carefully transferred Mallu to a rolling table and bore him away. "We will use *X-rays* to pinpoint the damage, then reinflate the sac. After that, he needs quiet and time to mend." She gazed directly into Kaln's eyes, her body carefully neutral. "No *fighting*."

"She did not mean to attack him," Jalta said. Her crewmate was pacing back and forth. "Mallu thrust himself between them."

"Whatever the intentions," Dr. Ames said, "it cannot happen again. Your captain is most fortunate that the rib did not puncture something more vital—like his heart."

Kaln wanted to flee, to be alone with her shame, but did not know where to go. Her head ached. The quarters they had been assigned were far away and she wasn't quite sure how to leave the ship and find her way back.

Dr. Ames gazed at her with the dispassion of a kochan-parent. "I think," she said finally, when Kaln could bear the silence no more, "you need to take a swim."

Jalta's head swiveled. Kaln could not believe that she had understood the human's words correctly.

"We have a number of excellent pools here on the *Lexington*," Dr. Ames said. "Why don't you try out the one on this level? It is just four doors windward down the corridor. Our Jao consultants report that the salts are perfectly balanced."

A swim. Kaln felt like it had been forever since she'd had that luxury. Her muzzle itched and her nap felt desiccated, absolutely stiff with dirt.

"When you are done, check back here," Ames said. "Your captain should be better by then."

Jalta tugged at her arm, and the two of them left to find the promised pool.

Wrot stopped at the office complex inside the refit facility and inquired about Tully. The human was busy in his own small allotted space, he learned from the adjunct on duty, two doors down. Wrot thrust his head into the compact, over-lit room. "Come with me," he said without preamble, blinking against the brightness.

Tully looked up from his comboard. He had golden hair, not unheard of among his kind, but not overly common either. It had grown rather long recently, giving him a ragged incomplete look. "Pretty busy here," he said, leaning back and tapping a pen against his chin. "Tons of stuff piled up while I was in the mountains. Can it wait?"

"We have trouble over at the ship with the three Krants," Wrot said. "I could use—as you humans say—backup."

"Goddammit," Tully said, rising. He keyed his comboard off and circled his desk. His jinau uniform was rumpled. "They haven't been here more than a few days. Couldn't they wait at least a week to start a ruckus?"

"They are traumatized," Wrot said as Tully ducked past him into the corridor. "Surely you can understand that. They lost their ships and most of their crew, which would be devastating to anyone, but especially so to Krant, which is not rich in assets."

The two of them hurried down the hall, then descended the stairs. Sounds of the refit assaulted their ears as they came out onto the work floor, the screech of saws cutting metal, the pounding of hammers, the buzz of wood being cut. The smell of fresh paint and scorched metal filled the air. "So what were they doing out there," Tully said, "if they couldn't afford to mix it up with the Ekhat?"

"They were part of a three-ship task force, dispatched from a Jao base to check out signals that indicated Ekhat activity in the nebula." Wrot headed toward the outside door at the opposite end. "It is difficult to correctly calculate framepoints in such an environment. One of the three ships was destroyed in transit, the second by the Ekhat they encountered there, probably the Melody, which is not the same faction that attacked Terra two years ago. The third ship fatally damaged the Ekhat vessel, but barely survived the engagement itself, too badly damaged to do anything more than make transit back to the base while the point locus was still active."

"So they are soldiers?" Tully trotted around the massive Earth subs in their immense wooden cradles and waved to a few of the workers as he passed.

"Yes, though all Jao undertake a form of what you would call military training," Wrot said, keeping up despite his age. "So you might say that we are all soldiers at some point in our lives."

Tully fell silent as the two of them dodged ladders, stepped over electrical cables, detoured showers of sparks from the welders perched on ladders and scaffolds overhead. "The crazy bastards would traumatize anyone," the human said, "at least anyone sane."

Once they reached the great ship, they were passed through Security immediately. "Status of the difficulty with the Krants?" Wrot asked the stocky human sergeant on duty.

"Krant-Captain Mallu has been taken to the medical bay on Deck Fifty-Seven," the sergeant said. "I haven't received an update on his condition."

"The other two?" Wrot asked.

"Swimming on the same deck. I posted a guard to keep an eye on them—discreetly."

"Sounds like it's all been resolved," Tully said. He shoved his hands into his blue uniform's pockets. "You don't need me."

"We are going to be traveling with these Krants for some time," Wrot said, leading Tully to a lift station. "It is necessary to achieve at least a rudimentary level of association with them."

"They don't like humans," Tully said. "They already made that clear back in Aille's office."

"Which is why it must be you and not me who makes them see reason. Humans are going to matter on this assignment, you and Caitlin most of all. They must acknowledge your right to serve if this is going to work."

They stepped into the lift and the doors closed. Tully stared at him with those unsettling blue eyes. "You want *me* to bring these—goobers—into association?"

Despite his many years of proficiency with English, Wrot wasn't quite sure what "goobers" signified. Humans were so endlessly inventive with language. He flicked an ear. "You and Caitlin."

The lift whooshed upwards. Tully held onto the internal rail to steady himself. He looked distinctly unhappy. "You don't want much, do you?"

Wrot leaned against the humming wall. "Anyone who can bring the mountain Resistance leaders into association can deal with a few backwater Jao."

"I understand the Resistance because I grew up with them," Tully said as the door slid open. "I know where they're coming from, but I haven't got a clue about these guys."

"Nor have they about you," Wrot said. "It should make for, as your species would say, an even playing field."

They padded down the hall, then spotted a uniformed guard at the far end. "You should find the senior-tech and the terniary-commander there," said Wrot. "Go in and reason with them while I check on Krant-Captain Mallu. Teach them how to deal with humans."

"Gee," Tully said, his shoulders slipping into his characteristic reluctant slouch, "may I?"

That, like much Tully said, was rhetorical, and not entirely respectful, either. Reflecting that the human was fortunate that Yaut was not nearby, Wrot left him there and went to the medical bay.

Kaln broke the surface of the little pool and floated. Here, in this deliciously balanced water, she could almost forget her shame. The salts mixture was reminiscent of her homeworld of Mannat Kar, though the saturation was not nearly as strong. She closed her eyes and thought of storms, spray flying in her face, giant swells that carried one far out to sea. She tightened her timesense so that the soothing moment stretched out. The ache in her head—eased.

Then her nap prickled, breaking her concentration. Flow abruptly resumed its normal rate. She opened her eyes, turned, and realized one of those runty humans was watching her from the wall by the door.

"What do you want?" Her voice rang hollowly in the echoing space.

"I came to see if you needed anything," it said. It had a shaggy golden thatch on its head, and seemed vaguely familiar. Without facial striping, though, it was difficult to be certain of its identity.

"If we wish something, we will request it ourselves," she said stiffly. "Go away." Then she plunged beneath the cool surface again. Jalta was swimming along the bottom, his body as sinuous as one of *manks* that swam Mannat Kar's seas. It was quite a decent pool, better than any they'd possessed on their lost Krant vessel. How strange to find such a civilized luxury on a ship built at least partially by primitives.

When she judged enough time had passed for the creature to have taken itself off, Kaln surfaced again. The obnoxious beast was still there, hunkered down, arms crossed, watching with those horrid static eyes.

"I sent you away!" She heaved out of the water and stood dripping at the pool's edge. Light reflected crazily off the water to the walls and ceiling. "We require nothing from you!"

"I just had word that your captain is resting comfortably," it said, brandishing a pocketcom. "I thought you might like to know."

Her good ear flattened and she could not think what to say, awash all over again in her shame.

"Do you want to see him?" the golden-haired creature said.

Jalta climbed out of the pool too and stood, sleek and wet, beside her. "When we do, we will find him ourselves!" Kaln said, whiskers bristling. "We do not need your assistance!"

"Is that the Jao way, to refuse association when it is offered?"

"What would a stub-eared thing like you know of association?" Her body slipped toward pure *rage* and she felt unreasoning emotion take hold of her again. The throb behind her eyes returned, even more savage than before.

"More than you, it would seem." Its Jao was heavily accented but grammatically correct.

Jalta stiffened. "You dare offer insult to us?"

"It is only an insult if it is true." The creature straightened and regarded them steadily, hands shoved into folds in its dark-blue clothing. It was not especially tall for its kind, nor heavily muscled, yet possessed a sinewy sort of grace and seemed very sure of itself. "Is it?"

"All Jao seek association," she said, her angles gone to *disbelief*.

"So I have been told," the creature said, "though I am always willing to be instructed."

"That is not my responsibility," she said, then shook the water from her nap so that the air filled with flying drops. "You must seek instruction elsewhere."

"Wrot has assigned me to you," the creature said, its face and uniform now wet from her spray. "And I am also under Preceptor Ronz's orders to join the crew, so—" It rocked back on its heels. "—it would seem that we are, in the human vernacular, stuck with each other."

"Not," Kaln said, her white-hot anger rising like a deadly high tide, "if I kill you!"

"True." Its alien face crinkled into a curious expression that she could not read. "I must warn you, though, that more experienced Jao than you have already tried with obvious lack of success." Its strange grimace broadened. "Just think of me as your very own fraghta."

Kaln launched herself at the creature, but it slipped tantalizingly just out of reach, much more agile than its appearance indicated. "*You* intend to—instruct *us*?" she bellowed, hands clenched.

"I told Wrot I was too busy to take you on," the creature said blithely, "but he insisted, so here I am."

It was not to be borne! All the terrible events that had come of their ill-fated expedition crashed in upon her. Kaln snatched up her maroon trousers and donned them again with savage jerks, blood thrumming in her ears. The Bond had summoned them here to this primitive world like errant children, quartered them away from the remnants of their crew, then foisted this—this—*beast* upon them as a moral guide? She felt as though the top of her head would explode.

"Calm yourself, Senior-Tech," a Jao voice said from the doorway.

She whirled upon the newcomer. It was one of the Jao from the meeting with Terra's governor, a highly ranked individual, according to the service bars incised upon his cheek. "This has nothing to do with you!"

"Actually, Tully is here at my order," the intruder said mildly, his lines indicating *bemused-inquiry*. "So the situation has a great deal to do with me."

"Wrot, it seems they do not want a fraghta," the human said. "I had always heard that it was an honor to be assigned such an advisor."

"Do you hear how it speaks to us?" She glared at this Wrot-whoever-he-was. "Kill it now before it shames you any further!"

"A fraghta?" Wrot's wiry old body eased into the angles of *consideration*. "I had not thought of that before, but actually that is a close approximation of what this situation requires."

"What situation?" Jalta asked, his own lines hopelessly jumbled.

"You will have to work closely with humans on this expedition," Wrot said, "without killing them out of hand."

"But they are savages!" Kaln said. "One does not work *with* a savage!"

"They are not savages," Wrot said, his body gone to *stern-disapproval*. "They are sapients, technologically accomplished and fully capable of association under the right circumstances." He gazed at her implacably. "Can you say the same for yourselves?"

Kaln bristled. "You criticize Krant now!"

"Actually," Wrot said, "I am only criticizing *you*, unless all Krants behave this badly." He studied her, his eyes flickering green. "Do they?"

The shame of this day's actions came back to her, losing control and injuring her captain, being sent off to swim away her anger by a human as though she were a child too young to have emerged into society. What would her kochan-parents have said about all this? Her hands clenched. "No," she said in a strangled voice. "Krant is an honorable kochan. I was taught better."

"You cannot make yourself of use here," Wrot said, "unless you are able to work closely with humans. Tully, who at one time had quite a bit to learn himself about working with Jao, will assist you. The three of you should listen carefully to him."

Him—it was male, then. She hadn't been sure about that. She batted at her bad ear, frustrated. Those many service bars meant that this Wrot outranked both of them. "I—shall—endeavor to do so," she said grudgingly.

The native made a strangled noise, shook his head and said something in his native language.

"Speak only Jao in the hearing of your new charges," Wrot said. "That is respectful, and besides how else will they learn?"

"I said—" The human appeared to struggle with the translation. "I will be—*damned*."

The last word had still been in his own indecipherable tongue. She glared at him, whiskers bristling.

"The term—does not translate easily," he said. "It means something like 'doomed to eternal punishment.'"

"Well," Kaln said, somewhat mollified, "that would be proper."

And then the stub-eared creature led them to a food hall for something to eat.

CHAPTER
6

The next morning, Caitlin moved into her quarters on the *Lexington*. Ed was morose when he dropped her off, kissing her right there on the tarmac in front of Jao and human alike with a passion that curled her toes. She felt her cheeks heat.

"Damn Jao," he muttered against her neck as supply trucks rumbled past just a few feet away. His warm breath tickled all the way down to her knees. "Spiriting a guy's wife off to the far reaches of the galaxy on a whim just when he's gotten used to having her around!"

She laughed, though her heart was racing. Facing east, the morning sun was in her eyes and made it difficult to focus on his face. "Maybe you're just a little too used to having me around." She pressed her cheek to the broad expanse of his chest and drank in the sense of calm strength he always exuded. He smelled of aftershave, as usual, laundry detergent, and, for some reason, orange juice. Must have spilled some on his jacket that morning. She sighed and clung to him, her fingers smoothing a wrinkle in his shirt over and over. "Maybe you'll appreciate me even more when I come back."

If I come back, she thought, and knew that he was thinking the same thing. They'd both traveled to that Ekhat ship two years ago, had stood together in that terrible ear-splitting place and heard the insanity of what the aliens had to say—right before the pair had ripped themselves to shreds for having been defiled

61

by non-Ekhat contact. There had been at least one Ekhat ship in the nebula where the *Lexington* was headed. The Krant ships had destroyed it, but there could be more.

Ed's arms tightened until she couldn't breathe, but then he released her and stepped back, his shoulders resigned. Above all, he was a soldier, she thought. He knew where a soldier's duty lay, both his and hers. She was just as much a warrior as he was these days, only her weapons were papers and words.

His gray eyes narrowed. "Just see that you do come back," he said in his officer's voice.

Caitlin smiled tremulously, her toes still curled from that kiss. "Like anyone could keep me from it!" She hoisted her travel bag's strap onto her shoulder, then watched him climb into their black car and drive away without looking back. As one of the top commanders of the jinau, he had meetings in New Chicago over the next three days. The *Lexington* was scheduled to lift before he could return.

At least, humans had calculated that was when it would leave. The Jao, who disliked the notion of chopping time into discrete bits and then fussily counting them, were talking about "flow being very close to completion." Somewhere in the middle of the two widely disparate attitudes about time lay the truth. The *Lexington* would take off when all supplies were loaded and personnel were in place, in other words, when the vast ship was ready, and not a single second before.

Caitlin passed through Security to enter the refit facility, then again at the ship herself. Such a grand lady, Caitlin thought, as she walked up the ramp, the *Lexington*'s massive gray ribbed hull obscuring the sky. So many hopes were riding with her. Earth had been lucky last time in the battle with the Ekhat, cobbling together a ramshackle defense that proved mostly effective, but the Chinese people had paid the price. And luck could only take them so far before it gave out. Preparation was a much better ally.

At the top of the ramp, she encountered the ship's captain, Dannet krinnu ava Terra, a middle-aged Jao female with a great deal of Ekhat combat under her belt.

"Mrs. Kralik," Dannet said. Her stance declared this meeting an *irritated-distraction* to the human's experienced eyes. "I felt you would come soon."

Dannet was handsome by Jao standards, with a powerful frame

as well as a strongly marked *vai camiti* that boldly stated her origin, despite her adoption of her new taif's designation. The three broad stripes slanted across her nose and eyes at that precise angle indicated "Narvo," to anyone with much knowledge of Jao culture.

Narvo had also been the kochan of Oppuk, the late and unlamented governor of Earth, who had abandoned Earth to the Ekhat when the attack came. Years before, he had murdered Caitlin's brother in a fit of pique because his Jao accent had been lacking, then later broken her arm as casually as one snaps a twig. He was dead now, but his kochan was very highly ranked. Members of it worked at various positions all over Earth. She often wondered how much they blamed her for Oppuk's disgrace and death.

To deepen the fragile new association between Pluthrak and Narvo, the current governor, Aille, a former Pluthrak, had applied to Narvo for an experienced captain, once the *Lexington* was under construction, with the understanding that he or she must join Earth's new taif. Dannet had come, apparently willing, but seeing that *vai camiti* was always chilling. It was like looking back through time into Oppuk's unsane face. Though she had no idea how closely the two were related, Caitlin avoided the Narvo female whenever possible.

"Call me Caitlin," Caitlin said, summoning her diplomatic skills. She let her angles assume *wishing-to-be-of-use*. "We are crewmates now. Formality will not be necessary."

"Formality has its uses," Dannet said, regarding her with an indecipherable expression. Her body had now gone classically *neutral*. "Do you know the way to your quarters?"

Thank the gods, she did, having inspected them several days before. "Yes."

"Then I will leave you," Dannet said. "I have much to oversee." She continued on down the ramp, her stride businesslike, resplendent in Terra-blue trousers and gleaming blue harness.

"Gives you the willies, don't she?" a voice said out of the shadows just beyond the great hatch. A hand extended.

"Rob!" Caitlin took the proffered hand. "I didn't know you'd come aboard."

The dark face of Rob Wiley, former Resistance leader, grinned back at her, sporting a gold front tooth. Good dental work was nonexistent back in the mountains and he'd been taking advantage of its availability since accepting the position of one of the two subcommanders heading *Lexington*'s ground force complement. "Boarded most of my troops this morning."

"How's that going?" she asked as the hatch closed behind them.

"Damned weird," Wiley said, slinging Caitlin's bag over his own shoulder and then falling into step beside her. "If anyone had told me two years ago that I would share command of anything with a freaking Jao, I'd have sliced their liver out and served it to them for breakfast."

"Is Brel making it difficult?" Their footsteps echoed across a patch of bare deck plating. Busy crew members, human and Jao, bustled past in both directions, paying them no attention. He directed her to the nearest lift station and punched for the car.

"Not on purpose, but I never know what that rascal is thinking," Wiley said as they waited. "He says almost nothing, and I can't figure out what all that stupid dancing around means. I've tried to learn a few of the basics, but I think you have to be born to it."

Or at least exposed at a very early age, Caitlin thought. She'd acquired a Jao guard when she was three, not a positive experience, since it meant she'd been a virtual political prisoner a good deal of her life. But it had left her the Earth's most fluent human in Jao bodyspeak.

"I can tutor you," she said. "We're bound to have some downtime on our hands during the voyage. From what I hear, it takes a few days on the trip out to set up frame travel and then jump."

The door opened and they stepped into the blue-lighted space. It was much larger than the standard human elevator, probably one of the heavy-duty lifts for handling combat equipment and troops, spare parts and supplies. The doors whooshed shut.

"Deck Forty-Six," she said. Her stomach lurched as they shot upwards, faster than humans liked, just one of the many Jao influences in this huge ship. Why set the lift to half-speed just to make humans a tiny bit more comfortable?

She wondered how long it would take her to get used to it, or if indeed she ever would.

Mallu was feeling somewhat improved, but the human medician wouldn't discharge him from her care.

"I want to swim," he said, restless in the hard human-style bed, rather than curled up in a proper soft pile of *dehabia*. The medical bay was never quiet, with beeps and hisses and attendants fussing about him all the time. He longed for solitude. His chest ached, though he was trying to disregard it.

The female regarded him with an indecipherable expression. "You need to stay here for—" She broke off and muttered a few words to herself in her own language as though peeved. "—for some time longer." She crossed her arms over her chest. "I will let you know when that particular flow is complete."

A Jao stuck his head into the room and glanced over at Mallu. "He looks better, Dr. Ames."

"No thanks to our Krant-captain," she said with a flick of her head that was almost meaningful. "He wants to be out and about, in fact, insists upon it."

"We Jao are tough," the newcomer said. "Perhaps he is ready."

Mallu realized he recognized him from that meeting with Preceptor Ronz and Earth's young governor, Aille krinnu ava Terra. He lay back against the pillow and chased the name around his foggy brain. They had not been introduced, but he'd picked up the name from the others' comments. Wram? Wral? No, Wrot krinnu ava Terra. That was it. A scarred old veteran of the original battle to take this planet, and now a member of its nascent taif.

"Not that tough," the medician said. "The original injury he suffered in the battle with the Ekhat was never adequately treated. It was just a matter of time until he collapsed. The Krant-captain needs a bit longer to heal."

Wrot crossed the room to stand by the human-style bed. Mallu got a good look at the numerous bars of service incised on his cheek. Impressive. He sat up, though the motion wrung a sharp jolt from his healing ribs.

"Two days, then?" Wrot asked.

"I cannot answer that with any certainty," she said. Her alien face contorted into a startling display of naked teeth. "I am good at this, but not that good." She twitched the thin white cloth back over Mallu's legs. "Just not yet."

"Flow feels almost complete," Mallu said, lying back again to ease the stabbing pain in his chest. Urgency teased at him. The situation was about to complete itself. "This ship will lift soon. I can feel it. We must get our crewmates aboard and situated."

"I will handle that," Wrot said. "Is there anything else?"

"Check on Senior-Tech Kaln and Terniary-Commander Jalta," he said. "I have not seen them since—" He broke off, then gestured at his chest. "—since this happened. The loss of our ships and then the summons that diverted us to this world rather than returning home has affected them both. Kaln suffered a head injury in the battle, which seems to have impacted her judgment. I fear she needs close supervision."

"They accompanied you here when you were brought in," the medician said. "Both seemed agitated so I sent them off to swim."

And they had no doubt been wandering the vast ship on their own ever since, Mallu realized. Not good. Kaln was so moody since the battle with the Ekhat, she might do or say almost anything. If another human offended her or even just got in her way, there might be dire consequences. What if she killed one? Even though they were a conquered race, the local authorities seemed to set great store by these spindly creatures. There would be repercussions and even more shame. Without conscious volition, his body assumed the lines of *distress*.

"I saw them a short time ago," Wrot said. "I assigned Major Tully as their escort soon after this happened so they have not been unsupervised."

"Is this Tully a human?" Mallu asked.

Wrot's body signaled *affirmation*.

"Then it may be dead," Mallu said.

"Oh," Wrot said, "you do not know Tully, possibly one of the most stubborn humans alive, and that is saying a great deal. They are a marvelously recalcitrant species." He pulled out his pocketcom. "They have to do everything their own way, and I am quite certain Tully would never be so obliging as to allow your tech to kill him."

Goddamn Jao. Tully doggedly followed as the pair entered the engine room, exclaiming to one another over the technology in words far beyond his everyday Jao vocabulary. After eating yesterday in one of the Jao food halls, some nauseating concoction involving raw fish that probably tasted even worse than it smelled, not that anyone could have persuaded him to try it, they'd prowled the ship for endless hours.

He'd located the Krants' quarters early on, but except for a brief nap, during which he'd stationed himself outside their door, they'd refused to stay there, exploring the *Lexington* with a relentless tenacity that spoke to him more of avoidance than real interest. It was plain that the female, Kaln, feared the Krant-captain would die and was trying with all her might to think about anything but that.

For now, he'd been letting them run, just as one let a frightened horse gallop out its fear before gathering the reins and turning its head back to the stable. His patience was about at an end, though. He had a lot of last minute details to oversee for Baker Company's deployment to the *Lexington*, and he needed some real sleep, more than a ten-minute catnap.

Kaln knelt on the deck and peered under a bank of controls. She rapped so hard with her knuckles that read-outs flickered. Two startled human techs headed over to intervene. Tully's pocketcom buzzed and he fished for the black plastic device as he went to join the fray. "Yes?"

"I assume you still have our Krant friends in sight," Wrot's voice said in English.

"Affirmative," he said, "though I'm getting mighty tired of their faces."

"Conduct them back to the medical bay," Wrot said. "Their captain wishes to assure himself of their good behavior."

"They haven't killed anyone yet, if that's what you mean," Tully said. "I've been running interference for them all over the ship, keeping the crew away from them, them away from the crew as best I could."

One of the human techs was bent over, arguing with Kaln, who had pulled off the back of the console and was peering into a maze of colored wires. Eyes flashing green, she looked up at the man and flattened her good ear.

Tully sighed.

"Wise," Wrot said. "Bring them up." The com clicked off.

Yeah, Tully thought, just like that. He inserted himself into Kaln's line of sight. "We have to go back to the medical bay," he said. "Your captain—"

"He is not dead!" the big female said. Her body stiffened.

Tully waved a hand. "No—"

"It was that human's fault!" she cried, shoulders rising. "The creature was too insolent to be borne!"

The other Jao, Jalta, was just watching, his spine at a peculiar angle, signifying something, no doubt, though Tully hadn't a clue. He was suddenly very sick of these two Jao and this half-assed babysitting assignment.

"Stand down!" he barked in Jao, schooling his tone to imitate Yaut. Gods knew he'd heard him often enough over the last few years. He caught and held Kaln's flickering green and black gaze. "You will not further shame your kochan with such wanton behavior!"

Jalta backed away, while Kaln froze, one dark-napped hand still on the wires.

The human tech, a youngster no more than twenty with fair skin that had gone even paler, was sweating. He clenched a wrench in one hand as though he wanted to give her a solid whack on the head. "Sir, I don't know exactly what's going on here, but if they pull those dynamo wires, we'll be hours getting them reseated and tested." He glared over his shoulder at Jalta as well. "It could mean we won't lift on time!"

"You are upsetting our techs," Tully said, "for no reason beyond idle curiosity, which will stop now."

Kaln's hand dropped. She handed the protective cover to the young human tech, who clutched it to his chest as though it were his firstborn and backed away. Her whiskers bristled as she came upright. "You will not speak to me or any other Jao in such a disrespectful manner!"

"It has been given to me to instruct you on how to conduct yourselves in this mixed crew," Tully said carefully, the blood pounding in his ears. Jeeze, negotiating with rebels had been a hundred times easier than this. It would have been less of a challenge to talk a clam out of its damned shell. He cursed Wrot's ornery hide for putting him in this position. "That is one of the ways, as a member of the governor's service, that I make myself of use." Without knowing exactly what the posture meant, he let his body assume his best Yaut-imitation of a Jao instructing someone very dim. "You will listen and do as I say!"

Jalta dropped his gaze, his stance gone to what seemed to be *neutrality.* Kaln loomed over Tully, her functional ear pitched at an unsettling angle, not *pride* exactly. He'd seen that often enough to know. Not *anger* or *rage.* Something else.

If it came down to hand-to-hand, he thought, holding his ground as she advanced upon him, he was confident he could take her. Jao were strong, but not as agile or fast as a human in good physical condition. They tended to underestimate humans in general—and Tully's military assignment meant that he'd trained extensively against Jao soldiers. As long he didn't let her get a good grip—

With heart-stopping abruptness, she turned away. "Lead us back to the medical bay, smoothface. We would see our captain for ourselves."

By leading, of course, he would be assuming an inferior position. Jao deemed it an honor to go last and, of course, "smoothface" was a sly insult, pointing out that he had no incised bars of service as would a Jao of similar rank. "My full name," he said with a sudden flash of inspiration, knowing that to force the knowledge upon her was a form of power, "is Major Gabriel Dorran Tully."

Her eyes flashed green as some restless alien sea, then she fell in behind him.

Wrot suddenly felt it, the pull of events, an alteration in his timesense. Somewhere, faraway, factors had shifted. Something important had changed, something that had to do with this impending exploration. It was *time* to act.

If what the Preceptor suspected was true, then the Lleix had survived, but as the sudden need for haste pressed in upon him, he knew that, for whatever reason, they might not have much longer. The Ekhat had been in that nebula. Krant's ships had destroyed the vessel they encountered, but there could easily be more investigating its disappearance. Many more.

He slipped out of the medical bay into the hallway, then used his pocketcom to contact the *Lexington*'s new captain, Dannet krinnu ava Terra.

"Terra-Captain," he said, when her gravelly voice answered, "there has been a change. Do you feel it too?"

"I felt a slight increase in urgency," she said.

Several crewmen hurried past, Jao and human, lost in discussion. "Because the Preceptor has shared more of his concerns with me," Wrot said, "it is possible I feel the change more strongly."

"You could tell me what you know," she said testily, "then I would no doubt experience it in equal measure."

"The circumstances are not mine to share," Wrot said. A pallet of supplies was being towed by a sturdy human female jinau to a nearby storeroom. He edged out of the way. "Only the Preceptor can authorize their dissemination."

"Would your answer be the same, had I not been born of Narvo?" she asked.

"You are Terra now," he said stiffly and set off for the nearest lift. The strange urgency tugged at him, making his nap itch, his whiskers unsettled. Some unfortunate flow was trying to complete itself. They must leave now, or as close to now as could be managed. "That is all that matters."

"So I was told," Dannet said, "though, thus far, I have not always found it to be true."

"Some maintain long memories concerning Oppuk's misdeeds, but you have been given command of this great ship," Wrot said as he jogged down the corridor, weaving around more crewmen, "the largest vessel ever built by Jao. Why should you not feel trusted?"

"I make myself of use," she said, then fell silent, obviously waiting for him to lead the conversation in a more productive direction.

"How soon can we lift?" he asked, turning at an intersection and dodging a pair of humans towing crates stacked on wheeled platforms.

"The last of the supplies are being loaded now," Dannet said. "I will recall all personnel not currently on board. We can lift as soon as everyone has reported."

At her words, he could feel things shifting into place, conditions being satisfied, edges coming into alignment. They would leave shortly, though he had no way to tell at this juncture if it were soon enough. "I will fetch the rest of the Krant crew," he said, "then return myself."

"Will that be sufficient?" she asked, acknowledging his superior perception of the situation's flow.

"It will have to be," he said.

CHAPTER
7

In his secluded office at the edge of the base, Preceptor Ronz felt the new urgency like a sharp prickle down his spine, an irresistible twitch that commanded his feet to move, to take him somewhere *else*. He stared blindly at the curving quantum crystal walls, trying to see beyond. The situation had altered.

He located his pocketcom under a pile of flimsies and contacted Wrot. The crafty old veteran answered immediately. "I feel it, too," his voice said through the device. "Something is quite definitely trying to complete itself."

That could be good or ill, the Preceptor reflected. There was no way of knowing. All he could tell for now was that faraway variables had shifted and it was time to act. He rose restlessly from his chair, knocking over a stack of paper reports. "The ship must leave as soon as possible," he said.

"I am already working on it," Wrot said. Ronz could detect a note of excitement in the old warrior's voice. "Fortunately, Terra-Captain Dannet's experience has stood us in good stead. She has prepared well. I have been running checks since I felt the flow turn. The ship's critical systems are up and running, most supplies already loaded. Subcommanders Brel krinnu ava Terra and Rob Wiley had the foresight to load their equipment several solar revolutions ago, including the space assault modules and ground tanks. All personnel not currently on board have been summoned."

"Fortunate, indeed." Ronz looked down at the plastic com's

rectangle in his hand, trying to make his mind pull up any critical lingering details. Nothing could be left undone. "I do not have to tell you how important this is."

"If you are right," Wrot said, "only our human allies can bargain for us in this situation. Those you seek will not be pleased to have us on their trail again."

"No, they will not," Ronz said. "It is your job to help Caitlin and Tully make them see the possibilities here, the many ways we could now be of use to one another as the Lleix once were to us, so long ago."

"Before they kill us for hunting them to the point of extinction," Wrot said sourly.

"Yes," Ronz said. He stalked about his office, round and round and round, utterly unable to be still. An immense opportunity for association loomed before them, if only they could make use of it. He longed to go and put his hand to the task himself, but could not spare his attention here. "That would be best."

Feeling the new urgency, Aille collected Yaut and went out to the *Lexington*'s vast construction yard to watch. The last of the supplies were streaming in. Lines of jinau and Jao soldiers strode purposefully toward the huge ship, their kits slung over one shoulder, talking among themselves with excited gestures.

Cables were being cast off, power lines withdrawn, scaffolding rolled away. The last-minute screech of tools was fading with only the final few touches here and there on the vast hull being administered. Everyone, human and Jao alike, seemed to feel the change in conditions just as strongly. It was *time*.

To do what? his brain demanded. Aille was keen to learn what Ronz was planning. Just who did the Preceptor expect to discover in that nebula in the section of space sometimes called the Sangrel Deeps? What could possibly lie hidden there worth all this hurry and secrecy? The Jao encountered sapient species from time to time, though rarely those accomplished enough for space travel or as infernally clever as humans. Still, word of such discoveries usually disseminated throughout the many Jao kochan as tales of interest rather than being withheld with this degree of fierce security.

The Preceptor joined the two of them outside the refit facility. His back bent with age, he watched silently as activity surged around the great ship. Everything had to be cleared away so the *Lexington* could launch.

"I do not suppose you can tell me now?" Aille said, letting his angles go to *urgent-polite-inquiry*.

The old Jao gazed at him benignly, his body exquisitely neutral, as only those of the Bond could manage, his eyes barely flecked with green. "When flow completes itself, you will be, as a human would say, the first to know."

"I do not find that reassuring," Aille said. "You are risking a great resource on this mystery venture. The *Lexington* will be urgently needed when the Ekhat decide to sweep back through this system, which could happen any time."

Yaut studied them both, but did not comment. His posture reflected *restrained-curiosity*. The fraghta clearly wished he were going.

As do we all, Aille thought. Something interesting was out there, something worth all of this commitment of resources, as a human would say, all this fuss. If his responsibilities were not so pressing, he would have named himself a member of that crew and gone off adventuring with them, no matter if he were invited or not.

But Terra was restless, and there was much still unresolved. He could not leave for the length of time this voyage would consume. His nascent taifs were coming along, but would fall apart without constant reinforcement and supervision.

Workmen, having just dismantled a huge scaffold, were carting the components back into the refit building, and the three of them moved aside.

"Much is being risked that much might be gained," Preceptor Ronz said, standing closer to Yaut. "And I am not going either. Keep that in view. There is far too much demanding my attention here."

The flow of supplies was lessening now, and there were gaps in the lines of the reporting troops. The mood projected by one and all was industry and purpose. Both of Terra's taifs were united on this matter, whatever it turned out to be.

The door-field behind them faded and Wrot krinnu ava Terra appeared, shepherding a group of battered Jao clad in Krant maroon, evidently the remnants of the crew from the ill-fated ship. Aille estimated there were about thirty, some obviously still recovering from injuries incurred during the battle. They seemed dazed and reluctant, walking slowly, gawking at the *Lexington*'s immenseness.

What could they have possibly seen to prompt this mission? Aille wondered. And how could they be unaware of it? Mysteries wrapped in mysteries. The only thing one could say for certain was that the Bond did not play politics. What they planned might be very long-range, but it was inevitably for the good of all kochan.

He just wished he were going to be one of those allowed to swim in this intriguing new sea.

On board the *Lexington*, safely installed in her new quarters, Caitlin heard her pocketcom buzz over on the bunk where she'd tossed it. She set her digital picture frame, which was stuffed with endless photos of Ed, on the little bureau built into the wall and then activated the loop. The first image came up. *Ed all kitted up in his dress uniform for a formal reception, looking grave and dignified.* She flipped her com open.

"Caitlin?" Professor Kinsey's voice said. "I hear you're leaving."

The digital image shifted. *Ed on their delayed honeymoon, wearing jeans and a white T-shirt, barefoot on the beach under the bright Mississippi sun.* "Yes, Professor," she said, settling on the narrow bunk, eyes still on the display. "They're in a great hurry all of a sudden, something about the 'flow changing.'"

"I don't suppose you know what this is all about yet?"

The image faded and the next came up. *Ed laughing, brandishing a bottle of beer, surrounded by his fellow jinau officers in a New Chicago bar.* "No," she said. "Ronz wouldn't say, and Wrot won't tell us until he's good and ready, and who knows when that might be?"

He hesitated, and she thought that the pause said more than mere words. "You will take care of yourself, won't you?"

New picture. *Ed bundled up in a gray parka when they'd visited the Resistance camps on a good-will trip up in the Rockies last winter, holding out his hand to her.* "I will." She forced her voice to remain level. "It's a great opportunity, Professor. Whatever is out there must be really important. I'm honored that the Preceptor thinks I can be of use."

"Jao can be wrong," her mentor said softly. "Even the Bond, and what is good in the long run for them might well be disastrous for you personally. Keep that in mind while you're out there adventuring—please."

He was so right. She was going to be walking a very thin line on this mission between making herself of fullest use and merely surviving. "I will," she said. "Good-by, Professor."

"Until we meet again," he said in his stiff, old-fashioned way that never failed to charm her.

The pocketcom clicked off. She sat alone in her spare room, with only digital books, images, and music recordings to remind her of home. Weight allowances had permitted nothing more. This trip was to be all business.

The picture frame display continued to run. *Ed at the New Chicago Zoo, feeding an elephant*, then *Ed in their kitchen, looking up from his breakfast of eggs and bacon, grinning and rumpled from lack of sleep because they had spent the night making love after long weeks of separation.* It was too much. She couldn't bear any more and clicked the picture frame off. Resolutely, she turned her thoughts to what she needed to do that very moment.

The pocketcom would have to be recalibrated for ship frequencies, she thought, gazing at the slim black rectangle in her hand. Everything was changing, so she would have to change too, in whatever way made her most productive. She only hoped the Preceptor was right and she was up to the task.

Tully delivered the two Krants to the medical bay where Krant-Captain Mallu did indeed look much improved. Next to his bed, a monitor beeped softly. White-coated personnel slipped in and out of the room, intent on their duties. Kaln and Jalta approached the captain's bed and gazed down at him, edgy as though their skins didn't fit. For once, the female tech was speechless.

"His collapse was not all your fault," Dr. Ames said to Kaln as she filled in a form on a clipboard, then handed it to a male human aide. "It was mostly the result of his injury in the battle with the Ekhat. He should have sought treatment much earlier and not put himself at such grave risk."

"He is very stubborn," Kaln said, her single good ear twitching. She batted at the drooping one as though it offended her.

Tully's pocketcom buzzed. He flipped it open. "We are leaving soon," Wrot's voice said in English. "Perhaps even within the hour."

Having lived on Earth since the original invasion, Wrot dealt with human methods of time management better than most Jao. "What about the rest of the Krant crew?" Tully said, keeping a wary eye on Kaln and Jalta lest they get away from him.

"I just escorted them aboard myself and left them in their quarters," Wrot said, "though they are jumpy and disgruntled. They wanted to go home to Mannat Kar, their natal world. They don't understand why they are here instead."

"Why didn't the Preceptor send them back, then?" Tully tensed as Kaln glanced at the door. Was she about to bolt again? He maneuvered himself between her and easy escape.

"He has his reasons." Wrot's tone was noncommittal.

"Right." Tully scratched his head. The Preceptor always had his reasons and rarely felt moved to share them. The rest of them might as well be puppets dancing on strings as far as the Bond was concerned. Business as bloody usual. "If we're leaving, then I have to pick up my kit."

"Have your batman do it," Wrot said.

Sometimes Tully forgot that he held a command grade for real these days. As a spy for the Resistance, he'd skulked around military installations for years before Aille had drafted him into his service, pretending to be Private First Class This and Sergeant That. It was still a surprise to wake up each morning and find that he'd earned something real and honest, something lasting and all his own.

"Meet me on Deck Six once you're done," Wrot said. "My quarters."

Tully glanced at Kaln and Jalta. "What about these Krants I've been nursemaiding?"

"Leave them with Krant-Captain Mallu," Wrot said. "He can handle them now."

"Right." Tully clicked off, then punched in the code for his batman, David Church. He slipped out of the medical bay into the hallway, watching the furious activity as crewmen, both human and Jao, checked read-outs, monitored controls, hauled packages onboard and stowed them with a quiet intensity. The whole ship reverberated with activated machinery, passing feet, and voices. Damn, he could almost feel the completeness of the impending "flow" himself. Obviously, he'd been hanging around with Jao far too long.

"Church here," a voice said on his com.

"Church, this is Major Tully," he said. "Pack my things on the double, then run them out here to the *Lexington*. I have quarters on Deck Fourteen. We're about to lift."

"Already done, sir." David Church sounded aggrieved as though Tully had accused him of dereliction of duty. The tall, dark-haired youth from Oklahoma was only twenty-six, but took his responsibilities seriously. "Your ship quarters are ready for inspection."

"Great," Tully said. Of course it was already done. Church was more than competent even if Tully's head was still spinning with the suddenness of this whole thing. "Carry on."

"Yes, sir." The com clicked off.

Sir, right. That was him. Tully pocketed the device. Still a shock every freaking time someone said the word. He doubted he would ever get used to it.

Mallu slipped off the uncomfortable sleeping platform when the human medician was not looking. His ribs still hurt, but one of the assistants, a young Jao with a marvelously bold *vai camiti*, had strapped them tightly, and now he could at least breathe.

Kaln and Jalta watched him without comment, but the medician, Ames, caught sight of him out of the corner of one eye and intercepted him. "Will you stop that? You will undo all my hard work!"

He wavered on his feet, then took a few tottering steps around her. "I am fine," he said, though the blood pounded in his head. "It serves no purpose for me to remain here. I wish to go to my crew."

The two of them glared at one another, although he could pick up very little of her mood. Her eyes were static and her ears could not so much as twitch.

"Fine," she said abruptly and crossed her arms. Her naked cheeks were curiously red. "Go! Maybe when you collapse again, they will take you to one of the other medical bays where someone else can try to put you back together. I must warn you, though, that next time it will not be nearly as easy."

Kaln's whiskers curled with *alarm*. "Captain," she said, "perhaps—"

"No, no, go!" Dr. Ames waved a dismissive hand at him. "I am quite certain you know more of the medical arts and the state of your own internal organs than I do." She crossed her arms and took up a stiff-backed stance that seemed quite meaningful, though he hadn't the slightest clue what it signified. "*I* have only studied Jao physiology for the last ten orbital cycles and performed thousands of medical procedures, but *you* have been Jao all your life!"

Jalta stepped closer, his body hunched in *uncertain-misery*, quite a complex posture for one of their kochan. "Stay until you are dismissed, pool-sib," he said softly. "There is nothing for us to do now. The ship will launch, but, as far as I know, we are not required on the command deck. Let the medician carry out her function as best she knows how. I will see to our crew."

Mallu's legs gave way and Kaln leaped to seize his arm. Taking his weight, the tech levered him back to the dreadfully uncomfortable *bed*, as humans called it.

"You could," Dr. Ames said, "make yourself of use here by furthering my education. I have never encountered an injury of this sort before. Treating you will allow me to be of more aid to other Jao in the future. Of course, your death could be useful, too, as a cautionary tale for other injured Jao who do not wish to heed my advice."

"Captain, you must stay!" Kaln burst out. "Indeed, I will not let you leave!"

Mallu sagged back against the thin cloth covering and sighed. Even the shallow breath made his ribs ache.

"Smart female." Ames jerked her head toward Kaln. "You should promote her."

"For that," Mallu said stiffly, "I would have to have my own ship."

"When the time is right," Ames said, examining the readout on a medical instrument, "certainly you will get another command."

But, as a human, she had no idea of Krant's poverty or isolation, or how seldom his kochan acquired new ships. The last two had been purchased several generations before when a trading run had proved particularly lucrative. They had not encountered such luck again in a very long time, and his sense of flow did not indicate they would any time soon.

He had been entrusted with a great treasure and had let his kochan down. He needed to return home and lay his misfortunes before Amnst, the current kochanau. Delaying here only increased his dread of that final accounting for what he had lost.

But he said none of this. Kochan troubles were not to be spilled before alien primitives, even one that was a bit on the clever side, like this Ames. He closed his eyes and let a rising tide of dormancy overwhelm him. Kaln and Jalta were talking softly, while all around them, the great ship quivered in preparation for launching into the black night of space. There, at least, he would feel at home.

It was time. Dannet krinnu ava Terra settled into her chair and gazed around at the controlled bursts of activity across the command deck. The majority of the bridge officers were Jao, but about a third were human.

Narvo had sacrificed her promising career to this new taif as proof of its intent to fully associate with Pluthrak. So she would work to the best of her ability and captain their huge ship with its barbaric kinetic weapons. But her liking of the assignment was not required.

"On your order, Terra-Captain," her second, Pleniary-Commander Otta, said. His eyes danced with green fire. His stance was a sturdy version of *restrained-readiness* which betrayed his Nimmat origin.

"You may launch," she said with a careless flick of one ear, as though this were any other ship lifting for the first time and not a momentous occasion for both species involved.

"Proceed," Otta said to his bridge crew. They bent to their work and then the great ship roared into the sky.

PART II:
The Lleix

CHAPTER
8

The great devils, the Ekhat, had tracked the Lleix down. They were no longer safe in this out-of-the-way pocket of the galaxy where they had long ago gone to ground like terrified prey and where their ancestral guiding spirits, the *Boh*, could no longer look upon them.

That dire truth beat through the sprawling Lleix colony at the foot of the Valeron mountains as though all who had been conducting their safe respectable lives there now could think but a single thought between them. After more than a thousand local years secreted on this world, they had been discovered by their age-old enemies and no longer possessed sufficient flight-worthy ships to transport the bulk of their population elsewhere.

Young Jihan of the Starsifters *elian* watched as her mentor, Sayr, made his slow and careful way along the crushed stone path leading up the side of the mountain. Though tall with age, his pewter-skinned form was now bent, his dark aureole drooping around his seamed face like the dying petals of a flower. He was the wisest elder she knew, yet distress fluttered in her breast.

After much deliberation by her *elian*, he was going to present what she believed to be, at least partially, an erroneous conclusion. The readings the Starsifters had examined from the battle, the debris they had analyzed, had whispered far different findings to her than it had to the rest of the analytical society.

All agreed that it was the Ekhat who had penetrated the nebula and then fought the Lleix. Alerted by satellites put in orbit long ago, her people had launched their ancient ships, held together with little more than wire and red string for luck, fueled by prayer. There had been two intruding Ekhat ships. One, the Lleix had destroyed themselves, but the survivor fled and then inexplicably fought yet two other much smaller ships which had blessedly destroyed it. One of the newly arrived ships had exploded, but the second, badly damaged, fled the system without making further contact.

So—something else, actually *someone* else, had also been present out there in the swirling nebula which confused long-range instrument readings and reflected back scans. Something alien and cunning. The Starsifters had recovered genetic material from both the Ekhat and the Anj, a slave species sometimes employed on the great devils' ships as they carried out their wanton mission of destruction. A tiny amount of the trace organic material recovered after the battle, though, had not matched either and indeed did not indicate any of the usual enslaved client species used by the Ekhat.

In the Starsifters' Duty Chamber, she had studied the records, analyzing and reading, researching for days on end until she'd found a passing reference to a great evil from long ago which seemed to match what they had in hand. She believed the physical evidence traced back to a species that had actually fought for the Ekhat in ships of their own, rather than just crewing their masters' vessels. Despite the conclusions of her elders, she was certain it had not only been the Ekhat in that savage battle. Their wily handservants, the Jao, had been there too.

Her mentors, led by Sayr, disagreed gently, pointing out that the trace evidence was indeed only that—a trace, a single sample. There was only a forty percent match with the record, hardly conclusive, and besides the Jao had not been seen for over a thousand years. No doubt the Ekhat had grown weary of them, as they did all sapient species, and put them down. The devils they knew were bad enough. Jihan should not invoke ancient fears just to make herself important. The situation was dire at any rate.

Added to that, they said, was simple logic: The strangers had dispatched the second Ekhat ship. The enslaved Jao would never have done that. No doubt it was another faction of the Ekhat, who were notorious for refusing to tolerate even their own kind. Most likely, the Melody had fired upon the Interdict, or the Harmony upon the Melody. That, the elders could believe.

The Starsifters were an esoteric *elian*, highly specialized, attracting few of the youth emerging each year from the Children's
Court, then accepting almost none of those. She herself was the
youngest full member by over ten years and little regarded, for
all that she studied hard. Many of the elders had never seen an
Ekhat ship outside of recordings until the recent battle.

The last recorded incursion had taken place before she was
born, over thirty years ago, and had come to nothing with the
bizarrely articulated Ekhat ship sweeping through the nebula
without hesitation, evidently on its way to visit destruction upon
some other unfortunate world. She had viewed the terrifying
records repeatedly.

Before that, their last encounter with the Ekhat had been almost
four hundred years earlier, battling in another star system where
the Lleix had also maintained a refugee colony, now destroyed.
The survivors had fled here, joining the settlement already in
place, poor though it was, and now, as far as anyone on Valeron
knew, the Lleix survived nowhere else.

The wind gusted and she drew the folds of her brocaded robe
more closely around her body. The cold bit bone-deep and her
breath plumed in a white cloud. Ahead of her, Sayr ascended the
path to the waiting wheeled transport which would take him up
to the towering hall with its exposed beams, carved *Boh* faces,
and sacred pennants, situated halfway up the mountain.

Although no Ekhat ships remained in the area, at some point
they would seek their missing fellows. And when they did, they
would find the Lleix here, hiding. They had always known the
Ekhat would discover them at some point. It had been bred
into each generation, that knowledge, the understanding that at
any moment, they might have to fight, or flee, or perhaps even
surrender to extinction, as had so many other species under the
maniac ministrations of the Ekhat.

Only now they could not flee. They had lost two ships fighting off the Ekhat, two they could not spare. Their numbers had
grown since retreating to this hidden world, while the refuge
where they'd gone to ground was resource-poor. There were too
few ships and no way to replace them.

The Shipbuilders' *elian* was defunct. They had not been able to
recruit new members when there was no material for construction
and its last elders had died a number of generations before she

was born. The Shipservicers did better at replenishing their ranks, but even they could not craft the replacement parts needed when the necessary metals did not occur on this world.

Jihan paced back and forth, her short legs eating up the distance with swinging strides. Sayr was wrong. They were all wrong. It was not just the Ekhat, it was the Jao too, no doubt as bad in their own way as the great devils they served. Though it was forbidden, though she would break *sensho* by appearing without permission, she had to present the truth to the Han.

She set off up the winding path, determined to catch up to Sayr. She would make the elders understand before it was too late.

Grijo arrived early, but the Hall of Decision was already close-crowded. The Hallkeepers, a tiny *elian* of only three, had done their duty, lighting the space brightly so that the colored woods with their attendant carvings showed well. The silent *Boh* faces gazed down within, a reminder of what they had lost. Everyone was painfully aware that the ancestral spirits could not find the Lleix in this alien place. As had been true since their initial diaspora, they were alone.

All the *elian* were represented: Childtenders, Waterdirectors, Groundtillers, Stonesculpters, the most plentiful, down to the more obscure, such as the Gameconductors and Scentcrafters. Tall and well filled out with age, they still trickled in, one delegate each, always the most senior, who would take back the decision here rendered and disseminate it to the rest of the colony. Each assumed his or her place according to *sensho*, proper rank sorted out by age, the youngest and least experienced seated in the back.

Representing the Dwellingconstructors, Grijo climbed laboriously up to sit in the raised immense ornate chair in the center of the vast hall and then waited. As eldest of all, it fell to him to conduct the assembly. His bones were old, though his sight was still quite good, and he possessed the experience of many such sessions to help him maintain order.

Soon the Starsifters' representative, venerable Sayr, who was nearly his match in seniority, would present their findings and the assembled *elian* would be called upon to decide how next to proceed. As if there were any sort of real choice, he reflected. He feared there was not.

He gazed out at the assembled *elian*. The Lleix were a graceful, silver-skinned people with varying shades of aureoles framing their concerned faces, gold, silver, black, and even the occasional startling russet. Only the comeliest were allowed to produce the next generation, so that the Lleix physical aspect was uniformly pleasing. One and all, their black eyes were properly upswept at the corners, which some vain individuals accented with sticks of black *vahl*. Down to the last individual, their robes fell in properly draped folds, the styling unchanged in over two thousand years.

The great doors stood open so that the morning sun streamed in from the east, red and angry. It was the leading edge of winter, and even colder up here on the side of the mountain than down on the plains below. Grijo settled his blue and silver brocaded robe more closely around his age-thickened body. Propriety must be served, even if this turned out to be the long-feared Last-of-Days.

Two more representatives scurried in and took their place in the assembled ranks, Treebinder and Enginetuner by their robe patterns. Their aureoles fanned out about their faces, carefully dressed for this significant occasion. Dread seethed through the room, along with fear and loathing, so palpable Grijo could taste the emotions.

The Ekhat had found them. The impact of that knowledge was much like being told one was going to die before the next breath could be drawn. The incursion thirty-two years ago, though the Ekhat had seemed to take no notice at the time, had probably marked their location for later action. Thirty years was but a gust of breeze to an Ekhat, the tumble of one leaf to the ground. No one knew exactly the length of a single Ekhat's life-span, but it was apparent the devils measured their plans in thousands of years.

A solitary figure appeared in the doorway and stood, awaiting recognition, its face in shadow. Grijo stood, his sinews paining him, and the great hall went silent but for the whisper of heavy robes and shuffling bare feet. "Have the Starsifters arrived at a conclusion?" he asked, holding his head high, his back straight.

"We have," the figure said, and Grijo recognized the voice of Sayr, an old and highly respected authority on the esoteric flotsam of space.

"Present your findings." Grijo settled back carefully in the ornate chair, which was noteworthy for its size and carvings, not its comfort. The Lleix did not intend their leadership to find itself too eager to sit here.

"It was most certainly the Ekhat," Sayr said, taking the center of the room, gazing at the circles of benches filled with his fellow Lleix, all well grown. His aureole, limp with age and long ago darkened to pewter, drooped around his wise face. "We cannot yet say which faction, though in the end, it will not matter. The Interdict is no better than the Harmony, the Harmony no better than the Melody. All seek our extermination."

A ripple of anguish ran through the assembled representatives. Many heads turned away, as though they could not gaze upon this bearer of such unwelcome news.

"What shall we do?" one youngster with an uncommonly red aureole cried, a head shorter than all the rest.

Grijo saw by the patterns on her robes that she came of the Foodsculptors, an impoverished *elian* of the arts who obviously had no one older and more experienced to send. "Hush, daughter," he said. "That is what we have assembled here to decide."

Hakt of the Shipservicers made his way through the ranks of benches and stood beside Sayr. He was good-sized for his age, sturdy and of pleasing demeanor, every fold of his robe in place. His pale-silver aureole fanned his face. "We have made what repairs we can," he said. "Two of our ships were lost in the engagement and cannot be replaced. We have stripped them of all that could be salvaged."

"What of our numbers could be transported to another system with the ships still in service?" Grijo asked.

"Less than a hundredth," Hakt said. He glanced up at the unseeing *Boh* faces.

So few. Grijo had suspected it might be so. He closed his old eyes, filled with grief. That would not save even a tenth of the *elian*, who held in trust all of Lleix wisdom and culture, and of course there was no question that the *dochaya* would have to be left behind.

"I would also speak to the Han!" someone cried.

"Jihan!" Sayr's cracked old voice was filled with reproach.

Grijo opened his eyes again, saw a restless young figure in the great doorway, outlined in the early red sunlight, shifting from foot to foot. She darted forward with unseemly haste to stand beside Sayr, looking sorely out of place, her head not even reaching his shoulder. "What is this?" Grijo said.

"Jihan is the junior-most member of our *elian*," Sayr said, "with a dissenting opinion on the analysis of the recovered debris. She should not be here and she knows it." He turned to the youth with great dignity. "Return to the *elian*-house, youngest," he said. "We will speak of this later."

"The Han needs all of the information to make an informed decision," the youthful Starsifter said. "It was not just the Ekhat stalking us this time. It was also the Jao!"

"Jao?"

"The Jao?"

The odd name echoed through the vast hall, different on each tongue. Grijo could feel the radiated puzzlement. He himself did not recognize the designation, though he could see the youngster expected otherwise. He leaned forward, taking care to keep the folds of his robe properly arranged. "What does that mean?"

A Historykeeper rose from her bench, her robe encrusted with scenes of events that had taken place so long ago, no one remembered. "She names the architects of our destruction," she said, "from two thousand years ago. They drove us from system after system until finally, what was left of us fled here into the nebula to Valeron."

"They are the handservants of the Ekhat," Jihan said. She gazed about the hall, her aureole quivering with indignation. "They must have come to finish the task they left incomplete so long ago."

There had been something about a servant species...savage and relentless...Grijo cudgeled his mind, seeking to remember long ago lessons in the Children's Court.

"I have researched the records. Our last contact with them was a little more than a thousand years ago," Jihan said, her fingers quivering as she belatedly twitched her robe into an almost acceptable configuration. "They were the ones who drove us from our Last-Home, Sankil."

Once the Lleix had held fourteen systems, traded with all manner of species on faraway worlds, built ships so vast and swift that other species commissioned them to build their own fleets. The markets in Lleix cities had been rich with fine scents, exotic fabrics, and imported woods. The tales of that long-ago abundance were still told, so fancifully embellished, though, even Grijo, who wished to believe, had trouble crediting them. His people had prospered under the benevolent spiritual guidance of the *Boh* and never known war—until the Ekhat came and harried them, system after system, from the lush favored worlds they had once called home.

Now they had taken refuge on this one resource-poor planet,

concealed within the nebula, so isolated, they had thought—hoped—obviously deluded themselves—that the Ekhat would not detect them here. Nor had they, until now.

"There is very little physical evidence for the presence of the Jao," Sayr said, "only a few scraps of organic tissue that survived the explosion of the smaller ship. What we do know is that the remaining Ekhat vessel fought a second battle sometime after our ships withdrew. If it had been the Jao, surely they would not have attacked their masters. They would have fought *for* the Ekhat, not against them."

Alln of that dreaded *elian*, Ekhatlore, rose, robe garish with bloody scenes of their ancient enemy. His aureole was so faded with age that Grijo could no longer make out its color. The elder gazed about the assembled representatives, gathering their attention until the hall quieted. "The Ekhat fight one another just as avidly as they seek to exterminate extraneous species. If they fought someone else, it must have been a second Ekhat ship."

Jihan turned back to Grijo. "If I am right," she said, "and these Jao do come after us here, we will not be prepared!"

"Child," Alln said, "since we left the *Boh* behind, we have been prepared for two thousand years to die at the hands of one or the other of these barbarians. What more would you have of us?"

She looked up at him, indeed at all of them, for she was the youngest, and therefore smallest, present. In spite of her brashness, she was a promising child, he thought, with her classic silver aureole, though her robe-draping was positively haphazard.

"I think we should find a way to live, not die," she said. "And to do that, we first have to understand the Jao."

"No one understands them these days," Alln said. "There must have been a Jaolore *elian* once, but it obviously died out when there was no longer any necessity for it."

"Then we need a new one," she said. Her black eyes glittered as she faced the array of elders.

A new *elian*. That happened but once in a lifetime for most Lleix, Grijo thought, sometimes not even then.

"There is little evidence for the presence of the Jao in that battle," Sayr said. "And if we could not defeat the Ekhat, how would we do any better against the Jao, even if it was them? Would not our efforts be better spent readying our ships to take a portion of our population to new safety?"

The assembled representatives muttered and turned to one another, arguing in low, intense voices. Grijo, his thoughts whirling, sat back, the prickly chair creaking under his weight, and tried to come to some conclusion himself.

Then speakers rose and one by one made their points, to be replaced by those of opposite views. Voices, though never raised, were fiercely eloquent. Ekhatlore thought perhaps young Jihan was right, while many other elders believed she was unused to the rigors of logical thought and merely sought to make herself important beyond her height. It was pointed out repeatedly that even the Starsifters themselves did not support her.

Outside, the morning light gradually transformed from its fierce red into a thin gold that did not warm at this elevation. Stiff and uncomfortable, Grijo watched it change, creeping through the day until the shadows had gone long and purple and yet nothing was resolved.

Finally, he heaved onto his feet again and the hall fell silent. "We have reached no accord," he said, "which in itself is a measure of the direness of this turn of events. Therefore, we must accommodate both views." He motioned to Hakt of the Shipservicers. The elder rose. "You will ready our ships to transport what portion of our population they can to another world," he said. "Consult the ancient charts for a possible destination. Requisition whatever you need of the other *elian*."

Then he turned to Jihan. "And you, outspoken child, will form a new *elian*, Jaolore," he said. "All of the colony's records are to be at your disposal. You may recruit any who are willing from the other *elian*, especially Ekhatlore."

Her silver aureole wilted with amazement. "Me?"

"You have put yourself most unbecomingly forward for one of your tender age and girth," Grijo said, "and you have boldly gainsaid the elders of your own *elian*, who have far more experience to make sense of the situation in which we find ourselves. This is a chance for you to redeem yourself. Make what you can of it. I doubt you will ever get another."

Jihan made herself respectfully small, lowering her head, averting her eyes, flattening her aureole. "I regret the necessity of what I did," she said, "but I felt I had no choice."

"Many times down through the ages the Lleix have had no choice," Grijo said, heaving back onto his feet. "And the sum of all those have led us to this, which may well be the Last-of-Days." He waved a hand in dismissal. "Go and form your new *elian* while you can, daughter."

"It is not the Last-of-Days!" the youth said with all the audacity of her inadequate years and experience. "I will not let it be!"

And she turned with inelegant recklessness so that her robes actually fell *open* and headed back down the mountain.

CHAPTER
9

Jihan knew the Starsifters would learn of her disgrace from Sayr. So, after leaving the Han, she descended the mountain and then wandered the city's river promenade with its sculpted waterfalls and elegantly pruned trees, trying to order her thoughts before confronting their rightful anger. Wind-borne spray from the falls soaked her face and robe as she passed, but, already numb with the shock of what she had done, she did not heed the chill.

The moment when she had broken *sensho* played endlessly in her mind, the stunned expressions on the Eldests' faces, the heavy silence that had hung like a shroud afterward. Now she feared what the elders of her *elian* would say when she faced them. Quite simply, she had committed the unthinkable. Had anyone ever behaved as badly in the entire history of the colony? She had made herself infamous. Why had Grijo not simply remanded her graceless self to the *dochaya* the moment she dared contradict her elders? Even the sharp wind blasting down off the mountain could not clear her whirling head.

It was less than six years since she'd been released from the Children's Court. She was so junior, it was amazing the Han had listened to even a word of her prattling. Now she'd been assigned this immense responsibility and she knew full well that she was inadequate. Form a new *elian*? It was obvious that she hardly knew how to function in the one that had already accepted her.

Finally, hungry and exhausted, she headed for home, following the winding path even as the promenade's evening lights blinked on. The temperature had dropped with the setting of the sun and now each breath seemed laced with ice crystals. The air crackled with cold. Few individuals were out, evidently preferring to remain in-house with their *elian* and contemplate the devastating return of their ancient enemies in private.

She turned up the path leading to the structure where she had dwelled since being accepted. It was modest, only a single story constructed of *giln*-wood with a few carved finials above the eaves, a sharply pitched roof, and a garden for day-to-day nutritional needs, mostly bluebeans and bushes of pavafruit. The remaining stalks were now dried and brittle with the arrival of cold weather.

The Starsifters' single spacecraft was not here, of course, but kept out on the colony's landing field. It had been called into use only rarely down through the years since the Lleix had fled to this world in the nebula. Long-range data and the analysis of debris from space were largely irrelevant in times of peace.

But this was no longer a time of peace. She opened the doors of the dwelling and stepped inside, pausing to inhale the familiar homey smells of evening-meal, evidently roasted sourgrain and spiced mealnut tonight. A servant clad in a gray shift glanced at her, then looked down as though Jihan were a rudely intruding stranger. Passing through the deserted Application Chamber, she found two of the elders, Sayr and Kash, seated in the house's communal kitchen, finishing small mealnut cakes.

Sayr looked up from his privileged place closest to the radiant heat-source. His entire body drooped with weariness. "Young Jihan, come in," he said, dark-pewter aureole flaring. "We have been discussing your reassignment."

Miserable, she threw herself at his feet, arms clutching her head, making her body as small as possible. "Forgive me!" she cried into the gleaming wooden floor. "I did not mean to disgrace the *elian*. I was just so—worried!"

"Gently, child, gently," Sayr said from above, then took her arms and pulled her up to face him. "Strong emotion clouds the intellect, and you will need all of your reason now."

She sat back on her heels, hands clutched to her chest, rocking with distress, unwilling to rise. "I do not—know—what to do!" she said brokenly. "The responsibility is too great!"

"Evidently it is not," Kash said, coming up to stand beside

Sayr. Her bulk was not as magnificent as Sayr's as she was only of middling age. Still, she was far taller than Jihan. "They would not have assigned such a task to you, otherwise. The Han is never wrong. You must seek within yourself for strength and plan how best to accomplish your task. Anything else will only shame the Starsifters even further."

Jihan gazed at the two of them, her mind whirling. Think, she told herself. What would Sayr do in her place? "I need the records," she said finally. "The ones dealing with the Jao."

"You have already reviewed ours," Kash said, "but you should copy them for your new *elian*." Her black aureole stiffened as she considered. "Next you must go to the Ekhatlore, then the History-keepers." She set a steaming bowl of roasted sourgrain on the communal table next to Jihan. "Whether you are right or wrong—and I do believe that you are in youthful error—it will be beneficial to the colony to have all the relevant information in one location."

But Jihan was not wrong. The chemical signatures of the debris recovered danced in her head: weapons' traces, DNA data, even the wiring and metallic composition of the blasted hull. The hated Jao were back. She would not let them succeed this time. Somehow, the Lleix would survive and force the wretched Jao to perish instead.

None of the other Starsifters would speak with Jihan the next morning beyond a grudging response to her inquiries after records. This *elian* had taken her when they accepted almost no one these days, and then she had shamed them, not only by breaking *sensho*, but also disputing their analyses before the Han itself.

The remaining eight resident Starsifters had now assumed classic *oyas-to*, the disciplinary mode dreaded by all youth where one's elders simply refused to acknowledge someone so inharmonious and disruptive to their inner peace. She had experienced that form of correction from time to time, especially right after she had first entered the *elian*, in response to minor infractions, but this was far worse. She knew from the subtle shifting of eyes that no one saw her from the moment she entered the Morning Room, with the exception of Sayr and Kash, and even they only responded with the briefest of words, then turned away.

Chastened, Jihan went to the Duty Chamber, rummaged through the archives, copied and copied. It had all been so long ago, almost a thousand years since the last Jao sighting, more than two thousand since the Ekhat had set their savage handservants upon them and thereby driven the Lleix from their array of jewel-like worlds. The Starsifters had only records of chemical traces, genetic markers, metallic compounds, engine signatures, and weapon patterns. Nowhere did she find an actual image of these hated warmongers. For that, she would have to go to the Ekhatlore or the Historykeepers.

The three unskilled servants from the general labor pool who were repairing an outside wall for the Starsifters moved aside as she left the *elian*-house, but even they did not look at her. Jihan clutched the case with her copied records close to her robed chest. It was not to borne! she told herself. Even the unassigned disapproved of her actions!

She lowered her head and stalked past them. They were great clumsy things, well along in years and yet without status because no *elian* had ever recruited them. She did not have to heed their disapproval, yet it rankled that news of her wantonness had spread even into the *dochaya* where the unassigned lived at the far edge of the city.

Jihan decided that she would not-see, too, and adopted *oyas-to* with all she passed as she made her way from the modest district of the Starsifters to the rarified quarter which housed the great *elian* like Dwellingconstructors, Childtenders, and Ekhatlore.

The Ekhatlore *elian*-house was massive, rising three stories with fanciful embellishments on the eaves and along the roof's peak. Gaily colored flags fluttered, one for each venerated member in residence. Ekhatlore attracted hundreds of youths each year at the Festival of Choosing and took five or six, never more, and occasionally no one at all. Jihan had always been leery of them, feeling as though stretching their minds to understand the Ekhat made them a bit like the great devils themselves.

Would the same happen to her now if she comprehended the Jao too well? She shuddered, then presented herself at the public doors which were half-again as tall as those of the Starsifters. A youth in an elegantly brocaded robe opened them. His folds fell perfectly as though sewn into correctness. His aureole, an impressively deep black, stiffened. His silver skin gleamed as though freshly oiled, while his upswept eyes regarded her with the chillest of courtesy. "Yes?"

"I am Jihan, formerly of the Starsifters," she said, hastily twitching her own robe into a more pleasing configuration. Really, she thought with chagrin, she was presenting herself with no more sophistication than if she were wandering the streets in her children's shift. "I have been charged by the Han to form a new Jaolore *elian* and so must consult the Ekhatlore records on that species."

"Ah, yes," the youth said. "After the Han adjourned yesterday, it was said someone of little consequence and even less dignity had broken *sensho*. Our elders could speak of nothing else the whole evening." He stepped aside so that she could enter, holding back his robe so that she would not brush against him.

Within, the Application Chamber, an architectural element present in all *elian*-houses, was anything but standard. The exposed rafters were a bright blue, the furnishings richly carved, with sumptuous woven mats and padded leather benches. Stern *Boh*-faces had been carved into the walls so that the traditional guardian spirits seemed almost present within the house itself, a reminder of what had been lost. The subtle astringence of steeped herbs filled the air.

She stared around the impressive room, clasping her case with its precious cargo, so nervous, her aureole only fluttered about her face.

"We have been expecting you," a deep voice said from the shadows. The youth who had conducted her inside glanced over his shoulder, then, head down, backed gracefully out of the room.

She turned as an elder entered, Alln, himself, resplendent in his robe of bloody scenes as he had been the day before. He was taller even than Sayr, almost as tall as old Grijo, Eldest-of-All. She inhaled deeply to steady herself, feeling the blood thrum in her ears. He was so massive, so magnificently old. "Do I have your permission to search Ekhatlore's records for mention of the Jao?"

"You do." Alln settled on a padded bench, then regarded her steadily, which in its own way was as disturbing as the determined not-seeing of *oyas-to* inflicted upon her at the Starsifters.

He had the classic Lleix upswept eyes that compressed to gleaming black slits when his attention was focused, a mark of comeliness. His oiled skin was very bright, shining in the vast room's dimness. She felt a child again, newly released, wandering the gaudy, loud Festival in desperate hope of attracting favorable notice and an offer of occupation.

"You have sacrificed your future for this, shortest," Alln said. "Therefore, by the worth of what you have given up, I feel you must be sincere."

"Do you believe that I am correct about the return of the Jao, then?" Her aureole stirred with hope.

"I cannot say," Alln said. "I am not a Starsifter, so those recovered bits of *this* and minute traces of *that* mean little to me. I do see that *you* believe, though, and in light of what you have sacrificed, that is a powerful statement in your favor."

She bent her head, overwhelmed.

"You cannot explore this possibility alone, though," Alln said. "Our records are extensive, far greater than one could sift alone in any reasonable amount of time, and there is reason to believe that we do not have a great deal of time to deal with this issue."

"But I am an *elian* of only one," she said softly. "I have no others to assist. Even if the Festival of Choosing were tomorrow, it would take time to train any that I accepted."

"Ekhatlore understands that," he said. "Grijo said up at the Han that you might recruit from other *elian*, so we have decided to release one of our number to you."

She raised her head, startled.

"We assign you young Kajin," Alln said. "He is quite—"

"No!" a voice cried behind her, belonging to the youth who had met her at the outer doors. "You cannot expel me! Such things are never done except for cause! I have given no cause!" The elegantly clad youth darted into the Application Chamber with unseemly haste, his aureole standing on end. Evidently, Jihan mused, he had been listening in the passageway beyond, hardly the behavior of one who wished to be thought exemplary.

"This is not expulsion," Alln said with great gravity, "it is reassignment in a time of great need. You should be honored that we believe you can assist in this momentous task." The elder sat back on his bench and regarded them both impassively.

"No one is ever reassigned!" Kajin glared at the Ekhatlore elder with a shocking lack of respect. "I have never heard of such a thing!"

"Your years are still very few," Alln said. "Just because you have never heard of a practice does not mean it never occurs." He gestured at Jihan. "All *elian* must work together in this time of trouble, each fulfilling its function. Have you forgotten that this may well be the Last-of-Days?"

Kajin's hand went to the front of his richly brocaded robe as though its folds were in disarray, which they were not. Even in his distress, he had preserved his dignity. "But this—creature—does not represent a real *elian*. That was just an excuse for the Starsifters to rid themselves of someone who could not behave properly! Everyone is talking about it across the city! She contradicted her elders and broke *sensho* before the entire Han!"

"She has put aside personal ambition," Alln said, rising to stand straight and tall, using his impressive height to its best advantage. "This child has traded her Starsifter future for what she believes is in the Lleix's best interests. How can you look upon her and do less?"

"I do not believe in her fantasies!" Kajin said. "I can serve best by performing my duties here!"

"You have no more duties with us," Alln said and stepped closer. "Your robe."

Kajin stared at him dumbly, his aureole limp. Then, finally, with trembling hands, the youth stripped out of his lavish Ekhatlore robe, folded the heavy material with reverence, then laid the bundle across Alln's waiting arms. Naked, he was slight, slighter even than Jihan, though, because of his height, she was certain he was senior to her by at least a few Festivals. She realized then that she still wore her Starsifter robe.

Kajin would not look at her. She suddenly felt indecent, standing there in her false clothing while he had none. She shrugged out of the beautiful gray cloth with its silver brocaded starbursts. She had no right to wear it now. Alln had been speaking to her too. She was just too dull-witted to grasp his words' relevance at first.

She bent her head, fingers tracing the starburst pattern one last time. "Could you have this returned to the Starsifters?"

Alln bent his head too, a great gesture of respect from one so lofty. "Indeed we will."

"And—" She inhaled, thinking hard. "Might we borrow two lengths of unadorned fabric until we can get a Patternmaker to design a motif for our new *elian*?"

"That would be most appropriate," Alln said. He turned and a waiting servant scampered forward. "Bring unworked cloth for these Jaolore," he said. "And see to their needs as long as they are researching our records."

*   *   *

It was not to be borne! Kajin could not make his mind work, could not process that he had been cast out, that the only meaningful occupation he'd ever had in his entire life was at an end and seemingly on a whim. As if it were not bad enough that the Ekhat were coming back to murder them all! Now he wasn't even going to be allowed to die with his true *elian*.

What could Alln have been thinking? That ran through Kajin's mind over and over. One simply was not removed from his *elian* without cause! And he had given no cause. Indeed, he had worked tirelessly to learn what the ancient records said so that they could be ready when—not if—the great devils who ate the universe, the Ekhat, returned.

Now they had come back and instead of being allowed to share his observations and correlate information with the rest of the Ekhatlore, he had been discarded to start over in a lowly new *elian*, one without even robes or a house to call its own. He simply could not process the stunning change in fortune.

Jihan was bent over a viewer. The bones in her naked spine stood out like knobs. "Here!" she said, eagerness vibrating through her voice. "This is what they looked like!"

A servant entered the room, bearing several bolts of undecorated cloth. Kajin snatched one and wrapped it around his body before looking. Lack of clothing made him feel like an unreleased child again, playing at choosing *elian* in the Children's Court.

The viewer was showing squat, muscular creatures with mobile ears and snoutlike faces. Their bodies were covered in short fur of varying shades of brown. They wore leather straps on their upper bodies, stiff foot-coverings, and loose flowing garments from the waist down in various colors.

"The Jao!" Jihan motioned him closer.

"They were a client race," Kajin said reluctantly, dredging his memory for what little he'd encountered about them, "one engineered by the Ekhat into sentience. By all accounts, they were only bloodthirsty savages when the Ekhat first came across them."

The servant stood patiently behind them, waiting with the other bolt of cloth. Jihan did not seem to notice, so Kajin took the cloth and pressed it into her hands. She draped it across her shoulders with a distracted air. The viewer was playing a battle scene now. Lleix and Jao were dying messily. Explosions shattered a graceful Lleix city, demolishing houses and fountains and roads.

"They fight very well," Jihan said, her voice strained.

"Too well," Kajin said morosely. He watched shards flying through the air, buildings blasted into slag, stumpy Jao brutes advancing on terrified weaponless children.

"Are there any records of their language?" She abandoned the viewer to scan the index again, flipping through the embossed sheets.

"Perhaps," Kajin said, "but why would you think it matters? Surely you do not mean to stand in their shadow and reason with them?"

Jihan looked up at him, her eyes bright with purpose. "We should familiarize ourselves with their language so that, if they return, we can understand intercepted communications. After all this time, they will not expect us to possess that capability."

"What good will that do?" He twitched at his makeshift garment so that it hung marginally better. "Those few of us selected to leave Valeron, will. The rest stranded here will have no ships. Jao or Ekhat, our enemies will destroy us utterly without even landing upon this world, and we will be able to do nothing in our defense."

She regarded him with unnerving focus. "You really think not?"

"I know we will not," he said. "As it has always been, it is just a matter of time. For most of us now, this is the Last-of-Days."

"You are in error," she said, turning again to the index. "Information is strength, and somewhere in here is the knowledge that will save us. We only have to find it."

She was obviously younger by at least a few Festivals, yet he felt lesser in rank, as though her surety somehow advanced her past him. Had it been that way in the Han yesterday? She had broken *sensho* by gainsaying her Starsifters' elders, yet Grijo had not expelled her from the gathering. Instead, he had rewarded her with the mandate to form her own *elian*.

In ordinary days, it was considered a great moment when a new *elian* was created, but there was nothing ordinary about the return of their ancient enemies. None of them here would survive long enough to make this new *elian* anything but a momentary curiosity.

Jihan searched the Ekhatlore records far into the night. At one point, a doddering servant clad in a gray shift arrived with steaming pots of sourgrain laced with fragrant greenberries, a great courtesy of the house as visitors were rarely fed more than ceremonial delicacies. She ate hers without tasting, her eyes trained on the fascinating records. She would have made a better Ekhatlore than Starsifter, she realized. The fierce turmoil of these long ago events drew her as the dry statistics of chemical traces and compounds never had.

Kajin remained beside her, explaining references, helping her access the old-style recordings until they had tracked down most of the information concerning the Jao.

Finally, in pursuit of a Jao-language file, she stumbled across the record of a meeting between Jao and Lleix which did not appear to be a battle. Two thousand, two hundred and forty years old, it had taken place on Sankil, Last-Home, before the remnants of her species had fled to Valeron.

She turned to Kajin, who was so weary, his aureole clung to his head. "What is this?"

He peered over her shoulder. On the screen, the little figures of Jao and Lleix faced one another, speaking in foreign gibberish. "I do not know," he said. "I have never seen it before." He halted the recording. "It should have an embedded translation track."

She shifted impatiently from foot to foot, unable to be still, as he fiddled with the settings, searching the file.

"Now," Kajin said finally, "play it."

She punched up the file name. The screen blinked, and then the figures appeared again. They stood on a blue and green world filled with sumptuous vegetation, all unfamiliar species. A huge Lleix, magnificently old, stepped forward. Her robe pattern indicated Wordthreaders, an *elian* which still existed to negotiate conflicts between their own kind. Her silver aureole flared. "Subcommandant Breen," she said, "the Lleix have a proposal for you, one that will set your people free to come into their own, as they otherwise never will."

CHAPTER
10

Jihan could not take her eyes from the screen. Both of her small hearts beat wildly. This was obviously a critical moment when the meeting's potential had poised on the edge of proceeding either very well or very ill.

"We propose an alliance of our two species against our common enemy, the Ekhat," the Lleix said. Her movements were calm, yet her body betrayed itself. Much rode upon each word, and Jihan could read the import in every carefully restrained gesture.

The stumpy Jao shifted into an oddly elaborate stance, arms angled just so, head tilted, ears pricked forward. It wore a dull brown garment on its lower body, encasing both legs, but only straps across its brawny chest. A bright greenness flickered within its black eyes, alien and disturbing. "Why should we listen to you?" it said gracelessly. "If we do not obey our masters, they will destroy us as surely as they now rain destruction upon you."

"Because they are the great devils who eat the universe," the Lleix elder said. "They may refrain from slaughtering you for now, but it will not always be so. The Ekhat only want to be alone with their own magnificence. They do not even tolerate variation within their own species. You have seen how the Melody seeks against the Harmony, the Interdict against them both. In their crazed minds, all other species must be exterminated. If you do not ally with us, the Jao will surely be next to fall."

The Lleix elder stood alone, Jihan realized, while the Jao was

103

flanked by at least a hundred of its ugly fellows. Were they so cowardly that they required the numbers to be heavily in their favor before they would parley?

Three other Jao came forward and conferred with the one the elder had named "Breen." They were all armed with gleaming gray weapons slung over their shoulders and wore similar brown gar- ments. Their bodies flowed from one odd stance to the next and then the next as though they were conversing somehow without words, and Jihan was suddenly certain each position had subtle meaning.

The elder waited, her black eyes turned to the blue sky-bowl above as though seeking help from that direction. The area around her was undeveloped with no sign of buildings, roads, or agricultural fields. Small red and yellow flying creatures fluttered through the sky like scattered drops of fire. Water surged over a nearby waterfall, obviously, by its casual disharmony, left in its natural state. They must have arranged this meeting faraway from the vulnerable Lleix cities.

"We are willing to put all of our tech at your disposal and have each of our *elian* release an expert to advise your forces," the elder said finally as the Jao continued to confer. "You are already fierce warriors. No one could dispute that. The Lleix believe you can also be a great people. You have only to reach out for the freedom your Ekhat masters have never allowed you."

Breen broke off speaking with its fellow Jao and turned back to her. Its black eyes suddenly glittered green again, brighter this time as though lightning flashed inside that hideous skull. "The highest good is to be of use," it said, its ears pinned. "We make ourselves of use to the Ekhat who gave us all that we have. How do the Lleix make themselves of use?"

"It is also the highest good to live well as a people," the elder said, "to learn all that you can and then make of your lives something proper, beautiful, and accomplished."

"Beauty is of no use!" Breen advanced upon her, its eyes still shimmering dangerously. "Talk is of no use! Weakness and fear are certainly of no use!"

Jihan could see the Lleix elder trying not to retreat. "We will make ourselves of use to the Jao," she said clearly, "by freeing them from the Ekhat."

"To do what?" Breen's body contorted into a bizarre shape

which it held for several breaths. "We belong to the Ekhat! They made us what we are. What else should the Jao do but serve?"

"You should serve *yourselves*," the elder said. Her silver aureole was trembling. Jihan saw that she was afraid. The situation was plainly escalating out of control. So much depended upon that moment and the elder knew she was failing, not just herself, but her entire species.

"We want only to be of use," Breen said, "so in serving the Ekhat, we are serving ourselves!"

The Jao was angry, Jihan thought. Obviously, the elder was making it think in new and uncomfortable ways. It did not want its assumptions about the meaning of life challenged.

"Only go back to your *elian*," the elder said, "those among you who make decisions. Ask them to consider. That is all the Lleix desire."

"It does not matter what you desire!" Breen raised a sleek, deadly-looking weapon. "The Ekhat have decreed you vermin. Nothing is required here except that you die!" It discharged a bolt of shimmering red energy into the elder's body. She crumpled to the ground, twitching.

Jihan cried out in dismay, unable to restrain herself even though it had all happened such a long time ago. Then the Breen-creature turned toward the recording device and fired again. The screen flickered and went black. She settled back on her stool, head whirling, and turned off the machine, unable to bear more.

"So," Kajin said, his eyes elegantly narrowed, "those are the Jao."

The two of them copied files far into the night, packing the filled recording-flats into reinforced boxes provided by Ekhatlore. Jihan kept seeing that moment in her mind when the Jao had fired upon that brave elder, terminating all her wisdom and experience without a single regretful twitch.

The Jao were utterly savage, she thought. Everyone knew, of course, that the Ekhat were insane. Their minds were impenetrable. No one could have reasonable conversation with one of them, but, from what she had seen in the records, the Jao's minds obviously worked more like that of the Lleix. They could have understood the same sort of logic that Lleix lived by—they simply chose not to. In its own way, that deliberate turning-away was worse, almost as though they conducted their entire lives in *oyas-to*. The Ekhat could not be other than they were, but, with Lleix assistance, the Jao could have broken free and developed their own culture, but instead they preferred to be lackeys and slaves, tools for the Ekhat's legendary cruelty.

Jihan found the language files and copied them too. She meant to familiarize herself with their tongue so, if the Jao came back, she could translate intercepted transmissions. That would certainly be "of use," as a Jao would put it.

Kajin worked alongside her, grim and truculent, but thoroughly knowledgeable as far as the Ekhatlore system of files went. He had been invaluable in her search, she thought wearily. Alln had certainly known what he was doing when he gave this one to the Jaolore.

"Enough!" Kajin said finally, when, too weary to notice, she copied over an already filled flat. "We will have to come back and search more tomorrow."

He was right. She looked at his smudged face, then slumped over the viewer, covering her aureole with her arms. But where could they go? They had no *elian*-house. There were a number of abandoned structures, left from when an unneeded *elian* had died out, but she'd had no time to look for one. The research had seemed far more pressing.

Perhaps the Starsifters would allow them to sleep in her old quarters for just one more night. She lifted her head and gazed out the window. Blackness reigned. It was very late so they would not be there long.

"Leave the receptacles," she told Kajin as she tottered onto her weary legs. "We will appropriate an unused *elian*-house tomorrow and come back for them."

He went to the door, but then waited for her, as though she were the elder of the two.

Too tired to argue *sensho*, she went through, passing all the wonderfully appointed rooms of this residence without a glance, when normally she would have loved to explore. Opportunities to visit the private interior of another *elian*-house beyond the Application Chamber almost never came, and certainly not for one of her meager age.

They exited through the Application Chamber, which was now silent and clean, ready for the next day's business. She opened the huge doors and stood on the threshold to get her bearings. Chill night air rushed against her face. She could hear water rushing over stone in the stream just beyond the road.

To her surprise, the space outside the residence was filled with unassigned. They stood in rows, clad only in the brief gray shifts of unskilled workers, their black eyes reflecting the starlight, waiting clearly for—something.

She was afraid. This was so out of order. Unassigned did not wander the city by night. They went back to the *dochaya* which was their proper place. "Why are you here?" she said as Kajin emerged to stand beside her in the Ekhatlore doorway.

One stepped forward, a male so small, he must have been released from the Children's Court only a Festival or two ago. "We heard there was to be a new *elian*."

His aureole was skimpy, his bone structure unpleasing, his eyes large and utterly round. There had been any number of such homely children in her year. None of them had found *elian*. "Yes," she said. "It will be called Jaolore. We are amassing information concerning an ancient enemy who may well have returned to plague us again."

"Mistress, you are only one," the youth said. He glanced back at his fellows. "You will need many more hands and eyes. Choose from among us. We will work hard to make the new *elian* a success."

"No!" Kajin burst out. "These are drudges, fit for nothing but the most menial of tasks! You might select one or two for house servants, once we are more organized, but not to serve in the *elian* itself!"

Jihan gazed out over the unpromising group. The enormity of the task ahead daunted her. So much to do and so very little time in which to accomplish it. She had barely started, and yet any moment, the Jao might sweep back through the nebula to finish the task they had left uncompleted so long ago.

Kajin seethed beside her, his aureole stiff with rage, but Jihan found herself intrigued. She could go to other *elian* and request the release of more adults to work with her, but they would all be as insulted and reluctant as Kajin, having long ago made their choices of occupation.

These unassigned workers, though, they wished with all their might to be accepted—anywhere, even by an *elian* with no resources, headed by a shortest like herself.

"How are you called?" she asked the slight youth.

He cast himself to the frosty ground, making his body even smaller. Starlight gleamed on his gray skin. "I am Pyr."

"Then, Pyr, come with us," she said.

The rest cried out and surged forward. Jihan waved them back with both fists. "I will not select anyone else tonight," she said, "but I will evaluate our needs and then perhaps come to the *dochaya.*"

"You cannot mean that!" Forgetting himself, Kajin seized her arm in the manner of a thoughtless child who understood nothing of propriety, then dropped it as soon as he realized what he had done. "They are less than the sand beneath your feet! They are nothing!"

She remembered being a dazed child, sent away from the only home she'd ever known to wander the colony during Festival with no surety that she would ever achieve a place. Those accepted by an *elian* looked back upon that moment with great nostalgia, but what of the ones never selected?

"They are no different than you and me," she said firmly. "They wish to live a good life, to follow propriety in all things, and to offer their abilities to a good *elian*. They only have to be allowed the opportunity."

Pyr scrambled to his feet, his body pitifully thin. "You are wise, mistress!"

"The honorific used by accepteds is Eldest," Kajin said sourly.

"But you are surely senior to me," Jihan said, eying the difference in their heights.

"Pah!" Kajin stalked away into the chill night and the formerly unassigned Pyr hastily cleared his path. "Now and for always, I waive my *sensho* rights in this *elian*. I have no wish to lead a pack of fools!"

Pyr followed the new Eldest to the house of the Starsifters. He was unfamiliar with that *elian*. It was small, maintaining a modest but nicely kept establishment, and evidently did not often come to the *dochaya* seeking temporary laborers. Apparently, he had either not wandered past here during Festival or had not noted it.

Jihan, so tall and silver, so elegant, even in her unadorned robe, led the two of them through the silent house, past room after room, until she reached a small space containing only a sleeping platform and a small table and stool.

"I am youngest in this house," she said, "so I sleep here."

Youngests rarely had sleeping partners. That honor was reserved for the higher ranked. Even Pyr knew that. He dropped to the floor and stretched out, weary from a day's labors for the Childtenders in the Children's Court. The very young were so—energetic. He would not be sorry to leave such duties behind.

The room was small and cold without a window or electric brazier to make things more cozy. Tattered charts of elements and compounds covered the wall space, overlapping one another, and a crate of electronic modules had been shoved into the corner. Pyr turned on his back and gazed about the chamber. So this was what life outside the *dochaya* looked like. He'd never thought to see such wonders for himself.

"Surely you are not going to allow *that*—" The elder she had referred to as "Kajin" kicked Pyr in the side. "—to sleep here with real adults?"

Air whooshed out of Pyr's lungs. Black spots shivered in his vision. He curled around the shock and pain as though he could contain them.

"Desist!" The elegant Jihan darted between them, looming marvelously tall. "If you cannot behave properly, I will return you to Ekhatlore! I would rather recruit only from unassigned than deal with such crudeness!"

Kajin stared at her, his aureole stiff with outrage. "But Alln released me! If you send me back, Ekhatlore will not readmit me."

"You can always go to the *dochaya*," she said grimly.

Silence prevailed then. Pyr heard the ragged breathing of both as he pressed against the bottom of the sleeping platform. Misery overwhelmed him—to be the cause of so much strife between such notable adults! The shame was worse than the throb in his chest.

Jihan crawled onto the sleeping platform and turned away. Kajin paced the small room for some time before finally slipping up beside her.

Pyr huddled on the floor, aching, but wildly happy. He would suffer a thousand beatings if they led to this moment. *I have an* elian! he thought over and over, far too excited to surrender to sleep. *An* elian *has selected* me! *I have a place! I am no longer nothing!*

Jihan was wakened by Kash entering her quarters the next morning. She rolled over and saw the elder standing in her doorway, hands thrust beneath her robe. "You must find your own house today," Kash said. "It is not proper that you dwell here any longer."

For a moment, Jihan could not think why Kash wanted her to go, then it all came rushing back to her, the Hall of Decision, her very different results from the space debris analysis, the new *elian*—*her* new *elian*.

"Yes," she said humbly. "The Starsifters have been more than generous in allowing me to stay this long."

Kash turned away, already not-seeing. Three bowls of steaming sourgrain stood on the table. Gratitude filled Jihan. These elders had taken her in, taught her their craft and nurtured her development, expecting that she would do so for future Starsifters in turn. Now, all that time and careful teaching was lost to them. They would have to wait for Festival and choose again.

But she did not know what she could have done otherwise. She was right. It had been the Jao out there in that battle, along with the Ekhat. Not-seeing them would not make it any less true. They had to be ready, had to be as prepared as they could make themselves with the limited resources available.

On the floor, young Pyr stared up at the hot food. "Eat," she said, gesturing. "We have much to do today."

Seen in the daylight, Pyr's aureole was definitely more gray than silver and his skin dusky, a shade that was almost pewter. No wonder he had not been selected by any of the *elian*. Compared to Kajin's beauty, he was like a lump of granite beside a silver nugget.

But such things were no longer important, she told herself firmly. All that mattered now was that she organize her new *elian* and learn all she could about the Jao before they came back.

After they had eaten, she carried the bowls back through the just-stirring house to the communal kitchen. Early morning sunlight slanted in through the row of tiny windows below the rafters. Sayr was there, conferring with several other elders. All fell silent as she entered the homey room where she had spent so much time. She dropped to the polished wooden floor at his feet, wondering if he would acknowledge her. He was the one she had most offended against before the Han.

"You are leaving," he said.

She looked up. He was so very tall and wise. Immanent loss overwhelmed her. "Yes."

"This is a good thing," he said. "New *elian* bring the colony additional services."

"I did not chose this," she said, trying not to tremble.

"Your intellect chose," he said, "and your training. Never turn away from knowledge, no matter how unwelcome it might appear to be. Truth is always to be preferred to delusion." He rocked back on his heels, gazing down at her with those handsome narrow eyes she knew so very well. "You may be correct in your conclusions, but be aware that you went about this thing badly. Achievements are always judged by the methods used to accomplish them. Poor form makes it harder to gain others' understanding, even though, at the center of things, you may be right. Now, go and solve the conundrum of these Jao."

She rose, head still bowed, unable to speak.

"Walk with grace, Eldest," he said, then turned away.

She led Kajin and Pyr out of the house, knowing she would never return. There was nothing for her here now and so very much to do.

Outside, the day was quite chill, with leaden clouds blowing in from the mountains to the west. A scavenging flock of tiny blue hoppers with their dished faces scattered through the kitchen garden as the three of them exited the Starsifters' house. Jihan did not look back. Regret would not solve any of her many problems now.

They wandered the colony, taking note of abandoned houses. There were more than Jihan had realized. Most were very large, belonging to defunct *elian* such as the Shipbuilders, who had long ago known how to construct spacefaring vessels, the Watercrafters, who had once constructed fountains and ornamental waterfalls, and the Skyflyers, who had maintained a small fleet of personal aeronautical machines for the colony's use. The majority of the deserted structures were in bad repair with gaping holes in the walls, missing windows and doors, crumbled stonework, or collapsed roofs. Such would require large amounts of time to be made habitable. Even though her new *elian* was authorized to draw workers from the *dochaya*, that would take too long. They needed a space in which to live and work now with a minimum amount of restoration.

The Shipservicers were frantically busy over on the vast landing field beyond the edge of the colony to the east where the land flattened out into a vast plain. They were repairing the ships damaged in the recent battle, refitting others long unused so that they might carry away at least a tiny portion of the Lleix to relative safety.

So that this would not be the long forecast Last-of-Days.

But even if a hundredth of their numbers survived by fleeing, the Ekhat and/or the Jao would just hunt them down and kill them somewhere else. It was a neverending cycle and the end would surely come sometime, if not now.

And it would certainly be Last-of-Days for those stranded behind here on Valeron.

Finally, she sat down to think on a bench before the Waterdirectors' sprawling house. One of the largest in the entire colony, they were an industrious *elian*, responsible for the colony's clean water supply, as well as sewage and flood control. Long ago, those functions might have belonged to three separate *elian*, she thought wearily. Now they were combined.

Kajin settled beside her, but only on the bench's edge as though avoiding closer contact. His moody silence bore the flavor of recrimination. If she had not broken *sensho* up on the mountain, neither of them would be in this predicament. What if they never found the right house, she asked herself. What if they just wandered the colony day after day until the Ekhat and Jao came back to slaughter them all? Her aureole clung to her head in misery.

"Eldest?" Pyr said meekly, crouching at her feet.

She turned her attention to him. He was still wearing his unassigned's gray shift. She must apply to the Patternmakers for actual robes, just one more task as yet left undone. "Yes?"

The youth's meager aureole flared to its best advantage. "I know of a structure that might do."

"You!" Kajin jerked his unadorned garment back as though contact with the youth might contaminate it. "You would not even know how a decent *elian* is run, much less what one looks like from the inside!" His fine face was scornful as he drew back a hand to cuff the youth into silence.

"No!" Jihan bolted to her feet. "Let him speak!"

CHAPTER
11

"He is no longer unassigned," Jihan said. "You will accord him the respect of a youngest!"

Pyr looked up, refusing to flinch. "Unassigned wander the colony every day, seeking work, if no one comes to the *dochaya* to secure their labor," he said. "Such—as I was—see many houses on a regular basis, while those who have their own *elian* mostly stay home unless they have outside tasks. I remember a small structure that may well suit your—our—needs."

Well, it might be no better than what she had found so far, but she might as well look. "Lead us there," she said.

Pyr hopped to his feet, almost wriggling with joy, and started off down the winding street. She followed the youth, with Kajin lagging behind. They passed the magnificent facades of Ekhatlore and Historykeepers, the eloquent architecture of the Distributionists. The sight of the huge houses, so very old and lovingly maintained, saddened her. The Ekhat, the great devils whose music was destruction, would sweep through and raze everything. If only the Lleix possessed the might to destroy them instead!

And then she expanded that wish to include the Jao, who in their own way were worse, because they'd had the chance to escape the Ekhat's control and had chosen instead to remain slaves.

Other Lleix gave them disapproving looks as the three passed, then quickly turned aside. Admittedly, they were an odd group, she and Kajin with their blank, hastily draped robes, homely Pyr

113

in his ragged unassigned's shift. Word must have spread about her transgression because all *elian* had been represented up at the Han. Quite literally everyone knew how badly she had conducted herself.

But Sayr had said, despite her graceless breaking of *sensho*, she might well be right. She held onto that, and the fact that Ekhatlore was willing to aid her. She could only go on from here, make the best of what circumstance provided.

"This is it," Pyr said suddenly.

Jihan looked up from the inlaid stone road. They had stopped before a small tidy house at the western edge of the colony, surrounded by large dried-up gardens. Huge windows swept from floor to ceiling. The interior must be flooded with light at all times of the day, she thought. Most *elian* sought privacy. How strange.

Faces, though not *Boh*, had been carved into a series of posts supporting a covered area around the front so that the membership of the former elders seemed still to be present. Each face seemed wise and knowing like the Starsifter elders Jihan had forever left behind. She felt another pang at the enormity of what her actions had cost.

Kajin scowled. "What kind of *elian* lived here? There is so much wasted space!" He stalked into the empty gardens, crunching through dead weeds. "An establishment of this modest size would not require such a large garden."

"I have been told that this belonged to the Flowercultivators," Pyr said softly. His skimpy aureole flattened in respect and he did not look at Kajin. "They have been gone for some generations now. I do not know how many, but the structure is still solid."

Flowers grew wild along with other weeds. Jihan had never heard of an *elian* organized for the sole purpose of cultivating such a thing. Her thoughts whirled as she followed Kajin into the gardens. What had the flowers been for? Who made use of them? She gazed at the abandoned house with its barren gardens. There was no one left to ask. Unless they had left records behind, she would never know.

Inside, the rooms were orderly and a fair amount of dusty furniture remained. She even found a few bolts of leftover cloth featuring fading patterns of blue, yellow, and purple flowers. Huge empty glass containers occupied each room as though waiting for something.

The colony had lost an interesting function when this *elian* died, she thought. And there were many empty houses now, each marking a group which had once contributed a valued quality to the whole and now was lost forever.

Like Jaolore. There must have been an *elian* devoted to the study of the Ekhat's client species. If it had survived, now they would be so much further ahead in understanding and preparing for the menace that was surely sweeping their way.

"This will do," she told Kajin and Pyr, and relief swept through her. She dispatched Kajin back to Ekhatlore to retrieve their copied files and beg the loan of several viewers. Pyr, she ordered to the *dochaya* to select servants to clean this dusty house so that it would be fit for habitation again.

She herself would go to the colony's central commodities warehouse and draw food supplies to last them for a few days. Also, she would stop at the Patternmakers to request a simple pattern for Jaolore so that they could go decently clothed. The rest would have to wait. The Jao were coming and it was upon her head to do what she could to make the colony ready.

Her head swirled with plans. First, she must study the Jao's barbarous language. Then they would be able to conceal nothing in their transmissions.

She would have Kajin teach Pyr how to run a viewer, then the two of them could sift records faster. At one point, there must have been a Jaolore. A great deal of that information would have been subsumed by Ekhatlore. They would have to pull it back out again.

There was too much to do, too much! She felt twitchy with dread. So much responsibility and so little with which to work!

A short time later, she looked out one of the huge windows and saw Pyr returning with five unassigned, ranging in height from very slight to quite tall, each individual utterly homely in his or her own way. She met them at the door. They filed into what must have once been the Application Chamber and gazed at her with expectant black eyes. All decisions fell to her now, even the assignment of their labor.

"I know these five well, Eldest," Pyr said with a modest sweep of one hand. "They will work hard."

"If they do not," Jihan said, "we will find others who will." She gazed at them critically. "The two largest of you shall come with me to the Commodities Warehouse, and the rest will sanitize the house while we are gone. Cast nothing aside unless it is damaged. We have limited time to replenish supplies."

She headed for the door, but none of them moved.

"Mistress," the tallest said, when Jihan turned back, "is it true that you might select more unassigned for membership in this *elian*?" The speaker was female, grown into respectable height, a full head taller than Jihan, but possessed of an oddly ragged brown aureole which seemed plastered to her head.

Pyr gazed at Jihan steadily, almost hungrily. He wanted—something.

She had broken tradition by accepting him, but he was still young, barely out of Festival. It was not beyond the bounds of reason that she put such a youth to work as a full-fledged member of her new *elian* in this time of extreme need.

But these others were hardened unassigned. No one would ever take any of them. The proper way to increase Jaolore would be to wait until Festival came round, but it would not occur again until the next warm season, a very long time from now. And any helpers she begged from established *elian* would be at least as resentful as Kajin, perhaps even worse.

"Perhaps," she said. "It remains first to see how my acceptance of Pyr works out, and how hard each of you works. But Jaolore needs more members and soon, so—"

The three designated cleaners scattered through the house without waiting for her to finish, while the two tallest stepped outside, plainly ready for the trip to the warehouse. She heard water running, cabinets being opened. Work was already in progress even as her words hung in the air.

Well, then, that was good. She rearranged the folds of her blank robes so that she would not look unkempt, then headed out into the frost-laden air. A few flakes of snow sifted down from the leaden clouds. She curled her bare toes against the chill and then hurried on. The unassigned followed.

Over the next few days, the house's organization slowly came together. Under Jihan's orders, Kajin trained Pyr to work the viewer, and then both of them passed only the interesting bits on to her. She consulted with the Patternmakers so that Jaolore could look respectable and worked out their comestibles allotment with the Distributionists.

The five unassigned worked so diligently that she was amazed no *elian* had ever taken them in. Their physical appearances, though seedy and plain, would improve with a better diet, and she thought they could not have looked so bad during their Festivals of Choosing. It was generally believed that all who deserved an *elian* found one, but she was no longer certain that was true.

Young Pyr worked the hardest of all even though he had now received his place. When he had finished examining Ekhatlore records for the day, he joined the five servants in restoring the house, clearing weeds from the vast overgrown gardens, fixing battered bed-platforms and cabinets, and retrieving abandoned supplies from the underground storage areas left by the Flower-cultivators.

Jihan had to order him to sleep each night and still he rose before all the rest and was already at work when she found him the next morning.

Their meager store of information about the Jao grew. Two hundred years after the fatal meeting, when the Jao had refused assistance from the Lleix, the savages had disappeared from the recorded encounters for almost eight hundred years. There were many records of battles with the Ekhat, whole colonies exterminated, ships destroyed, but the Jao were strangely absent.

Then, a mere thousand years ago, in the battle that had driven the Lleix to take refuge on a resource-poor world inside a nebula, the Jao had appeared again. Jao ships had destroyed the last of the fourteen Lleix worlds. Jao weapons had exterminated nine-tenths of their population.

Half of the surviving Lleix had fled to Valeron, leaving the Jao behind in a series of jumps that also had left a number of their own ships wandering forever lost.

They had left behind the stars and hidden on this occluded world for the last thousand years. Until three hundred years ago, there had been no sign of the Ekhat. Although Valeron was not a particularly welcoming world, they had believed themselves safe.

Jihan realized now, though, that with or without the Ekhat, the colony was slowly dying. Critical *elian* passed away every generation and knowledge was lost. The colony lacked the mineral deposits and ores needed to craft replacement parts for machines and ships. *Elian* like the Skyflyers died out for lack of support so that her people were ever more rooted to this barren plain at the foot of the mountains.

What had the Jao been doing out there in the nebula with the Ekhat? Why had they fired upon their own masters? Were they trying to break free, as the Lleix had once counseled them, or had the Ekhat finally turned upon them too?

So many questions and so little data with which to resolve them. It made Jihan's head spin each time she tried.

The only thing of which she could be certain was that it would be useless to attempt parleying with the Jao. That brave elder had tried long ago and her effort had led only to slaughter. It was clear that the Jao would interpret any hesitation as weakness. The Lleix must meet them with all possible force when the moment came.

She consulted with the Weaponsmakers, who armed the colony's spaceships. Under their direction, the crews had fired upon both the Ekhat and the Jao ships, destroying one and damaging another, so their tech, though ancient, was still effective.

"We are fewer every generation and there seems to be a nev-erending river of Ekhat," the Weaponsmaker Eldest, Branko, told her. He was amazingly tall, almost equal to old Grijo himself. His robe was carefully draped, the decorative pattern a simple and severe lightning bolt. "They will return in ever greater numbers and then it will finally be Last-of-Days."

"It will if we just give up!" She bolted to her feet, dislodging a tiny table in the Weaponsmakers' Application Room. A silent servant appeared from a side corridor to right it, then retreated back into the shadows.

"We have never just 'given up,'" Branko said stiffly. "But it is understood that the Last must come—eventually."

"*I* do not understand that!" The recent facts she had absorbed and was attempting to correlate whirled through Jihan's head: sav-age Jao words for which there were no Lleix equivalents, starship statistics, firing patterns, chemical signatures, population trends, death rates, records of ancient encounters. "We must work together so that the Last-of-Days will not come!"

"You are still quite short," the Eldest said, his tone condescend-ing, as though she had just emerged from the Children's Court. "Greater height will eventually grant you better perspective."

If she lived to achieve greater height. The Ekhat and the Jao were coming back! Jihan stared at the oh-so-proper draping of the Eldest's robes, his carefully raised aureole, the heavy lines of *vahl* around his eyes and accenting the bridge of his magnificent nose. He was static, going nowhere. The whole colony was going—nowhere! They would send off a few ships with a mere fraction of their population, then just sit here and wait for the Ekhat to incinerate the rest of them! Frustration flooded through her and she had to force herself to be civil.

"I require your records about battles with the Jao," she said, her gaze turned to the floor. "They will be quite old, at least a thousand years old, and many older."

"Access will be provided," Branko said. "Will you take refreshments with me?"

And because it was polite, because that was what two Eldests did, even when one was half the size of the other and had nothing in the way of wisdom or experience to offer, Jihan agreed. She settled back onto a painted bench while servants offered platters of spiced mealnut cakes and newly squeezed halla pulp. The two Eldests discussed the weather, the lacking quality of cloth produced these days and the latest crop of children accepted into various *elian*, anything but the certain destruction waiting to pounce upon the colony out there in the black cauldron of space.

And the whole time, Jihan seethed.

When Jihan returned to the Jaolore *elian*-house that night, the building smelled quite fresh with boughs of pungent purpleleaf tacked up in strategic locations and the wooden floors polished. They still creaked when she stepped inside, but she imagined that in another day, at the present level of industriousness, even that would be remedied.

Pyr waited for her in the Jaolore Application Chamber, his aureole newly fluffed, draped in a length of undecorated cloth. He looked quite the proper little adult, she thought, despite his inherent homeliness.

She handed him a stack of recording-flats, then passed a weary hand back over her limp aureole, trying to think what must be done next.

"You must rest, Eldest!" Pyr handed the flats off to one of the servants, who was now clad in a clean shift, she noticed with approval.

"No." Jihan stalked through the hallways into the long communal kitchen in the back. Spices filled the air. The lights were mellow. Two of the servants looked up from a low table where they were eating, but there was no one else. "I do not have time for such." She glanced around the dimly lit room. "Where is Kajin?"

Pyr followed her into the room, but his gaze was downcast, his demeanor subdued.

She stopped. "Where is he?"

"Gone, Eldest."

Pyr's voice was so soft, she thought she hadn't heard him correctly. "Gone? Where?"

"He did not tell me, Eldest." He inhaled deeply, still averting his face.

She tried to think. "Did he train you on the equipment as I requested?"

"Yes, Eldest." Pyr's round eyes looked up and glinted momentarily with pride. "I have been practicing and can operate the viewers quite well."

Then where would Kajin have gone after that? She'd given him no further instructions. "He must have thought of another *elian* likely to have records of the Jao," she said finally. "No doubt he will return shortly."

"No doubt," Pyr echoed dutifully, although his tone belied his words.

There was more here than the youth was saying. "You will be honest with me," she said sternly. "We cannot waste time on smoothing over ruffled feelings."

Pyr went very stiff. "Kajin said that it does not matter how much information you collect on these savages, we will never be able to fight them off."

There had to be more, she thought. "And?"

"He refuses to be part of such—foolishness." Pyr's voice was barely more than a whisper. "You violated *sensho*, so he says that he owes you no respect. He would not say where he was going, but he threw off his robes and left the house in a great temper. I followed him across the city, keeping to the shadows. Kajin has removed himself—to the *dochaya*."

Obviously Kajin would rather be without an *elian* than under her control, she thought numbly, but he did not have the right. She had not released him, so now *he* was the one breaking *sensho*. "File these new recording-flats with the rest," she said. Her fingers tugged at her robe, improving its drape. She must look her best.

"I will be back soon," she told Pyr and the servants.

"Shall I go with you, Eldest?" Pyr asked, still hunched in misery.

She started to say no, but young Pyr knew the *dochaya* as she did not. "Yes."

And the two of them set off through the night.

The *dochaya* was crowded, filled with building after low graceless building where the unassigned kept themselves when not needed for gainful employment. Each structure they passed emanated unpleasant smells and was marred with filth. Jihan stopped at the edge, surveying the mess visible through an open door. Bowls and eating utensils were scattered about the floor, along with ripped shifts, bits of broken stools and benches. "Why do they not clean their quarters on the days they do not find work?" she asked Pyr.

He stared at the ground, shivering with remembered distress. "They are sad, Eldest. They think only of leaving."

The night wind gusted, howling around the buildings. Unassigned gazed at her hungrily as the two of them passed. Why, she wondered, were they milling outside when they should have been within, sleeping, making their bodies ready for the next day's work?

The *dochaya* was large, stretching around the eastern edge of the colony, bordering the landing fields themselves. She hadn't realized its true extent. Servants came from here and returned when they were no longer needed. Those without employment applied at the *elian* each morning for occupation. It was rarely necessary for anyone of her rank to enter this place.

And Kajin was here? She would never find him among so many.

"Wait, Eldest," Pyr said when they had reached the center. "I will make inquiries."

The youth disappeared into the dark maze of ramshackle buildings. She walked up and down as a few late unassigned trickled back from the city in their ragged shifts, obviously having worked late. Jihan shuddered. This could have been her fate as well. She'd received only one offer during Festival while better favored children sometimes had twenty and thirty. She'd always been grateful to the Starsifters for accepting her, but now, seeing this desolation, she knew she had not been grateful enough.

Wind caught a fragment of a shattered crate and sent it skittering against a building. Unassigned stared at her, but did not speak. The night was clear. She gazed up at the nebula's crimson haze, trying to imagine the Jao and the Ekhat lurking out there, persistent down through the long years, waiting ever so patiently for the opportunity to murder them all.

Finally, Pyr emerged from the shadows between the two closest buildings, Kajin in tow.

"You acknowledged me as Eldest," she said. The former Ekhatlore looked utterly dejected, naked and weary. "You have no right to be here. I have not released you."

Unassigned murmured as he passed, their eyes reflecting the scant diffused starlight that filtered down through the nebula's haze. "Forgive me!" Kajin said and cast himself at her feet, making his body small.

Then she understood. The *dochaya* was far more dreadful than he had expected, too. She held herself stiff and proper as she thought Sayr would have, under similar circumstances. "We will have no more of this foolishness! Jaolore has far too much work and not enough hands as it is."

"All my life," Kajin said, his voice muffled against the dirt, "I wished only to be Eldest of Ekhatlore. I received forty-seven other offers during Festival, but chose them above all others. I was—distraught that they released me."

She could well imagine him a favored choice, the many *elian* courting him because of his comeliness and grace. "You have a chance now to make a difference in the colony's future," she said, twitching at her robe to improve a fold. "To ensure that we even have a future. We must understand these Jao in order to defeat them. I cannot waste more time chasing after you."

"Eldest, you will not have to," Kajin said.

They returned to the *elian*-house to spend the rest of that night, and many days and nights thereafter, analyzing and studying their implacable and terrible enemy, the Jao. The more Jihan learned, the more she was alarmed. In many ways, these Jao were worse than the Ekhat. Their minds were less impenetrable. They'd had the opportunity to be different and yet they chose to obey their vicious masters and exterminate sapient species all across space.

They must have a weakness, she told herself over and over again. There must be a way to destroy them utterly. She would spend her life, or what was left of it, seeking it out.

And so, under her direction, the Lleix prepared.

PART III:
The Voyage

CHAPTER
12

The *Lexington* thrummed and hummed and even quivered from time to time, a persistent reminder to Caitlin that, no matter their ultimate mission, this was also a shakedown cruise. Something could very easily go wrong. Every time she ventured out of her cabin, crew were rushing about to regulate *this* better and adjust *that*, or check on *those*. Even on the third day into the mission, her awareness of their lack of experience added a frisson that kept her nerves unsettled.

She was also highly aware of the vast variety of life contained within the great ship, everyone intent upon his or her own task, all striving together to make the odd-ball gestalt work. She, of course, had no ship duties and Terra-Captain Dannet had made it clear through disapproving postures that such extraneous crew as herself were not welcome upon the command deck without a compelling reason. So Caitlin kept to her quarters, when she wasn't tutoring Rob Wiley, and dug through the data from the misadventures of the Krant ships in the Sangrel Deeps nebula, trying to perceive what Ronz suspected.

The readings and statistics obviously concealed something important, which had sent the usually careful Jao scrambling in what was, for them, a headlong, almost reckless, return to the scene. Damn Ronz, she thought fretfully, going through the files on her personal computer for the umpteenth time. Why couldn't he have just told her what—or who—he thought they might find there? He'd let Wrot in on the secret.

On the shelf above her desk, her husband smiled down at her from in front of a temple, an image she'd taken when they had traveled to Amritsar, India, representing Aille. It had been hot as blazes that afternoon and perspiration sheened his forehead. Then the scene shifted to their wedding day. They looked both ecstatic, though her arm was still in a cast, and overwhelmed. Missing him with a fierce ache that took her breath away, she switched off the digital display in order to concentrate.

Think! she told herself. All the clues were there. She just had to assemble them correctly. The engagement had involved two Ekhat vessels, two Krant ships, and the mysterious third party. Readings inside the planetary nebula, reflected by the dust and gas, were misleading and fluctuated from second to second. It had been difficult to pinpoint the location of one's own ship, never mind the enemy's.

But, as Preceptor Ronz had indicated, impacts on the Ekhat ships had been recorded during the battle which could not have originated from either Krant vessel. She computed the trajectories over and over, but the results always came out the same.

That third ship out there in the haze had fired upon the Ekhat. *The enemy of my enemy is my ally?* She squinted at the replay. It was like standing outside in a storm at night, she thought, and watching the rain sheer around something invisible. The shape was suggested as much by what *wasn't* there, as by what was.

Who else would have participated in such a battle and then left without contacting the surviving Krant ship? Not another Jao vessel. No matter how estranged a *kochan* might be from mainstream Jao culture, they were too practical to leave a damaged vessel that might be repaired and returned to use.

A rival Ekhat faction wouldn't have fled either. Even though the Harmony—which was itself divided into factions—the Melody, and the Interdict had fought viciously with one another for millennia over how best to achieve the Ekhat's on-going extermination of all other sapient species, they would never abandon another Ekhat faction's vessel to be destroyed by inferiors. Most likely, if it was no longer flight-worthy, the crazy bastards would want to blast it themselves even if it cost their lives.

So, it couldn't have been the Jao or the Ekhat. Her fingers

drummed on the room's built-in desk, out of sync with the great ship's droning engines. Then who was left? She'd had access to Aille's database since being added to his service several years ago. As a result, she knew that other sapient species occurred throughout the galaxy—this arm of it, at any rate, which was all any Jao knew and only a smallish part of it at that. But if sapience was common enough, advanced technological ability was not. The devilish Ekhat made it their practice to stamp out such cultures when they were in their infancy, never giving them a chance to reach the next stage in their development.

The door chimed. She sighed. Understanding was so close! She could feel the answer hovering just out of reach, waiting for her to open her eyes and recognize it. Letting it go now meant she would have to start all over again, but faced with the monotony of ship-life, she had to welcome any diversion. She reached over to the command board and toggled the door open.

Gabe Tully stood out in the corridor in his dark-blue jinau uniform, hands clasped awkwardly behind him. Lean and tan from his recent weeks in the mountains with the Resistance, he shifted his weight from foot to foot like a teenaged kid picking up a blind date for a dance.

Behind him, crewmen rushed past, talking to one another. He glanced over his shoulder. Tully and Caitlin had never been close friends, even though they were both members of Aille's service, but he'd come a long way since she'd first seen him as a closely monitored Resistance prisoner in Yaut's rough charge. Intrigued, she waved. "Gabe, come in. I haven't seen you since we lifted. How are things going?"

He flushed, then stepped just inside, looking like he might bolt. His eyes appraised the compactly arranged room. Spartan as her quarters were, she thought, they were still probably bigger than his. The Jao didn't see any point on wasting resources on luxury—except of course for pools.

"What can I do for you?" she asked, when he didn't speak.

"I—" His gaze dropped to his boots. "Ed asked me to, you know—"

"Oh, I see." She sighed, certain she could just hear the conversation back on Earth that had prompted this visit. Was she ever going to pin Ed's ears back when she got home! "My gallant husband made you promise to look after me."

"Yeah," Tully said. His blond hair was combed, his uniform clean and pressed. He looked almost as presentable as if he had a *fraghta* to look after him like a high-ranking Jao. Knowing his indifference to traditional spit and polish, she thought his batman David Church must labor night and day. Poor man.

"So," Tully said, "are you, like, okay?"

"I'm fine, Gabe." She smiled and shook her head. "You don't have to worry about me, no matter what Ed said. I managed for years before he came along, learned to tie my own shoes and everything!"

"I don't mind," Tully muttered, "though it always seemed to me that you did a pretty good job of taking care of yourself."

The moment stretched out, silent and awkward. Not much opportunity for learning the social graces when you grew up in the mountain Resistance camps, she supposed.

"Maybe you can help me with something, though." She gestured at the scene frozen on her computer screen. "I don't have much to do while we're in transit, beyond tutoring Rob Wiley in Jao bodyspeak when he has time. So, I'm trying to figure out what we're going back to the nebula in such a hurry to see."

"Something's got their tails in the wringer for sure," Tully said, dropping into Resistance camp vernacular. He edged closer to peer down at the image she'd frozen from the end of the battle when the Ekhat ship had been heavily damaged and about to implode. "I've been wondering about that, myself, not that Wrot or Dannet will tell a lowly grunt like me anything."

"Actually, I don't think even Dannet knows and it's eating her up. She's even testier than usual, and that's saying something. As near as I can tell, the Preceptor only told Wrot."

"And why is that?" His earnest green eyes sought hers. "You understand the Jao better than anyone I know, growing up under their thumb like you did. What would make the Preceptor keep this a secret even from his own kind?"

"I went to Ronz before we lifted and asked him outright. He refused to tell me, said expectation of any particular outcome might change what we find, or do, when we find it, which makes no sense." She paused. "And I suppose it might—for a Jao. I think he's in error about the human reaction, though. Withholding information just makes us crazy with curiosity."

"I bet that's exactly what the old devil wants," he said, sitting on her bunk, "to keep us occupied like stupid hamsters on an exercise wheel, running all the time and getting nowhere."

She had to laugh. He had a point. There was very little she would put past Ronz and the Bond. "That's entirely possible!"

"But that doesn't explain why he wouldn't tell the Jao," he said.

"If the information were controversial somehow," she said slowly, trying to fit the pieces of evidence together and make a recognizable pattern inside her head. "If knowing this information would somehow change everything, Ronz would keep it to himself until he was sure he was right. The Jao don't process new conditions very well. He wouldn't want to upset everyone needlessly."

"Change everything?" Tully said.

"Yes." She turned in her chair. "But what would do that, I haven't a clue."

"Well, accepting humans into a new *taif* changed everything," he said.

"Because it meant recognizing that we were more than clever savages incapable of self-rule." Caitlin tapped a finger on her chin. "Gabe, they admitted at the briefing that a third sapient species fought in that battle. If this was just a standard First Contact scenario with an unknown species, they would know what to do, and they certainly wouldn't drag an untried ship half-filled with humans along with them to do it. Instead, it looks like Ronz knows, or at least suspects, who these folks were. It must be a species they've encountered before. If so, returning to that system in the *Lexington*, which is a new design, would conceal the fact that we have Jao with us."

Tully's eyes narrowed. "Do you know who it is?"

"I can't quite put it together yet, but I've been searching the databases and I'm going to keep digging." Restless, she got up, leaned against the wall and crossed her arms.

"Wrot may not like that," he said, grinning. "He'd say that if the Preceptor wanted you to know, he would have told you."

"Then Ronz shouldn't have drafted me for this voyage," she said. "He knows what humans are like. We can't leave a puzzle unsolved when all the pieces are scattered right in front of us. It's just not in our nature!"

After Tully left Caitlin on Deck Forty-Six, he took the lift up to Seventy-Two, deep in Jao Country, to fetch the three highest ranking Krants. They were taking their morning swim, which should put them in the best mood possible, not that he expected it to be all that good. They were a recalcitrant lot at the best of times and this situation hardly qualified as that. They were put out as all hell at being dragged along on this seeming wild goose chase into the Sangrel Deeps, and quite rightly too, as far as he could tell.

Wrot had contacted him that morning—ship-morning, that is—and assigned the remnants of the Krant crew to his command while aboard ship. His unit, Baker Company, specializing in reconnaissance, had no mission on the *Lexington*, beyond eating their heads off and getting into trouble, so they were training on Weapons Spine C to man the new guns. Jao had little patience with anyone sitting idly by when they could make themselves of proper use and expected ground troops to put their hands to whatever needed doing while in transit to an assignment. They neither shared nor tolerated the human tradition that made sharp distinctions between different branches of the military. As far as the Jao were concerned, a soldier was a sailor was an airman was a spaceman, and would damn well do what he or she was told. And do it properly, and do it now.

Unlike the cobbled-together tank artillery that had proved so successful in the Terran battle against the Ekhat, these guns had actually been designed to be used on a space-going ship. They combined the best of Terran and Jao tech and exuded an air of deadly blue-steel efficiency. And there was the possibility that the Krant crew, experienced with space battles, might even be able to show the human complement a thing or two.

Or they might just sit in the corner and pout. That was entirely possible. Then it would be up to Tully to maneuver them into answering his authority. Yaut certainly could have done it, and Tully had been trained by the old fraghta. He just had to dig deep and think what Yaut would do in his place.

Tully squared his shoulders and stepped off the lift when the doors opened. The corridor was redolent with Jao salts. Even if he hadn't consulted the ship's directory, he could have just followed his nose to the pool.

Two sleek wet Jao emerged from a doorway, harness looped over their shoulders, conversing with one another, casually unclothed. The Jao's lack of a nakedness taboo took a bit of mental adjustment for humans. One of the pair glanced at him, then with a contemptuous flick of her ear, passed by without acknowledgment.

She had an unusual *vai camiti*, the markings mostly on the left side of her face, leaving her right eye unmarked. Where had he seen that before?

"*Vaim*," he said, using the Jao greeting proper between two equals: *We see each other*. It burned him to be ignored as though he were just so much flotsam and Yaut had warned that he must establish himself from the first. Too many Jao still regarded humans as little more than flunkies, fit only to clean up and do grunt work that required muscle.

They stopped, staring down at him, ears and arms toggled at an angle he deciphered as probably *annoyed-disbelief*. Yaut had regarded him in that fashion on a daily basis for weeks, and occasionally even the much more patient Aille.

"You dare to speak so, stub-ears?" the female said, her body rigid.

That off-center *vai camiti*, it denoted Jak, he suddenly realized, a high ranking kochan which had lost status on Earth since Pluthrak had arrived. He attempted a rough rendition of *waiting-to-be-instructed*. "If you rank above me," he said in Jao, striving to get the angle of his neck correct, "I am willing to be enlightened. I am Major Gabriel Tully, Commander of Baker Company." Forcing his name upon them unasked was a slyly rude tactic. Yaut would have cuffed him soundly for it, but Yaut wasn't here.

The other Jao, a male, was more traditionally marked with a stolid but recognizable facial pattern denoting Kaht, if he wasn't mistaken, a midlevel kochan. "Oh, it is one of the Pluthrak's boorish little humans," he said with a dismissive wave of one hand. "I have always heard that he lets them run quite wild. No doubt, this one has become accustomed to flaunting itself unasked without correction."

"This is both a human *and* a Jao ship," Tully said, realizing it might be better to let minor breaches of manners like this go unless he wanted to spend all his time forcing traditional Jao into association. Him and his big mouth. He had much bigger battles to fight, but he'd provoked this confrontation and had to see it out. "The giving and receiving of names is a courtesy among my kind."

"In case it has escaped your notice, we are not your kind," the female said stiffly.

"No, but we serve together on the Bond's ship," he said, "both seeking to make ourselves of use to the Preceptor. How will we accomplish our mission, perhaps even fight alongside each other, if our two species cannot observe even the simplest of courtesies? Or, perhaps, you do not care if this assignment is completed successfully."

The Jak's ears drooped into *uncertainty* and the angles of her body altered. "I rank as sennet-subprime," she said, then stalked off down the corridor. The second Jao followed her without a backwards glance.

Tully stared after them. No name, but he'd obtained a rank, and one below him at that. A sennet was the equivalent of a human platoon leader, and subprime would meant something like assistant, or second-in-command. Maybe this hadn't been such a mistake after all. He straightened his shoulders and entered the pool room.

It was not the fragrant seas of Mannat Kar, Mallu thought, but the pool had nicely balanced salts and was in truth far more satisfying than the facilities on their late lamented ship. He swam on the surface slowly, carefully, letting the water support his healing ribs so that the pain was minimal. Jalta dove next to him, surfacing immediately, then stared over at the door. Mallu followed his subordinate's gaze. It was one of the humans, the one with bristly yellow nap on its comically round head.

"Krant-Captain," the graceless creature said, crossing the room to kneel beside the pool. It was dressed in crisp jinau blue and the trousers' fabric promptly soaked up splashed water. The human didn't seem to notice.

What was its human-name? Tutty? Tucky? Mallu floated over to the side of the pool and held on, reluctant to heave himself out of the water and endure the ache of his injury unless it was necessary. Behind him, Jalta plunged to the bottom and joined Kaln who was racing back and forth beneath the roiling water, working off nervous energy.

Reflected light danced across the ceiling from the water. "You and your crew have been assigned duty on Weapons Spine C for this mission," the human was saying in accented, but quite passable Jao, though it was making no attempt to move correctly. "We are running firing drills in a short while, so you need to report for training."

Mallu flicked an ear, thinking. It would be good to be busy

again, to have something useful to do to take his mind off his failure to return to Krant with his ship. "My crew numbers are too few to handle such an assignment."

"Yes," the creature said. "That is why you have been added to Baker Company, which is my command."

Mallu froze.

"They are waiting for us." The human stood and gazed down at him with those horribly static eyes.

The shame of it flooded through Mallu. They had placed his crew under the command of a *human*? Far better that they had all perished back in that vile nebula at the hands of the Ekhat than to be so dishonored! He heaved out of the pool, grunting at the bite of pain in his side.

Jalta popped back to the surface and gazed at him, *unease* written into the angle of his pool-sib's ears. "Fetch Kaln," Mallu said without explanation.

Other Jao were arriving to swim and the room echoed with their voices. Mallu met none of their eyes and kept his head down as he retrieved his harness and trousers from the hooks on the wall, putting them on while his nap was still soaked rather than endure the pain of shaking the water out of his nap. After a few breaths, Kaln and Jalta joined him, dripping, carrying their harness and trousers.

"Do not ask!" he said when their bodies hinted at *question*. Prudently, they shook themselves and dressed. Then he gestured to the creature. Blast its ears, what *was* it called—Tunny? Turly? Kaln had told him its name back in the medical bay, but now the alien sounds had slipped his mind, and he could not lower himself to actually ask.

The human stood aside, waving them to the door. "Head to Weapons Spine C," it said.

"We are required?" Kaln said, her angles *confused*.

Her mental balance was still precarious and Mallu hesitated to impart the disturbing news of their demotion to her. He turned to the human. It stood to one side, hands shoved into concealed folds in its trousers, gazing pointedly over his head and *refusing to lead the way*, he realized. The wretch was employing Jao disciplinary techniques as though it had been born to them. One of the Krants would have to go first. He turned to Kaln, who was lowest ranked, and motioned her forward.

All her lines went to *incredulity*. Her eyes blazed with green fire as she glanced at the human and made no move to obey.

"You toured the ship while I was—indisposed," Mallu said, as though they were back on their own vessel and this was merely another order to be followed. "Lead us to Weapons Spine C."

Kaln turned to Jalta as though to protest and Mallu cuffed her good ear. The rapid movement pained his ribs and made him gasp when he spoke. "Weapons Spine C, Senior-Tech!"

Kaln's angles shifted from *incredulity* to *guilt*. With a snarl, she pushed Jalta aside and lurched through the door into the hallway. Mallu motioned Jalta after her, then followed himself, not deigning to notice what the vile little human did.

The four of them entered the nearest lift and rode down to the assigned Weapons Deck in silence. Kaln kept glancing at the human with such distaste, Mallu thought he might have to discipline her again.

They got off on the proper level and found the rest of their Krant crew milling before a row of great guns, muttering and asking why they had been summoned. A number of humans in jinau uniforms were staring.

The yellow-napped human stepped into the center. "Listen up!"

The milling stopped and all the humans present fell into rows, assuming a rigid stance, shoulders back, arms straight, heads high, obviously a codified posture appropriate to the situation.

"I am Major Gabriel Tully, Commander of Baker Company," the human said in Jao, "and a member of Aille krinnu ava Terra's personal service."

Names, names, names! thought Mallu crossly. This species was obsessed with them, forcing their slippery syllables upon hapless bystanders at the slightest provocation. With their bland, almost indistinguishable faces, it was no doubt the only way for them to tell one of their fellows from the other with any degree of accuracy.

"Because everyone on this ship must make themselves of use, all Krant-crew aboard has been assigned to Weapons Spine C, which is under my command."

Mallu's crew stiffened and he saw *amazement*, *confusion*, and outright *hostility* in their postures. He stepped forward, trying to project *dignity*, but the pain in his ribs thwarted his ability to achieve the proper angle. "Whatever comes, you will not shame Krant!" he said, his ears flattened in *admonition*. "You will put your hand to whatever you are asked, and you will do it to the best of your ability. Show these dry-footed primitives that whatever they can do, a Jao can accomplish faster and better!"

One by one, his crew regained control of their emotions and schooled their bodies to a mostly respectful neutrality. Kaln stood stiffly before him, betrayed by her drooping ear, but otherwise credibly restrained.

Tully turned to him, his naked lips twisted in a strange grimace that Mallu could not interpret. "Very good," the human said. "Now we are ready to start." He leaned closer and lowered his voice. "By the way, Krant-Captain, you might want to bear in mind for future reference, that while Baker Company is one-quarter Jao and three-quarters human, all the humans with whom you will be working speak excellent Jao."

Startled, Mallu glanced at the rows of waiting jinau. One of them in the front, small in stature with startling red fur on its head, closed a single eye in what seemed to be a deliberate gesture.

CHAPTER
13

Kaln stood speechless while the insufferable Tully divided up the Krant crew and assigned them to teams in his mostly human unit to operate the individual gun mounts. Only Krant-Captain Mallu remained apart, ears stiff, still hunched against the obvious ache in his ribs.

Tully gave a quick orientation for the Krants: There were fourteen kinetic guns on this so-called "spine," which was actually a weapons deck. Each required a seven-man crew: one in charge of fire control radar, four to load the projectiles, a single gun operator, and one to supervise the whole process.

She, in fact, was the only Krant allotted to this particular team, Gun C-Six, though some of the other mounts had been assigned two Krants. Feeling exposed and picked upon, she shuffled behind the six jinau, one Jao and five humans, waiting before "her" designated station. Several of the humans glanced over their shoulders at her with what seemed to be curiosity in their nasty, static eyes, but the Jao, a stocky middle-aged fellow, pointedly turned away as though tales of her bad behavior had spread throughout the ship.

The one named Tully went on to explain firing procedure in Jao, but she was having a hard time making herself follow his words. By the Beginning, he was only a primitive! As a scion of Krant, she had traveled the stars since emerging from her natal pool, had even fought the Ekhat and survived to tell about it. What could such as he possibly say that was worth her attention?

The gun mount itself, though, was sleek and deadly, crafted of a blue-gray metal which she assumed was an iron alloy. She found it oddly alluring, for some reason. Tracks had been laid into the floor so that the mount could be retracted, as it was now. Bizarre.

"—bulkheads have been reinforced for ramming," Tully was saying. He gestured at the far wall. "We found that strategy effective when the Melody attacked Terra two years ago. Ekhat ships are particularly vulnerable to structural damage."

Kaln felt ill. He was talking about actually *smashing* this ship into an Ekhat vessel! She should have known it would come to something ludicrous like that. Humans were only one evolutionary step away from clouting one another over the head with clubs.

"Senior-Tech?" one of the human crew said in Jao. The creature seemed to be female, small-boned, shorter than most of the others. A strange shade of vivid red fur topped her head.

Kaln realized suddenly that Tully had stopped talking. The gun crews had reported to their assigned stations to run firing drills. Everyone on her own crew was murmuring as they stared at her, waiting. Evidently she had missed something and a response of some sort was required. She blinked.

"I asked—which position would you like to take?" the human said, her tone respectful. "I am charged with supervising this gun as well as several others. You can serve in any capacity you wish; gun captain, gun operator, take the fire control radar, or work in the *magazine*." That last word was human. Either there was no Jao equivalent, or the female wasn't fluent enough in Jao to know it.

The little figure gestured at the gun. She looked inadequate for a soldier of any sort, as though the first strong wave she encountered would sweep her away. "You have experience fighting in space as most of us have not," the female said, her body carefully still. "We would like to take advantage of that."

"I—have not worked on this sort of weapon before," Kaln said. Her mind whirled so that she could not focus. She reached out and touched the cold metal. She did not want to be here, most certainly did not want the responsibility of trying to make this hodgepodge of species work together as an effective crew. "I will train to work in the *magazine*." Whatever that was. She hadn't the faintest idea, but one place she had no wish to be was surely as good as another.

"All right," the human said. "I rank as 'lieutenant.'"

Kaln's good ear flinched at the brash presentation of rank unasked, but then realized the female had at least not forced her personal name upon the Jao. And she had read the service bars incised upon Kaln's cheek correctly as senior-tech, impressive for a primitive.

The rank itself was typically human. One of the Jao with experience dealing with humans had already explained the bizarre customs involved to Kaln and the other Krant officers. The term "general" could mean almost anything, since as well as being a military rank it was a common term. The same for "major." The term "captain" was more tightly focused, but was still maddeningly vague. It could serve as a verb as well as a noun. Thus, a ship could be "captained" as well as having a captain—but the captainer might not actually have the rank of a captain.

Likewise with the term "lieutenant." It could either refer to a specific rank or, more fluidly, to a relationship. Thus, apparently, one general—a very high rank, that was—might still serve another as his "lieutenant."

It was all very frustrating. Only the term "colonel" seem to have any real precision. Unfortunately, there didn't seem to be that many colonels.

"The magazine is below," the lieutenant said. "Access is through this hatch." She gestured at a circular opening in the floor as one of the humans climbed down a ladder and disappeared. Kaln followed, filled with foreboding.

Light flooded the chamber below, brighter than Jao eyes liked. Peculiarly-shaped objects of some sort were stored neatly in sturdy racks on one wall. Kaln stared at them blankly. They resembled missiles, in their shape, but she could see no sign of any propulsive mechanisms. She had no experience with kinetic weapons. As a military option, such tech seemed no more effective than surly children flinging rocks at one another.

A human almost robust enough to be a Jao turned to her. His hide was darker than most of the others, a mellow shade of brown. "Those are depleted uranium sabot rounds. They will penetrate any Ehkat armor we—you Jao, I should say—have ever encountered."

Kaln was able to follow that much of the logic, although the thought of meddling with radioactive material was a bit unsettling. Still, she assumed that by "depleted" the human meant that the uranium was no longer very dangerous.

"In times past," the human continued, "we would have had to load powder as well. But we use liquid propellant, these days." He pointed to a mechanism. "That's the hoist that lifts the rounds into the firing chamber. It's configured now for sabot rounds, but can be changed if we use other ammunition. High explosives, for instance, or incendiary rounds. For space combat, though, that's pretty unlikely."

So, apparently, they had different types of missiles. Kaln couldn't really see the point to that. Throwing rocks, even explosive or combustible rocks, was not going to defeat the Ekhat. The first enemy ship they encountered would make very short work of them.

But at least then her misery would be at an end. Flow stretched out so that everything was slow and murky. Kaln would rather have been anywhere but here and now. The room seemed to be buzzing.

A hand touched her arm. "Senior-Tech?"

Kaln recoiled, then normal flow reasserted itself. She saw the red-topped female who had designated herself as a lieutenant.

"I think you should view one of our vids before assuming your duties here," the human said, withdrawing her hand. "It is a standard requirement for all jinau troops during what we call basic training, titled *Battle of the Framepoint*."

Wrot prowled the great ship from one end to the other, poking his nose into the engine room, the command deck, the living quarters, and the food halls, sampling the mood of the mixed crew. Emotions varied from excitement at being summoned to such a faraway location to apprehension over what awaited them, and always among the humans simmered insatiable curiosity. Their capacity for sheer inquisitiveness never failed to surprise him despite his long association with the species.

Certain decks had been designated Jao, others human. The two did not mingle much off-duty, which made sense since their recreational activities and dietary habits were vastly different. But the tendency of the two contingents to keep to themselves concerned him. They all had to pull together, braiding the strengths of their two species so that they were stronger in unison than either could ever be alone.

Tully had begun accepting Jao into his reconnaissance unit over a year ago, which was highly unusual and considered an experimental policy by the Bond. Such Jao were technically considered jinau, which normally would have been a grave demotion. Only Jao of the lowest-ranked kochan would ever consider making such a choice. Typically, Tully's Jao jinau resigned from their natal kochan and joined the Terran taif.

The new taif was turning out to be much more successful than anticipated, though. It seemed, despite their reputation, a number of low kochan had given birth to individuals who had the potential to be far more than merely competent dullards. These often became a credit to Terra Taif once they had the opportunity to make themselves of more use with increased responsibilities. Humans were quite fierce in their belief in the value of the individual over the group, and although Wrot would never go that far, it seemed that encouraging individuals to make the most of their innate talents, whatever their origins, possessed a certain merit.

In the ship-afternoon, Wrot dropped by Deck Forty-Six's food hall to meet Caitlin Kralik and Rob Wiley and answer some of their questions, if he could. The room was mostly empty at the moment, just a few humans scattered about, seated at green-covered tables, many consuming that vile sludge called "coffee." Just the reek of it was enough to ruin his appetite.

Heads turned as he passed, but no one hailed him. Caitlin and Rob Wiley were seated at a table in the far corner, their backs to a vidscreen streaming a view of the stars ahead of them from the command deck. The former member of the Resistance was a brown-skinned man, wiry, but still strong for his age. A twisted scar across the heartward side of his face spoke eloquently of old battles and the man's long-standing fight for survival.

"*Vaist*," the human woman said, using the inferior-to-superior form of the greeting, I see you. She rose, bowed her head and positioned her arms into the graceful curves of *recognizing-authority*.

Her slight stature compared to his own species was deceptive, Wrot thought ruefully. Inside, he knew this one was made of steel. Even Oppuk krinnu ava Narvo had learned that, to his utter misfortune. The Jao shook his head, a bit of highly useful human body-language he'd acquired long ago. "None of that, girl," he said. "You're just trying to make me feel old!"

"Well, you must be in charge," she said. "I know the Preceptor told *you* who's out there in that nebula. He certainly didn't tell me."

"He told me what he suspects," Wrot said, sliding onto the chair across from Wiley. It creaked beneath his weight, the furniture in here intended for human dimensions, not Jao. "Which is hardly the same thing, and it would be pointless to run about spreading rumors and getting everyone all excited until we know the truth of it."

"You wretch!" she said with a placating smile. "You and Ronz both know how miserably curious humans are! You're just trying to make us all crazy!"

Wiley's dark face was watching the exchange with half-lidded eyes. He'd been slowly changing his attitude toward Earth's conquerors since being reinstated in the military by Aille, but the old Resistance fighter had spent too many years fighting Jao to unbend easily. Distrust and enmity toward Terra's previous foes ran deep in his character. He leaned back in his chair and laced his hands over the slight paunch he'd been developing since gaining access to a decent diet.

"So you admit that there's something to get excited about," he said, using Wrot's words against him. Despite his lack of Jao postures, the former Resistance fighter managed to convey *craftiness*.

"More like some*one* to get excited about," Caitlin said. She'd angled her arms and body in a sketchy approximation of *sly-expectation*, hampered by her seated position.

"You'll either see what Ronz suspected when we get there," Wrot said, refusing, as a human might say, to rise to the bait, "or none of us will see anything but gas and dust and debris. First, though, we have to reach the proper coordinates and make our jump."

"Two more days until transition is what I've heard," Wiley said. He narrowed his dark-brown eyes. Though lacking green fire, they were oddly expressive. Wrot could almost see the questions burning inside the grizzled old fighter's head. "And here I thought space travel was supposed to be so blamed fast. I swear I could have walked to the Rockies and back from Pascagoula already."

"Terra-Captain Dannet is being rightfully cautious," Wrot said. "She understands the dangers inherent in emerging in the nebula all too well, so she'll position the *Lexington* at the coordinates needed for optimal safety before giving the go-ahead to activate the framepoint."

"Just a lot of fancy talk, if you ask me, for 'we're not there yet,'" Wiley said, shoving his chair back.

Caitlin smothered a laugh with one hand, cueing Wrot that the statement was meant to be humorous. Unfortunately, the implied wit eluded him. He had spent over twenty years on Terra, as humans reckoned such things, but their humor was difficult to grasp. All too often, though he had diligently studied the art of joking, he just did not "get it." Perhaps Caitlin would explain what he'd missed later.

"At any rate, Rob has some concerns," Caitlin said. Her blond hair was tied back, her manner forthright. "Serious ones that I hear a number of the human crew share. I wanted you to have a chance to answer."

Wiley gave Wrot a hard look. "I think the reason your Bond filled this ship with humans was that they don't expect us to come back. Losing a ship full of jinau wouldn't be such a big problem as losing one crammed with high-status Jao."

Wrot's whiskers wilted into utter *bafflement*. "Leaving aside the matter of deliberately sacrificing several thousand highly trained jinau troops," he said, "do you really think Preceptor Ronz would just throw away this expensive new ship on a mere whim?"

"I think no one knows what goes on inside his head," Wiley said stubbornly, "except maybe another Jao."

"Certainly not this Jao," Wrot said.

Wiley ran a hand back over his tightly curled graying hair. "Then just come out with it. What the hell could be so freaking important that the Bond would risk all our lives just to go take a poke at it?"

"Something that could change everything, if it's really there," Wrot said.

Caitlin inhaled suddenly. She sat forward in her chair. Her blue-gray eyes turned to Wiley. "And I'm betting this is something that would not be glad to see the Jao."

"And why is that?" Wiley gazed at him with a sour expression. "What did you lot do to *them*?"

What we used to do to everyone, Wrot thought morosely, even though the Jao's wholesale slaughter of alien species under the direction of the Ekhat had ended a thousand years before his own birth. "Humans are here because Preceptor Ronz thought they might be useful, given what we may find in the nebula," he said. "Think! Would he risk members of Aille's own service if it was only to throw away their lives on a useless gesture?"

"He has you there, Rob," Caitlin said.

"Then tell us what we're getting into!" Wiley said, bolting to his feet as if he could no longer be still. "It's not fair to keep us in the dark!"

Humans couldn't see as well as Jao at night, Wrot reminded himself. A Jao kept "in the dark" wouldn't mind, but the experience might be frightening for a human. "I will tell you as soon as I know for sure," he said. "I cannot promise anything more."

"I damn well knew he'd say that!" Wiley shoved his chair back so that it squeaked on the tile floor. He stalked out of the food hall, limping a little from an old war injury that hadn't healed well.

Caitlin stared after him. "That was rude, but he has a point, Wrot."

"It won't be much longer," Wrot said, shaking his head human-fashion. It wouldn't do any good to discipline Wiley for his discourtesy. Bringing him, and the rest of the Resistance, into association had been tricky and would be an on-going process for some time to come. Many of those holed up in the mountains made Tully, who came from the same background, look positively mellow in comparison. "Once we jump, then we will all know what is—or isn't—there."

"What if I guess first?" Her body had gone startlingly neutral, a deliberate choice on her part.

She was good at Jao games, he thought, and who really knew the full measure of what she had learned during her childhood as Narvo's prisoner? If any human could figure out what Ronz suspected, it would certainly be her. "Then I hope you will do the Preceptor the courtesy of keeping the information to yourself," he said, lowering his voice so that only the two of them could hear. "There are pressing reasons to not to tell anyone, especially the Jao aboard, until and unless we absolutely must."

"All right," she said. Her expression was inscrutable. He could discern nothing of her thoughts. Impressive. "I promise."

At that, Wrot relaxed a bit. Unlike many humans, Caitlin was as good as her word.

Tully kept a close watch on the Krants as his unit ran firing drills so that they would be proficient if and when the time came. The Krant Jao started out stiff and standoffish, but soon lost themselves in the rhythmical process of cycling together the ammo, then feeding the shells into the hoist and loader drum. He noticed that several Krants volunteered, in fact, to train as gun operators and seemed to be naturals despite their lack of experience with kinetic weapons.

He'd assigned Krant-Captain Mallu as gun mount captain on C-Eleven. The poor bastard had already had more than enough bad luck, losing his ship and then sacrificing his ribs to save Aguilera's hide. Tully just couldn't bring himself to shame the Jao any further by ranking him as a mere team member, and his still-healing injury prevented him from taking on more strenuous duty. He was betting Mallu could learn what he didn't already know on the fly and Eleven's crew would cover for him until he knew the routine. No one advanced among the Jao to ship-captain without a full measure of brains.

At any rate, Tully had drawn enough ammo to give the operators a feel for the ordnance, and the firing stats were impressive, especially for a crew just coming up to speed. Tully walked up and down the line of fourteen weapons. Despite the vents, the air was filled with the scent of hot oil, burnt propellant, and heated metal. The guns were blue-steel beauties, whose design had been inspired by the jury-rigged tank weapons used back in that now-famous Battle of the Framepoint, but were specifically crafted for this ship. And they were far more powerful. The guns used in the Framepoint battle had been 140mm tank cannons. These were 500mm guns, larger than the main guns on old-style human battleships. Half of the other artillery-spines sported Jao energy weapons, but Tully figured these alone ought to be enough to take care of whatever was waiting for them in the nebula.

Tully didn't believe for an instant that the *Lexington* was on the trail of one of the Ekhat factions, or even two factions. Ronz wasn't the sort to get all hot and bothered over the Interdict or the Harmony or the Melody, no matter how bat-crazy the aliens were. For the Jao, the Ekhat were business as usual. This, whatever it turned out to be, was something entirely different.

Voices rose, audible even over the roar of firing guns. He signaled and one by one the crews shut down their weapons. Close to the middle, a dark-napped Jao in maroon harness was shouting at Lieutenant Caewithe Miller. He shoved his hands into his pockets and headed that way. It was one of the Krants, of course. Tully's jinau Jao either got along with humans or he booted their tailless behinds out.

"What is the difficulty?" he said in Jao when he reached the

Number Six mount. The Krant was stalking about, looking murderous even to someone not well versed in postures.

The red-haired lieutenant's blue eyes stared over his shoulder. Her face was flushed. "We seem to have a difference of opinion, sir."

Miller was from Atlanta, and didn't usually have much of a southern accent. But Tully had noticed before that the accent tended to come to the surface when the woman was agitated, either from pleasure or anger. Right now, it was pretty pronounced.

Tully locked his arms behind his body, rocked on his heels and did his best rendition of Yaut's *waiting-to-be-informed*. He turned to the Jao. It was, he saw now by the droopy ear, Senior-Tech Kaln, making trouble yet again. He repressed an oath. "Yes?"

"They are doing it wrong!" Kaln blurted, her good ear flattened.

"It?" he said politely. Were those angles indicating *desire-to-kill*? His hand inched forward to rest upon his holstered sidearm.

"Loading the weapon!" She paced up and down, waving her arms in no posture he'd ever encountered. "The lifting device—it is so—slow, so—inefficient! We could do better!"

He glanced at Miller for an explanation. "I sent Senior-Tech Kaln back to my quarters with Private Cupp to view a documentary about the Battle of the Framepoint," she said, back stiff, shoulders braced. "I thought it would help if she could see for herself how effective kinetic weapons can be against the Ekhat when properly deployed."

"And?" he prompted.

Kaln turned to him. "I saw!" Her eyes danced with that characteristic green lightning Jao displayed when they were all worked up about something. "It is nothing like throwing rocks after all!"

"Throwing rocks?" he said and glanced at Miller, who gave a slight shake of her head.

"Kinetic weapons!" Kaln said. Her shoulders flexed and he realized suddenly that the angles of her stocky form weren't indicating *desire-to-kill* after all, but raw *excitement*. "I thought you were merely throwing things at the enemy, like children fighting, but this is infernally clever! The Ekhat shield against energy beams, but they will never anticipate such sheer blunt-force savagery!"

"I...see," Tully said, very much hoping that he truly did. "And you wish to improve the loading process?"

"The hoist is slow," she said, gaining sufficient control of herself finally to stand still. "It limits how rapidly the loader drum can be filled which also restricts the number of rounds fired in a battle."

The gun crews were all staring and he could feel the tension from both the humans and Jao. He could just about read their minds. These Krants had just shown up and already they wanted to run the show. However, Kaln was a senior-tech, he thought. That rank indicated true ability, and female Jao were traditionally more proficient at handling technology than the males.

How strange, though, that she should want to do something new, to craft an improvement that a human would even say was "creative." Jao usually had little ability to visualize things-that-were-not, what they called *ollnat*. "If you will draw up a plan for improvements," he said, "I will examine it for feasibility, and then if it looks good, we can take the suggestion to Terra-Captain Dannet."

Kaln's black eyes glittered green with emotion.

"For now, though," he said, "we will finish the drill."

Lieutenant Miller turned back to the crew. "Load her up!" she said in English.

Kaln joined the crew down in the magazine and the great guns went back to work.

CHAPTER

14

That night, using Aille's access codes, available to her as a member of his personal service, Caitlin sat in her too-quiet quarters and pored over Jao archives, downloading old file after file, reading and listening until her head swam. Finally, she sat back and massaged the bridge of her nose, thinking. One thing was for sure—Jao had absolutely no gift for narrative. Dry facts and understatement were all you got. She suspected a lot was hidden between those lines.

The Jao had been around a long time as a sovereign species, and before that they had existed for an even longer period as slaves to the insane Ekhat. Oddly enough, the Jao records did not reflect triumph at having escaped such bondage, nor seem particularly ashamed of their origin. It was what had been and nothing could change that, and it had happened to no one now living, nor had anyone currently in existence taken part in the Ekhat's wholesale slaughter of intelligence across the galaxy.

So there were no holidays to celebrate their hard-won independence, no days of remembrance, and their own enslavement had certainly failed to make them sensitive to the injustice of doing the same to other species, now that they themselves were free.

To the Jao, it was simple: the strong should rule, and the weak should make themselves of use. The only reason humans had achieved any measure of equality with their conquerors was that they had proved themselves more trouble to dominate than any other species the Jao had ever encountered. In the end, it had been considered easier to bring them into association so they could make themselves of use that way.

And not all Jao were in agreement with that decision, even now. Many kochan believed the Bond was making a mistake in allowing Terra to form its own taifs. But since the two most powerful kochan—Pluthrak and Narvo, each for their own reasons—supported the Bond in the matter, the others acquiesced.

None of this told her, though, who was likely to be lurking in that nebula, so she dove back into the records and ferreted out name after name of other conquered worlds. It would have to be someone with the technological prowess to wander the stars and stand up to the Ekhat in a fight. That seemed to eliminate all of the known conquered species. The Jao freely admitted that humans were the most technologically advanced species they'd ever come up against.

But that only covered the species encountered since they'd freed themselves from the Ekhat. What about before?

Under the direction of the Ekhat, they had obediently exterminated developing sapience wherever the Ekhat sniffed it out. The archives contained only the bare bones of these campaigns with poker-faced Jao droning on about how many ships and troops had been involved in an extermination operation. They rarely elaborated beyond that sort of dry but gruesome detail.

One name cropped up over and over, though: the Lleix. They had been an advanced civilization, spacefaring, and inhabited a number of planets. According to the records, the Lleix had fought gamely and inflicted terrible losses upon the Jao even as, inch by inch, they lost their homes.

They'd had advantages that Earth had lacked, especially spaceships and a population spread across multiple worlds. Exterminating such a species would be difficult. Even if you took out the majority of their settlements, what were the odds that somewhere a pocket of these hardy, resourceful, and highly intelligent folk had survived?

Then she stumbled across a file depicting an ancient parley with the Lleix that took place on a grassy slope beneath a star far more orange than Sol. The Lleix was humanoid in shape, though stockier, and its head was encircled by a fleshy crown more like the calyx of a flower rather than anything resembling hair or fur. It was dressed in an elaborately decorated robe as though attending a ceremony. Its face was smooth and round with only the smallest suggestion of nose. No ears were visible and it appeared to be completely hairless. Tall and silver-skinned and alone, it approached the Jao representative.

Caitlin tapped into the audio and heard the Lleix propose that their two kinds form an alliance and turn against "their common enemy, the Ekhat." The Jao and the Lleix had far more in common with one another than the Jao had with their terrible masters. Would it not make sense for the Jao to free themselves and devote their resources to making a good life for their own kind rather than exterminating species who had done them no harm?

"We are willing to put all of our tech at your disposal," the silver-skinned one said, speaking grammatical, though heavily accented, Jao. "Have each of our *elian* release an expert to advise your forces. You are already fierce warriors. No one could dispute that. The Lleix believe you can also be a great people. You have only to reach out for the freedom your Ekhat masters have never allowed you."

The argument continued until the Jao representative lost patience and killed the Lleix. The alien crumpled to the grass and its corpse was abandoned there unceremoniously.

Caitlin froze the recording. She remembered having heard the story about this particular species long ago. The Lleix were the ones who first put the notion of the Jao freeing themselves from the Ekhat into their thick-skulled heads. Jao, who disdained *oll-nat*, would never have devised such an innovative idea on their own. And even so, the concept of liberation had taken hundreds of years and many generations to work through Jao culture and sufficiently motivate the great kochan before they actually came up with a plan and acted to make it happen. But by then the Lleix were all dead.

Or were they?

Perhaps that was who Ronz suspected had joined the battle back in the nebula and then run away. And if it was a long-lost remnant of surviving Lleix, the last people they would want to see would be the Jao.

That would explain why the Preceptor had loaded up a new ship of decidedly unJao design with humans and sent it back to investigate. The Lleix would not recognize it as being of Jao origin and humans could front any negotiations so that the Lleix wouldn't be so likely to attack them out of hand.

Caitlin's thoughts whirled. If she had it right, no wonder Ronz and Wrot wanted to keep the notion quiet. Humans had odd ideas, as far as Jao were concerned, about persecution and the value of liberty. If this story got out, the human troops aboard the ship were bound to sympathize with the Lleix if it came to a shooting match.

And what would the Lleix do, when they learned the *Lexington* housed a complement of Jao as well as humans? If their performance in the recent nebula battle was any indication of their capability, they might simply drive the *Lexington* out of their space, then pack up their colony and lose themselves again. By the time anyone on Earth figured out what had happened, it would be too late.

That meant the diplomatic contingent on board would have to be especially persuasive, she thought. They would have to reassure the Lleix that the Jao had not hunted them down this time merely to finish what they so long ago started; that together, they would be stronger still, forming a three-part alliance to stand against the Ekhat.

Caitlin of course was meant to be one of those diplomats and did not feel nearly golden-tongued enough for such a challenge. She punched in a call for Wrot, ready to share her theory with him. If she was right, she had a lot to learn about the Lleix in a very short time. Blast Ronz! He could have told at least her what he was thinking. He should know her well enough to understand that she could keep a secret—except from her husband, of course, and he wasn't here.

Abandoning the chair before her console, she curled up on her bunk and hugged a pillow to her chest. God, did she ever wish Ed *was* here right now. Two years of marriage had accustomed her to not having to shoulder emotional burdens alone anymore. Though the two of them were often parted by their jobs, they were in constant contact. This would be so much easier if she could bounce ideas off his practical mind while deciding how to approach this.

She rolled over on her back and stared up at the gray ceiling, feeling the thrum of the great engines. Well, she told herself, she'd gotten along for many difficult years before Eddie Kralik came her way and she could certainly do it again. But she didn't have to like it.

When Tully checked up on the whereabouts of the three ranking Krants the next morning after breakfast, he managed to interrupt Jalta's swim long enough to learn that Kaln was down in one of the magazines on Spine C, tinkering with the hoist.

If she'd been human, he wouldn't have been surprised, but in his experience, Jao just didn't have ideas about how to improve devices, and if one did occur, no self-respecting Jao would go so far as to act upon it. They were skilled operators of technology as well as competent craftsmen and repairmen. They fought fearlessly and clung to honor, as they defined it, like a human would to his pants when caught naked on a public street. But they usually regarded anything smelling of *ollnat* as childish or even barbaric.

Yesterday, though, Kaln had somehow gotten an idea on how to enhance the hoist and now she was exploring it. Even if she was wrong and thoroughly screwed the device up, Tully was fascinated. Most Jao, left on their own, would spend their free time swimming, arguing kochan history, or lounging about on a soft pile of *dehabia*, and most techs would have occupied themselves with the study of operating manuals. The more he knew of this particular Jao, the stranger she seemed.

He left orders for Baker Company to report for firing drills at 14:00, then went down to Spine C to see what Kaln was doing. Fortunately, he found Caewithe Miller already there, supervising. She was young for an officer. Like most of her generation, she'd grown up under Jao rule and didn't have the same chip on her shoulder carried by those who remembered the brutality of the Conquest first-hand. That gave her an edge in dealing with mixed human and Jao troops.

Along with her own ability, of course. By now, Tully was almost certain that the little redhead was the most capable subordinate officer he had in his unit. And he was even more certain that his assessment wasn't influenced by the fact that Miller was also, by a country mile, the best-looking one too. Tully was by no means immune to the young woman's attractiveness, but he was quite disciplined about such things. He always had been, even before he got Yaut's relentless training.

The great gun mount was locked into the hull, ready for action.

Miller was squatting, peering down into the magazine. She glanced up, then sprang to attention. "Sir!"

Freckles stood out on her face. Between those and the bright blue eyes and the red hair and the general prettiness of her features, Tully actually had to struggle a little to keep his mind on business.

"At ease, Lieutenant," he said. "How's it going?"

"Okay, I guess." She glanced at the open hatch. Banging could be heard from below. "If her adaptation works, it may be ready to try later, if that's all right."

"We're running another drill at 14:00," he said. "Tomorrow's the day we jump and we have to be sharp. No telling what's waiting for us in that nebula." He leaned over the opening. "Senior-Tech Kaln?"

The dark-napped Jao below paused and looked up, good ear pinned. The floor was littered with parts. "I am busy." Her tone brooked no interruption.

"This mount has to be up and running by—" He broke off, trying to gauge how to explain 14:00 to someone who did not understand measuring time in quantified amounts. "—a little after mid-sun."

"Do not be ridiculous," she said, holding up a silvery rod and squinting at it. "There is no sun on this ship. Even a dry-foot like you should know that."

"We are running firing drills—later," he said. "And not a lot later. You have to reassemble the hoist in time for that."

"It will be done when it is done," Kaln said, turning back to the scatter of disassembled parts.

"No," he said, trying to channel Yaut, "it will be done on time. Even if I cannot feel the flow of this situation, I know you can, and you will either have the improvement finished or the hoist reassembled in its former condition in time for the drill. Do I make myself understood?"

She threw down the part in her hand with a clank and scrambled back up the ladder to stand before him, shoulders braced, whiskers bristling.

Yaut, he thought, trying to remember the proper stance for someone being defied as she loomed in front of him, a head taller. *Yaut, when Tully had done something particularly clueless by Jao standards. What had that looked like?* He dropped one shoulder, angled his head, curved his arms.

Kaln's eyes blazed green. Caewithe Miller edged away, her own arms locked behind her back, her gaze prudently on the back wall.

The Jao froze. If she'd been a dog, Tully would have said her hackles were raised. Time seemed to stretch out as Kaln attempted to out-stare him, but he'd been trained by a master. He concentrated, noting her *vai camiti*, camouflaged by dark-brown nap. It was actually quite bold, sweeping across her face at a rakish angle.

"This is important," she said finally. Her whiskers wilted. "I know how to make the device better."

"I am impressed that you have an idea to improve the technology," Tully said, not relaxing his stance. "But the gun mount must function in time for the drill. We will jump soon and no one knows what we will find when we emerge from the framepoint. It could be the Ekhat. It could even be something worse. We have to be ready."

Kaln suddenly dropped her gaze to her maroon boots. "On a Krant ship, such—changing—would not be allowed." Her voice was low.

Indeed it would not, Tully thought. "Do you often get such ideas?" he asked, grasping at the edge of something intriguing in this conversation that was still eluding him.

"Occasionally," she said, "but no one is interested in improvements. Things work as they are meant to, as they always have. That is good enough. Anytime I changed something, no matter how well it functioned afterwards, I always had to put it back."

"I see," he said, and he thought that finally he really did. She was a Jao maverick, the proverbial square peg trying to fit into an exceedingly round hole, gifted with a least some measure of creativity while born to a species that had little use for such interests.

"Humans respect the power of *ollnat*," he said, "but the gun mount must be ready for action." He considered the situation. "I will assign a ship-tech to assist you."

Her eyes glittered with that enigmatic green fire that must signify something, though he had no way to understand. "That would be helpful," she said. The lines of her body shifted into a posture he'd never seen on Yaut. Skies above only knew what it was. He certainly couldn't ask.

He nodded to Lieutenant Miller, then left Senior-Tech Kaln to her self-appointed task.

✳   ✳   ✳

Flow increased. Somewhere, something was about to come together and Wrot had a fairly good idea just what that was. The jump into the nebula would be tomorrow and then they would all know whether the Preceptor's suspicions were justified.

Part of him hoped Ronz had made an error, that this would be some new species, never before encountered. If so, the Jao would have a "clean slate," as humans liked to say, no preconceptions, no more than the usual fears at encountering unknown sapients. First contact would be much easier than dealing with the mayhem the Jao had long ago sowed under the Ekhat's direction.

Caitlin Kralik had sent him a message last night, requesting a meeting "at his earliest convenience." That expression amused him, as much about humans did. A Jao would never care if a desired interaction were "convenient" or not. His kind would accept an invitation from a subordinate if it were deemed necessary or advantageous, and ignore it otherwise. Humans, though, were a different breed. No one understood that better than Wrot, who'd fought in the Conquest and then spent over twenty years afterward living among them.

He sent word that he would drop by her quarters, then indulged in a quick morning swim so that his wits would be at their sharpest. Caitlin had been sniffing at the edges of the matter ever since they'd left Terra. It was not inconceivable that she'd figured out their mission.

"Wrot, come in," Caitlin said, when he presented himself, his nap still damp, at her door.

"*Vaim,*" he said. We-see-each-other, a greeting between those of equal status. By naming her so, which she was not in this situation since he had *oudh*, he rendered her a great compliment.

Dressed in jeans and a navy-blue shirt, she resembled a jinau. Her face was flushed with excitement. She stood aside as he entered, then eased into the graceful lines of *appreciation-of-bestowed-favor*. "*Vaim*, yourself, old man," she murmured, starting in Jao and then ending in Standard English. She had the air of a mischievous child. A hint of simple *pride* crept into her lines though she quickly suppressed it.

"You know," he said, taking her console chair. She sat across from him on her bunk.

"I think so," she said, drawing her legs up and hugging her knees. "You'll have to tell me whether I'm right."

Humans were so much more limber than Jao, he thought ruefully. He cocked an ear at her, waiting.

"It's the Lleix," she said. "The species who first put the notion
of freedom into your minds."

It would never do to underestimate this one, Wrot told himself.
Her childhood exposure to Jao culture had made her infernally
clever. He wondered if humans would ever be recruited by the
Bond. If so, she would probably be the first selected. "That is what
we suspect," he said, "but there is no way to know until we jump."

"If it is them, they won't welcome us," she said. Her face had
gone pink in the cheeks, a reliable indicator of excitement for
her kind. "They'll be afraid, or angry, or both."

"That is, as humans say, an understatement," Wrot said. "So, if
Ronz is correct, we will have to proceed carefully."

"Why proceed at all?" she said. "Why not just leave them in
peace? If they wanted to be found, they wouldn't have left after
the battle."

"The Ekhat have already rediscovered them," Wrot said. "At some
point, they will be back with as many ships as it takes and then
this colony will perish. For the sake of our *vithrik* and all those
who died so long ago at our hands, we should make ourselves
of use and save these."

"How will we even speak to them?" she said. "The only file I
found with an audio track had them communicating with your
representative in Jao, for all the good it did them."

Once the Lleix had even gone to the trouble of learning their
enemy's language to try to forge an alliance. That indicated much
about both their desperation and resourcefulness. Wrot closed his
eyes, thinking hard. That meeting had been so long ago, no Lleix
would remember how to speak Jao now. They'd certainly had no
reason to maintain the skill.

"I do not know," he said finally, "but they are an intelligent species with something of humanity's ability to visualize that-which-
is-not, otherwise they would never have glimpsed the possibilities
in the Jao that we could not see for ourselves. Perhaps you and
your fellow humans can connect with them on at least that level."

"Are there any restricted files dealing with the Lleix?" she
asked, her eyes upon a digital photograph of her mate, Ed, on
the shelf above Wrot's head. "I have Aille's access codes, but you
must have the Bond's."

Now that she had guessed the truth, she should have access to everything so that she could make herself of the fullest use, should the Lleix be waiting for them in that nebula. Still, Wrot hesitated. Caitlin thought she understood the full grimness of the Jao's former existence as tools of the Ekhat, but he was quite certain she did not. If he gave her access, she would see for herself in gruesome detail all the terrible actions they had carried out long ago under Ekhat rule, and once known, the knowledge could never be taken back.

It would be a burden she would have to carry all her days. He understood that in this moment, even if she did not.

But they all had to make themselves of use, Wrot and Caitlin and Tully and Dannet and the Krants, no matter how painful the path was. *Vithrik* allowed nothing less. He turned his chair around and then added his code to her authorization on the computer. "What you learn here," he said over his shoulder, "can be shared with no one without Bond permission, not even Ed." He turned back and met her startled blue-gray eyes. "Can you handle that?"

"But Ed has very high clearance," she said. "Surely—"

"Not without Bond approval," Wrot said, "and that may never be granted. Ronz would require as good a reason to authorize him as I have with you now."

Flow slowed as she took some time to think it over. Wrot appreciated that about this particular human. Plagued as she was with her species' endless curiosity, she still understood what kind of commitment this would be. She did not rush into big decisions like a child newly emerged from its natal pool.

Finally, she sighed. "I don't want to know things I can't tell Ed, but I don't see that I have a choice. I need as much information as possible if I'm going to do any good here."

"I think you are right," he said and validated her access.

CHAPTER
15

Mallu heeded the summons to Spine C for additional training, reporting with Jalta, Kaln, and the rest of his reduced Krant crew. His own position as Gun C-Eleven's captain was much more interesting than he had first thought. The great kinetic weapons packed immense force and he could see how they might even be more effective in some situations than energy weapons for which the Ekhat would have shields.

His ribs still ached, but not as much, though a number of postures were still difficult. However, working with humans as he was, postures weren't required and mostly he didn't even bother trying. The creatures seemed oblivious to them anyway and their own postures were too chaotic to interpret.

Jalta was working at the far end on Gun One with no more fuss than if he'd been one of these stub-eared humans. Mallu had been braced for trouble from Kaln, but oddly enough she seemed to be fitting in with her own crew. At least, she had taken a position in the magazine of her gun mount and stayed down there most of the time. As far as he could tell, there had been no more commotion.

His other Krants were also doing fairly well. He'd only had to discipline three so far, and those for minor infractions. That was fortunate because he could feel the flow of this journey increasing. Something was about to happen and they all had to be ready.

His gun crew knew what to do far better than he did, in actuality, so at first he observed the other captains as their crews struggled to increase their efficiency, then watched for the same problems with his own personnel. Those under his responsibility were all human, infernally quick and more agile than Jao, but also more easily distracted. He soon realized that part of his job was to keep them focused, and that was not so hard.

When the drill was completed, Tully called a meeting of the gun captains and read off the stats. "Excellent," it said. Then Mallu corrected himself mentally—*he* said. This particular individual was male. He was beginning to be able to reliably tell the genders apart, which seemed important to humans. Males apparently disliked very much being taken for female. The opposite mistake elicited an even more indignant reaction.

Tully said something in his own language. Most of the gun captains, who were all but one human, chuffed, shook their heads, then dispersed. Tully turned to Mallu and switched to Jao. "We jump next-sun. Everyone is to be on duty at that point."

The nap behind Mallu's ears prickled with dread. *Lexington* was a new ship, and unless he were mistaken, this would be its first jump, a tricky enough situation even if they weren't heading into a planetary nebula. The moment swept back over him, three Krant ships emerging in the nebula, but only two surviving as the third miscalculated, jumped too deep in the targeted star, and was crushed and incinerated. Then, before they could orient themselves, his own ship had taken critical damage from the Ekhat even as its remaining fellow Krant vessel was blasted into fiery splinters. He still felt that terrible moment when he knew they were outclassed.

Tully was watching him closely. "Terra-Captain Dannet is very experienced," he said. "She came to us from Narvo."

Mallu's ears swiveled. He found himself surprised that a mere human had read him so well. "It is difficult to surrender control to others when one is accustomed to wielding it oneself."

"I understand," Tully said. His lean body was very straight, almost *respectful.*

The human and Jao jinau were filtering out of the spine, leaving behind only a small maintenance force to service the guns. His Krant-crew did not follow them, milling about instead, looking to Mallu for direction.

Kaln approached Tully, which initially alarmed Mallu until he saw that her good ear was *indecisive.*

Tully consulted the sheets in his hands, rustling through them as though in search of something. "You were right," he said finally to the waiting tech. "Gun Mount Six had a fourteen-percent increase in efficiency."

Kaln glanced at Mallu, her eyes smoldering green.

"I will recommend the upgrade be applied to all the *Lexington*'s kinetic guns when we return to Terra," Tully said. "I will need you to document the process so that it can be implemented wherever appropriate." He glanced at Mallu, his lips stretched into an unsettling grimace. "Be careful, Krant-Captain. Terra Taif may just try to steal this one from you." Then he followed the rest of the jinau out of the spine.

Mallu was baffled. Kaln was not an object which could be stolen. Was that a sly insult? Whatever did the annoying creature mean by such a comment?

Kaln, however, stared after Tully's retreating form with an odd hint of *longing* in her lines.

Jump Day. That's what Caitlin called it to herself as she left her quarters to make her way up to the *Lexington*'s bridge the next morning. Heavens only knew what the Jao were calling it. "Today," most likely, or simply "now." They were as unsentimental about such things as it was possible for a species to be and still qualify as sapient. She supposed the Ekhat had bred that quality into them back at the beginning of their uplift. It wouldn't have done for slave soldiers to waste time mooning about the sadness of extinguishing so much promising life or always wanting time off to commemorate some event.

She had done her homework on the Lleix as well as possible with the resources at hand and uncovered more records of Jao attacks against Lleix colonies and ships. The Lleix had fought valiantly, extracting a high price for each system yielded. The Jao had been indifferent to their plight, efficiently exterminating them at every turn, noting statistics but little more.

If the Lleix had gone to earth on a planet concealed in the nebula, they would expect no quarter from the Jao and would certainly give none. Any envoys from the *Lexington* would have to hide Terra's association with the Jao as long as possible, if they even managed to arrange a first contact. The Lleix were bound to be painfully skittish of alien intrusion.

What would such a culture be like after all this time? Yesterday, Wrot, having validated her conclusion, had asked her to use her university training in the study of human history under Dr. Kinsey to speculate. The Lleix, if she was right, had been in exile, concealed in this extreme environment for many generations.

Their society might well have become rigid and highly ritualized. Something like that had happened to the Jews during the Babylonian period, after the destruction of the Second Temple. She could visualize them embracing control over every aspect of everyday life in an effort to give their existence shape under such harsh conditions.

The Lleix elder trying to convince the Jao to free themselves had been beautiful in its own way, regal and silver-skinned. Would she ever get the chance to talk to one? And if she did, how would she make up for what the Jao had done to them so long ago? She knew full well how deep humanity's bitterness ran, based upon a much briefer struggle with a far better outcome. The Jao, persecuting them down through the years, must have seemed like evil incarnate to the Lleix.

All around her, the great ship brimmed with activity as she headed for the command deck. Creating a point locus was said to be intricate, not to mention tricky, and everyone was understandably nervous.

Figures darted in and out of doorways as she passed, their faces, both Jao and human, focused and intent. Several exited the lift at the end of the corridor as she entered, then grasped the rail, steeling herself. "Command deck," she told the controls. The cab soared upwards, as always, too damn fast. She sighed and held on.

When the lift stopped, Tully got on, blue jinau cap tucked under his arm, chuckling. His hair was combed, his uniform spotless. His batman, again, she thought. Bless the man. He deserved a promotion.

"Okay," she said as the door closed, "what's so funny? I could use a good laugh today. I've got ravens racketing around in my stomach instead of the proverbial butterflies."

He shook his head, unable to wipe the smile off his face. "Caitlin, I'm not sure this would help."

"Try me." She seized the support bar as the lift again raced upwards and even Tully braced himself. Blasted Jao and their cast-iron innards. These contraptions had to be set at least five times as fast as a human elevator. Every time she got on one, she felt like she was on a theme park ride whose main purpose was to frighten the wits out of a person.

"All right," he said as they arrived at the command deck. His eyes crinkled at the corners with suppressed merriment. "Don't say I didn't warn you, though."

They stepped out into controlled confusion. Voices, both human and Jao, rose and fell. Crew darted back and forth from station to station in the bridge's oddly shaped space with no right angles that satisfied the Jao's need for "flow" in their architecture. Sensors beeped and blinked and whistled, warning of dangers Caitlin had no wish to know.

Terra-Captain Dannet glanced over at them in the midst of conferring with an officer. She said nothing, but her angles shifted subtly toward *displeasure*. She had the affect of a lioness, all muscle and deadly grace mingled with the attitude that any second those within reach could become prey. Just the sight of the former Narvo made Caitlin want to retreat.

She had stayed out of Dannet's prickly way up to this point on the mission, but her rank entitled her to be up here during such a momentous event and, attitude or not, she wasn't going to be faced down.

"Over here," Tully said in her ear. She nodded and followed him to a station not currently being manned.

"Okay," he said, his voice still low, his green eyes gleaming with amusement. "I just left my company down on Weapons Spine C. They're on duty in case trouble is waiting on the other side for us, though the turrets themselves are retracted during the jump. I was inspecting the gun mounts and I kept getting jittery rumors from my people about jumps going bad. They've heard that ships were found completely inverted with the hull compressed into a solid core and the exterior of the ship on the outside like a gutted corpse. Their crews were in the same condition, skeletons inverted so that they were a bloody mess."

Caitlin swayed. "Oh, my God!" She glanced around at the busy command crew, mostly Jao but sprinkled with humans. Lights blinked. Displays flicked from setting to setting. Business as usual. Each crew member seemed focused upon his or her task, apparently unconcerned that they might all be dead in a few minutes.

"Yeah," Tully said, "that was my unit's general reaction. They were pretty spooked, but I'd never heard anything like that the whole time I worked on Aille's service. So I traced the stories back until I found out that they all originated with Kaln and Jalta. I just checked with Wrot and asked him how likely that kind of accident was to happen."

"Well?" She felt her heart hammering. Over at the front of the deck, a Jao navigator was calling off coordinates. Things were in motion. Her palms began to sweat.

"Wrot told me that they made it up," Tully said, a smile tugging at the corners of his lips. "It's the Jao equivalent of a damned tall tale. We're dealing with a bunch of Jao hillbillies!"

She sagged against the wall. "Wrot was sure?"

Tully nodded. "He said sometimes there is an accident, and a ship is lost during a jump—but then the ship is never heard from again. No one knows what happens to such ships."

"So why are the Krants trying to get everyone all upset?" she said, peering over shoulders blocking her view. Dannet was discussing a set of readings with a subordinate. Were they about to jump?

"It may be their idea of a joke," Tully said. "Jao do have a sense of humor, but it's not anything like ours. I'm going to have my guys start telling Pecos Bill and Paul Bunyan stories to the Krants and see how that goes over."

Caitlin had never heard of "Pecos Bill," though she was vaguely familiar with the Bunyan mythology. She supposed she'd have to listen in on a few of the stories.

"First framepoint generator set," a stocky Jao with a well-marked *vai camiti* said. "Waiting on response from next in sequence." Beneath their feet, the ship vibrated like a purring tiger.

"Come on," Caitlin said, taking Tully's arm. The mood of anticipation on the command deck was infectious. She could almost feel the so-called increasing "flow" of the moment herself. "We're going to miss all the fun."

"Yeah," Tully said. "I can't wait for the part where we emerge inside the photosphere of a damned star. That's Christmas and Halloween all jumbled into one terrifying moment."

"Second framepoint generator set," the Jao said calmly, as though they weren't readying to leap into hell. The vibration kicked up a notch, more like trembling now as though the *Lexington* were a racehorse confined in the starting gate, about to jump out and gallop down the course.

Caitlin's heart hammered. Why hadn't she stayed in her quarters until things either went properly—or didn't? At least then she wouldn't be staring into the barrel of the gun, so to speak. Her clenched fingernails bit into her palms.

Dannet turned and gave her a long appraising look from the captain's central station. That slanting Narvo-patterned *vai camiti* was still off-putting every time she saw it. Caitlin made herself meet the gaze, allowing her lines to indicate only *mild-interest*.

"Come closer, Envoy," Dannet said with a hint of *wicked-enjoyment* in the cant of her ears. "You will not see the process properly from back there."

Caitlin was suddenly certain that she did not want to see any of what was going on, did not in fact want to be here on this untried ship, jumping into what was most assuredly trouble. Ed had been right. She should have stayed home.

"Thank you, Terra-Captain," her dry mouth said, and her legs carried her closer. She would *not* disgrace herself, she told herself, fighting to hold onto the shape of *mild-interest*. Even more important, she would not disgrace humans in this creature's dancing, green-fire eyes.

Tully sauntered after her, hands in his pockets, though the invitation had not included him.

"Third framepoint generator set," the navigator said, gaze trained upon the readings. "Waiting on Four."

Now the ship shook as though caught in the riptide of some violent sea. How many generators did it take? Caitlin wasn't sure, though she'd read a general file on the process several days ago. All useful knowledge seemed to have leaked out of her head in the last few seconds. Sometimes it was four, she thought she'd read, sometimes five?

"Fourth set!" Even the navigator sounded excited now, and it took a lot to make a Jao show emotion while doing his or her job. They tended to be phlegmatic about such things.

The viewscreen was filled with scintillating stars, scattered before them like a field of diamonds. The ship rocked as unseen forces acted upon it. Each of the framepoint generators seemed to be pulling the ship in a different direction.

Caitlin realized she was breathing too fast and tried to slow down before she hyperventilated. It was just a jump, she told herself. Jao did it all the time without turning inside out or getting irretrievably lost. Otherwise they'd never have made it to Earth and caused misery for humans for more than the last twenty years.

"Fifth set!" the navigator said. The rocking escalated into a frenzied motion that mimicked the bucking of a frightened horse and Caitlin had to catch hold of an empty chair for support before a vacant station. She glanced at Tully, who looked white-faced himself, but still managed to wink at her. He'd thrown his arms around a support pillar.

"Stand by," Dannet said calmly, as though the bridge crew was merely about to conduct a staid tea party. The ship's insistent motion did not seem to affect her at all. Riding it out like an experienced sailor on a ship's deck in heavy weather, the former Narvo flicked an ear. "You may jump, Navigator Sten."

At his station, Sten pushed a lever and the great ship *jumped*. Caitlin felt her insides *fling* themselves forward, abandoning *where-they-were* for sheer *in-betweenness*, which her senses queasily interpreted as *nowhere-at-all*. She looked down at her hand holding onto the chair. It seemed almost transparent and yet solidly there, two conflicting states in one. Which was impossible, her stunned mind insisted. She dropped into the chair and huddled over her clenched fists, feeling impossibly thin and altogether ill.

The bridge crew, both human and Jao, were working, murmuring readings, making adjustments. The bucking had stopped and the ship hummed as it made its way through—what? Caitlin felt as though she were riding a horse over a brick wall. The horse had leaped and was sailing through the air now. The ground was far below and they all had to land sometime, didn't they?

Her hands grew more transparent and even the Jao began to show signs of stress, muttering, stiffening their whiskers, flattening ears, darting to one another's stations, arguing quietly but strenuously over settings. The ship began to shake again, gently at first, then more insistently with each passing second.

Dannet herself prowled the bridge, stopping to correct a human crew member and adjusting settings on that console, then pulling a protesting Jao from his seat and taking his place, handling the controls herself.

Jumping into a nebula was technically harder somehow. Caitlin remembered that one of the Krant ships had been destroyed in the attempt. But Dannet was one of Narvo's finest ship captains, a gift to Terra Taif to atone for the crimes of Oppuk. Her skills should be superb. Narvo would never shame itself by providing anything less.

Ears flattened, Dannet furiously altered settings. The officer she'd displaced protested from the floor and she backhanded him without taking her eyes off the display. That sort of casual violence, which could easily have been cause for legal action in a human military force, was taken for granted by Jao. The junior officer made no further protest. He simply sprawled on the deck, half-dazed.

The shaking worsened as though the ship were trying to exist in a dozen different places simultaneously. Maybe they *were* going to turn inside out before it was all over, she thought queasily. How could the Krants have made up such a story anyway? There must have been a grain of truth in it somewhere. Everyone, including the Jao, admitted that their species had little capacity for *ollnat*.

Tully's face had taken on a faint green sheen as he gripped his pillar with both arms. Caitlin's muscles cramped. *Lexington* shuddered one last time and then the shaking abruptly ceased. The air altered, becoming more breathable. They were—somewhere.

Thank God, Caitlin thought. She glanced down at her hands. The skin and bones were definitely all where they should be, at least for now. The screens had gone white, probably because they'd emerged in the photosphere of a blasted star, she thought shakily, and there was nothing to transmit except a searing blaze of solar combustion. She'd seen that for herself once, when one of the Ekhat factions, the Interdict, had traveled to Earth's system to warn for its own inscrutable reasons of the imminent arrival of the maniac Harmony. That ship had emerged from Sol in a white-hot ball of flaming solar gases, shedding streamers of fiery plasma as it headed outward.

The *Lexington* had to look much the same at the moment. Was it just her imagination, or was the hellish heat encasing them actually heating up the bridge? She blotted her suddenly perspiring forehead with a sleeve.

"Hull temperature receding from critical," a Jao officer said, his voice neutral, but his whiskers limp with *relief*.

The white viewscreens gave way to a swirl of red gas and dust, interspersed with black starry spaces which seemed to somehow have a meaningful shape. The nebula?

A second later, alarms went off. Caitlin lurched to her feet, gazing around the bridge. Had the heat penetrated a weakness in their never-before-tried shields? Were they about to burn up?

"Ekhat ships, five of them, Terra-Captain," one of the bridge crew, a balding human, said. His face had gone pale as watered milk. "Dead ahead."

PART IV:
The Battle

CHAPTER
16

Third-Note-Ascending was having trouble integrating with her mate again. Manifesting at a mere half-tone above Third's own mental signature, Third-and-a-Half-Note-Ascending was keeping his distance so that their mental fields could not properly synchronize. It was a willful act on his part, she was quite sure, not something over which he had no control. Like many males, he was finding the needs of sexual submission unsettling.

The result had been blatant discordance since entering the conductor's pod this duty cycle. She could not think well under such circumstances and strongly suspected Half could not think at all.

Without warning, the song-klaxon transmitted a note three octaves below her own mental tuning, powerful and pure, lasting six long breaths, a mighty contribution to the Ekha. Somewhere in this sector, an infestation of non-Ekhat sapience had been sterilized from a world. The entire ship, even the serviles, stopped to contemplate the beauty of the moment. The next such note might not come for quite some time. Each musical interlude had to be properly analyzed and savored.

Third did not recognize the singers, but her admiration surged. They were magnificent. She must corral Half and make him submit so that when their opportunity came to contribute to the on-going Melody composition, they would match such brilliance.

Half seemed not to have noticed the splendid performance. He was spidering on his six legs around the ship's conductor pod

like a newling, poking at this, fiddling with that. A possibility
existed that she had chosen her mate unwisely. She might have
to terminate him, before another of the ship's mating pairs rose
to dominance. She was still reluctant to do so, however. Half
had a great deal of promise, to go with his obstreperous nature.
It would be tedious to begin anew with another mate. The final
result might well be a lesser coupling, which would most likely
result in the same outcome of submission to another pair.

Manifesting even a half-tone higher or lower would ruin the
composition-in-progress, over time, sending the ship's Ekhat neuters into paroxysms of disgust and giving either one of the two
other mating pairs the surge they needed for dominance. Like all
females, Third was intensely aggressive. She would far rather rend
her own limbs from her body than have it done for her by a rival.

Third sometimes wondered what her existence would be like
had she been one of the far more numerous neuters produced
by Ekhat mating pairs. Less anxious, certainly. But there would
also be much less in the way of exultation.

Crossing the conductor's pod, which was suspended high above
the control pit, she surveyed sensory input screens scattered
across the far wall. The vile dust and gas in the planetary nebula
obscured the readings, reflecting beams back upon themselves,
slowing down what should have been an easy search for whatever
menace lurked here.

Below, small gray and black patterned Anj slithered about in
the control pit. Only one quarter the height of an Ekhat, when
they stood on their hind legs, they were nevertheless competent
with mechanics when not paralyzed with fear. The latter happened
all too often, of course. But it had long been Melody policy to
breed serviles for fear, accepting the drawbacks. Terror quickened
the servile reflexes, alleviated tiresome delays, and left the Ekhat
more time for composition.

Something lurking in this area of space had silenced a Melody
ship in the not-too-distant past. The lost notes had left a void in
the composition presently being conducted in this sector of the
galaxy. The remaining ships would have to parcel out the missing
tones among themselves and fill in where necessary. A heavy burden. There was no room for error in the Melody. Every note must
express itself to perfection or the music that was their life would
veer into cacophony, making them as unfit to exist as the Harmonies.

Are you still examining that ball of rock? Half said as the two circled one another. *It cannot be the source.*

Perhaps the True Harmony once harvested here, Third said, searching for an opening in the other's mincing gait in order to close. She could feel the electric tingle of his mental field approach and retreat, never quite near enough for the two of them to think effectively in tandem. *It would be like that faction to waste a few random notes here and thus encourage the native sapients to fantasize themselves capable of attaining the Ekha.*

Below, three of the little Anj became agitated, keening to one another in their atonal babble. They slithered over and under one another, squabbling, checking controls, fighting one another to adjust settings. Third noted their discomfort, but did not investigate what had occasioned it. Such matters were not the responsibility of Conductors. She had to keep her coupling's mind clear for the music that was the divine Ekha—if she could ever force Third-and-a-Half-Note-Ascending to function properly.

Twelfth-Note-Descending entered the pod so that Half had less room to circulate. Twelfth's mate, Tenth-Sharp-Ascending, followed. Both of them seemed so closely synchronized that even their great red eyes blinked as one. The sight enraged Third when she considered her own shameful state of discord. It frightened her also, of course.

Still, Third and her mate still held the edge of ascendancy, she thought. *What?* she demanded, and was heartened to hear Half's voice at least speak in modulation with her own.

Debris, Conductor-of-the-Moment, Twelfth and Tenth-Sharp said, their voices twining beautifully. *The chemical signatures indicate both Ekhat and Jao, along with Lleix, whom we had thought to be completed long ago.*

Jao and *Lleix,* Third said. This time, Half's voice lagged behind hers by a good quarter of a beat. The short hairs between her eyes itched. Disgraceful! Had her rivals noticed and been emboldened as a result? They must have!

Those tuneless rebels infest no worlds in this sector, she said, desperately trying to make her single brain work out the conundrum of their former serviles partnering with a supposedly extinct species. This time, Half did not even attempt to speak at all, remaining silent as though this discussion did not concern him.

No, indeed, said the synced pair of rivals. *So the question becomes, why would they venture into this environment with all its inherent dangers, and when did they become allies?*

Half was eyeing Tenth-Sharp, and Third took advantage of his inattention to move in so closely that their bodies brushed. With a sudden surge, their mental fields finally merged and fell into sync. She was no longer just her woefully singular self. She was part of *they*, and *they*, each augmenting the other, were much more capable of bold, forceful decisions.

Half's body took up her confident stance, every movement precisely mirroring Third's. The two of them spoke together in exquisite modulation. *Send probes to the ball of rock we have detected. Let us listen to the leitmotif playing down there before we extinguish it forever.*

Is that expenditure of resources necessary? Twelfth asked. Her tone had a desperate tinge. She too had recognized the full merging of her rival. Her mate Tenth-Sharp stood completely paralyzed. *Why not just destroy the planet and be on our way?*

By the end, her voice was quavering hopelessly. The time had come. As a single organism, the newly synchronized coupling leaped forward. Half wrestled Twelfth into immobility while Third gouged out one of her rival's eyes. Then, she dug deeply into the brain and severed her former rival's cerebral tree.

Because, Third/Half said, claws dripping with hot white gore, *it is too soon in the composition for another major note.*

That left Tenth-Sharp, but like most males in the final sub-mission, he was almost completely paralyzed. Half was able to terminate him with no assistance. Quite easily, in fact. His own now-sure knowledge of coming termination lent him strength along with exultation.

Twelfth/Tenth-Sharp, lying quite dead upon the floor, would dispute no longer. Neither would the other mating pair on the ship, now that dominance was established. Most likely, they would terminate themselves before Third/Half did so. She regarded the bleeding corpses with pleasant excitement. It was good to establish dominance so early in a mission. She had never done so before. Such quick violence stirred the Ekha profoundly.

Third/Half ordered the Anj to release the probes, then the two of them spent a few moments dabbing spangles of white gore upon one another's face and shoulders. Half was now in full submission, reveling in the ritual. She was sure he would be a superb mate, until her pregnancy allowed her to terminate him. He would exult in his own final rending.

But that was still some time away. It would take several couplings before she could be assured of continuing the Ekha line. For the moment, there was still the menace in the nebula to contend with.

All through the rest of the duty cycle, Third/Half practiced for the approaching moment when they would contribute to the Great Song. They sang their combined notes, so deliciously close, until the ship's hull vibrated at the frequency of their booming voices. By now, in their own chambers, the last remaining coupling pair would be paralyzed if they had not already rent themselves. Dominance was total. Down in their pit, the little Anj pranced and shouted in rapture.

No other note had come through on the song-claxon, indeed might not for some time, but the spaces between notes were equally meaningful. Out in the blackness of space, Melody ships were hunting the universe for lesser intelligences. The entire ship was poised, ready for their part in advancing the Ekha.

The planetary probes did not return on schedule, which was puzzling. Something, or someone, must have interfered. Third/Half had just sent word to the other four Melody ships to move in closer and assume orbit around the planet when the Anj down in the control pit positively exploded with chirps.

Third/Half leaned over the railing. "What is the meaning of this cacophony?"

"A ship, Great One!" an Anj said, looking up to the pod, while doing its best to stand on its stunted hind legs and utterly failing. Its fellows mobbed it, pulling it down.

"We have five ships, single-brain!" Really, the Anj were so dim, it was a wonder they could even consume nutrients or reproduce.

"Not Melody ship!" the Anj said, struggling back to the top of the slithering pile of bodies. It chittered hysterically in its own language, unable in its distress to communicate sensibly. "Other ship! Other!"

"From the planet?" Third/Half strode over to a screen, but could detect nothing untoward.

"No, Great One," the Anj said, gaining tenuous control of its inferior self. Its squishy little face contorted with fear as it gazed up to the Conductor's pod. "From the star!"

Third/Half's hands reached for the controls and brought up a view of the sun in this system. Were more Melody ships coming to investigate? Irritation surged through the linked pair. *They* had been given Conductor's rights in this matter. No one else should be intruding to impose their sensibilities upon the situation.

But that was most certainly not a Melody ship shedding fiery plasma as it emerged from a point locus in the system's sun. The shape was huge and solidly oval, lacking the characteristic angles of Ekhat construction. It was not a Jao ship either, though there was a hint of their pedestrian esthetics in its flowing lines.

Anticipation of tuneful ecstasy flooded Third/Half. It was so seldom these days that the Melody had the pleasure of destroying a hitherto unsuspected species, and one so relatively advanced! What lovely music she and Half would make while reducing this ship to its constituent atoms!

The monstrously large ship was coming very fast, though, and already maneuvering to fire weapons. Below, in the control pit, the Anj were screaming, fighting one another in their frenzy to bring the Melody ship up to readiness to respond.

One ship against five, Third/Half mused. It would be a woefully short battle, but the note they would contribute afterwards to the Great Song would be magnificent. She would probably be assured of dominance for at least four or five more mating cycles. And already she was one of the oldest females of record.

CHAPTER
17

Pyr approached Jihan as she was working early that morning in the Jaolore Duty Chamber where the main tasks of the *elian* were carried out. Thin gray sunlight, half obscured by clouds, slanted in through the old house's tall glass windows. The heat-source was blazing comfortably, though the day was quite chill without. Wind coming off the mountains blasted along the eaves overhead. She should acquire flags to signify the number of residents, she thought, looking up at her young subordinate. One by one, she was seeing after the proprieties.

"Eldest!" Pyr said, when he'd caught her eye. His hands were dithering in agitation. "Come quickly!"

The former unassigned was filling out, his aureole brightening, his dull skin gaining a bit of luster. Whether the improvements came of a better diet or his pleasure in finally being accepted by an *elian*, she thought he looked almost presentable these days. She straightened, then turned away from the viewer where she'd been going through yet another cache of fragile ancient records, this lot from the Historykeepers. "Yes?"

"A representative of the Starwarders is here to see you!" Pyr's meager gray aureole stood on end. "She says there is reason for haste!"

Jihan adjusted her new robes with their simple but tasteful design, the outline of a Jao ship. Jaolore might be only a small *elian*, but she would conduct their affairs with decorum. Satisfied that she would not shame her associates, few though they were, she followed Pyr into the Application Chamber.

The spacious room had been swept clean, the wooden floor polished by industrious servants acquired from the *dochaya*. It smelled pleasantly of herb-scented oils, though as yet there were only two scavenged benches for seating. A female of middle height looked up from contemplating the barren gardens through the window. Outside, a few flakes of snow drifted out of increasingly leaden clouds. The sunlight was rapidly being occluded.

"Greetings...Eldest," the visitor said, as though the honorific passed her lips with difficulty, and settled on one of their battered benches with exaggerated care.

"You honor us," Jihan said, taking the seat across from her and wondering what could be so important as to bring a Starwarder to Jaolore. Surely they had enough responsibility patrolling the system during these troubled times to keep them busy. "Shall I call for sustenance?"

"I am Hadata," the newcomer said with indecent haste, then glanced at Pyr whose mouth gaped at the breach of protocol. She glanced at him. "Do not presume to judge me, child!" Her expression darkened as she turned back to Jihan. "However did you come to accept such an unpromising creature? His skin is positively gray! Surely even the *dochaya* could provide better." She waved a hand when Jihan opened her mouth to protest. "No, no, it does not matter, and the situation is far too dire to be remediated by having him scrounge up a bit of biscuit."

Off to one side, Pyr had gone stiff with shame. Anger suffused her, but no matter what had happened among the Starsifters, Sayr had never once given way to crudely raising his voice, much less to graceless shouting. She would conduct herself with the same propriety.

"We do not require service," Jihan told the youth when she was sure of her voice. "You may go." Pyr lowered his head and bolted from the room.

"That was badly done," Jihan said as soon as he was gone. "We are a new *elian*, but I have never heard it said that outsiders may criticize the choices of an Eldest."

"You wish to speak of proprieties?" Hadata's magnificently upswept black eyes regarded the Jaolore shrewdly, and in them, Jihan saw again how badly she had behaved up on the mountain, her disgraceful breaking of *sensho*. By now, everyone in the entire colony knew what she had done. That brash moment would shadow all of her days. She might be an Eldest now, at least in name, but her achievement of the rank was tainted. Shame tingled up through her face, dried her mouth, flattened her aureole.

"Never mind," the Starwarder said abruptly, gazing out the window again, plainly seeking to alter the course of the conversation. "Such matters pale in light of current troubles."

Her visitor's manner stilled. She closed her eyes, then opened them again, and it was as though another, more practical, Starwarder had entered the chamber and now gazed out at her. "As a former Starsifter, you have ship training. Therefore, we petition Jaolore to grant us your service in this crisis." The Starwarder's fingers twitched an errant fold in her robes back into place. Her expression was bleak. "We have been maintaining a presence in orbit around Valeron since the battle. Yesterday, we detected an incursion into our space, vessels entering our system through a point locus in the outer layers of the sun, as is necessary when journeying between star systems."

Framepoint travel. Jihan had read of such, both in the course of her recent research and during her Starsifter training, though it had been many generations since the Lleix had dared to travel in such a bold manner. "Is it the Jao?" Her aureole stood on end.

"Child, no one believes that nonsense you were spouting up on the mountain." The Starwarder rose, arranging her robes into proper folds with great care. Her hands were shaking. "It is the great devils, themselves, the Ekhat!"

Jihan found it suddenly difficult to breathe. Her mind struggled to think and she felt ill. This was too soon! The colony was not yet ready to protect itself or flee. "Then—it is Ekhatlore that you want, and Weaponscrafters."

"They have been alerted, but several Starsifters have already come forward to help crew Starwarder ships, and Sayr suggested that you be recruited," Hadata said. "You have been trained to operate the Starsifters' vessel and data stations, and we have grown too few. We cannot adequately staff our remaining ships, so our Eldest asks that you help crew the next ship to be launched."

The Starsifters' vessel had been ancient and small, meant only for the gathering of data and retrieval of minute portions of debris for analysis. Piloting it had been one thing, traveling upon one of the Starwarders' ships was bound to be quite another. Jihan found herself trembling. "Is it your intention to attack these ships?" If so, they would die even sooner than their fellows upon the planet.

"The Ekhat have not assumed orbit around our world yet," Hadata said. "Thus far we are only observing their actions so that we can relay information back to the Hall of Decision. It is possible that they might pass by, as they did once before, though not probable."

"I see," Jihan said, trying to gather the shreds of her disarrayed thoughts. So much needed to be done! How would she ever fulfill so many responsibilities?

"The few remaining mass transports are being readied," Hadata said. "Representatives of each *elian* will be sent on them to another system, if the Ekhat allow us enough time. You should choose one among you for that honor."

It would have to be Kajin, she thought numbly. Poor untutored Pyr would perish from embarrassment to be thrust so amongst his betters, and Kajin possessed skills from his Ekhatlore training which should be preserved. "When will he need to report?"

"Word will be sent," Hadata said, turning back to the windows and the worsening snow outside. The pale flakes were beginning to accumulate and obscure the abandoned gardens. "For now, you and I must make haste."

Jihan excused herself and went to find Pyr, who turned up in the communal kitchen, abjectly scrubbing the floor. "You must dispatch me back to the *dochaya*," he said without looking up, when she entered the homey room with its smells of herbs and simmering blueleaf stew. "I have no wish to shame Jaolore further."

One of the servants, modestly clad in a gray shift, glanced at the two of them from the larder, then slipped out of the room.

"You do not shame us," Jihan said when they were alone. "I forbid you to take any notice of what was said back there. Her remarks were based solely upon your appearance, which has no bearing upon the quality of your work here."

He sat back on his heels, still not raising his eyes. His fingers clutched the damp rag to his scrawny chest.

"Tell Kajin that he has been chosen to represent Jaolore in the exodus and he is to ready himself for departure," Jihan said to Pyr, "then keep up your studies until I return."

If she ever returned, she thought, then went back to accompany

Hadata out of the Application Chamber into the morning's frost-ridden air. That was by no means certain.

Fortunately, her meager piloting skills were not required on the Starwarders' patched ship. Hadata took the pilot's seat and Jihan found herself relegated to one of four unoccupied data stations. She was surprised to find the vessel little bigger than the Starsifters' only functioning vehicle and in no better operating condition. Every aspect of the ship was worn and cobbled-together. The first data station she tried to activate no longer worked at all.

And the Starwarders had not exaggerated when they said they lacked trained crew. Only two other Starwarders were on board, so that less than half the ship's functioning consoles were manned, even with the addition of Jihan and Lliant, a sturdy male recruited from Ekhatlore to employ his expertise. Even in this crisis, he had taken the time to groom himself, his eyes heavily outlined in vahl, his robes freshly scented with herbs and carefully draped, his silver skin gleaming, obviously just oiled.

The Ekhatlore did not greet her when she came on board, only looked away and feigned preoccupation with buckling his harness, despite the fact that Jihan was an Eldest, technically outranking him and due at least minimum courtesies. *Everyone knows of my untoward behavior,* Jihan thought, gazing at his lowered head, then resolved to put the shameful past behind her. It was not what she had done before—and she had been right that day, however much she had flaunted protocol—it was what she would do from now on that mattered.

She was apparently the last to board. Hadata ran through the preflight checks, and then, without warning, the little ship lifted, the ascent much rougher than any launch Jihan had experienced with the Starsifters. She was thrown against the restraining harness repeatedly until her chest ached and she had to gasp for breath. The noise was overwhelming, louder than a hundred storm winds screaming down from the mountains. She closed her eyes and endured until the engines' roar eased, then fought nausea until the artificial gravity clicked on. At that point, she was finally able to turn her attention to the data station as the ship assumed orbit.

Via a real-time view, Valeron swam far below, a green and gray ball obscured by clouds. From this vantage, she thought, the colony did not seem so exposed. After all, it occupied just one small location, tucked at the foot of towering mountains. That was the only such spot her kind occupied on the entire world. Might not the Ekhat overlook them?

But their ancient enemies had not missed the Lleix the last time the Ekhat had broached the system, when the most recent battle had taken place. It must be obvious that they had gone to ground here. The devils would search until they located her people. Or, more likely, they would simply render all of Valeron uninhabitable with a massive plasma bombardment. The records were full of such loathsome tactics. Apparently the Ekhat did not value planets capable of sustaining life, precious and rare though they were. The monsters wished only to be rid of the "taint" of lower life-forms so that they could rule alone in their increasingly pure and perfect universe.

Hadata crossed the tiny control deck to alter the settings on one of Jihan's monitors. "There," she said, pointing as the new readings came up. "Do you see?"

Five hideous shapes appeared, characteristic of the Ekhat disdain for beauty in form. No one would ever mistake one of their awkward looking ships for anything else.

Lliant abandoned his station and peered over their shoulders. "Blast us all," he said softly. His black eyes glittered with anger. "It really is them."

Jihan realized she also had been hoping the Starwarders were wrong, or the Ekhat had already gone, but they were here. Last-of-Days might well be in progress.

She punched in a vector assessment on the closest ship as she had been trained to do when retrieving debris for the Starsifters. The numbers came back, chilling. The Ekhat were on a course heading directly for Valeron. She turned to Hadata, who was monitoring a station on the other side. "They are coming."

Hadata reached over and checked the readings for herself. "Eldest-of-Us-All!" Her eyes widened. "They have held their position steady out there until now. Is it just the one or all of them?"

Jihan ran more numbers. Each time, the results were the same. "All five ships approach," she said, though her throat had trouble producing the words. Lliant sank back into his seat with a muffled curse. Jihan looked at the four of them, the three Starwarders and the Ekhatlore. "What shall we do?"

"What little we can," Hadata said, and went to transmit their findings back to the Starwarders' *elian*-house.

Jihan watched the readings with a terrible fascination. According to numerous historical accounts, the monsters were obsessed with rhythmic noise, which they called "music." Were they singing one of their dreadful songs even now as they approached, intent on destroying what was left of the Lleix? No wonder her kind considered patterned noise of any kind an abomination when it inspired such genocidal mania.

She continued to monitor their dreadful progress until, across the cabin, Lliant pushed back from his console. "Another ship!"

Jihan's blood dried to powder in her veins. As if five of the hulking monsters were not enough to destroy every house and individual on the planet! "I still have readings on only five," she said, her fingers flying over the uncooperative controls as she widened search parameters. "Where do you see it?"

"Quadrant zero in the photosphere of the sun," Lliant said. "It is emerging through the system's point locus."

Hadata glanced back at them, aureole limp with disbelief. "Another Ekhat vessel?"

"Probably," Lliant said, his shoulders hunched as if against an expected blow. "It is too soon to tell."

Who else could it be, though, Jihan asked herself, except the Jao? Who were no better than Ekhat.

The emerging ship shed streamers of fiery plasma and for a moment a roundness was visible, then was obscured again by the fierce bright whiteness. Jihan blinked. "That was not an Ekhat ship," she said, evaluating the stats as they came back to her. "The shape was wrong and it is positively huge."

"You are being misled by the enveloping plasma ball," Lliant said, his eyes intent upon his own screens. "It always distorts initial readings when the Ekhat jump into a system."

Lliant was an Ekhatlore with years of study completed since being accepted by his highly regarded *elian*. All reason dictated that an experienced expert must understand the situation better than Jihan, yet she knew what she had seen and it had been nothing like the long spindles, angular gantries, and inverted tetrahedrons of an Ekhat ship.

The white ball of solar fire separated fully from the photosphere and shed additional plasma. The dark shape was momentarily visible against the brilliance of the sun again. It was not angular and deceptively fragile, crisscrossed with girders, but almost round and solid with long protrusions. *It is not the Ekhat,* she told herself, but refrained from speaking the thought aloud. Ekhatlore held *sensho* in this situation. She would not shame herself by claiming to know more than Lliant did.

Plasma closed around the vessel again so that it was occluded. Lliant returned to his own data station and studied the figures coming in. His aureole stiffened. "It *is* very large," he murmured, "massing far more than any Ekhat ship ever detected according to the Ekhatlore archives."

But it wasn't the Jao either, she thought. She knew the sleek lines of their ships too from her research since forming Jaolore, and there were no records of any of this size. "Someone else participated in the last battle," she said hesitantly. "I thought from the readings it was the Jao, but whoever it was, they fired upon the Ekhat ship, not us."

Hadata and Lliant, along with the two Starwarder crew members on the other side of the cabin, stared at her. "Perhaps this ship belongs to a species entirely unknown to us," she said. "The Ekhat must have many enemies. This could be one of them."

"No," Lliant said. "The Ekhat will not tolerate any resistance. They destroy everyone they come in contact with. All their enemies are dead."

Plasma exploded off the newcomer and that incredible shape was visible again. And the ship was already maneuvering, coming about, readying itself for—what? Excitement mingled with dread thrummed through her.

She checked the vectors of the Ekhat ships again. "The Ekhat are turning back," she said.

"They are going to engage the new vessel," Hadata said.

"Then they must not be Ekhat," Jihan said. "They are someone else, highly advanced, by the size of that ship, another intelligent species."

"They could simply be another Ekhat faction," cautioned Hadata. "Although I think that unlikely, given the radically different ship design."

"Even if you are right and they fight the Ekhat," Lliant said sourly, "that does not mean they will win. And if they do survive, that does not mean they will befriend the Lleix."

Remember the Jao and what they did, Jihan told herself. Whoever these new creatures were, they might battle the Ekhat simply to have the pleasure of exterminating the Lleix themselves. Just because they were not the Ekhat did not necessarily mean they would be friendly.

The last of the white-hot plasma streamed from the huge ship and Jihan focused her instruments on those strange flat projections all around its hull.

"Bizarre design," Lliant muttered as his fingers flew over his station's controls. "Is that part of its propulsion configuration?"

Then a series of energy signatures flared along the protrusions. Jihan ran a hasty diagnostic. "No," she said. "I think they might be weapons platforms."

"Surely not," Hadata said. The Starwarder abandoned her seat again to peer at Jihan's screens. Her aureole wilted. "There are far too many."

Brightness blazed. One of the Ekhat ships suddenly changed vectors as it took some kind of hit.

The battle was engaged.

CHAPTER
18

Whatever Terra-Captain Dannet had expected to find when the *Lexington* emerged from the point locus, Tully didn't think it was five Ekhat warships. Adrenaline exploded through his veins as an apparently unruffled Dannet ordered Navigation to plan a withdrawal back into the star's photosphere, then directed Spines C through E to fire as soon as they acquired targets.

Tully darted into the lift, glancing one last time over his shoulder at Caitlin Kralik. She had hastily surrendered her seat to the working bridge crew the second the situation made itself clear, and was now standing beside a support column. Her hands were clenched, her eyes trained on the terrible sight on the viewscreen. The doors closed and the lift raced downwards, leaving his stomach several levels behind.

His unit was already in action by the time he reached his post in Spine C. They were loading sabot rounds into the huge guns, as they had diligently practiced, and setting targets with the fire control radar. They'd already started firing. The boom of the great cannons was deafening in the confined space. He grabbed a set of noise dampening headphones from the rack by the bulkhead hatch, then turned on his mike. "Report!"

"We're concentrating fire on the two closest hostiles, sir," Caewithe Miller's voice came over the headphones. "Do you have additional orders?"

"No. Carry on." He slid into the seat before the central monitoring station and strapped himself in. There were no visible fumes, but there was still an oily reek in the air, even with the air conditioners working full bore.

On the screen, one of the Ekhat ships seemed to vibrate as it took one hit after another. Tully knew what was happening aboard that enemy ship. Even the big sabot rounds fired by a 500mm gun weren't massive enough to actually jolt the Ekhat vessel. Instead, they'd be punching through the hull and turning the interior into a fiery charnelhouse. The jittery motion of the enemy vessel was actually a byproduct of internal explosions, as the many flammable substances aboard the enemy ship ignited.

The Ekhat were firing back with laser weapons, but seemed to be retreating. Then Tully realized it was actually the *Lexington* retreating—deeper into the photosphere, where the enemy's lasers would be almost completely ineffective. For all her aloofness, that Dannet was a clever rascal. He'd never thought to be grateful for a sly Narvo, but he surely was today.

Two of the Ekhat ships accelerated after them, growing noticeably larger in the viewer again. "What are they trying to do?" he muttered, calculating vector assessments as the massive guns boomed and boomed.

"Stand down!" a voice came over the command channel from the bridge. "*Lexington* is maneuvering to come about. Spine C's vector will be marginal."

"Cease fire!" Tully said and the guns on their deck fell silent. Sweat rolled down his neck and soaked into his collar, so that he was both hot and chilled. He could feel vibration relayed throughout the ship, though, as another weapons deck took up the firing pattern as they now had more effective trajectories. Probably Spines E or G, or both.

Over at Gun Eleven, Mallu pulled off his ear-protectors. The Jao's dark-bay body was still, frozen in a posture that Tully felt he ought to recognize, but didn't. His thoughts were chasing one another around in edgy circles and his bones still rang from cannon fire. He removed his own headset, unbuckled the safety harness, and trotted over to the krant-captain.

"I do not understand," he said to the Jao, who had logged far more space combat than anyone on his team. "Why are they following us into the star? Our kinetic weapons will still be effective at that depth, but their lasers won't work inside the photosphere."

"They will try to force us too deep," Mallu said, "hoping that we will be swept down into the supergranular cells where the pressure and temperature are too high to withstand."

"Oh." Tully remembered reading the accounts of Terra's famous Battle of the Framepoint. Several of Earth's cobbled-together ships had been lost that way. He swore under his breath, making Mallu give him a sharp look. He didn't care. This was utterly bat-crazy, traveling through suns and then fighting battles on the naked edge of destruction.

"Spines B, D, F, and H, stand down," Dannet's voice said over the P.A. "We have reentered the photosphere. Spines A, C, E, and G, fire when you have acquired targets."

Mallu put his headgear back on and Tully followed suit. The gun teams resumed their positions. Lieutenant Miller was trotting down the line, overseeing the work.

The great cannons started firing again. By then, Tully had returned to his supervisory station, wishing he were down in one of the magazines, loading and loading, doing something physical and useful. He felt like a blasted fifth wheel up here, keeping an eye on the process when everyone else was doing all the work. And, face it, he longed to have an active hand in blowing those Ekhat bastards into atoms. He flat wanted to kill something!

He dropped into his seat, refastened the harness, and studied the screen. The two Ekhat ships were still closing. Fire control on all weapons decks that could be brought to bear was concentrating now on the closest. The awkward looking vessel took hit after hit, and he saw explosions around the periphery. Shapes were blown out of the ship by venting gas. Some of them looked like bodies, though the carcasses were much smaller than the Ekhat he remembered from that harrowing expedition two years ago. But it was hard to tell, because they were incinerated so quickly. They'd reentered the photosphere and nothing material was going to survive outside of a ship's shielding for more than a few seconds. Soon enough, as they plunged deeper into the star, that would become milliseconds.

Not only were the great guns doing their job, but the Ekhat were obviously having trouble realizing their effectiveness and adjusting tactics to compensate. Then the targeted ship suddenly disintegrated. Its structural integrity had become too compromised by the accumulated effect of the sabot rounds. Hundreds of them would have smashed into the vessel by now.

Once a ship started to give way inside a star's photosphere, the end was astonishingly quick. The star's own nuclear fury completed the destruction in what seemed like no more than an eyeblink.

Cheers went up all along the firing line. Human cheers, not Jao. The Jao weren't given to useless demonstrations of emotion.

"Stay focused, people!" Tully called at them. "Target that second ship! We're not done yet by a long shot!"

The second ship rushed toward them.

This was supposed to be a diplomatic mission, Caitlin kept telling herself over and over as the *Lexington*'s bridge seethed with action. And, if things had gone according to Ronz's plan, she would have known what to do. She, who had never even fired a Terran handgun, had no place in this harried battle. No doubt, Terra-Captain Dannet would prefer her to leave, thereby eliminating a potential distraction. But Caitlin could not bring herself to bury her head in her snug cabin while the ship's crew fought to survive.

That would seem cowardly, she thought, and she was not only her father's daughter, but Ed's wife. She could not behave like a scared little mouse during this crisis and then expect to maintain the crew's respect afterward, not to mention her own.

A human male called for Dannet and the Terra-captain moved rapidly to his station. Unlike a human commander, who'd most likely have remained in his own seat during the action, Dannet had been moving around the bridge constantly. But then, human officers had to pay a lot more attention to the needs of morale than Jao did. They needed to project the appearance of stolid unconcern for their own safety, where the Jao simply took that for granted.

The boldly striped Narvo face studied the screen, then Dannet keyed on her mike, broadcasting to the entire ship. "The lead vessel has been destroyed," she said, as casually as if she were discussing the balance of salts in a pool. "Focus fire now on the next-in-line."

The human members of the bridge crew cheered and Dannet's body lines went to pure *annoyance*. She was still relatively new to Terra, and not very familiar with the habits of humans.

For different reasons, Caitlin also thought that exuberance was out of place. Certainly premature. There were still at least four more Ekhat ships out there, just waiting for *Lexington* to make a mistake. And this was an untried ship, she thought, blood pounding in her ears, and, for the most part, a green crew. They were bound to make mistakes. That was part of the learning process.

She realized with a start that her own lines and angles had gone to *repressed-dread*, which any Jao on the bridge could read. With an effort, she composed herself and assumed a credible, if shaky, version of *determined-confidence*. And, as she had found down through the years, her feelings shifted somewhat toward what her body was trying to say. She felt less frightened, more able to cope.

The Ekhat ship charging after them was no longer firing. That was good, she told herself, wasn't it? None of the Jao crewmen watching the viewscreen seemed to think so, though. Their lines had gone mostly to *alarm*.

It was rushing toward them very fast, the image growing and growing. If it didn't look out, it was going to—

With a shock, Caitlin understood. "My God. It's going to ram us," she said under her breath.

"All decks, lock down!" Dannet ordered over the P.A. Her ears had gone to *concern*, an indication of her abstraction.

The nearest Jao bridge officer glanced up at Caitlin. "Find a seat and strap in," he said, his eyes ablaze with green. "That location is not optimum for your safety."

Her face heated. She was just standing there, waiting for instruction, for someone else to save the day, like a two-year-old who'd escaped from the nursery and was wandering in traffic. All around the multilevel bridge, voices rose and fell, relaying readings, recommending adjustments, and she understood none of it. She felt so damned useless!

Spotting an empty station, she moved into the seat, which was oversized for human dimensions in order to accommodate Jao members of the crew. Her hands shook a little as she buckled the safety harness around her waist and across her shoulders. In the viewscreen, the image of the Ekhat ship grew until all she could see was the infamous characteristic inverted tetrahedron. Her heart raced and she felt the sickening zing of adrenaline in her veins. If the Ekhat ship was trying to ram them, then *Lexington* should retreat, shouldn't it?

The rest of the bridge crew had taken similar precautions. "Gun mounts retracted and locked on all spines," a human woman said off to Caitlin's left.

"Prepare for ramming," Dannet said.

"Maneuvering," a Jao said on the far side of the bridge. Amber lights played across his muzzle.

Dannet watched the central viewscreen and the on-coming Ekhat vessel with a hint of *gleeful-anticipation* in the line of her spine and the cant of her whiskers. Was the former Narvo insane? Caitlin wondered suddenly. Her predecessor, Oppuk, certainly had been. Or had Narvo sent her to the new taif with secret instructions to scuttle the *Lexington* at the first opportunity? The ship would never return and all across the galaxy Jao would say it was the human crew's fault.

"In position," the Jao said. "All decks confirmed locked down."

"Then reverse course and accelerate," Dannet said.

Accelerate? Startled, Caitlin craned her head. The Ekhat ship was growing nearer, according to the viewscreen. Shouldn't the image be shrinking if they were trying to avoid a collision? Surely Dannet wouldn't—

A human officer was counting down the seconds to impact, though the words meant nothing to the Jao. They already knew when it would take place, feeling it in some way that a human never would experience.

She wanted to look away, but couldn't. The Ekhat ship with its bizarre configuration, as though it were constructed from a child's Tinkertoys, didn't look that dangerous compared to the massive *Lexington*, but—

The Ekhat swept closer and closer.

There was a hideous crash that wrenched her neck and rattled her bones so that it seemed her brain was ricocheting off her skull. She was thrown against the harness with bruising force. The camera feed went black and it took several seconds for someone to switch to an alternate view.

The Ekhat ship was disintegrating in an almost leisurely manner, gantries separating from one another, crushed tetrahedron spinning, gas venting, small explosions here and there. Then the flotsam burned, winking out with a flash so bright, it hurt her eyes. They had lost their shields in that moment, Caitlin realized with a jolt, then wondered how stable their own were after the crash.

"Damage reports coming in," a human male said from across

the bridge, his voice hoarse. "So far, shields have retained ninety percent integrity."

So far? Caitlin didn't like the sound of that.

"Point of greatest impact?" Dannet asked, rising from her command chair, not a whisker out of place.

There was a moment of silence as the bridge crew recovered their composure enough to punch in queries on their screens. "Spine C," someone reported.

Tully heard a klaxon wailing in his ears. He tasted the coppery bitterness of blood in his mouth.

Hands reached down, removed his harness, and hauled him to his feet as though he weighed nothing. Jao hands, he realized, trying to clear his head. His vision was fuzzy as though someone had just clouted him in the head.

"Y-Yaut?" But that made no sense, he thought, trying to get his bearings. He was on the *Lexington*, not back in Pascagoula.

"—must command your troops!" the Jao was saying. Tully finally got his eyes to focus. The Krant-captain, Mallu, was peering into his face. The Jao's eyes crawled with green. "This deck is venting atmosphere. If we lose hull integrity, the ship will be vulnerable to the star's plasma. *Lexington* will be lost!"

"Damage control!" Tully husked, then looked about. Dazed soldiers, both human and Jao, were struggling out of their safety harnesses. At least one of the guns had something wrong with it, judging from the haste with which its crew was emerging. From the distance, Tully couldn't determine the exact nature of the damage. A fire had probably started in the turret. Such a fire didn't pose a threat to the whole area the way it would have if they'd been using old-style powder instead of liquid propellant. The moment the fire was detected, the propellant would have automatically been diverted from the area. But it could still kill any crewman trapped inside.

"Lock those vents down!" he called. "There must be some fractures!" He stumbled to help, pulling the less injured to their feet, shoving them toward emergency lockers that held the needed sealant. Mallu was doing the same, though he could see now that the big Jao was also hunched in pain. The collision had done his healing ribs no good.

Tully tried to make his dazed brain think. If Spine C lost hull integrity, Dannet would have to jettison it to save the ship. The fact that it was manned mostly by humans would make her decision easier, probably—it was obvious that Dannet had no liking for humans—but she'd do it just as quickly if the crew had been entirely her own people. The Jao did not select ship-captains for their sentimentality and tenderness.

"Weapons Spine C, report!" a voice was saying over the clamor of the alarm.

Tully grabbed Lieutenant Miller's arm as she moved past him, headed for the emergency lockers. She had a cut above one eye and blood was trickling down her pale cheek. "Shut that klaxon off!" he said into her ear, having to shout.

"Weapons Spine C, report!" the voice repeated. Tully thought it might be Dannet, but it was hard to be sure with all the racket. Was the rest of the ship any better off? By whatever gods were out there, he hoped so.

He dropped into his seat, letting Mallu and the other gun captains supervise damage control for the moment. Baker Company had drilled repeatedly on safety procedures over the last few days, along with loading and firing the great guns. They would handle the situation, especially with Miller overseeing them. Bloody-faced or not, the young lieutenant was conducting herself in a calm and controlled manner.

Abruptly the klaxon shut off and he felt limp with relief. Now maybe he could string two thoughts together.

He turned his mike on. "Weapons Spine C, reporting," he said. "We have—" He turned and surveyed the long narrow deck. "—fairly severe damage. Gun C-12 is out of commission, for sure, and the same is probably true of one or two others. There are no visible hull ruptures"—that was a stupidly unnecessary thing to say, since if the hull was visibly breached inside the photosphere they'd all be crisped bacon by now—"but there are certainly microruptures. We are working to find and contain the leaks now."

Before him, the screen seemed to shrink and swell. He put a hand to his forehead and found a painful lump and the warm stickiness of blood. Great, he had probably knocked out what little brains he possessed. Yaut would—

He sighed. Yaut would say to get over himself. He would say: *Make yourself of use. Take care of your crew.*

"Secure damage, then report," a Jao voice, not Dannet, said. "We have dispatched additional crew to assist."

Someone pounded on the hatch that provided entrance to the spine from the main body of the ship. From the sound, they were using a big wrench for the purpose. "Can you release from your side?" a faint voice called. "We can't get it open."

Oh, swell. They were trapped. Tully went to the hatch, trying to twist the handle with both hands. The handle turned well enough, but the hatch remained firmly shut. The impact of the collision had probably warped the hatch entrance. Not much, but enough to keep the door sealed.

"Major!"

He turned to find Kaln staring at him with a peculiar hunger. "Gun Six is functional," she said, her good ear standing tall. "We may still fire at your discretion."

Fire at what? Oh, gods, he realized the Ekhat were still out there. "That is…good," Tully said, trying to cudgel his brain into making sense of the chaos around him. "But we have no such orders at the moment, Senior-Tech. Carry on with your inspection of the rest of the guns."

He returned to his station. "Shall we acquire targets?" he asked the bridge.

"Negative," the voice said. That was perhaps Otta krinnu ava Terra, Dannet's Second up on the bridge. What humans would consider an executive officer. "Proximate targets are already destroyed. The remaining three are staying clear of the photosphere for now."

Destroyed? "We—rammed them?" he said in a daze.

"Affirmative."

And lived to tell about it, at least for the moment. Tully found that a little astonishing, even though intellectually he knew that ship speeds inside a star's photosphere were slow enough to make ramming a tactic that could be distinguished—barely, anyway—from outright suicide.

"I'll be damned," he said, forgetting that the line was open.

"I have no doubt that such an event is inevitable," Otta said. "Complete your damage control activities, then report back."

"Yes, Pleniary-Commander," Tully said, his face heating. A Jao with a dry sense of humor was about as astonishing as surviving a ram inside a star.

Behind him, he could hear someone outside whacking the hatch with what sounded like a crowbar along with a chorus of steady cursing. That wasn't likely to do any good, if Tully's assessment of the cause of the problem was accurate. They needed to blow that hatch, not bang on it.

He turned to look for Caewithe Miller, but she was already there. She'd brought two able-bodied crewmen with her. One of them was carrying a portable drill.

"I think we'll need to drill and set explosive charges, sir," she said. "In order to get the hatch open, I mean."

"Yes, I think you're right. See to it, Lieutenant." He didn't bother to ask what she planned to use in the way of explosive material. Miller would know what she was doing. Tully still had a lot of injured crewmen he needed to get ready for evacuation in case the damage control teams couldn't seal the hull leaks.

"Exiting the photosphere to go after the remaining Ekhat vessels," Dannet's voice said on the ship-wide channel. "All decks prepare."

CHAPTER
19

Third-Note-Ascending's ship assumed a low orbit above the star's photosphere, allowing her two minor conductors on the accompanying vessels to pursue the bizarre interloper as it retreated back into the sun from which it had emerged. Its unexpected intrusion had already altered the note she had been so carefully planning to transmit, once this system was scrubbed free of infestation. She and Third-and-a-Half-Note-Ascending must now consider the implications so that their presentation would reflect the battle and subsequent routing of a minor sapience accurately. How else could the Melody truly know itself than through its works?

Below in the control pit, the little Anj gibbered and howled as they sought to repair the damage the strange ship had inflicted before sinking back into the swirling photosphere. The brutes had actually *flung* things at them, a form of primitive tech that had proved oddly effective.

They had also fired laser weapons that matched the energy signature of the Jao. But the Jao, notoriously dull brutes that they were, had never employed anything like the solid projectiles that had taken out the Anj breeding gallery on this ship.

An immature and still nameless Ekhat crew member broached the conductor's pod with suitably nervous mincing steps. *Lead Conductor,* it said, not meeting their combined gaze. *Readings are inconclusive, but it would seem one or perhaps even both of our ships in pursuit have been destroyed.*

That is not likely, unless they fired upon each other, Third-Note-Ascending said, Third-and-a-Half's voice in perfect sync. *Which is also not likely.*

It is not, the nameless drudge said, remaining prudently out of reach. *Nevertheless, that is what the readings seem to indicate.*

There must be more. *And?* Third said, slowly circling her think-mate.

The enemy ship seems to be approaching.

Then we will destroy it. Third/Half was again contemplating the marvelous note she would contribute once this business was concluded.

It is very large.

Perhaps a quarter variation on the originally planned note with a slight tremolo at the finale would properly reflect the loss of the two Melody ships.

It masses more than our three remaining ships combined.

Its rising concern was unseemly. *These creatures hurl bits of metal to defend themselves,* she said, abandoning Half to stalk about the drudge's quivering form. *Are we to be wary of such?*

You know best, of course, it said, realizing its error and retreating. *Only give your orders and they shall be obeyed.*

Summon a replacement. Then terminate yourself. Your hesitation is a source of discord in our melody.

At once, Lead Conductor. The immature crew member signaled the service pool to send a replacement, then gouged out one of its eyes and began probing within for a key synapse.

Not surprisingly, it bungled that also. It collapsed onto the deck, bleeding badly but still breathing. To her annoyance, Third was forced to reach into the wound and sever the cerebral tree herself.

Clean this up, Third/Half said to its replacement, going back to their consideration of the forthcoming creation.

Down in the control pit, the Anj were screaming. Their fear was pleasantly aromatic, filtering throughout the entire ventilation system. Third/Half turned as one to the viewing tank as a monstrous-sized ball of plasma emerged from the star.

Maintaining the enveloping sheath of plasma as *Lexington* exited the photosphere was not technically difficult. It simply required modifying the same force shields that protected the ship within the photosphere. The problem for Terra-Captain Dannet was psychological. In the past, she had always been trained to shed the fiery plasma as soon as possible when emerging from a point locus, lest the ship's overtaxed shields fail.

But the notion of retaining the plasma ball as a protective shield had occurred to the human members helping in the design of *Lexington* from the very beginning. The *Lexington* had powerful kinetic energy weapons and the Ekhat would be totally reliant upon lasers. Maintaining a plasma ball around the ship would degrade the effectiveness of the enemy's lasers without significantly affecting the *Lexington*'s own guns. Not as well as a star's photosphere, of course, of which the plasma ball would be just a tiny fragment. But it might be enough to make a difference in a hard-fought battle.

Dannet understood the logic. Still, it seemed unnatural. She was no more prone to enjoying novelty than any Jao.

Spine C was down, having taken the brunt of the ramming, but the other kinetic weapons decks were still functional. She directed them to acquire targets and fire at will.

The guns wouldn't be as effective out here in open space, naturally. Fighting inside a star's photosphere required the combatants to draw very close to each other, and their velocities dropped as well. Outside those conditions, in an open vacuum, the combatants would draw much farther apart and their velocities would increase. For all the savage effectiveness of the sabot rounds in close quarters, at these ranges and speeds the great majority of rounds fired would miss their targets. The shells were not missiles, with their own guidance mechanisms. They were very primitive weapons, when all was said and done.

As for Spine C, if there was too much damage, it would be necessary to jettison it for the good of the ship. That provision had been foreseen also—in this instance, by the Jao members of the design team. All of the spines were designed so that they could be jettisoned from the ship. In effect, since the design of the *Lexington* ensured that almost all battle damage would first be inflicted upon the spines rather than the main hull, those huge spines added another highly effective layer of armor to the vessel.

That might also require jettisoning the crew members in the spine, of course. That would be regrettable, but casualties were a given in war. Any war, much less the brutal and all-out struggle for survival that was the never-ending war with the Ekhat. If the need arose, Dannet would give the order to sacrifice the spine's crew without a moment's hesitation.

Lexington edged out of the photosphere, looking for the enemy. If they could take out at least one of the Ekhat ships before they lost the protective shielding of the plasma ball, they would add to their advantage. As Dannet's human subordinates would say, "help level the playing field."

The first time she'd heard that expression, she'd been puzzled. Once the logic was explained, she could see the meaning of it. But what sort of contorted mind would imagine a playing field for athletics tilted in the first place? As was so often true with humans, the saying was clever and irritating at the same time.

Carefully, she restrained herself from slipping into a body posture that would project her annoyance. She had been warned when she was offered the assignment by the Narvo leaders. A great honor, of course, to help Narvo to overcome the stain left by Oppuk. That was so, even when the honor would have to remain unspoken, since she would be formally leaving Narvo to accept membership in the new Terra Taif. But she would also, they told her, be accepting a lifetime of aggravation—and if she reacted improperly to such, she would add to the stain rather than helping to remove it.

And so it had been. Thus far, at least, and she saw no reason to expect the situation to improve.

Her Second spoke up. "Damage Control reports they are still unable to evacuate Spine C." Otta looked up from his screen. His whiskers and the cant of his head displayed *concern*.

"That will be unfortunate," Dannet said, "should we be forced to jettison. How is hull integrity in that sector?"

Otta studied the stats. "Eighty-one percent, up from seventy. They are effecting repairs from the inside."

"I see." She strode over to the tank displaying projected positions for the Ekhat ships, reduced to probabilities at the moment because of the distortion produced by the fiery plasma. Weapons systems were not the only things degraded by maintaining the shield.

"Inform Tully that we may be required to jettison Spine C soon," said Dannet. "We cannot risk a hull integrity in the spine worse than ninety percent, with a battle coming very soon."

"Jettison?" Caitlin Kralik said, crossing the command deck, her tiresomely unchanging eyes focused upon Dannet. The human's lines and angles had gone to *baffled-disbelief.* "But..."

Other human bridge crew watched her pass, then returned to their work, industriously not-noticing. Unexpectedly wise of them, Dannet thought, punching up a new set of readings.

"There is a whole company down on Spine C," Caitlin said, "including a member of Aille's personal service and the remnants of the Krant crew. You cannot just cast them off! They would fall into the sun without a shield!"

"Your perception of the situation is most likely correct, Mrs. Kralik," Dannet said, remembering to use the peculiar human honorific taken by mated human females. Her own lines were carefully schooled to *cool-indifference.*

That took some effort, as skilled as Dannet was at body posturing. She had disliked this particular female even before arriving on Terra and joining the new taif. Everyone in her natal kochan was aware that Caitlin Kralik had been instrumental, somehow, in pushing Oppuk past the bounds of sanity. How else explain what happened? Madness, common among humans, was rare among Jao. Among any Jao, much less a Narvo *namth camiti.*

Dannet was younger than Oppuk, but still remembered him visiting her natal compound while she was training. He had been magnificent with a rakish *vai camiti,* strong and decisive. He had certainly deserved better than the ignominious death at the hand of a primitive he had suffered on Terra.

The very primitive, in fact, who was now in command of the crew in Spine C. But that was irrelevant to Dannet's present concerns.

"That is a decision that must sometimes be made," she said, "A few lives versus the survival of an entire ship."

"It has not come to that yet," Caitlin said. Dannet saw how carefully the little human female was now controlling her lines and angles. She had gone blatantly *neutral* as only the Bond could manage. "Send more crew members to get them out of there."

"I have already dispatched as many as I can spare," Dannet said, settling into her command chair. She itched to correct the feisty human, but the governor of Terra was sure to disapprove. As this one was a member of his personal service, it should fall to him to discipline poor behavior—unless Mrs. Kralik made herself insufferable before all here on the command deck.

"This ship holds thousands," Caitlin said, her body still classically *neutral*. "Surely, you can—"

"Are you challenging my leadership?" Dannet's voice was soft, yet pitched for all on the command deck to hear. She assumed the lines of *polite-inquiry*. It was crucial that she not leave herself open to the slightest criticism later, which would inevitably reflect back upon Narvo. *Say it*, she thought, though she kept any indication of her thoughts from her posture. *Say the unforgivable.*

"Decks E and G firing," the munitions officer said, as though his captain were not totally occupied with Caitlin.

"Your leadership is beyond question, Terra-Captain," Caitlin said. "This is, of course, your command and I will now leave you to it as I should have done when the engagement started. Please excuse me." She strode toward the lift, taking the gaze of most of the command crew with her.

The opportunity slipped away from Dannet like a wily sea creature diving into sunless depths. She had been so close to provoking the human into an unwise statement, but Caitlin had dodged the trap. And neither had she maneuvered the human into association, as Pluthrak was always so cleverly doing.

Dannet forced herself to seize the possibility provided. "Mrs. Kralik."

Caitlin paused, and looked over her shoulder. "Yes, Terra-Captain?"

"I have no desire to see unnecessary casualties. Please make yourself of use and go to Spine C. Warn Tully that we will jettison the spine if he cannot bring hull integrity back up to ninety percent."

Caitlin nodded. "Thank you. How much time does he have? He will need a human time frame, you understand."

More irritation. Dannet knew that humans insisted on breaking the flow of time into arbitrary and meaningless fragments. But she did not yet have the needed experience to provide an approximate translation of her own time sense.

One of her human subordinates was standing nearby, and came over. That was Melonie Brown, the female officer who attended to many of the ship's mechanical needs. She had some formal human title—Engineering Officer, if Dannet remembered correctly.

"Tell him he has twenty minutes, Ship-Captain," she said softly. "We have that much time before reengaging the enemy. If Tully can't reestablish ninety percent hull integrity within ten minutes,

he probably can't do it at all. And that gives him ten more minutes to evacuate the spine, which should be enough."

The specific units meant nothing to Dannet, but she had already
discovered that Brown was capable and had an excellent knowledge of the *Lexington's* design and structure. She would accept
her judgment in the matter.

She even remembered to do the little head jerk—they called
it a "nod"—that served humans as a crude equivalent of either
command-to-make-it-so or *full-agreement*. Or perhaps both. As with
all human gestures, it was maddeningly vague. "Tell Tully what
she says, Mrs. Kralik," Dannet commanded. "In twenty minutes,
if hull integrity has not been restored to ninety percent or better,
I will jettison the spine."

Caitlin jerked her head, and left the deck.

Interesting. Apparently the "nod" gesture was also the equivalent of *obedient-acknowledgment*. Despite her Narvo preference for
straightforwardness, Dannet was pleased with herself. She didn't
think even a Pluthrak could have elicited more association out
of such an unpromising situation.

And there would be more such situations, she thought, turning
back to the projection tank. This was going to be a lengthy voyage. Her sense of flow predicted when they would likely return
to Terra, as conditions now stood, and that time was not what
a human would term "soon." Before it was over, if all went well,
much of the damage caused by Oppuk would have been repaired.

It was unfortunate, of course, that Dannet would never have
the pleasure of receiving formal recognition of her work from
Narvo. But that was an inevitable part of the work itself. As she
had been fairly warned. Far more important was that she make
herself of use. To Narvo, to the Jao—and even, she was now
coming to accept, the humans who were part of her adopted taif.

Jihan saw that the largest alien ship had fallen back into the
sun. Perhaps it was running away from the Ekhat's superior force,
using framepoint travel, or perhaps it was even immolating itself.
The Ekhat were known to be casually suicidal, after all. Who
could say how unknown alien species might behave?

Either way, five Ekhat vessels remained in the system and the
Lleix were facing them unaided. The realization terrified her even
more, and she had not thought that possible.

Then, two of the ungainly ships of the Ekhat devils followed the huge vessel into the sun. Lliant and Hadata looked at one another blankly. Time stretched out as no one on the tiny Starwarder ship spoke. Even the recycled air lay heavy in Jihan's lungs. "What—does this mean?" she asked finally into the silence, thinking that the Starwarders or Ekhatlore would understand this turn of events far better than a former Starsifter.

Lliant's black eyes turned to her. "They must be pursuing the intruder back to its home."

So the great devils could visit death and destruction on yet another species. Whoever they were, it might be their Last-of-Days also.

Hadata piloted the little ship closer, the crew observing, which was all they could do. This vessel carried no weapons heavy enough to be effective against the Ekhat. Three of the devils' vessels remained in low orbit above the sun, their angular shape in stark black outline against the star's brilliance, plainly visible.

Then, a huge blob of fiery plasma emerged from the sun, rising slowly. It would be one or both of the Ekhat returning, Jihan thought, back from their grisly errand. It had taken very little time.

But the shape was so massive, so round, unlike the Ekhat design, spindly, angular, and long. "It is the intruder," she said, hardly able to breathe.

"That cannot be," Lliant said, his fingers flying over the controls, taking readings, evaluating what little data came back.

The immense vessel soared toward the remaining three Ekhat, still enveloped in the deadly plasma. "They mean to use the plasma as a weapon, I think," Jihan said. "They will engage them." She tight-beamed the bizarre sight back to Valeron for the Starsifters, Starwarders, and Ekhatlore. Jaolore had not yet set up a receiver for such data. As with so many other things since Jaolore's rushed formation, there had been no opportunity.

"What happened to the two Ekhat ships that were pursuing it?" Lliant said.

Who was manning that ship? Jihan kept asking herself. It resembled nothing that belonged to the Jao. Were these new creatures as bad as the Ekhat, or perhaps even worse? It was entirely possible.

The huge vessel was firing again, no doubt from those strange flat extrusions which were not visible at the moment. The closest Ekhat ship abruptly changed vector—as it was hit, perhaps—then returned laser fire, which seemed to have no effect.

Three against one. Massive as their ship was, the newcomers could not possibly prevail against such numbers, and the other two ships could return at any moment. The Ekhat would finish them off and then turn their attention back to Valeron.

The others fell silent again, sitting rigid before their screens in grief and shock. However this battle turned out, the Lleix and their way of life were already dead, but for the moment those on this ship were the only ones who knew it.

Down in Spine C, at Tully's order, Mallu took charge of the work of trying to restore hull integrity. He let his timesense stretch out as he worked, so that the mad rush to attend to damage seemed almost leisurely, allowing him to detect details that might otherwise have escaped his notice. Major Tully was still struggling to open the hatch, so he did not consult the human's judgment any more than strictly necessary.

Jalta had been stunned by the collision and was sitting propped up against a bulkhead, bleeding from a gashed shoulder. Up and down the line of great gun mounts, the human lieutenant named Miller and Senior-Tech Kaln were coordinating that work, certifying which guns could return to service and organizing dazed, but able-bodied crew into new groupings to operate them. At least two of the fourteen guns were completely out of commission. Unsalvageable, according to Kaln, by anything short of a repair dock.

Mostly, Mallu was impressed by the way the majority of the humans ignored their own injuries and helped with the repair work or aided their more badly wounded fellows. He was unaccustomed to the species, and could now see that their appearance had fooled him, at least to a degree. There was something both fragile and vaguely comical about humans, to an untutored Jao eye. He had not expected them to show such determination and resilience in the middle of a fierce battle.

The air had quickly grown stale, filled with the stink of shorted out wiring and acrid smoke, and it was very hot. All around him, the humans' naked faces gleamed with moisture as though they had just come from swimming. A curious side effect, evidently, of their biochemistry under stress.

Then Tully called him over to his screen. "Dannet is trying to retain the plasma sheath as we emerge from the photosphere."

Mallu had gotten accustomed enough to human speech to

understand that the tone of Tully's remark was one of admiration for Dannet's cunning. For himself, Mallu thought he understood what the Terra-captain was trying to accomplish. Laser weapons were ineffective against the *Lexington* as long as they were enveloped in the fiery plasma, but the kinetics could still be utilized. At the present moment, only five of the guns were operational on Spine C, but Kaln and the human female officer named Miller had them manned and firing.

"Gabe?" a faint human voice called from the other side of the jammed hatch.

"Caitlin!" Tully turned away from the screen, then shouted something back in the slippery native tongue.

The voice answered, still speaking in Terran. More precisely, the Terran language called English, which seemed to be the dominant one. Humans had a bewildering variety of tongues.

Tully moved over to the hatch, crouched to press his ear against it, and listened for a short while. Then he turned to Mallu. "That is Caitlin Kralik," he said. "She has just come from the command deck. Dannet is ready to jettison this spine, if we don't contain our damage. She says we have less than seventeen minutes left to bring integrity back up to ninety percent."

By now, Mallu had learned to translate the rigid human time terms into meaningful concepts. Closely enough, he thought. He looked up and down the long narrow deck, gauging the progress of the Jinau and Jao crewmen, working together to repair the damage. For the first time since he'd encountered them, Mallu felt some genuine liking for humans. As baffling and aggravating as they so often were, it was now obvious to him that they were also capable of subordinating their petty concerns and associating with others—Jao as well as their own kind—for the sake of the mission.

For the first time, also, he essayed one of those crude and imprecise human body gestures. A "shrug," they called it. "If she must, then our deaths will make themselves of use by preserving *Lexington*. There is nothing worse than losing a ship." He still felt the hollowness incurred by the loss of his own command. "I am almost certain that we will not be able to restore sufficient hull integrity in the time allowed."

"That's what I figured myself," said Tully. "I think we'd need at least an hour, more likely two or three."

He stood up abruptly. "To hell with that damn Jao stoicism," he growled. "Our deaths will be of no fricking use to anyone on this highly misbegotten ship, especially ourselves. But our lives certainly will!" He turned his head, seeking something, then pressed a stubby ear to the metal, apparently listening. "We are damn well getting out of here!"

The human was so overwrought that he kept sprinkling his Jao conversation with incomprehensible Terran terms. Mallu moved closer, his whiskers limp with *bafflement. Lexington*'s design was unfamiliar, heavily influenced as it was by Terran esthetics. Perhaps he was missing an obvious alternative that could get them out in time. "What can we do from this side that we have not already tried?"

Tully looked at the two human crewmen who had been working at the hatch earlier. They had ceased that work some time back, and had spent the time since doing something incomprehensible.

One of the two crewmen nodded at him. "It's ready, sir."

Tully hammered on the metal hatch with his fist. "Caitlin!" he cried. "Get away from the hatch! You and everybody else out there! Do you hear me?"

Mallu heard the Caitlin female's muffled voice responding with what he took for an affirmative. Puzzled, he wondered what Tully was planning.

Tully stepped back and motioned at Mallu to do the same. "Stand back!"

Still confused, Mallu did as instructed. A moment later, at a gesture from Tully, there was the sharp cracking sound of a contained explosion.

The hatch sagged open along the side where the hinges had been. Mallu could see now that the two crewmen had placed explosives charges of some kind.

The whole thing was obvious, in retrospect. Mallu hadn't realized what they were doing earlier because...

It was so monstrous. Inconceivable, until he saw it done. They might have condemned the entire ship! With the hatch unable to be closed again, there would be no easy way to seal off the wound caused by the spine's jettisoning.

At first, he was too enraged to speak coherently. Then he began shouting at Tully.

But Tully shouted back, and after a moment, the meaning of his words penetrated.

"—stupid Jao bastards, you're worse than idiot kamikaze! Thankfully, this ship was designed by humans. You think we're dumb enough to build a ship designed to break apart in a crisis—and not make provisions for the safety of the crew?"

He went back to utterances in which the words "Jao" and "stupid" and "bastards" intermingled freely. But did so while spending most of his time and energy waving crewmen forward to escape through the now-open hatch.

"—get those people out of the turrets, Lieutenant Miller! Kaln, you murderous maniac, quit firing! We've got to get them out of there!"

Mallu could see Kaln in the distance, obviously hesitating and reluctant to obey the order.

One of the two crewmen who'd done the work at the hatch—what humans called a "sergeant," if Mallu was reading their equivalent of rank stripes properly—leaned over and spoke softly.

"The ship is designed to seal itself off from a jettisoned spine with a lot worse damage than a blown entry hatch, sir. This won't make any difference at all to the integrity of the *Lexington*. All it does—maybe—is let us survive."

And that too was obvious, now that Mallu thought about it. Humans were simply not Jao, no matter how bravely they might conduct themselves. They would take the time and spend the effort to establish safety provisions that Jao would ignore.

The first crewmen began emerging from the gun turrets. Most of the other crewmen in the spine were already lined up and beginning to pass through the hatch. The sergeant—his name was Andrew Allport, Mallu remembered—was now helping one of the more badly hurt of the crewmen through the hatch. The door was still not fully open, so passage through it was a bit difficult for someone impaired by wounds.

One by one, they squeezed through the blasted door, the Jao having a harder time because of the breadth of their shoulders. Mallu hoisted Jalta to his feet and pushed him through just behind Kaln, who was aiding, not one, but two humans who had suffered broken limbs. Tully was hanging back, evidently intending to be last. He even had a brief argument with the small female officer concerning the matter. Apparently, she'd planned herself to be the last one out of the spine.

Very brief. For all his fondness for mocking Jao habits, Tully had something of those Jao attitudes himself. As he passed through the hatch, Mallu could hear Tully behind him.

"—on your feet or on your ass, Miller. That's your only choice, and either way you're going through that hatch first. Now why don't you do something useful instead of wasting my time and yours?"

Now out of the spine, Mallu turned and peered back through the hatch door. The red-furred lieutenant's face seemed even paler than usual. Her jaws set, she nodded abruptly, and went through the hatch. Mallu helped her through. Tully followed closely behind.

A new alarm sounded, pitched excruciatingly high. Only the dead could have ignored it.

All up and down the deck, explosive bolts blew between the inner wall and the outer ship. Mallu recognized that sound. The long narrow weapons spine lurched as its supports were severed one by one.

"Let's get out of here before we get caught by the shield plates," Tully half-shouted. Looking, Mallu saw that some sort of protective plates were emerging from slots he'd never noticed and were closing rapidly across the hatch in the narrow space that separated the entrance to the spine from the main hull. From what he could see, such plates would cover the entire base of the spine. No wonder Tully hadn't been worried that destroying the hatch would compromise the integrity of the hull. For all the speed with which they were closing, the shield plates were massive, much thicker than the hatch had been.

Mallu followed Tully through the rapidly dwindling space. Behind them, the shields locked into place with a metallic clang. Then there was a rasp and the last of the connecting bolts were severed. The alarm's tone rose, even more strident. Mallu batted at his tortured ears.

"Gabe, are you all right?" A human female with yellow head fur—"hair," the humans called it—was kneeling beside the major, peering at his head wound.

He answered in Terran, then the female looked at Mallu, her curves and angles gone to a splendid rendition of *profound-gratitude*. "You have accomplished much good work here today, Krant-Captain."

How could a human move so elegantly? Mallu stared. Her posture was perfect, effortlessly double. He felt like an uneducated clod.

Medicians were evaluating injuries and taking the wounded away for treatment. A Jao medician stopped to check Mallu, but he waved him on. His ribs ached, nothing more, as far as he could tell, beyond a scrape he'd somehow picked up on his left leg. There were many who needed immediate attention far more than he did.

The ship shook as though they had taken a hit. He lurched to his feet and bent over Tully as a medician dabbed the cut on the Terran's forehead with antiseptic. "I am going up to the command deck," he said.

"Not without me!" Tully struggled to his feet, then swayed. Mallu caught his arm and then together they wove toward the nearest lift.

CHAPTER
20

Tully took the lift back up to the bridge, bracing himself against the wall as the deck indicator flashed, watching Mallu on the other side of the cab. The Krant-captain was in obvious pain, standing bent over to ease his ribs. One of the legs of his maroon trousers was torn, the skin beneath abraded and seeping that odd orange shade of Jao blood. Tully wondered how the Jao had acquired the injury. In all likelihood, though, Mallu wouldn't know himself. Things had been pretty chaotic and confused in the spine for a while.

Tully's own head throbbed where it had collided with the bulkhead, but he was almighty grateful not to be left behind in the weapons spine as the jettisoned section drifted toward immolation in the blazing white-hot heart of that star.

The lift stopped abruptly. The door opened and they ventured into controlled chaos, Tully taking the lead out of respect. The scattered viewscreens displayed only a blaze of filtered light. Tully craned his head. The ship must still be enveloped with plasma. Was Dannet's crafty plan working?

There was some sort of stink in the air. Subtle, but still noticeable. Overheated wiring, maybe. Low voices were arguing at the far end. Then heads turned as he and Mallu stepped onto the bridge. Terra-Captain Dannet looked up from a display she was examining. Her body posture was not one Tully was familiar with. Or didn't think he was, anyway. It wasn't always easy to tell, because the different great kochans all had their own variations on Jao body language. Like so many dialects, as it were.

"Major Tully and Krant-Captain Mallu," she said, stating the obvious as Jao never did.

Tully waited, but the captain could seem to think of nothing else to say.

"My crew are being looked after," he said, assuming a Yaut-like posture. *Readiness-to-serve*, he hoped, or perhaps *respectful-attention*. He never could get those two straight. "I thought I would report in person. We come to make ourselves of use."

"The command deck is already fully staffed," Dannet said, turning back to the display. Her ears twitched and came together. "But you may remain and observe, if you wish."

Was that just a hint of *approval* in the line of her spine? Tully, not for the first time, wished he were more fluent in bodyspeak.

Lexington reeled suddenly like a boxer who had taken a punch. Tully almost fell into the lap of a startled Jao female, catching himself at the last second against the nearest console. Mallu did better, riding out the pitching motion, having apparently developed better "space legs" through long practice.

The ship took another hit, though not as massive. "All three enemy combatant ships firing," a human woman said, eyes trained upon her display. "Minimal damage on our end. The plasma diffuses their lasers."

If the damage was minimal, what had caused those tremendous jolts? And now that Tully thought about it, lasers weren't really impact weapons to begin with. The answer came on the heels of the question. Dannet had ordered evasive action.

Tully winced when he considered just how extreme that "evasive action" had to have been to move an object as massive as the *Lexington* so quickly that even the internal gravity controls were overloaded. Dannet's pilot was handling the huge craft as if it were some kind of old-style human fighter plane in a dogfight! That was Charles Duquette, who didn't even have the excuse of being a Jao.

The bridge stilled but for the ever-present beeps and clicks as the instruments cycled. A Jao was calling out distances in hundreds of *azets*, a Jao standard of measurement. They were all waiting for…something. Tully wasn't sure what.

"Desired proximity achieved," the Jao officer finally said. Tully thought he recognized Sten krinnu ava Terra, the ship's navigator. "All three enemy vessels are now inside our plasma sheath."

Dannet took her own command seat, Tully and Mallu seemingly forgotten. "All kinetic weapons decks, maximum fire when you have a target!"

Tully edged behind a support pillar so that he wouldn't be in anyone's way. He also wanted to stay out of Dannet's sight as much as possible. Even though she'd given them permission to stay on the command deck, Tully had no desire to trigger a change of mind on her part. He and the rest of his company had nearly given their lives in this battle. He'd damn well earned the right to be here. So had Mallu.

Visual input had been pretty much useless as long as the Ekhat remained outside the plasma ball, but now that *Lexington* had closed with them, Tully could just make out dark, oddly articulated outlines in the swirling inferno, as well as the ruby blaze of their lasers, still targeting them.

Kinetic rounds were making Swiss cheese out of the nearest vessel, while the answering Ekhat lasers were severely degraded by the plasma. *Lexington* maneuvered to give the surviving kinetic weapons decks a better angle, and then Tully detected several small explosions at the base of the nearest tetrahedron. The strobe of their lasers faded and the ungainly vessel drifted away.

Was it dead? Tully looked around at the deck. Everyone was focused upon his or her task. Several stations were unoccupied, though. He turned and motioned to Mallu, gesturing that the Krant-captain should take the nearest one.

Mallu flicked an ear, then slid into the indicated chair, pulling on headgear as though he belonged there. Tully hunkered beside him, using the Jao's bulk to keep himself out of Dannet's sight.

"What is happening?" he asked Mallu in a low voice.

The Jao listened. "The closest Ekhat is drifting back into the photosphere," he said. "If their shields hold, and we survive the battle with the remaining two, we will have to go in after them."

"Great," Tully muttered. He dabbed at his aching head with the back of one hand and then stared at the sticky blood. Whoever thought up all this insane sailing around inside suns ought to be shot. Oh, wait, he told himself, that had been the Ekhat. No wonder. They were bat-crazy to begin with.

All the same, he had a new respect for the Jao, stiff-necked imperialists that they were, for fighting the good fight all these years against the Ekhat's murderous insanity. They looked positively like good old homeboys in comparison.

"The Ekhat are still battling the intruder," Jihan said, hunched over her instruments.

"But it is so outnumbered!" Hadata leaned over Jihan's shoulder. Lliant got to his feet and joined them.

Like the Lleix, Jihan thought. The universe seemed to produce more Ekhat than any other species. "Two of the Ekhat ships followed it into the sun, but did not return. They have either fled the system or been destroyed. Now the newcomer has resurfaced from the sun's photosphere, sheathed in plasma, and closed with the remaining three Ekhat ships so that they are all inside the plasma ball."

"Such ships are designed to withstand contact with plasma," Hadata said. "It cannot defeat them that way."

"Their weapons will burn it into slag!" Lliant said, his fingers gripping the back of Jihan's much patched chair.

"Perhaps not." Her aureole flared with excitement. The strategy in this strange battle was so different from anything she had come across in the historical records. The newcomer could not possibly be another Ekhat faction, and neither could it be their despised lackeys, the Jao. Everything, the design of the monstrously huge ship, the strange armament, the peculiar tactics, all pointed to some species never before encountered.

She detected an explosion, then one of the Ekhat ships drifted out of the plasma back toward the star, wobbling eccentrically, clearly not under power. "Only two left!" she said, her voice a hoarse excited whisper. Two out of five, when even one of the monstrous vessels was enough to destroy an entire planet. Were the long-lost guardian spirits looking after the Lleix, after all?

"That cannot be!" Lliant said, turning away.

She gazed across the cramped cabin at him. He was elegant and educated, his robes perfectly draped, his manners precise, but his mind was closed. "It is just possible that we do not know everything about the universe," she said. Lliant stiffened, but resumed his station and did not turn around. "At one time, before the Ekhat rained destruction upon our many worlds, murdering our future, we knew more than we do now. One only has to walk the colony and view deserted house after house to comprehend how very much we have lost through the long years of our exile."

"Jihan!" Hadata said, slumping in amazement at the Jaolore's effrontery.

Exasperation flooded through Jihan. "What I said is true," she said, "and pointless avoidance of the facts will not make them any less valid." She stiffened her aureole, sitting up straight to make the most of her meager height. "And there is no reason to look so shocked. I have not broken *sensho* by saying any of this." She gazed into Hadata's lovely upswept black eyes. "I am an Eldest. No one else here can say that for themselves."

"Eldest of a pack of *dochaya* fools!" Lliant said under his breath.

Hadata lowered her head and returned to her pilot's seat. "Indeed," she murmured, "not that such things will matter once the Ekhat dispatch this newcomer and turn their attention to Valeron."

It might not come to that, Jihan thought with just a trace of hope. The outsider might triumph, giving them at least more time to evacuate Valeron, but she kept the outlandish notion to herself. Events would proceed, regardless of what she or any of the others thought. Then they would all see who was right.

Clever, clever Terra-captain! Mallu thought, hunkering over the sensor board. It was well known that energy weapons were ineffective inside a star's photosphere, but, until now, that disadvantage had applied to both sides battling in such an environment, Jao and Ekhat. With the addition of kinetic weapons to their arsenal, Dannet was using the plasma to give them a huge advantage.

The disabled Ekhat ship, however, had not plunged back into the star after all, he realized from the readings. It had established a very low orbit and no doubt they were racing to complete repairs and rejoin the battle.

Dannet couldn't maintain the plasma ball indefinitely. *Lexington* would have to make maximum use of the advantage while it lasted.

Two Ekhat ships remained in play. Tully edged higher, gazing into the screen with an odd hunger. "*Jesus!*" he said.

Mallu flicked an ear in irritation. "Speak Jao or at least comprehensible English," he said. Then, grudgingly: "Please."

"That was just the invocation of a—sacred name," Tully said. "A wish for—luck. The content is emotional, not indicative."

Superstition, then. Mallu managed to keep his whiskers from bristling with *indignation*. As though that sort of primitive nonsense could be of any use in this situation! He punched up a real-time view on the station's screen. The nearest Ekhat ship had taken continuous heavy fire from their kinetics and was now breaking apart, the angular gantries spinning off on trajectories of their own, the tetrahedron imploding. Gas vented, then the shields failed spectacularly and the metal components were melting into slag from the high temperatures. Scattered remnants spun lazily toward the star.

"One left!" Tully said. The peculiar tracings of yellow nap above his static eyes rose.

But *Lexington*'s plasma protection was dissipating quickly, Mallu saw by the readings. Hull temperature was plummeting.

"All laser decks, go to full power," Dannet ordered. Her ears were pinned in unabashedly singular *concentration*. "Fire at will."

Lexington shook and Tully sprawled on the deck at his feet. Dannet glanced aside at him, but said nothing. Despite the Terran's attempt to conceal his presence, Mallu knew that she'd been aware of him all along and had just chosen for the moment to say nothing.

Klaxons went off. Emergency indicators flickered into life. "Taking damage on decks twenty-eight through thirty-three," a human male said.

Now that the plasma sheath was dispersing, they were again vulnerable to laser fire, but then so was the remaining Ekhat vessel, and *Lexington* was heavily armed with both kinds of tech. Commands raced through Mallu's mind, maneuvers and tactics he would try if he were in charge.

As he was unlikely to be—ever again.

"*Jesus!*" Tully said again, his eyes trained on the main viewscreen where the ruby strobe of Ekhat laser weapons was clearly punishing *Lexington*'s shields.

Obviously, the name's invocation was of no practical benefit, but, flashing back to his own ship's crippling, Mallu was almost of a mind to try it himself.

"All decks, lock down!" Dannet ordered, buckling herself in. The rest of the command deck crew hastened to obey. Some of the humans had gone quite red in the face. Others were noticeably paler.

"Cut speed to one quarter," Dannet said. "Come about ten degrees."

Mallu levered Tully up from the deck, wincing at the pain in his ribs. "Over there!" He shoved the human toward another empty station.

"But—" Tully turned back to him.

"Fool!" Mallu buckled the safety harness around his own shoulders. "We are going to ram!"

Tully dove for the chair and fumbled at the straps. In the viewscreen, the Ekhat ship grew larger and larger until all that could be seen was a close-up view of the tetrahedron believed to carry the main Ekhat living quarters.

Careful, careful, thought Mallu as the blood thundered in his ears. Ramming in open space was extremely dangerous, given the speeds involved. They could not strike the other vessel solidly, or, despite the new ship's massive construction, *Lexington* would take fatal damage as well.

Dannet consulted the readings. "Come about two degrees more, Lead-Pilot Duquette."

For some reason, one of the humans was counting down the diminishing distance in Jao. Mallu did not know why. It was quite obvious when the *Lexington* would collide. Flow indicated that it would be—

—now.

The deck heaved and everything, including his body, was impelled savagely upwards and back. Unsecured writing implements, cups, coms, electronic tablets, and anything else not tied down flew across the huge cabin, pelting unwary crew. His teeth clicked so hard, he thought he might have broken one. The safety harness held, biting deep into his shoulders and chest, but the wave of pain from his healing ribs made his vision white out.

When he could see again, the command deck was dark, save for a few blinking red lights. Pain flickered through his body like heat lightning. He had to breathe shallowly. Voices were calling, reporting, demanding, but faraway, almost as though they had nothing to do with here and now. Something had shorted out and he could smell the burnt metal reek of the wires.

He turned his head, surveying the damage. Terra-Captain Dannet was struggling with her harness. Mallu freed himself and went to help. The Terra-captain did not acknowledge him, only lurched to her feet as he disengaged the harness, eyes blazing with green fire. "Damage Control, report!"

"Damage Control parties dispatched to Decks Fifteen, Seventeen, and Thirty-Two," a hoarse human male said. "Weapons Spine F is experiencing some atmosphere loss, but hull integrity is still ninety-three percent."

Across the command deck, lights flickered back on, though not all of them. Officers unbuckled their harness and hastened to check unresponsive crewmen. Mallu inspected Tully, who seemed dazed, but not visibly injured.

In the viewscreen, the Ekhat ship spun crazily, too fast for its station-keeping jets to stabilize. Mallu understood at once that Dannet's maneuver had worked perfectly—given the skill of the human pilot. The *Lexington* had missed the main body of the Ekhat vessel entirely and collided with one of the outlying gantries. The gantry had been torn off, of course—but, more importantly, the enemy ship had been sent into an uncontrolled spin. Ekhat fire control was simply overwhelmed. There was no longer any way they could aim their lasers from such a rapidly rotating vessel. Their internal gravity controls might even be collapsing, which would produce massive injuries on the Ekhat and their slave crewmen.

The same spin, of course, would bring every part of the enemy vessel under the *Lexington*'s guns, if—no, once; Mallu could see that the pilot was already at work—the range was close enough.

Less than two minutes later, it was. The *Lexington* was positioned no more than three *azets* from the Ekhat ship. "All kinetic weapons decks, begin firing," Dannet said, pacing back and forth before the screen.

Lexington vibrated as the big guns on the two remaining kinetic energy weapon spines started firing. More than two dozen 500mm cannons sent a stream of depleted uranium sabot rounds into the spinning enemy vessel. It was like watching a piece of metal in a lathe being cut into ribbons. Pieces of the Ekhat vessel went flying in all directions, the pieces getting larger with each passing second. Then, suddenly, the whole ship just disintegrated.

Fifteenth-Note-Flat and First-Note-Ascending stalked about the conductor's pod of their ship in a savage temper, having already slaughtered everything living within reach. The vessel was spinning out of control and the brainless Anj down in the control pit seemed unable to remedy the situation, no matter what the two think-mates threatened.

Who *were* these intruders? There was no record of any ship with such bloated dimensions and they fought like no other species ever encountered by the Melody. It was intolerable. They must be tracked back to their nest and exterminated.

The ship shook with repeated blows. The intruder was hammering them to pieces by lobbing chunks of simple matter, distressingly dense, all the while also employing more traditional energy weapons. Their own weapons were returning fire, but it was impossible to target with any accuracy while spinning at this rate.

An explosion rocked the ship as another one of the solid rounds impacted with some critical sector. The interior gravity flickered on/off/on, so that their feet drifted off the deck, then they were slammed down, only to lose contact again a heartpulse later. The end of the next flicker brought an increase in gees and Fifteenth suffered a broken lateral joint as they hit the floor, which made their mental synchronization difficult. First hastily broke her own joint so that they could still think in tandem.

Down in the control pit, the Anj were squealing, rising up off the floor, then being crushed by the erratic gees. The noisome stink of their vital fluids filled the air. Then the gravity cut out altogether and they were pinned against the hull by centrifugal force. Fifteenth lost synch with First and found his thoughts chasing themselves round and round like small terrified vermin. The note, he thought. Now they would never get to sing their perfect note. The composition in this quadrant would remain woefully incomplete.

Something *cracked*. Fifteenth glimpsed the black of raw space through the parting cabin walls, along with the colored gauzy red threads of the nebula, dim faraway stars, the sun of this system, then blackness again as they spun and spun. Atmosphere vented with a whoosh, and then there was nothing left to breathe.

CHAPTER
21

Tully assisted where he could as the bridge crew set about restoring order. Every so often, he glanced over at Dannet's Narvo-striped face as she directed the hunt for larger portions of the wrecked Ekhat vessels to ensure nothing had survived. Some of the Ekhat's lasers were still firing from time to time, probably on automatic, because they were even targeting other Ekhat debris.

Tully figured most of the pieces would wind up in the sun in fairly short order, but he admired Dannet's ferocity. It was good to see Jao bloody-mindedness turned upon their common enemy. Humans knew only too well how focused they could be from the conquest of Terra.

He watched the Terra-captain as she steered the bridge crew back on task, stern and uncompromising and deadly efficient. By all that was holy, she had outmaneuvered and outfought five fricking Ekhat ships! She was amazing. The Bond had certainly known what it was doing when it turned command of this ship over to her.

Despite being Narvo. Or...more likely, *because* she was Narvo. Uncomfortably, Tully finally admitted to himself a truth which he knew was accepted by all Jao. Narvo was one of the two greatest of the Jao kochan, along with Pluthrak. But where Pluthrak's stature derived from their subtlety and multiple associations, Narvo's came from something much simpler. They were the great warrior kochan of the Jao. In purely military terms, by far the mightiest.

Professor Kinsey had once commented that insofar as the Jao kochans found a parallel with the caste system of the Hindus, Pluthrak was the equivalent of the Brahmin priests and Narvo of the kshatriya warriors. The analogy hadn't meant much to Tully at the time, but he could see the logic now.

Dannet's notice lighted upon him. "Major Tully," she said, crossing the deck to stand by him. Her eyes blazed down at him, flickering with green, and her ears were positively dancing. Something was going on inside that alien skull.

"Yes, Terra-Captain?" The knot on his head ached dully.

"You were stationed in Spine C. So now your unit has no function." Her ears kept flicking to odd angles, lowering abruptly, then rising again, as though her thoughts were racing.

"Not while we are in space, Terra-Captain." He kept his body very straight, trying for simple neutrality. "We took some injuries and at least two fatalities that I know of, but I can assign personnel to fill in wherever you have a need."

The Jao's eyes had gone to almost pure green now. He suspected her of finding something in the situation amusing, and unfortunately, things that amused the Jao could give a human nightmares. "Though heavily damaged by our fire, one of the Ekhat ships survived," she said abruptly, "or at least a substantial portion of it. That section has achieved a low orbit around the star and its shields appear to still be functioning, suggesting that it may yet be manned. Load the functional portion of Baker Company into assault craft and investigate whether any of the crew live."

Tully's throat went dry. "And—what is our mission? Take the survivors prisoner or finish the job?" He devoutly hoped for the latter. He'd met a pair of Ekhat face to face once. They were barking insane.

"It has been hundreds of years, as humans term such things, since the Jao captured an Ekhat ship. Even longer since we secured live Ekhat." She settled into a Yaut-like stance, *extreme-sternness*, perhaps, or *admonition-to-duty*. "If any Ekhat survive, they will attempt to terminate themselves rather than face captivity. It is your responsibility to prevent this." Her gaze turned to the screen. "Interrogating them could provide valuable information."

Question an Ekhat? He shuddered as he tried to visualize the process. "Jesus!" he muttered involuntarily, running fingers back over his aching head. Even his hair hurt.

"Are you requesting support from one of your mythical talismans?" Dannet said. "I assure you that this *Jesus*, whatever it is, cannot assist you in this matter."

"No, Terra-Captain, indeed you are right," Tully said, his mind whirling.

"You have your orders," Dannet said, and turned away.

He saluted her back, trying to preserve the shreds of his dignity, then went to round up the rest of his unit. They didn't know it yet, but they had a lot to get done.

The Starwarders' ship observed the end of the great battle as closely as the crew dared. The notion that the Lleix might survive this latest Ekhat incursion was heady. "All five destroyed?" Lliant said, his aureole fluttering with amazement. "That is not possible!"

"Analyze the readings then yourself," Jihan said. The newcomers' victory was improbable, true, but Lliant's continued incredulity angered her with its foolishness. She reminded herself that an Eldest, however short or newly named, should never give way to sharp words.

"Who—*are*—they?" Hadata whispered from her pilot's seat. "Where did they come from?"

"And what do they want?" Segga, one of the other Starwarders, said from his station at the back. The other two stayed out of the discussion, sullenly doing exactly what was required and nothing more. It was clear they had no wish to be here.

What, indeed, did the newcomers want? wondered Jihan. Her nerves crawled with uncertainty. Were they as vicious as the Ekhat or perhaps even worse? They certainly fought with an unparalleled fierceness, suggesting that if the Lleix resisted them, their people could expect no quarter either.

During the battle, the huge ship had lost a section, one of its strange flat extrusions that seemed to carry weapons. The piece drifted away from the battle and would eventually be pulled in by the star's gravity. "If we can get closer to the debris field," she said, studying the data, "I can take some readings, then beam the information back to the Starsifters. They might be able to tell us more. Perhaps there is some information on this species buried in the ancient records."

"You are not going to try to convince us that these creatures are Jao?" Lliant's voice carried an implicit sneer.

"No," Jihan said, spreading her fingers across the console and gazing steadily at them. He would not provoke her! "Whoever they are, they do not resemble what I have learned of the Jao." All those days spent learning the rudiments of the Jao tongue had been wasted, she thought regretfully. They would have to start all over with this species.

"Maneuvering in that closely will be precarious," Hadata said from her pilot's seat. "I am reading a great deal of debris, much more from the Ekhat than from the newcomer."

Jihan rose and crossed to Hadata, leaning over the other's shoulder to point at her screen. "Match course with that huge piece there," she said.

"It is passing very close to the Ekhat debris field," Hadata said, nevertheless making the suggested course corrections. "There are still a number of large sections. I am not certain how close we can safely get."

"Will we be in danger of collision?" Lliant asked.

"I will endeavor to prevent that," Hadata said.

Jihan studied the spinning Ekhat flotsam. Perhaps they should also try to take some readings from—

A red energy signature flared as a laser beam speared the flat section, vaporizing a fair amount. Hadata's startled black gaze turned to Jihan. Her hands flew to the controls, plotting a new vector away. "They are still alive!"

"They—cannot be," Jihan said, her mind whirling. "That section has lost hull integrity. You can see as it spins—it is open to space."

The energy signature flashed again, this time incinerating a broken girder from one of the Ekhat wrecks, hardly a threat by anyone's standards.

"It must be an automatic mechanism," Lliant said, "firing at anything within range. Ekhatlore has records of such."

"That could include us!" Hadata said, her hands flying over the controls.

Jihan headed back for her station, but the little ship jolted violently. She stumbled and then fell full-length to the deck, her head ringing, aureole collapsed around her face. Her arm, which had taken the brunt of her weight as she fell, throbbed.

"We have been hit!" Hadata cried.

The cabin filled with the unpleasant reek of burnt electronic components. Someone in the back section was crying out hoarsely, one of the other Starwarders, Jihan thought groggily. She had not gotten the female's name.

"T-take us back to Valeron!" Lliant said, coughing and waving away smoke. His face had smashed into his control panel and blood trickled down his cheek. He lurched out of his seat and went to check on the two back stations. One, a very short male, obviously quite young, sprawled on the floor, his head twisted at a bad angle. The other was still murmuring in pain, then her voice trailed off and she was ominously silent.

Lliant returned, wiping his hands on his robes. "They are both dead," he said, his face scrunched in disbelief.

Jihan pulled herself up into her chair with her remaining good hand, cradling the damaged arm against her chest, the taste of blood in her mouth. Her vision blurred, came back into focus. On her screen, the Ekhat energy signature flashed again, then the newcomers' ship answered by firing upon the spinning fragment, vaporizing it. Her pulse pounded as she feared it would then also fire upon them, but they were masked by the bulk of the flat extrusion. The vessel cruised on, massive, black, and deadly, evidently seeking out the last of the surviving Ekhat, putting an end to even the possibility any still lived.

"We have taken damage to our engines," Hadata said, punching in command after useless command. She turned in her seat to look at the rest of the crew. "This course is headed for the sun."

Lliant lurched to his feet, elegant draping forgotten. "Pull us out!"

"We do not have enough remaining power," Hadata said.

"Then it is the Last-of-Days," Lliant said, "at least for us."

Why did everyone always just give up? Jihan thought crossly. Her breath hissed as she tried to find a comfortable position for her injured arm. "Then we do have some power?" she said, gritting her teeth against the stabbing pain.

"Not even enough to put us into a stable orbit, much less take us back to the colony," Hadata said, her aureole drooping.

"I have piloting experience," Jihan said. "Let me try." She and Hadata traded stations and then she used her Starsifter skills, one-handedly plotting the course of every bit of flotsam out there, the newcomer, and—

She blinked. "Something fairly large has assumed low solar orbit," she said, doing the calculations again just to be certain. "Yes, there!"

Hadata came back. "I—see," she said, "but it is part of an Ekhat ship. What possible good could it do us?"

"If we shut down all extraneous equipment, I think we will have enough power for minor maneuvering," Jihan said. "We can rendezvous with that fragment and avoid being drawn into the sun."

"Rendezvous with an Ekhat?" Lliant lurched to his feet. His face was rapidly darkening with bruises and his lip was split, giving his words a slur. "Are you insane?"

"Would you rather burn up?" Jihan said. Her arm throbbed. There must be emergency medical supplies onboard. She needed to apply a pain-dampener so that she could think clearly. "If we hide there, we can summon one of our ships," Jihan said. "Perhaps the Starsifters or another Starwarders craft."

"You would bring them to the Ekhat too?" Lliant snorted. "They should have thrown your body off a cliff that day you broke *sensho* in the Hall of Decision! You do not deserve to live among civilized people!"

"Silence!" Hadata said. Her head hung as she visibly searched for the correct words to fit the situation. "Jihan is an Eldest and also has Starsifter experience. She has more right than you to determine policy."

"She will kill us all!"

"We are already dead," Hadata said. "It only remains to take our last few breaths."

Giving up again! Anger helped Jihan focus. "Lliant, stop babbling about dying and find the medical supplies. I have broken my arm." She thought through the rising haze of pain. "Hadata, contact the Starwarders and Starsifters and see if any ships can come after us." She sighed. "I will do my best to conserve what power we have left for maneuvering."

Lliant glared at her, not moving.

"And stop pouting," she said, awkwardly using her undamaged hand to shut down unneeded systems, one after the other. Most of the lighting was unnecessary, she thought, most of the heat. They were left with a few amber emergency lights that turned their silver skin sallow. "After all, it is entirely possible that you may get your wish. Despite our best efforts, we very well may not survive."

After the fighting was over, Caitlin and Wrot tracked down Tully in one of the sick bays.

"I just came in here to check on my people," Tully said, as a doctor insisted upon him lingering long enough to get his head wound cleaned. "My skull's tough and I have orders to carry out."

Caitlin wrinkled her nose. The bustling med center reeked of antiseptics and blood. The worst of the injured had already been whisked away for surgery, though, and orderlies were cleaning up. Most of the rest of the patients in here now suffered from only minor wounds.

Wrot leaned in and examined the gash in the back of Tully's scalp for himself. "That is not too bad," the old Jao said noncommittally.

Tully looked a bit wan, Caitlin thought, but with typical Resistance stubbornness, he'd stay on his feet until he keeled over.

The doctor shook his head as he laid aside bloodied cotton. Caitlin knew his name—Michael Bast—but hadn't ever really spoken to him. He was young and gawky as though he hadn't quite got his full growth. His face had gone quite pale after the events of the last few hours and he was apparently compensating for his nerves with an overly serious demeanor. Caitlin guessed, due to his youth, this was most likely his first time in combat.

"After a crack on the head like that," Bast said, glancing up at Wrot, "I would advise rest for at least twenty-four hours."

"No can do, Mike," Tully said, flinching as a bandage was applied. "Baker Company has an assignment." He smiled crookedly at Caitlin and Wrot. "Got to make ourselves of use and all that."

"Not if you've been knocked senseless!" she said, then she couldn't help her curiosity. "What kind of assignment?"

"Going to take assault craft and check out a bit of Ekhat junk that's established low orbit around this star," he said, sliding off the exam table. His blue jinau uniform was splotched with blood. He tugged to straighten his shirt. "Probably nothing, but then again unmanned wreckage should just plunge into the sun, so maybe Dannet is onto something." He shook his head. "After beating the odds like she just did, I can't deny that her instincts are all in the right place."

"You think some of them are still alive?" Caitlin said, overwhelmed with the possibilities. "My god, why doesn't *Lexington* just blast them from here?"

"Survivors will most likely be helpless," Wrot said thoughtfully. "This is an opportunity to take prisoners, which comes very rarely when fighting the Ekhat."

She remembered the only time she'd ever seen Ekhat in person back in Terra's solar system and shuddered. She'd had nightmares about that grisly encounter for months. "But when we parleyed with the Interdict, the two speakers killed themselves afterward," she said, "because they couldn't endure the taint of simply having talked to us—and that meeting was of their own accord."

"You must take great care to prevent that," Wrot said to Tully, as the human struggled to get his arm through his jacket sleeve. "As Caitlin points out, they will wish only to die."

She took the jacket and held it for him. From the way he winced, he must be bruised from end to end. "Take me along!" she blurted. All three turned to stare at her, the doctor, Wrot, and Tully. "I'm trained as a diplomat. Let me try to talk them down from committing suicide."

"You've got to be kidding," Tully said, shaking his head. "Ed would skin me alive."

"And me as well," Wrot said. "At any rate, you are not here to speak to Ekhat. You and I both know that Ronz had a different mission in mind for you. It's necessary, more than ever at this point, for you to remain onboard and hold yourself ready, should the need for your skills arise."

He meant if they encountered the Lleix, but so far there had been no sign of them. Even if they had been here, the sight of five blasted Ekhat ships had probably sent them running for cover back out into the galaxy.

Caitlin sighed, able to tell from the stubborn angle of Wrot's head that she couldn't argue her way out of this. The old Jao might have gone "native" to a startling degree in the twenty-odd years he'd made his home on Earth, but at his core, he was solidly Jao. He had *oudh* in this situation, which meant she would stay on the *Lexington* and make herself of use any way he saw fit. She just hoped her opportunity came before she went stark raving bonkers from inactivity.

The great ship had taken damage, Dannet thought, but fortunately not too much. She prowled from station to station on the command deck, reading the stats for herself, craving unfiltered data. Most of the damage, they could repair themselves. The mission, whatever it was, could continue, though no one had seen fit to trust her with its true nature.

That bit of flotsam in low orbit, though, that was intriguing. It would be interesting to see what Baker Company found and what Wrot krinnu ava Terra would order her to do about it when they reported back.

She still felt some resentment that he had *oudh* and she did not. For all their fine words, Terra Taif had obviously not forgotten Oppuk krinnu ava Narvo's deeds. It would be a very long time, if ever, until her Narvo origins were forgiven and she was judged upon her own merits.

But…this had been a magnificent battle. And the ship which fought and won that battle—this odd, misshapen and hybrid vessel that she had initially thought was both grotesque and dubious— had proven itself. Her ship, now. Neither she nor anyone else would doubt that any longer. Her place in Terra Taif might be questionable, but not her place in the *Lexington*.

She had deduced Wrot was seeking contact with the species that had manned the other ship in the previous battle, but perhaps that vessel had only been passing through this system. She saw no evidence of them now, though, whoever they had been.

At any rate, diagnostics had detected a single habitable planet in this system. Nebula gases reflected all attempts to scan the surface from this distance, but after they had finished the tiresome mopping up from the battle, they would be at leisure to take a closer look. Perhaps that would yield some useful information.

Their trajectory was still not promising, Jihan told herself, but with precise firings of maneuvering thrusters, they might—just— intercept the wrecked piece of the Ekhat ship with its own orbit. So far, all efforts to contact one of their other Lleix vessels had failed. The hit they'd taken must have damaged the Starwarder transmitter. They were on their own.

Lliant by turns sulked in his seat, then stalked about the rapidly cooling cabin and harangued her. The surviving Starwarder, Hadata, simply hunched over the screens in a daze, punching up useless vectors, until Jihan finally shut the systems down to save the ship's precious power. What little they had might be enough, but then again it might not. They could not afford to waste any.

What they would do, should they be successful by using the Ekhat debris to keep from falling into the sun, she did not know.

That bit of ship was in a stable orbit, which was very unlikely without conscious direction. Someone had lived long enough to make it happen and she had no wish to make their acquaintance.

But it seemed, if the *Boh* were watching, they would.

PART V:
The Wreck

CHAPTER
22

As they approached the Ekhat wreck, Jihan was forced to divert more and more of their dwindling power supply to the shields. Solar radiation at this proximity was deadly.

Lliant was of little help, mostly just mumbling about the Ekhat, huddled in one of the chairs, his robes rucked up in a shocking fashion. Hadata had regained some of her composure, but continued to look to Jihan to direct their actions as the only Eldest on board.

The two remaining Starwarders were, as Lliant had reported, quite dead, one from a broken neck, the other from severe burns taken when the power surge had shorted out the electronics of her ship station. Jihan bullied Lliant until he stirred himself to remove their bodies to a storage area, then left him to fret.

With the application of an herbal pain-dampener, Jihan's arm proved not to be as badly damaged as she'd feared. Muscles and ligaments seemed to be torn, but she did not believe the bones were broken after all. She now had limited use of it, which was enough for the moment.

The ship's interior cooled rapidly with most of the power shunted to the shields and thrusters. Her bare toes curled against the numbingly chill metal underfoot. Her fingers stiffened, gone clumsy as a child's, increasingly hard to use. She had shut off the emergency lights, so now, seated in dimness, the only light came from the instrument panels. Their shadowed faces were uniformly grim.

She took successive readings as they neared, then her aureole flared as she detected energy traces from the Ekhat derelict. The hull had been holed by the newcomers' extraordinary weapons and could not possibly contain an atmosphere, yet electrical activity was evident. Could it be automatic, like the fragment of ship that had fired upon them? If so, they could be hastening to their deaths.

But they had no choice. Their trajectory had them headed into the sun, whatever they did with their limited resources. They had to make the best of what opportunities were given them, which admittedly, wasn't much. At this rate of power depletion, their shields would give out before they hit the photosphere itself. They needed to protect themselves from the radiation almost as badly as they needed to escape the sun's gravity. That derelict could shade them if they anchored on its dark side.

Sitting back, her head spinning, she turned to Hadata. "We need to secure this ship to the derelict."

The Starwarder raised her head, black eyes shining. Her aureole did not stir. "We have magnetics."

"Magnetics will be of no use," Lliant said bleakly, eyes slitted almost shut. He was rocking as though in pain. "Ekhat do not employ iron alloys in their ship construction."

"By some physical means then," Jihan said. "What can we use?" She touched the barely responsive Hadata. "Think!"

"We have—grapples," Hadata finally said. "But they cannot be deployed from inside. We would have to—" She broke off, staring at the rapidly approaching Ekhat wreckage in horror. "—suit up and go—outside—and attach them by hand."

"No!" Lliant lurched to his feet. His bruised face was contorted with emotion. "I will not!"

Jihan wished she had brought poor homely Pyr in the Ekhatlore's place. She had no doubt her *elian's* youngest would have put his hand to anything required without a single protest. "Is this *fear*?" she said. "From one who is convinced that he is already dead?"

"I will suit up," Hadata said quietly. "Even death out there will be better than falling into the sun."

"And so will he," Jihan said, "because if he refuses, I will push him out the air lock in his naked skin!"

His startled gaze turned to her. He was taller, more heavily built, and she had an injured arm, but she felt the blood pounding in her throat and knew that she had all-out fury on her side. She could see he recognized that too. "Well?"

Lliant rose and stripped out of his Ekhatlore robes with sharp, angry motions, casting the brocaded fabric aside. Then he and Hadata suited up while Jihan painstakingly maneuvered them ever closer to their objective with delicate firings of their remaining thrusters.

The Ekhat derelict grew larger and larger in the screen as they approached. It would dwarf them, once they came alongside. Jihan could not take her eyes off it. Were there survivors who had detected the little ship on a docking course that would rendezvous with them? Was anyone left alive to fire upon them?

If so, the Starwarder, the Ekhatlore, and the Jaolore were about to come nose to nose with the infamous great devils who ate the universe.

Kaln krinnu ava Krant was pleased to be assigned to an assault craft dispatched to investigate the Ekhat wreckage. Though the *Lexington* had taken damage, the immense ship had survived with minimal casualties. Compared to the previous battle, in which Krant had lost one vessel in transit, a second to Ekhat fire, and had a third irreparably damaged against only one of their enemy's ships, this action was a resounding success. The Terra-captain's audacity dazzled them all, and these humans—well, they fought much better than Kaln would have ever credited, had she not seen it for herself.

Mallu was assigned to this mission, too, though Jalta had been left behind with the medicians, recovering from a shoulder wound. She noticed, as Baker Company filed aboard down in one of the hangar bays, most of the rest on this mission were humans. But, there were also a smattering of Jao who had joined Terra Taif and now wore the dark-blue jinau trousers, and they all seemed to be in association. Not perfect, of course. She saw a bit of jostling for position on both sides, not to mention some brashly angled Jao ears, but the two species appeared to have a solid working relationship.

And, even more intriguing, these humans didn't look down on Krant either. She remembered how Tully had listened to her ideas about improving the hoist. That would never have happened on a Jao ship, especially one not owned by her kochan.

It was possible that humans just didn't know enough about Jao to understand Krant's low ranking, but, whatever the reason, the end results were the same. For the first time in her life, she felt like an equal among others outside her kochan.

Lieutenant Caewithe Miller settled on a bench seat next to Kaln, checking a hand-held. She was diminutive, even for a human, but Kaln had watched her direct her subordinates very capably.

"Have you ever seen an Ekhat?" the human female asked, turning dead-white eyes with those strange centers upon Kaln. The color varied among humans. This one's were a shade of blue.

Kaln's good ear flattened in *surprise* and she felt even the damaged one stir a bit. Maybe sensation would return to it after all. "Only dead ones," she said.

Miller's posture seemed almost *attentive*. "They look huge in the vids."

"Most are very large, yes," Kaln said.

Miller glanced over at Tully, then grimaced, baring her teeth. "Not as large as Paul Bunyan, I bet."

"Pool—Bantyam?" Kaln tried to replicate the sounds, but did not think she got them quite right.

Warning beeps sounded. The hatch closed, then the assault craft lurched forward, heading for the retracting hanger bay doors. "You have not yet heard of Paul Bunyan," Miller said, "and Babe the Blue Ox?"

"Are they members of the *Lexington* crew?" Kaln had not been concerned with names when she worked down in the magazine with the gun mount crew. Mostly, since coming onboard, she had dealt with Major Tully, and he had never mentioned these particular individuals.

"No, no," Miller said. She glanced at a device on her wrist. "Well, we have some time to—" She grimaced again. "—kill, as a human would say, before we reach our objective, so let me tell you about Paul Bunyan and Babe."

Kill time? Kaln had heard that humans were time-blind, but why did that make them think they could actually do away with any portion of it? Perhaps they were crazy, after all.

"This happened long ago," Miller said, "on Terra, when humans moved into a wilderness and needed to cut down a forest quickly. Paul was what we call a 'lumberjack.'"

She went on to relate an improbable but quite interesting tale.

Evidently conditions on Terra had once favored the exceptional growth of occasional individuals. On a trading run, Kaln had once seen examples of gigantism on a lush planet that belonged to the kochan of Hij, but those marine creatures were scarce, having been hunted into near extinction. This "blue ox" sounded much bigger anyway. She listened carefully to Miller's soft voice with its pronounced Terran accent, trying her best to understand, and soon realized that other humans seated close to them were paying attention, too.

By the end of the narration, some were even adding details, as evidently the female's memory proved faulty in several respects. This Pool Buntyam supposedly had an enormous appetite and consumed amazing amounts of some comestible called "flapjacks." Once he had even spilled an entire boatload of a vegetable called "peeze" into a hot spring to create a huge amount of "soup" for his workers.

Then several jinau, both male, argued vociferously, about the exact size of this "ox," which, Kaln gathered from the tasks it reportedly carried out, was some sort of beast of burden. One human said it was "seven feet" tall, while the other insisted no, no, it measured "seven feet" just between its eyes.

Kaln blinked. "What do the records say?"

Miller exhaled a long sighing breath. "The records from that era were very poorly maintained," she admitted. "So no one can say who is right."

"Perhaps we can find stored images," Kaln said.

Miller closed one eye in what seemed to be a deliberate, if baffling, gesture. Her fellows chuffed. "Perhaps," she said.

Kaln realized then that they were all amused, even the jinau Jao. Not a word of that improbable story was true. Evidently, humans relished the stringing together of such impossibilities. It was just *ollnat*, but cleverly done. Kaln had always had a secret fondness for the invention of such tales, even though the practice was considered juvenile. She would remember that for the future and concoct some wild series of events for their ears.

"Now," Caewithe Miller said, "would you like to hear the story of Snow White?"

That equally unlikely tale was just ending when Tully came back, Mallu behind him. "Listen up, people," he said in his heavily-accented Jao. "We are closing with our target." He paused, gazing around at the assembled jinau and Krants. "Preliminary readings indicate that there well may be survivors on the derelict."

A murmur arose from the humans. The Jao spoke with their bodies instead, indicating *unease, fierce-determination*, or *willingness-to-be-of-use*. Kaln realized her own lines and angles had gone to *stubborn-pride* and made herself assume something less provocative. She had no wish to have her ears boxed and Mallu certainly would have disciplined her, had he noticed.

"We have about *fifteen minutes*," Tully said as the craft fired maneuvering jets. The specific terms were gibberish to Kaln, but she got the sense that the mission would be underway very soon.

"Make ready," Tully said. He returned forward.

You cannot be ready for the Ekhat, she thought. She felt the moment approaching as she studied her fellow Krants. Each had fallen into a single posture now, as had she, as though they all had but a single thought between them: *readiness-to-die*.

Mallu got up and followed Tully aft. He'd had an idea and wanted to discuss it. Lingering just outside the cockpit, he caught the Terran's attention and then Tully motioned him forward into the cramped space separated from the main cabin by a bulkhead.

"Yes, Krant-Captain?" the human said, settling back into his seat across from the pilot.

This was a delicate matter, Mallu thought, and he was not a trained negotiator, but Krant had no other official voice here but his. He would just have to do his best. "That derelict is valuable," he said, his lines gone to *desirous-of-favor*, for all the good it would do. As nearly as he could tell, humans were oblivious to the niceties of bodyspeak, outside of a few like Caitlin Kralik.

"Really?" Tully scratched the yellow thatch on his head, then turned to the growing image on the viewscreen. "No one told me that."

"By being first to investigate," Mallu said, "Baker Company will receive booty rights."

"Thank you for enlightening me," Tully said, then picked up a sheaf of papers and leafed through them.

Now, thought Mallu. He only hoped he had the right words. Krant had not exactly ingratiated itself with this particular Terran so far, but Tully was a member of Aille krinnu ava Terra's personal service and therefore highly regarded. "But Baker Company is not the only group present on this mission." He glanced back at the crowded cabin. "Krant is here too, though admittedly in fewer numbers."

Tully turned back to him with just a hint of *inquiry* in his angles. That seeming posture must be only by chance, Mallu cautioned himself, and then pressed on. "Krant suffered a hard blow when we lost three ships to this nebula," Mallu said. "We are…"

This would be almost impossible to say to another Jao, but Tully was different. "A poor kochan. Very poor. Our two planets do not produce much in the way of exportable wealth."

Tully's head dipped. "You want a share of the spoils," he said.

"Yes, Major," Mallu said.

"Is that common practice among the Jao?"

How else would it be done? Mallu wondered. But he had enough experience with humans by now to realize that some Jao practices he'd always taken for granted, as if they were a law of nature, might have alternatives.

"Yes. The kochan present at the action divide whatever spoils might be obtained in accordance with their respective numbers."

That was…not quite a lie, but close enough to make Mallu uncomfortable. The reality, as all Jao knew, was that numbers as such were only one of the determinant factors involved in these affairs. Status, resources committed, all those things also came into play. Put so many Pluthrak or Narvo or Dano to divide the spoils with an equal number of Jao from Krant or another desperately poor kochan, and the members of the great kochan would come away with most of it.

But, at least formally, humans placed great store by the social virtues they called "equality" and "fairness." So perhaps in this situation, Krant might be able to get a better outcome.

The human pressed his fingertips together and bowed his head, obviously considering. "I do not understand the way these things are handled among the Jao," he said finally, "and I do not wish to make a mistake, but I will certainly consult with Caitlin Kralik when we return. She is much better versed in such matters."

He gazed up then into Mallu's face. If only Terran ears were more expressive, Mallu thought, then he would have some idea of what Tully was thinking.

"And I would need to consult with representatives of both of Terra's taifs about the distribution of any wealth earned in this action," Tully said. His mouth had a strange quirk. "Perhaps, though, something could be done about your ships. We might even be able to work out some kind of deal to construct new ones to replace those that were lost."

"Like the *Lexington*?" Mallu said, his ears now frankly *astonished*. With even one ship like the *Lexington*, Krant would no longer be poor.

"I think it comes down to association," Tully said. "Would Krant wish to associate with Terra Taif?"

Mallu stared at him. *Association?* With this bizarre new taif, most of whose members were humans and not Jao? Had someone asked him the question before he arrived on Terra, Mallu would have dismissed it immediately as madness. But now...

He'd only been thinking in terms of getting as big a share for Krant as possible, of whatever spoils might be derived from the Ekhat derelict. But now that Tully had raised the issue of association, Mallu found himself intrigued.

And then, as he continued to think about it while Tully waited silently, his intrigue deepened. He could see how far removed his initial notions—prejudices, to call things by their right name—had been from reality.

Item one. Terra Taif was certainly not as wealthy and powerful as one of the great kochan like Narvo or Pluthrak, but it was far more wealthy and powerful than any single-system kochan Mallu had ever heard of. It was certainly wealthier and mightier than Krant, which had been driven to the point of desperation by the loss of three ships, any one of which would have been dwarfed by *Lexington*. And Mallu knew that Terra Taif was planning a *fleet* of Lexingtons.

Item two. For all the derision that most kochan felt toward Terra Taif, the two greatest of those kochan—Pluthrak and Narvo—were already in association with it. The name-founder of the hybrid kochan-to-be was Aille, once a scion of Pluthrak recognized as *namth camiti*. And while Aille had formally severed his ties to Pluthrak, it was perfectly obvious that the relationship remained close and warm.

Narvo...The common assumption was that Narvo's association with Terra was a formality. Something Narvo had been forced into because of the shame brought upon the great kochan by Oppuk. But the more he saw of the situation, the more Mallu was coming to think that Narvo was quite serious about developing the association—if for no other reason than the fact it brought with it, indirectly, an association with Pluthrak.

How else explain Terra-Captain Dannet? Her abilities as a military leader were now obvious—and must have been obvious to Narvo itself when the kochan sent her here. Surrendered her, and her talents, to the exotic new taif. Talents which, to a kochan like Narvo, were more precious than anything.

Third item—the Bond. For the first time in Jao history, the Bond of Ebezon had agreed to affiliate with a kochan or taif. While the affiliation was understood to be temporary, there was bound to remain a residue and a closeness even after the affiliation was formally severed. And the Bond was at least as powerful, in military terms, as any of the great kochan, if not perhaps as wealthy.

It was astonishing, really. Now that experience allowed Mallu to see things clearly, it was obvious that Terra Taif—dismissed by most Jao as an irrelevant freak—was already better positioned in Jao society than the great majority of kochan.

It was certainly better positioned than Krant! Which meant that Krant would gain greatly from an association with Terra Taif.

Allowing, of course, for two unknown factors—the prejudice of Krant's own elders, and the attitudes of Terra itself. Why would they have any great desire to associate with such as Krant?

As he ruminated, Tully had been watching him closely. Now, he made that lip-twisting gesture—a "smile," they called it—that seemed the most fluid and varied of all the human gestures.

"Interesting idea, isn't it?" said Tully. "I'll raise it with Caitlin, first chance I get. And, one way or another, I'll do my best to make sure Krant gets a fair share of the loot." The lips twisted a different way. "Insofar as you can apply the term 'loot' to what looks like a wreck, anyway. Speaking of which..."

Tully cocked his head sideways a little. Mallu wasn't certain, but he thought that gesture was the human version of *sudden-consideration*.

"We're supposed to try to capture a live Ekhat," Tully said.

"Yes, I know. It is not likely we will succeed."

"Won't break my heart if we don't, either. But we're supposed to try, so try we will. But I've *seen* one of those monsters while it was alive—two of them, in fact—and it'd be easier to capture a Tyrannosaurus alive than one of them."

Before Mallu could ask, Tully shook his head. "Never mind the reference. Very big predatory animal. The point is, it won't do any good to point a laser at one of them and say 'hands up.' We've got to take it down in a way that completely immobilizes it *without* just killing it."

The solution was obvious, of course. Almost impossible to do, but obvious. "We need to shoot off all of its limbs. Otherwise it will suicide."

"What I figure—and there's no way we'll be able to do that with lasers. So."

Tully bestowed on Mallu a variety of big smile—"grin," he thought it was called—that the Krant-captain did not think boded well for his immediate future.

"I'm putting you in charge of the special bell-the-Ekhat detail."

Mallu wondered what bells had to do with anything involved. Tully turned away. "Follow me. I want to introduce you to the key members of your team."

He led Mallu to a small dining area, what the humans called a "mess hall." Nine human soldiers and two Jao were sitting at the tables.

"Bringmann. Kelly. Greer. Front and center."

Three of the human soldiers stood up. All of them were male, and two of them were very large for humans.

Tully waved his hand at Mallu. "I believe you know Krant-Captain Mallu. I'm putting him in charge of you guys. Your team—you'll love this, boys—is assigned to capture an Ekhat. Alive."

The faces of all the human soldiers became distorted. Mallu didn't recognize any specific body gesture, but the gist of it was clear enough—the human equivalent of the *shocked-disbelief* posture of the two Jao soldiers.

Tully shrugged. "Look, the orders come from on high. Don't take it personally, Bringmann. Mallu's got experience fighting them and you don't."

The smallest of the three standing jinau nodded.

"Krant-Captain, these two corporals"—Tully pointed to the two large ones—"are Thomas Kelly and Dennis Greer. They're the unit's recoilless rifle specialists."

Mallu stared at them. They were easy to tell apart, because Kelly was very dark-skinned. "And a recoilless rifle is...?"

"Hard to describe. Kelly, Greer, show him."

✳   ✳   ✳

Once Mallu saw the weapons and had their operation explained to him, he felt a surge of sympathy for the Jao soldiers who'd fought in the conquest of Terra. Like most Jao who'd been far from the scene, his impression of Terran military capability had been shaped by the knowledge that they used kinetic weapons almost exclusively. Primitive stuff, as you'd expect for a primitive species.

Watching what the *Lexington*'s big guns had done to five Ekhat ships had drastically shifted his views on the matter, of course. But seeing such an obviously deadly version of a kinetic weapon adapted for ground combat brought it even closer to home.

Such a recoilless rifle—the jinau called it "an 84mm goose"— had originally been designed to destroy human tanks, apparently. But they'd adapted the munitions to serve for shipboard operations. In fact, they had a bewildering variety of munitions, whose distinctions—HEAT, HEP-T, Anti-Personnel Tracer, Armor-Piercing, and there were two or three others—soon had Mallu hopelessly confused.

It did at least become clear why both of the soldiers were so large, by human standards. The concept of a "recoilless" rifle in microgravity was...

Very flexible.

The one named Dennis Greer grinned widely when the subject came up. "Yeah, well. It's tricky. If you don't know what you're doing, firing a goose in null gravity is likely to leave you spinning in circles."

"With a busted neck," added the other one, Thomas Kelly. "It helps, of course, to have as much body mass as possible."

Mallu had gotten intrigued by now. The weapons might actually have a chance of attaining their goal. And he could see other uses for them. "Why not use Jao soldiers, then?"

Both human soldiers chuckled. "Jao don't really take to the things," said Kelly.

"Bunch of snobs, you ask me," said Greer.

Mallu looked from one to the other. Then, even though he suspected the subtlety would be missed by the two soldiers, adopted the posture which he thought came closest to the meaning of their chuckles. *Amusement-at-folly.*

"You have simply never met the right Jao," he said. "Wait here."

✳   ✳   ✳

He came back shortly with two of his Krant soldiers in tow. Both of them were large by Jao standards, which meant they were much larger than even Kelly and Greer.

"These are Urta and Naddo." He pointed out one from the other. "Teach them how to use the gooses."

He interpreted the expressions on Kelly and Greer's faces as the human equivalent of *expectation-of-silliness-from-others.* "You need not be apprehensive," he said. "We are Krant. Not—what was the term?"

"Snobs?"

"Yes, that one. Tully once told me we are hillbillies. He was rather exasperated, I believe, so he added the terms 'stubborn' and 'ignorant' as qualifiers. But I got the sense that 'hillbillies' itself was not derogatory."

Kelly's dark face displayed a large smile. The *grin* variety of the expression. "Not coming from Major Tully, anyway. You hear it coming from one of my homeys, be a different story."

The meaning of the last statement was obscure. But it was clear from the subtle shift in the expressions of the two human soldiers that they were willing to try to teach the two Jao how to use the very un-Jao-like weapons.

When Mallu reported back to Tully, he found the human officer in the assault craft's rather small command deck. The monstrous outline of the Ekhat derelict filled the screen now, backlit by the boiling inferno of the system's sun. The pilot, a human female named Kristal Dalgetty, looked over her shoulder at them. "Strap in, sirs. We are about to fire maneuvering jets."

As he strapped himself into his seat, Tully's mind was on the recent conversation with Mallu, not the approaching Ekhat.

Association with Krant...

On the one hand, it was obviously a dirt-poor kochan. Dismissed by most Jao, if not exactly sneered at, and with very little in the way of resources.

Fine. They were a bunch of backwoods hillbillies. Who cared? Not Tully, for damn sure. He'd spent most of his life as a Resistance fighter in the mountains. If not quite a hillbilly himself, at least a first cousin. Now that he'd fought alongside them, the Krant were okay in his book.

Besides, Terra Taif was fighting for status and respectability, far more than it needed wealth and resources. The fact was, although few of the Jao kochan were astute enough to realize it, that with its enormous population—Terra was by far the most densely inhabited planet in the known galaxy—and its technical advancement, Terra Taif was already more resource-rich than all but the great kochan.

What it *really* needed was simply...association itself. Terra Taif needed to develop the vast and rich network of connections and alliances and agreements and quid-pro-quos with other kochan that was the single most important fount of power and influence among the Jao. And if that started with bringing into its orbit an impoverished kochan on the fringes of Jao society, so be it.

Baby steps, and all that. As the assault craft neared the hideous-looking Ekhat wreck, Tully reviewed one hoary axiom after another.

The longest voyage starts with a single step. You do what you can.

There were a lot of them. Enough to keep his nerves steady, thankfully. That damn derelict really was uglier than sin. What was it about the Ekhat, anyway? The maniacs couldn't seem to do or make anything that didn't have a horrible appearance. If they made mashed potatoes, the mashed potatoes would look scary.

Jihan was anxious as she struggled into stiff protective clothing so that they could exit the vessel and attach the tethers. None of her experience as a Starsifter included actually working outside a ship, though, as a safety measure, she had been trained in the correct procedure. Hadata assisted her, but Lliant had turned his back, steadfastly not-seeing her, as though he had the right to *oyas-to* in this situation, which he most assuredly did not.

It did not matter, she told herself, easing the damaged arm into its sleeve. Nothing mattered except that they survive the next few breaths, and then the ones following. And, to do so, they had to clamp this ship to the derelict before they tumbled into the sun's photosphere or all the bad manners in the universe would make no difference.

Hadata settled Jihan's helmet onto her shoulders, then closed the seals. She heard a whoosh as the suit's systems activated, then she was alone with the sound of her own breathing. It seemed quite thunderous, but that was probably a byproduct of her tightly controlled fear.

The three of them walked clumsily then to the air lock, Lliant hanging back. She motioned him in before her, not trusting that he would actually leave the ship if she lost sight of him, even briefly. Once he was in the air lock, she stepped in and closed the door. The system cycled, and then they were face to face with the sun with its overwhelming, blazing presence and the looming Ekhat derelict. Despite the energy signatures she had detected from within, the wreck was holed, pitted, and scorched. It looked thoroughly dead from this vantage point.

They clipped their tethers to the Starwarder ship and then activated the suits' tiny maneuvering jets to launch themselves across. It was terrible and wonderful, all at the same time. Though the situation was indeed dire, Jihan felt strangely free in that moment, and the sun, on the other side of the wreck, was gloriously huge, swirling and flowing, in constant motion, almost alive itself. The nebula's gases prevented those on the planet's surface from ever seeing the solar system's star this clearly.

"It is so beautiful," she murmured, then realized she was going to miss the derelict and corrected her angle with a burst from her jets.

"You are insane," Lliant said, landing awkwardly feet-first on the wreck. "It is no wonder the Starsifters cast you out!"

Jihan made contact too, flexing her knees, then sprawled full-length across the alien hull, wringing a wave of pain from her injured arm. Hadata, wiser and more experienced, had halted just short of the wreck and now hovered, seeking the best spot to anchor her cable.

Each tether terminated in an explosive bolt. Of course, Jihan thought, if anything were still alive in there, sinking bolts into their hull might attract unwelcome attention. But they had no choice. It was either this or die in very short order. No matter how beautiful the sun was, she had no wish to dive into its heart.

Hadata activated her bolt and it burst through the plating. She tested it, then turned to Lliant. "Hurry up," the Starwarder said.

He knelt to position his, then fumbled the release, lost hold of the tether, and floated away from the hull. He was terrified, Jihan thought, feeling almost sorry for him. The Ekhatlore had studied the great devils all his life, but had never expected to come this close to them.

She edged closer to assist him. With an angry oath, he pushed her away. She spun off the surface, but fortunately had enough presence of mind to keep hold of her tether. Even without gravity, spinning, so that her visual field was filled with the ship—the derelict—the ship—in rapid succession made her dizzy. After a moment, though, she regained stability with her maneuvering jets.

"Idiot!" Hadata was saying. "You could have killed her!"

"What does it matter? We are all dead anyway!" With a choked cry, Lliant cast away his tether and Hadata launched herself to retrieve it. Face averted, the Ekhatlore floated above the derelict, arms clenched across his chest.

"You certainly *will* be," Jihan said, as the blood pounded through her veins, "if you try something like that again. I do not care how frightened you are!" Behind her lay the immense blackness of space laced with red and blue gasses from the nebula. Before her hung the sun and the damaged derelict. It was all overwhelming.

"Frightened?" Lliant twisted clumsily to face her, more than a body length above the pitted hull. Through his helmet, she could see how his aureole was flattened against his face. "The dead cannot be frightened."

Hadata fired the second bolt into the derelict, then turned to Jihan. "Let me have yours," she said.

"No, I can do it," Jihan said and maneuvered with her jets to return to the wreck. She selected a third site for the tether, roughly equidistant from the two bolts already seated, and had just positioned hers against the hull when a suited creature thrust its head through one of the jagged holes.

Lliant shrieked and then jetted back toward the Starwarder vessel.

Hands shaking, Jihan fired the third bolt into the hull.

CHAPTER

23

Jihan tested the line with her good arm and found it solid, then the creature—whatever it was—bowled into her and she floated away from the derelict again.

She twisted around. Lliant was headed toward the air lock and Jihan had no doubt that he was fully capable of sealing her and Hadata outside to save his own skin. "Go after him!" she called to the Starwarder.

Her attacker was too small to be an Ekhat, according to the images she had studied. Neither did it resemble a Jao. Its torso was long and sinuous with four stubby limbs a quarter of the length of her own, and it was shrouded in a white casing with a clear bubble on the end, not a proper environment suit with a helmet like the three Lleix wore. It would be about a third of her height, she thought, if they stood face to face, and had unblinking red eyes.

"What in the name of the *Boh* is it?" Hadata called as the beast ineffectively pummeled Jihan with all four limbs.

Terrified, Jihan kicked it away so that it sailed toward the end of the derelict. She was drifting backwards then and had to stabilize her position with the maneuvering jets.

When she could spare the attention again, Lliant had reentered the Starwarder ship and Hadata had propelled herself halfway back. Jihan feared the creature would right itself, as she had, and attack again, but it just skimmed on past the end of the derelict, limbs flailing. She watched, sick with fear, the rasp of her own overwrought breathing harsh in her ears.

Her attacker had no control devices, she realized, nor any safety line anchoring it to the ship. By thoughtlessly jumping her like that, it had just condemned itself to orbit the sun for a short time, then burn to cinders.

"Come on!" Hadata called. "There may be more of them!"

Shaking, Jihan used her jets to follow the other two back to their own ship. She saw Lliant reach the controls inside the air lock first. He appeared to be trying to trigger the seal without waiting for the other two, but Hadata got there in time to jerk him off and take over. Once Jihan made it inside the air lock, the Starwarder ran the cycle and then they were safe again, for the moment.

The artificial gravity inside the cabin felt wonderful, though the air was cold and stale. She no longer had the terrible sensation of endlessly falling and the walls blessedly protected her from the sight of the bloated sun, so dangerously near.

"What *was* that creature?" Hadata said, as she helped Jihan struggle one-armed out of her suit.

Lliant was already standing naked before a console, his shoulders hunched, his backbone knobby beneath his beautifully silver skin. He reached for his robes with trembling hands. "It was probably an Anj," he said, "one of the client species of The Melody."

With a jerk, he pulled the brocaded robes over his arms and shoulders, then fiddled with the draping, taking great care with the folds as though such niceties mattered out here, so very far from eyes that judged one's worth by such things. "The beasts are considered little more than vermin by their Ekhat masters, entirely disposable. Ekhatlore has never been certain that they were more than half-sapient, trainable, but not independently intelligent."

So it had given its life for masters who cared nothing for it just to perish in that gruesome fashion. Jihan shuddered.

"Now, what, Eldest?" Hadata asked, as Jihan kicked off the clumsy boots that were part of the environment suit.

She had been so focused upon avoiding their headlong plunge into the blazing heart of the sun, she hadn't thought much beyond stabilizing the ship. Jihan half-fell into one of the empty chairs, legs shaking, her aureole barely able to flutter, and stared at the screen. Her wrenched arm ached and she cradled it across her chest.

"We should check the most probable vectors between here and Valeron," she said finally. "Even though we cannot receive messages, at least part of our request for assistance may have transmitted. Perhaps one of the Starsifter or Starwarder ships is on its way to pick us up."

Hadata went back to the pilot's station, and then Jihan regarded Lliant, remembering how in his panic he had thrust her away. Any number of factors could have intervened, and then she could be falling into the sun along with the unfortunate Anj this very moment. Anger clouds the reason, she told herself. Sayr would have known what to say in this situation, how to impart wisdom without irrevocably shaming the miscreant.

But all she could think of was the endless depths and the roaring furnace to which the Ekhatlore had nearly doomed her. For his part, he hunched over his console, punching up stats, taking useless readings. She wanted to strike him, but that was not what an Eldest did when youngers behaved badly, and so she held onto that thought until her shaking subsided.

"We need food," she said finally and flicked her fingers at Lliant. "Go through the supplies and see what is available."

He rose without protest and went to the rear of the cabin.

Suddenly Hadata leapt out of her seat, staring at her viewscreen.

"Is someone coming?" Jihan asked. She struggled to her feet, wincing at her wrenched arm, then crossed the cabin to peer at the screen herself.

Hadata's hands twitched at her robes. "Yes," she said slowly, "but not one of ours." The Starwarder's eyes narrowed so that Jihan could barely see their gleaming blackness. "Three ships, all larger than any of our Starwarder or Starsifter designs, approaching on a vector that indicates they launched from that enormous newcomer."

The aliens had dispatched their own ships? Jihan tried to make sense of that. "What do they want?" Not to rescue three desperate Lleix, she was certain of that. Even if they'd intercepted their call for assistance, they wouldn't have been able to translate it.

Lliant returned with three dried rations packets in his hands. "They come to destroy what is left of the Ekhat vessel, of course," he said bleakly. "The very same hulk to which we just anchored ourselves. With care, they will be able to take us all out with a single volley."

He was most likely right, Jihan thought. What other reason could there be? "And, yet," she said, "if they merely want to destroy the derelict, could they not safely target it from their primary vessel? Why send three smaller, less heavily armed ships into potential danger? After such a battle, they can be under no misapprehension that the Ekhat will not attack if they are able."

"Perhaps they intend to parley with them," Hadata said, "or take prisoners."

"No one takes Ekhat prisoner," Lliant said with a weary shrug. "When they are cornered, they terminate themselves. They cannot bear the taint of contact with what they consider to be lower species. They even terminate themselves on the rare occasions that they initiate communication."

"We should stay in our ship and see what happens," Hadata said. "We are quite small compared to the derelict. It is entirely possible that they will not even notice us, concealed as we are in its shadow."

"And then what?" Jihan said. "We skulk here and die in perfect peace?"

Hadata's aureole sank.

"They are the Ekhat's enemy," Jihan continued, "as are we. They might render us aid, if we so requested."

"By the size and design of that monstrous ship, all we know for certain about them is that they are powerful." Lliant turned in his seat to stare at them with smoldering black eyes. "Power cares nothing for the weak. Whether they detect us or not, they will destroy us too when they take out the Ekhat wreck. Not that it matters." He twisted away again. "We are already dead."

"Stop saying that!" Jihan's anger resurged. "You sound like one of the hopeless unchosen from the *dochaya*, worse even! I have found them at least willing to put their hands to whatever is required, despite their unfortunate situation. I should have brought one of them instead!"

Hadata gave her a questioning look, but she ignored it. "I think," Jihan said, "we must contact these aliens, or else we will die, either like that Anj burning up in the sun, or when our air and power and supplies are exhausted."

"But what could we possibly say to them," Hadata said, "and how will we communicate? They most certainly will not speak Lleix or Ekhat."

"When the moment comes," Jihan said, "we will find a way to make ourselves understood." She tapped a finger against her forehead. "Two of us will go aboard the wreck to observe, if they do indeed dock with it. The other will stay behind."

"I will stay here," Lliant said.

"No, you will not," Jihan said. "There is no way I can trust you out of my sight."

The lead assault craft jinau pilot, Kristal Dalgetty, spotted what looked like a hangar bay on the sunward side of the derelict, so Tully authorized that approach.

"We will have to blast the door, sir," she said. "And that's bound to attract attention if any of them are left and they haven't already detected us."

"I'd bet a hundred dollars they know we're here." Tully stuck his head around the bulkhead. "Krant-Captain, come forward."

Mallu lurched to his feet and made his way past the rows of bench seats. All the eyes followed him, both Terran and Jao. "Yes, Major?"

"You have more experience at this sort of thing," Tully said. "What recommendations do you have about boarding an Ekhat ship?"

"Avoid it if at all possible," Mallu said immediately. Green lightning danced in those black, black eyes.

Tully barked a laugh, then cut himself off when it was all too apparent that Mallu had not intended the comment as humorous. "Unfortunately, in this case, we cannot avoid boarding since those are our orders."

Mallu sighed. That, at least, was a mannerism that Jao shared with humans and usually signified about the same thing. His ears canted at half-mast. "That should be a storage bay for the smaller ships they employ from time to time. They will defend it vigorously, if any of the crew have survived, but it should not have defensive weapon emplacements inside."

"All right, then, strap in," Tully said. "We will use that area as our insertion point." Mallu retreated as the pilot relayed the commands to the other two assault craft.

It required considerable laser fire from two of the three assault ships before the door was compromised. When the debris field cleared, Tully could see it hadn't burned cleanly off, but hung from what must be the Ekhat version of hinges. "Pretty solid construction," he murmured, gazing at the screen.

Mallu returned, his body gone to what Tully was fairly certain was simple, unadulterated *question*.

"We can get in," Tully said, "but not by landing the ships. We will have to transfer outside." He considered the situation. It wouldn't do to risk their transport to the Ekhat's nonexistent mercy anyway.

He nodded at Dalgetty. "Patch me in with the other two ships."

The pilot bent her sandy-haired head, working for a moment, then gave Tully a thumbs-up.

"This is Major Tully," he said. "We will board the Ekhat derelict, starting with this ship. Once all combat personnel have unloaded, pilots are to stand off two kilometers and wait for my orders."

He hesitated. "I know it will be difficult, but if anything is left alive over there, we want to keep them alive. Do what you can to make it happen, but not at the sacrifice of your own hide. Any questions?"

Nobody spoke up, so he had Dalgetty shut off the circuit. "Take us in," he said, then went back to join his troops.

Third-Note-Ascending marked the approach of the three vessels in the viewing tank, which still functioned in intermittent flickers. It was growing cold in the pod as environmental controls failed.

Five ships lost! Against a solitary alien vessel, albeit one large and heavily armed. It was hard to reconcile that development with any melody. The lost note still warbled inside her mind.

But now, when she could no longer go after them, the sub-sapients were coming to her. Anticipation sang through her blood, lightening her burden. She would meet them with Half, along with what Anj remained, and demonstrate what it meant to be part of the unfolding Ekha.

She tapped into her protective suit's audio circuits and directed all surviving serviles to assemble in the conductor's pod. Their certain terror was a pleasant leitmotif to the broad underlying bass line of the coming havoc. She had slaughtered all who had dared enter her presence earlier. The Anj knew that, but they would come anyway, because such was their place in the great composition.

Joy surged through Third and at least a hint of it must have made it through to Half, because he suddenly rejoined her. Their mental fields flared, then snapped back together. With so much to look forward to, it was hard even to regret the lost note.

CHAPTER
24

Tully had had a fair amount of training using suit jets to maneuver in open space. "Fair amount," at least, as his Jao instructors measured such things—which Tully himself thought woefully inadequate. But, there it was. Just one of a multitude of differences, some blatant and some subtle, between the way humans and Jao looked at things.

So, he spent a fair amount of his time passing from the assault craft to the Ekhat wreck cursing those same Jao instructors. He jetted over with the first group, as a display of leadership, although he mostly succeeded in delaying them. At one point, Mallu had to rescue him from one particularly ill-timed burst of his maneuvering jets.

Good thing he did, too, because otherwise Tully would have passed out of the shadow of the Ekhat wreck into full sunlight. That could have gotten dicey, very quickly. Theoretically, the suits could withstand solar radiation this intense for several minutes. But that was theory, and the theory of Jao engineers, at that. The suit was of human manufacture but much of the design was Jao—and Jao engineers had notions concerning "safety margins" that humans considered preposterous.

His jinau troops, along with the Krants, followed him silently, though he could just imagine the cursing that must be going on inside their heads also. But he didn't have much sympathy for them. Every soldier in his unit, human and Jao alike, had had quite a bit more training in ship-to-ship assault than he had. What made the whole thing ironic, in a bitter sort of way that Tully didn't find the least bit amusing, was that Tully himself had ordered the extensive training regimen. And had then—here he took some time to curse assorted civilian powers-that-be—been taken away from the training himself so that he could go play diplomat with the Resistance.

He saved a reasonable portion of his silent cursing for Terra-Captain Dannet, whom he'd enjoy giving a kick in the proverbial pants for placing his people in this situation. A few of the *Lexington*'s well-placed sabot rounds could have sent this hulk spiraling down into the sun where anything still twitching in there would never have troubled Jao or human again.

But they wanted to freaking *talk* to them? Ekhat were howling mad. Even Tully, who had once been dragged along on a mission to parley with the maniac faction that called itself the Interdict, knew that. How could Dannet be deluded enough to think anyone could actually have a conversation with one?

He pulled himself through the opening they had spotted that seemed to lead into the wreck's interior. It was a big, jagged tear in the alien ship's wall. From the looks of the damage, the tear had been caused by a massive internal explosion. The walls had been blown outward, not inward. One or more sabot rounds must have ignited something inside the ship when they pierced the walls.

That wouldn't have been hard to do. One of the vivid memories Tully had of his one visit to a functioning Ekhat vessel was the sheer *stink* of the thing. The interior of Ekhat ships were filled with organic compounds that no human or even Jao commander would have tolerated for a moment. Leaving aside the stench, such poorly contained substances were *dangerous*. But leave it to the Ekhat to fly around the galaxy in what amounted to a gasoline-filled tin can.

And they wanted to *talk* to these maniacs?

About what? "Why are you crazy, Mr. Ekhat?" If they got an answer, it would be incomprehensible anyway.

A large number of his soldiers were already inside the wreck. Most of them, in fact; Tully's "lead" had turned into a trail in the course of his clumsy suit-jetting across from the assault craft.

"The area is secure, sir," said Lieutenant Miller.

Tully took a little time to look around. What seemed to be green emergency lights glimmered along the curving walls, providing a minimal sickly illumination. The cavernous hangar interior was littered with twisted hulks that might have once been small ships, all drifting in a giant mishmash because the artificial gravity had failed. It looked like an automobile junkyard put through a giant blender. Bodies of creatures floated here and there.

One of them was recognizably Ekhat, despite being very badly damaged. The sheer size of the carcass was enough to establish its identity. According to the Jao, no other sapient species that they'd ever encountered was even close to being the physical size of the Ekhat. But most of the corpses were obviously not Ekhat. They were the torn and mangled bodies of creatures smaller than humans. Gray bodies, from what Tully could see through tears in their covering; long torsos, stubby arms and legs. The one face he could see that wasn't badly damaged reminded him of a weird cross between a caterpillar's head and that of an English bulldog.

But, no matter the species, the corpses had all suffered severe decompression on top of a lot of battle damage and were, in a word, disgusting. Gore, some of it a viscous white, but mostly an unsettling off-shade of red, drifted in globules through the debris.

Even Tully, who had fought with the Resistance for years and seen his share of death and injuries, found his stomach queasy. *Focus!* he told himself.

"All right, people. Let's move out toward that opening over there." Realizing, as soon as he said the words, that many of his soldiers couldn't see where he was pointing, he added: "Ten o'clock from the opening we came through."

"What is 'ten o'oclock'?" demanded one of the Jao, mangling the English term badly. It sounded like Kaln's voice.

Tully tried to find a Jao equivalent but couldn't. "Never mind," he said. "Miller, take the lead. The rest of you, just follow."

The redheaded lieutenant led her unit toward the distant opening. "Look for ones in spacesuits," Tully added. "Nothing could have survived in here without one."

"Yes, sir," said Miller patiently. The tone of her voice, though, practically dripped exasperation for superior officers who insisted on stating the obvious.

Tully chuckled. Damn, he liked that woman. Too bad they were in the same chain of command.

A strobing green flash suddenly came out of somewhere. Near

the dark opening, but not from within it. The laser blast charred a strut not far from Miller's head. She ducked into cover immediately, behind one of the wrecked vehicles in the hangar, and so did the soldiers following her. Swearing, Tully jetted toward them and tried to spot the attacker in there amongst the flotsam.

"We got a live one!" someone shouted. The rest of the jinau took cover behind chunks of wrecked vehicles. That wasn't always easy, because everything in there down to the smallest piece of scrap was in motion.

Before Tully could spot the location of the sniper, it all became a moot point. A wave of small white-suited forms wearing jet harnesses appeared from the far end. More green energy beams speared the dimness. A human screamed, but Tully couldn't tell who was hit.

Tully took cover himself, behind a nearby, half-destroyed... whatever-it-was. For all he knew, the Ekhat equivalent of an oversized toaster oven. His jinau were already returning fire. A lot of fire, way more than was coming at them.

Tully was pretty sure they weren't facing anything worse than a hastily organized sally by a few survivors. They might all be slaves—Anj, the reports called them—with not a single Ekhat among them. But from this angle and distance, he couldn't really tell anything. He kicked his jets back on and began working his way through the debris field, trying to get a glimpse of what, or who, had come at them.

He wasn't any more adept at maneuvering the suit through an enclosed space cluttered with haphazard wreckage than he had been maneuvering it through the vastness of space. But at least his clumsiness wasn't so blindingly obvious to anyone watching.

Jihan and Lliant returned to the Ekhat derelict, entering through the same hole through which the Anj had previously attacked. Her aureole was positively plastered to her head with dread. It was like crawling into the mouth of a monster, asking to be eaten. But no matter how bad the situation was, she told herself, you could only die once. Get on with it!

She pushed Lliant along ahead of her, never letting him elude her direct sight. The two of them floated through buckled corridors littered with grotesquely decompressed corpses. They were mostly Anj, but they did come across three carcasses of the great devils themselves. Spatters of white and purplish blood fouled their faceplates as they passed and could not be avoided. Even dead, with their limbs askew and their eyes ruptured, Ekhat were terrifying. If for no other reason, because they were so huge.

Without atmosphere, there was no sound, of course, but she suddenly detected vibration in one of the walls when she steadied herself at a corner. Something was happening, not too far ahead. She motioned Lliant in that direction. Then, by keeping one trembling hand on the gory bulkhead, she traced the vibrations' source and headed that way. They finally emerged onto a platform which looked down upon some sort of huge open chamber for storing small ships.

Fighting raged below amidst the pieces of shattered vessels. A small cluster of white-suited Anj were firing at a larger number of enemies from behind some wreckage. The Ekhat's little serviles were outnumbered and obviously getting the worst of it. She pulled herself forward to get a better look—then something coming from behind knocked her into the wall.

Her head impacted her helmet. Pain rocketed through her neck and shoulders, especially bad in her already wrenched arm. Gasping, Jihan twisted around and met the searing red gaze of a suited-up Ekhat, staring down at her from a short distance away. There was a second Ekhat, too, and they were accompanied by a crowd of seething Anj in their protective white coverings.

She was frozen. Those eyes were mad, burning with unreasoning hatred.

Lliant, who also had been shouldered aside, seemed frozen in place also.

But, for whatever reason—probably unknowable—the Ekhat ignored the two Lleix. The huge forms swept past them and the Ekhat dove off the platform toward the fighting raging below. The little mob of Anj followed. They ignored the two Lleix cowering against a wall also. Following their masters' lead in every respect, apparently.

Once the last Anj plunged off the platform, Jihan took a gasping breath. She hadn't inhaled at all, she realized, during the time she'd been in the presence of the Ekhat.

From the shaky sound of his voice, Lliant had been just as terrified as she was. But at least he hadn't panicked and tried to run. "I think," the Ekhatlore said, breathing hard, "we will be able to observe better from that part of the platform." He pointed to their left, where there was an overhang that would give them some shelter.

He'd even kept his wits, for a wonder. She activated her jets and headed to the overhang. Once there, she looked down. Flashes of light illuminated the dimness but it was difficult to follow the action without the references of a solid *up* or *down*, or any sort of noise to draw one's attention. There were only laser flashes in the swirling gloom, and fleeting glimpses of the combatants.

There was something else, too, but Jihan couldn't determine its source or nature. A number of very bright flashes, yellowish instead of green. They were much brighter than the laser blasts, whose only illumination was caused by the fact that there was still some gas and dust in the chamber.

Then she spotted the figure of one of the creatures fighting the Ekhat and their Anj slaves. It was bipedal, wearing a dark-colored spacesuit and was quite small, whatever it was. Not as small as an Anj but definitely smaller than a Lleix, much less an Ekhat. She couldn't see any of its features, because of the dim lighting.

As she watched, the creature brought up some sort of weapon and she saw that bright yellow flash coming from one end. A large number of flashes, she now saw, in very rapid succession.

Then the whole interior of the cavernous chamber was lit by some sort of flare. For the first time, Jihan could see clearly.

The sight paralyzed her again, for a moment. Down below, near the center of the chamber, the two Ekhat were in full fury. Their six great limbs extended, claws open, their hideous mouths agape—quite easy to see, with the transparent globes the Ekhat favored for helmets—and their red eyes glaring.

But the terror passed, almost at once, replaced by wonder. As she watched, the gigantic Ekhat forms began disintegrating.

CHAPTER
25

Tully bestowed a silent blessing on Caewithe Miller. The quick-witted lieutenant had fired a flare. Finally, they could see clearly.

The first thing he saw were the two enormous Ekhat storming into the chamber. God, he'd forgotten how big the damn things were! It was like facing some sort of mammoth-sized arachnids.

But before Tully even had time to finish gritting his teeth, Mallu and the special unit were already coming forward to face the monsters. Say what you would about the stiff-necked Krant, they were tough as nails. Tully took a moment to bestow another silent blessing, this one on hillbillies of whatever species.

The first to fire an 84mm recoilless rifle was one of the two Jao whom Mallu had added to the team. Urta or Naddo, from that distance he couldn't tell which.

Tully was impressed. With only the sketchiest and most rudimentary training, the Jao managed to hit his target dead on. The head of the second and somewhat smaller Ekhat pretty much came apart. The monster's brain—or whatever did for an equivalent—was destroyed instantly. The Ekhat's six huge limbs splayed out and the monster began a slow cartwheel toward the far distant wall of the chamber, spraying blood and bits of what were presumably brains everywhere. *Hot damn! One down, one to go.*

But Mallu shared none of his pleasure. The invective that followed was more colorful than anything Tully had ever heard coming from a Jao. He couldn't even follow most of it.

"—brainless crecheling, Naddo! You'll be lucky if you don't get served up as"—a term Tully didn't know came here; several of them, he thought; probably along the lines of *stinking filthy dog*—"food! Supposed to *capture* them, you idiot!"

But the object of his ire might very well not have heard him at all. Naddo had obviously not taken to heart the warnings he must have gotten from the two human corporals. "Recoilless" was an almost mystically vague term, applied to any sort of projectile weapon used in null gravity. The Jao soldier who'd fired that Deadeye Dick shot to the head was doing his own cartwheel toward the opposite wall. And not a slow one, either.

The other Jao fired. Urta, that would be. He missed the surviving Ekhat altogether and blew one of the nearby little slaves into pieces. And...

Began his own none-too-slow cartwheel toward a distant wall.

"—scrubbing decks till you keen in misery," continued Mallu, "you worthless"—here followed a number of Jao terms Tully was unfamiliar with. Probably the names of animals native to the Krant planet. Filthy, loathsome, disgusting vermin, at a guess.

Mallu, normally even-tempered, was obviously in a fury. More than anything he'd ever said, it was that which drove home to Tully just how desperately poor his kochan was. The Krant really *needed* whatever spoils value would come from capturing a live Ekhat.

Then Thomas Kelly fired. Mallu's tirade cut off abruptly. The human corporal's shot struck the surviving Ekhat at what amounted to a knee joint. The lower part of the limb was blown off and sent spinning rapidly at the same wall toward which Urta was headed.

Okay. One down, five to go. If they could sever all six of the monster's legs, they could probably take it alive. Whether or not that would lead to any sort of communicable interrogation was another matter. Tully thought that was about as likely as the proverbial snowball in hell. But it wasn't his problem—or the Krants'. They'd just been set to the task of catching the critter. Somebody else could try to figure out how to talk to the damn thing.

Unfortunately, the success of Kelly's shot made the rest of it harder. Some of the impact of that shot had been absorbed by the bulk of the Krant's body, of course. And while the huge creature hadn't been sent into the rapid spin of its now-severed leg, it was still sent spinning.

A slow spin, true—but an 84mm goose wasn't really a sharp-shooter's weapon. The damn thing was designed to destroy tanks, not shoot apples off spinning little William Tell's head.

Or was William Tell the guy who shot the bow? Or crossbow, whatever it was. Tully couldn't remember the stupid legend, which he didn't believe anyway.

But Dennis Greer's shot, coming right on the heels of that thought, proved him wrong. Or maybe the corporal was just lucky. Tully didn't care. Either way, another lower limb was severed and sent on its merry blood-spewing way.

Greer's 84mm round had blown off the rear leg on the same side as the leg that Kelly had taken off. If they'd been under grav-ity conditions, the monster would have toppled to the floor and been effectively immobilized. That couldn't happen in null grav-ity, of course, but the Ekhat was still pretty effectively crippled. Half-stunned, obviously, if nothing else. One of the wretched little slaves leapt to its master's side, trying to stem the bleeding of the front limb. The Ekhat rewarded it by taking off its head with one snap of the immense claws on its surviving front limb, then seized the torso and smashed it against the deck.

Why? Maddened by pain, maybe. Or maybe just murderous-maniac bat-crazy Ekhat. Who knew?

Or cared. Not Tully. All he wanted was that thing down and legless. What was most important was that, by sheer good luck, the monster's slam against the deck had largely nullified its spin. As a target, it was almost stationary.

As Kelly promptly demonstrated by firing a shot that took off one of the limbs on the Ekhat's opposite side. Three down, three to go. Of course, inevitably, the impact sent the Ekhat into a slow spin again. It was not a perfect universe.

Belatedly, it occurred to Tully that the problem with such a rough multi-limb amputation was that the monster would just bleed out. But there didn't seem to be much of its hideous-colored ichor coming out of the shredded limbs. Most likely—as was true of human and Jao fighting suits—the Ekhat's suit was designed to cut off blood flow in the event a limb was severed.

Humans and Jao used what amounted to automatic tourniquets for the purpose. The Ekhat being Ekhat, they probably used cauterization. But it didn't matter. Either way, there was a good chance the creature would survive having its six limbs blown off.

Guiltily, Tully realized he'd been so preoccupied by the fight with the two Ekhat that he'd ignored what else might be happening in the cavern. But, looking around, he relaxed. Miller had taken charge of that fight, and he could see she and her people were mopping up what was left of the Anj without much trouble.

They'd never been much trouble, really. Tully could only see two human casualties. One was obviously dead, the suit ruptured and the body surrounded by a cloud of blood-mist. But from the way the medics were working on the other one of them, Tully didn't think he or she was badly wounded. The Anj, he now realized—these Anj, anyway—must have never served the Ekhat as the kind of Janissary soldiers the Jao had been. They were probably just ship-handlers, as inept in a hand-to-hand fight like this as any similar group of human flight engineers would have been.

He had to fight down a completely inappropriate giggle then. He'd had a sudden image of human geeks sallying forth to do combat in ill-fitting spacesuits with pocket protectors.

He was helped in stifling the giggle by the sight of Mallu. Talk about maniacs! The Krant-captain had launched himself toward the writhing Ekhat with four other Jao.

Was he mad? That pair of claws could cut through Jao battle armor about as easily as it had taken off the head of the slave. The kind of light armor on a spacesuit, anyway.

But there was a method to Mallu's method, Tully realized, once the Jao struck the Ekhat. Between his mass and that of the other four Jao who hit the huge body a split-second later, they drove the Ekhat against a large nearby vehicle of some kind. If it was a vehicle at all, which wasn't clear. The design of the thing had a closer resemblance to a jungle gym than any vehicle Tully could think of.

But that design was perfect for Mallu's purpose. The badly injured body of the Ekhat, driven into the object by the momentum of five armored Jao warriors, was effectively immobilized. It wasn't spinning any longer, and while a bit of spin had been imparted to the vehicle-cum-jungle-gym, the object was too massive to be moving much.

Kelly and Greer's experience had enabled them to counter the recoil of the "recoilless" rifles, unlike what had happened to Urta and Naddo. They pushed off from nearby supports at the same time they fired their weapons. Kelly had used a deck stanchion, both times; Greer had used the bulk of a large wrecked vehicle. That pretty much counteracted the recoil. So they were both back already, and got to very close range, just barely out of reach of the remaining limbs.

Kelly fired again. Another knee-equivalent was turned into fleshy ruin and another lower limb was sent flying. Greer fired and the same happened to the limb next to it. The Ekhat's mouth, clearly visible in the helmet, opened in what looked like a screech. Then, with the one clawed limb remaining to it, the Ekhat began smashing at its helmet.

It was trying to suicide, Tully realized. And while that helmet seemed very sturdy, it wouldn't stand up for very long. Not given the insane strength with which the Ekhat was beating itself.

No way to shoot the knee joint, either. Or was it the elbow? Tully neither knew nor cared. Not the way it was waving around now.

Mallu must have reached the same conclusion at the same time. Mallu shouted something in Jao that Tully didn't catch. Then—Jao could be just as crazy as Ekhat, sometimes, he and all four of his soldiers launched themselves at the waving claws.

They caught them—more or less; snagged them, anyway—and for just a moment the limb was immobilized.

Greer had come to literally point-blank range. He couldn't risk aiming at the knees/elbows, because the Jao were close. So he took off the whole limb, right below what amounted to a shoulder.

A cloud of blood engulfed him. Mallu and the four other Jao, still holding the claws, drifted away. The Ekhat seemed to shrivel, like an insect caught in a flame. Then, its mouth agape in that same screech—what Tully took for a screech, anyway—the monster began beating its head against the object in which it was pinned. *Still* trying to suicide, even with no limbs left.

But "trying" was the operative term, Tully saw. Even a creature as huge and powerful as an Ekhat couldn't smash open a helmet designed to withstand combat in space, when it only had its torso muscles to work with and lacked any effective leverage.

And not even an immense and maniacally murderous Ekhat could remain conscious for very long, with all six legs severed. It had to be suffering badly from its own version of shock. Tully could see the mouth grow slack and the eyes turn a dimmer shade of red. A few seconds later, the creature was still.

So much for that. Now. How to keep the damn thing from bleeding to death? The Ekhat's suit had stopped the ichor-flow from the first five severed limbs. But the blast that took off the last limb, coming right at the shoulder, had created too large a wound for the suit's own resources. Ichor was spewing out, just like it would from a human or Jao arterial wound.

Mallu came up with the answer to that. A temporary solution, anyway. Whether it would keep the thing alive for very long was hard to say.

Lasers hadn't been of much use when it came to capturing the Ekhat. But they did just fine at cauterizing the monster's wound. True, any orthopedic and plastic surgeons assigned the task of restoring the Ekhat to its proper shape and vigor afterward would have cursed Tully and his crew. But Tully could live with that burden for...ever and ever and ever.

Miller came up to him. "They're all dead, sir. The slaves, I mean. Except for"—she pointed at a cluster of soldiers—"three of them over there. When the last Ekhat went down, they were the only ones left. They quit, then. Sorta turned into pumpkins, in fact. Dropped their weapons, curled into little balls and didn't do anything. I didn't see any point in killing them, so we've got them captured."

"Good work, Lieutenant," he said, feeling pompous but not knowing what else to say. There were some definite disadvantages to having the hots for a very capable subordinate officer. You were always a little at a loss for words, for which you compensated by acting middle-aged. Middle-aged and dull-witted.

But this was no time to be thinking about Caewithe Miller's ready smile and bright blue eyes—much less the small but very feminine body that lay hidden somewhere beneath her spacesuit. So Tully sternly told himself, and turned to address the others present.

"Good work, Kelly and Greer. Mallu, my congratulations."

Could he possibly sound any *more* middle-aged and dull-witted? He didn't think so.

CHAPTER
26

If the new aliens were triumphant, dare she ask for help? Jihan's injured arm ached abominably as she swung back to the overhang, then stretched out along it, peering into the maze of debris. She wondered who was winning and who in the name of the *Boh* these bold strangers could possibly be.

Lliant positioned himself behind her, watching back down the corridor so that they would not be surprised again.

The chamber was suddenly lit again very brightly by a flare of some sort sent up by one of the combatants. Jihan could finally see the newcomers clearly. They wore transparent helmets, similar to those employed by the Lleix, so that their heads were visible. They had no aureoles, which was unattractive, but hardly surprising. Instead, their skulls were covered with patches of fur in varying shades, mostly browns. Their eyes were large and round, white with tiny dark circles in the center like holes. To the last of them, they seemed to be shorter than Lleix. She doubted the tallest of them topped even herself. A magnificent Eldest like Sayr would have dwarfed them all.

Then a figure jetted past her, its movements more deft than the rest, and she stopped breathing. The creature's entire head was covered in dark brown fur. It had a prominent muzzle and green flecked black eyes along with those large infamous ears, which were swiveling even as it passed.

She turned to Lliant. "That—" she said, but could not find the words to finish.

Lliant pulled himself up beside her, gazing out over the platform into the battle. "Yes?"

The figure was gone, having fired at an Anj, then plunged back into the maze of debris. Blood hammered in her head. Alarm flattened her aureole so thoroughly, she thought it would never again straighten. Once again, the universe had turned itself inside out. The situation was far worse than she'd thought. "That—was a *Jao.*"

Tully hovered above the corpse of the other Ekhat. Its legs and arms had curled like those of a dead spider after Naddo's shot had destroyed its head. "Jesus, that's ugly!" he said with a shudder, then turned to Miller. "Lieutenant, send parties to search the rest of this hulk. Go through every compartment, open every door. I think we've run into whatever survivors there were who were still in shape to fight. But I might be wrong, and there are probably some Ekhat or Anj somewhere who are immobilized by injuries."

"Yes, sir. And what should we do with any we run into who aren't dead?"

Tully hesitated. Then decided that with one Ekhat captured alive, they'd already fulfilled that mission. One was enough. More than enough, if anyone wanted his opinion.

"If they're Anj—or any other slave species you might run across—try to keep them alive. If they're Ekhat, kill 'em."

She jetted off. Mallu and Kaln motioned him over to a bit of debris.

"Despite appearances, Major, much of this tech is usable," Kaln said. "We should take care not to damage it any—" She broke off, staring up at the curving wall.

Tully followed her gaze and spotted two figures in unfamiliar design suits surveying the battle scene. They had only two arms and legs, so were not Ekhat, but neither were they short and stumpy like the Anj. A second slave species? "Kaln, Burgeson, Nam, secure those two up there!" he said, motioning.

Nancy Burgeson, who was closest, swooped in to train her weapon on the pair. Kaln, along with Nam, one of the jinau Jao of Baker Company, followed to back him up. The aliens did not flee, however. Instead, they pushed themselves up so that they were floating more or less face to face with their captors, staring back at the trio with upswept black eyes.

*   *   *

These were *Jao*. Jihan's mind reeled at encountering yet another of their ancient enemies. But...

Most of the ones who had fought were of another species altogether, similar in conformation to the Jao, but easily distinguished by their smaller build and paucity of fur. Their faces were flatter, their ears tiny and stationary, when she knew from the records that those of the Jao were almost always in motion. And these particular Jao seemed to be under the command of one of the newcomers, the one with bright yellow head-fur. They were clearly following its directions, taking its orders.

Understanding flooded through her. Of course! The Jao had always been a slave species, and still were. For some reason, this particular group of Jao—perhaps all Jao—had fallen under the rule of another alien culture. So they served them now, not the Ekhat.

One of their captors, not a Jao, motioned with its slim gray weapon for her to approach. She turned to Lliant, who had not moved. His black eyes stared. "Come," she said. "We must do our best to make ourselves understood."

"They will kill us," Lliant said. "There is no need to communicate that."

"If they wished us dead," she said, "we would already be so. They want something else." She gestured at two of their captors. "Do you not see? Some of them are Jao!"

He groaned. "And you find that welcome news?"

"They are obviously communicating with one another," she said, hand fumbling at her controls. "Perhaps we can find the same frequency."

The closest Jao waved at her now. She pushed off and drifted down to it, if the chamber could be said to have a "down" orientation in any meaningful sense of the word under these conditions. Hurriedly flipping through the available communication channels, she listened to each for a breath, but heard only silence, static, silence. It was hopeless, she thought. Their tech was bound to be radically different. They might not even communicate in frequencies that could be detected by Lleix ears.

At her side, Lliant jerked, then looked at her. His black eyes gleamed. Had he found it? His mouth was moving as though he were trying to tell her something.

She clicked back to their common ship frequency. "—to five-thirty-four!" he was saying. "Dial to five-thirty-four!"

Fingers shaking, she did so. "—throw away your weapons!" a growly voice was saying. In Jao.

Lliant gazed at her expectantly. He did not understand, of course. He was an Ekhatlore. Quite properly, he had only studied the sly maniac tongue of the great devils. But she was Jaolore, however short the duration of her appointment. From long days of study, she knew approximately what those words meant, although they were not pronounced in the same way as the ancient recording. But that was not surprising. Languages changed, over time. She was lucky it was still basically the same.

"We—have—none—weapons," she said slowly, the alien syllables dropping clumsily off her tongue before she could quite complete the sounds. She remembered the records, how the Jao had simply shot down that brave Wordthreader Eldest when she had pleaded for alliance, and white-hot fear seared through her. *"Nothing is required here except that you die!"* the Jao had said to the Lleix elder. She had watched the gruesome scene so many times, she knew the dialogue on both sides, word for word.

Then she got hold of herself. She and Lliant could die in the next few blinks, that was true. But it was also true that without aid, they were soon to perish anyway, as indeed were all their kind, scrambling even now back on Valeron to send off a few of their number to dubious safety. Nothing was more certain than the fact that the Ekhat would return to extract vengeance for their lost ships.

The three were staring at her, two of them Jao, the other, one of the unnamed aliens. She noticed, off to the side, the newcomers had rounded up a few Anj and were guarding the little serviles, rather than exterminating them. How very strange.

Even stranger was that the aliens evidently intended to keep one of the Ekhat alive, even though they'd severed all of its limbs. For what possible purpose? she wondered.

But, whatever the aliens' intent, they had not fired upon her or Lliant. So at least they were not purely murderous. With a great effort, she put aside her useless fear and then jetted toward the alien who seemed to be in charge, the one with the yellow thatch of fur on its small head. Lliant followed, she noted with approval. If they were to have any chance of surviving, she would have to find a way to appeal to this alien creature.

✳   ✳   ✳

"Heads up, Major!" Burgeson called.

Tully turned to find the captured pair sailing through the debris field toward him.

"They do not seem to be armed," Kaln said as she trailed after them, good ear pinned, weapon ready. Nam krinnu ava Terra came too, his gun trained upon the aliens. "And, Major Tully, one of them managed to say so—in Jao."

In Jao? Tully studied the creatures. Did the Ekhat perhaps keep some of these—whatever they were—around as linguists or translators?

"Stop," he said in Jao, as the one in front neared. It complied, employing its suit jets for station-keeping. "How are you called?"

"I am Jihan," it said. He could see a strange fleshy serrated corona rippling across its head through the suit's helmet. Its skin was a dusky silver, its eyes gleaming black slits. If the two of them had stood face to face on the ground, it would have been head and shoulders taller. "You—rule Jao," it said, sweeping an arm toward Kaln and Nam, who both promptly looked affronted. "Jao—our—old enemy."

For a translator, Tully thought, the words certainly weren't coming very fluently.

Then it straightened, raising its head, seeming to tap into an inner store of words. "The Lleix have proposal," it said slowly, in heavily accented Jao, "one to set your people free to come into own."

"It must belong to the Ekhat," Burgeson said in English. "It's just as freaking nuts as they all are!"

"You already fierce warriors," Jihan continued carefully in Jao, obviously producing each syllable with a great deal of effort to get the sounds right. "No one could dispute. The Lleix believe you great people. You have to reach for the freedom Ekhat masters never allowed."

Mallu joined them, his ears wavering. "What is this?"

"I have no idea," Tully said. "Do you recognize the species?"

"No," Mallu said. "But the Melody may have many client races we have never encountered."

"Jao-slaves!" The alien, Jihan, gestured at the Krant-captain, then turned to Tully. "You rule now! You!"

Kaln's good ear twitched. "It believes we are your slaves," she said, and even with his poor ability to read postures, Tully was sure he detected a sudden *intent-to-commit-mischief* in her lines. The senior-tech jetted between him and the two captives. "You are correct," she said and pointed at herself, Mallu, and Nam, "we are but lowly Jao slaves." She swept her arm back toward Tully. "That, however, is Tully, master of many great ships and eater of Ekhat!"

"Now, hold on—" Tully began. Since first accepting Jao into his jinau unit, he knew full well that what passed for Jao humor was about as far removed from dry wit as you could ask for. And once they got amused by something, they almost always took it too far.

The alien stiffened all the way up to its corona. "This very one—eat—the great devils?"

"Yes—while still alive!" Kaln said, positively gleeful. She pointed to immobile body of the one surviving Ekhat. "Eat it still alive!"

Tully winced. Even if this creature were only an Ekhat servile, there wasn't any point in deceiving it. He raised his voice. "Kaln, this is not the time for—"

"We needing—help," Jihan said, its fleshy crown rippling. "All Lleix—needing help—now!"

Its companion hung back, regarding them with an inscrutable black gaze. Maybe they weren't Ekhat serviles at all, but captives. How was he supposed to figure this out? "You are *Lleix*?" he said, struggling to pronounce the name. The closest he could come was "Laysh."

"Yes, yes!" the alien cried.

Tully rolled his eyes. He was good at fighting, but he sure as hell wasn't trained for this. "Are there more Lleix on this ship?" he asked. If so, he thought, poor buggers, they were most likely all dead.

"No, on planet!" Jihan said, waving an arm. "Valeron! On surface!"

"But—" he began.

"Lord Tully rules twenty planets!" Kaln broke in. "He brews soup from lakes and straightens rivers with his bare hands!"

Tully turned to the Krant-captain for assistance, but Mallu was looking distinctly amused. Jao humor. Right.

"Kaln, go back to the assault craft!" he said desperately. If he understood the alien correctly, at least one of the worlds in this system was inhabited by these Lleix, which made this some sort of First Contact situation. That meant Kaln was screwing the proverbial pooch.

The tech gazed at him, eyes flickering with merry green fire. "Pool Buntyam," she said. "Tully is like Pool Buntyam!"

"Great," Tully said under his breath. Whose bright idea had it been to tell the Krants tall tales?

Well. His.

"And then there is Bab the green ox—" Kaln continued.

"Shut—up!" Tully said and glared Kaln into blessed silence. He closed his eyes for a second, trying to think. "This is way above my pay grade," he said. "We need to contact Caitlin and Wrot."

"Cat-lin and Rot?" Jihan said. "These rule—as well?"

"Yes, yes, Caitlin!" Kaln said, still clearly on a roll and enjoying herself far too much to let it go. "Queen of the Universe, ruler of all and possessor of many many fine green ox! Wrot is of course her faithfullest slave. She lives on a comet and uses stars to cook comestibles!"

"Queen?" Jihan said. Its corona fluttered.

"A queen," Kaln burbled on, "is a female ruler who—"

Tully reached over and punched Kaln's radio off. Then they all stared at one another, human, Jao, and Lleix. How in holy hell had Kaln even heard of "lords" and "queens?" He'd suggested that Caewithe Miller tell the Krants a few simple tall tales, not relate a goddamned entire fairy tale book!

He should have known better. With a name like "Caewithe," the lieutenant had to come from a family with one of those Celtic fetishes. Probably got fed ancient mythology with her mother's milk, and cut her teeth on legends as she was growing up. Could read runes by moonlight and recite the *Iliad* from beginning to end.

This, he thought grimly, was going to take some explaining.

CHAPTER
27

Caitlin knew something was up when the call came in, maybe even what wily old Ronz had suspected from the start because everyone was being very mysterious. Tully had summoned Caitlin and Wrot, asking that they meet him at the Ekhat derelict soonest, but declined to explain further.

She accompanied Wrot up to the bridge to formally request transport from Dannet. The mood was calmer than when last Caitlin had visited. A faint hint of singed wiring lingered in the air. Repairs were still being made, but most of the equipment seemed to be functioning.

Beside a damaged console, the Terra-captain was sitting on her feet, as Jao sometimes did when agitated, looking as though she could launch herself at any second. Her eyes were glittering, her spine angled to indicate *barely-repressed-curiosity*, whiskers quivering.

The back of Caitlin's neck prickled. The former Narvo knew something was up, too, had known it all along, but the Bond had given Wrot *oudh* over the noncombat aspect of this mission, not her. The Terra-captain had to play her assigned role.

Wrot waited, his body arched with *polite-request*.

"*Lexington* will transport you," said Dannet. She rose and stretched like a frustrated lioness. "We have completed our task of destroying leftover fragments from the battle."

Indeed, Dannet had been so thoroughly ruthless on that score,

Caitlin doubted anything bigger than a bread box was left drifting out there.

The bad part, she learned two hours later, was that she had
to suit up and go over to the derelict—outside—crossing naked
space. Why Tully couldn't just report to her and Wrot on the
Lexington was not being explained. He insisted they had to come
in person and would say no more on an open channel.

Well, she thought, in the space suit locker, as Wrot settled a
helmet over her head and then activated the seals, it had damn
well better be worth it. She didn't even want to think about what
Ed would say when he heard about this. The air rushed and then
she was alone with the sound of her thudding heartbeat.

She'd had the terrifying experience of boarding an Ekhat ship
of the Interdict faction several years ago and had no desire to
repeat the experience with a Melody ship, even if the wretches
were all supposedly dead.

Wrot gave her a quick course in using her jets, then tethered
her with a cord to his own suit. "I will do the maneuvering,"
the old Jao said. "You just, as they say, come along for the ride."

They cycled through the air lock, then Wrot towed her outside the *Lexington*'s huge curving hull. The star hung there on
her right, swollen and fiery. She could see its surface seething
as convection currents swirled, rose, and fell. Had they really
emerged into the system through *that*? She felt ill all over again,
a sensation not improved by the lack of gravity. Her stomach
kept trying to climb into her throat, and her mind insisted she
was falling, even though she knew logically it was not true. A
fervent new appreciation for gravity suddenly suffused her. She
would endeavor to enjoy it as it deserved, once she was back in
a civilized environment.

Don't look! she told herself. *Think about something else—yeah,
like that battered Ekhat derelict just ahead.*

But that didn't help much. Light gleamed through numerous
hull breaches, courtesy of *Lexington*'s powerful armament. The
huge bay door hung crazily to one side, anchored by a single
hinge, floating. Probably, she thought, one good tug would send
it careening down into the sun to incinerate—

That didn't bear thinking about either. She trained her eyes on
Wrot's blue space suit as he jetted assuredly toward his target.

Luckily for her, he probably had done this a hundred times, she told herself as they neared the access point.

Wrot maneuvered through the irregular opening, half manufactured doorway and half blast hole. She held her hands out as he towed her the rest of the way, then eased through the gap into dim green light. Inside, she found herself in a large bay filled with drifting fragments of—something. She craned her head, trying to make sense of the jumble of debris. Maybe this wreckage had once been shuttles. Maybe heavy machinery. Or maybe something only the Ekhat would understand.

A group of small sinuous creatures in white space suits floated off to one side, guarded by a trio of jinau. "Caitlin! Wrot!" Tully's voice called. "Up here!"

She looked around, then spotted a blue-suited figure waving at her from some sort of extension that had once overlooked the storage bay. "Use your jets," Wrot said, activating his own to head for Tully. "And avoid the wreckage. You could hole your suit on a jagged edge."

Taking a deep steadying breath, she activated her jets and wobbled tentatively after him, still tethered. When they reached the platform, she found Tully, Kaln, and Mallu, along with several unfamiliar jinau, one of them Jao and the other human, and a pair of suited figures who were...

Neither. To her relief, though, it was immediately apparent that they were not Ekhat. Abstractly, she knew that there was only one surviving Ekhat aboard the derelict, which had been very badly injured. But her one experience with Ekhat aboard the Interdict ship had been frightening enough to make her somewhat irrational on the subject. Even the wounded Ekhat would probably scare her silly. Fortunately, it was nowhere in sight.

"Who is this?" she asked Tully, trying at the same time not to careen into the wall. Wrot put out a steadying hand to stabilize her. "Were they part of the crew on this ship?"

"Beats me, Caitlin," Tully said. "I haven't been able to make heads or tails yet out of what they are doing here, and we haven't run across any more like them, dead or alive. They say they are Lleix and speak a bit of Jao, as it happens."

Lleix! Her heart lurched at the sound of that ancient name. Now that she could see them better, she could see that their appearance matched the record she had watched. The aliens were quite tall, even stately, built wide on the bottom, then more narrowly on the top, possessing two arms and legs and an odd crown of flesh across their heads that rippled apparently to the rhythm of the creatures' thoughts. The effect suggested the petals of a daisy, if a flower could move at will. Their faces were concave with only a nub of a nose and thin silver lips.

Two pairs of upswept narrow black eyes turned to her and the one closest spoke in an unexpectedly musical voice. "You are Cat-lin, Queen of the Universe?" The words were Jao, except for the English term "queen."

"What?" Caitlin glanced at Tully.

He scowled and shook his head. "I'm afraid there has been a complication," he said in English. "After we took them into custody, these Lleix mistook the Jao in my company for our slaves. In addition, our Krant friend over there"—he gestured at Kaln—"has been listening to tales of Paul Bunyan and picked this moment to reciprocate with a tall tale of her own. About Caitlin, Queen of the Universe, and her faithful Jao slaves."

The Lleix. Again, the enormity of it hit Caitlin. What had merely been suspected was now standing before her, and, with all that long, complicated history between the two species, it was amazing the creature hadn't simply fled screaming at the first sight of a whiskered Jao face. "I...see," she said, though she really didn't. "Paul Bunyan?"

"Pool Buntyam!" Kaln said. "He has the strength of twenty humans and prepares comestibles on a grill the size of a shuttle! He—"

Mallu seized the senior-tech's suit and shook her. "Enough!"

Wrot turned to Caitlin, eyes jumping with green fire. "This may not be entirely unfortunate," he said in English while the apparently puzzled Lleix looked on, their fleshy coronas in constant motion. "When the Lleix last had contact with the Jao, we *were* slaves—of the Ekhat. Better that they believe us now to be humanity's slaves than still under the control of the Ekhat."

"But—" she said, her mind whirling. "That's crazy! And it's wrong to start off by outright lying."

"This misunderstanding works in our favor, though," Wrot said in English. "We should take advantage of it. I believe the correct human term would be 'play along for now.' "

✳   ✳   ✳

For a creature with so much authority, this Cat-lin was very small, Jihan thought. She had expected an Eldest of magnificent proportions, towering far above them all. The Queen of the Universe seemed as slight as a youth about to be released for the Festival of Choosing.

"I am Jaolore," she said to the creature slowly, struggling to get each syllable as close to the pronunciation in the ancient records as possible. "This your slave, Rot?" She glanced at the Jao who had accompanied Cat-lin, assisting it—her?—"queen" evidently indicated the feminine gender.

"Jaolore?" Cat-lin said.

"My *elian* learn about Jao," Jihan said. "We know—from debris— from earlier battle—Jao come back." Her aureole flattened with anxiety. "Long ago, we fight Jao."

Unable to understand a single word, Lliant hovered at her shoulder, glowering.

"You need not fear them now," Cat-lin said, then conferred with the others in her own sibilant language before she resumed speaking Jao. "We will go to my ship and talk more there."

She must mean the amazingly huge vessel which had defeated the Ekhat. Jihan was both relieved at the thought of quitting this terrible place, lair of the monstrous Ekhat, and yet afraid to venture amongst so many unknown aliens.

Then she blurted, "Hadata!" She had almost forgotten the poor Starwarder, left behind, concealed in the derelict's shadow. "We must—" In her distress, the proper vocabulary eluded her. "Must—getting Hadata!"

"What is this Hadata?" Cat-lin said.

"Other Lleix, hiding," Jihan said. "Will die soon."

Cat-lin looked at the others. The Jao designated "Rot" spoke, then Cat-lin turned back to Jihan. "Where is this one hiding?"

"In ship, in darkness, outside this place," Jihan said.

"Show us," Cat-lin said.

Jihan took Lliant's arm. "We will go now to retrieve Hadata," she said, urging him back down the corridor.

It was entirely possible these aliens were just as bad as the Ekhat, yet they had taken the Anj prisoner rather than destroying them as they could have easily done, and they hadn't shot the two Lleix on sight. She could not imagine the great devils showing such restraint.

And they had defeated five Ekhat ships. That alone would hearten her people, should she ever make it back to the Hall of Decision to relate what she had seen. Please the *Boh*, all three of them, Lliant, Hadata, and Jihan, would have that honor one day.

Tully sent Caitlin back to the *Lexington* with Wrot to await the three Lleix. It made him nervous to have an untrained civilian bobbing around a barely secured area. If she slashed her suit or one of these little Ekhat serviles whom they might have over-looked popped up its head long enough to get off a few shots, Ed Kralik would have his skin. In addition, Tully had a lot of confidence in her and thought they needed her. Back on Earth, Caitlin had made a huge difference in the struggle to achieve respect from the Jao.

Burgeson and Nam returned with the two Lleix along with a third suited figure of the same configuration. One of them carried bundles of fabric over one arm.

"Finish mopping up here," he told Burgeson. "Kaln, Nam, you come with me back to the *Lexington*."

Of the three Lleix, only the one named Jihan seemed to speak any Jao. Tully was almost grateful for that. It might prevent further nonsense. He just wasn't accustomed to having to worry about Jao making stuff up. Such shenanigans weren't normally part of their nature, but Kaln had already shown herself to be gifted with *ollnat* through her reworking of the hoist mechanism. And then there was that whole business of Krants making up stories about ships being turned inside out in transit. They obviously had a penchant for *ollnat* that other kochan lacked. Looking back, he guessed he shouldn't have been all that surprised.

The Lleix obediently accompanied them to the *Lexington*, entering through the same EVA locker room. He worried that the ship's atmospheric mix wouldn't be right for them, but they were stuck out here with a damaged ship and were going to run out of air soon at any rate.

"Wait," he said to Jihan after the air lock had cycled and the alien was fumbling at its helmet. "We need to test your suit mix to make sure you can breathe our air."

"Jao breathe?" it said, black eyes narrowed into gleaming slits.

"Yes," he said, glancing at Kaln, who had already removed her helmet and was scratching her ears.

"Lleix breathe too, then," Jihan said. One of the others came to help and he realized that it had an injured arm.

Wondering how it could be so certain, he held his breath as the helmet was pulled off and the silver-skinned alien inhaled. When it didn't fall over gasping, the other two removed their helmets as well.

Caitlin entered the locker. "Bring them up to Deck Forty-Six," she said in English. "I've reserved a conference room, then we'll have to find them quarters."

"Does Dannet know we brought them over?" Tully asked as the Lleix struggled out of their suits. He couldn't help staring. They were taller than humans and sturdy, with massive pillar-like legs, huge four-toed feet and wide hips. Their trunks then tapered up to narrower shoulders, which were topped with long graceful necks and round heads. The most exotic aspect of their appearance was the odd fluttering coronas that ran across their crowns from ear to ear. The overall effect, wider on the bottom, attenuating up to their heads, was triangular, even pyramidal.

They were all completely hairless and silver-skinned. Their broad hands sported three fingers and a thumb. Their eyes were black and upswept, set in dished faces with only the nub of a nose and nearly lipless mouths. Ignoring his scrutiny, they assumed the robes they'd brought along. Nudity did not seem to trouble them, though they all three subsequently fussed with the drape of the fabric, seeming to have a rigid standard of dress to which they conformed.

He spotted none of the obvious body conformation clues as to gender, but, he told himself, it was entirely possible that they had five distinct genders or even just one. Time would tell.

"Wrot decided to report in person," Caitlin said. "But this is not Dannet's call. Wrot has *oudh* in this situation."

This situation. Tully blinked. Now that he thought about it, Caitlin had not looked all that surprised to find a new alien species hiding out here. The possibility of finding "this" must be what had Ronz so hot and bothered back on Terra that the Bond risked their fancy new ship on a mission to this misbegotten nebula. They damn well knew these Lleix were here! So what if five sodding Ekhat ships were here as well?

"Wrot will meet us in the conference room." Caitlin turned to the Lleix and let her body curve into a graceful Jao posture. Tully didn't recognize which one, but he had to give Caitlin credit. It did give the general impression of respect, at least to his eyes.

"Please accompany us," she said to the Lleix.

"Lleix needing help!" Jihan said.

"We may be able to provide that help," Caitlin said, then motioned at Tully.

Oh, yeah, he told himself, lowest ranked goes first according to Jao tradition and these Lleix seemed to know at least a bit about such things. Cat-lin, Queen of the Universe, could not possibly take the lead.

Hands shoved in his uniform pockets, he slouched through the door and headed for the nearest lift. The Lleix chattered to each other in musical voices, ran splayed fingers over the walls, examined the flooring and lighting. Though their legs were massive, they did not walk so much as glide, their movements even more lithe than Jao postures.

They were all dressed in stiff silver-blue robes brocaded with brightly worked scenes, each different. Hadata, the one who had been left behind, obviously deferred to Jihan while the third followed in their wake, uncommunicative. If it had been human, Tully would have said it was sulking, but with aliens, who knew what was going on?

The lift fascinated them, too, but they did not seem disconcerted by its rapid speed, like most humans. When it stopped, he led them out, then conducted the trio to the conference room where Wrot was waiting.

A full complement of guards in ship uniforms was already in place, but otherwise the deck seemed to have been cleared of extraneous crew. This might not be Dannet's show anymore, he thought, but the Terra-captain was still on the job.

He stuck his head through the door. Inside there was a gleaming black table surrounded by chairs that were going to be totally inadequate for Lleix dimensions. Caitlin squeezed past him, then stared in dismay.

"I, um, need to get back to the wreck," Tully said.

Caitlin turned back, put a hand on his shoulder, and squeezed. "Oh, no, you don't, mister," she said softly. "You're staying right here!"

"Hey, you've got your faithful slave, Wrot," he said. "What more do you need, Princess?"

"That's Queen Caitlin to you," she said and her blue-gray eyes gleamed. "And don't you forget it!"

Wrot saw them walk in, three tall gliding figures, silver-skinned, clad in silver-blue robes. Only a few file images had survived since the Jao had done their best to extinguish these people, his kind being unsentimental about such things. Now, out of their suits, he saw that they were as unlike Jao and humans as a species could be and still be built along the same general two-armed, two-legged plan.

The chairs in this room, though sized for use by Jao, who were generally bulkier than humans, were still too small. He dispatched three of the guards out in the corridor to fetch benches from the nearest pool room. In the meantime, they all stood around and stared at one another, the Lleix as frankly curious as the humans and the Jao.

"Lleix needing help!" the one who called itself Jihan said.

"Yes." Caitlin gave it her full attention. "You said that before. What is wrong?"

"The great devils have founding us!" Jihan said, its corona fluttering.

"But they are all dead," Caitlin said.

"Those now dead," Jihan said as the three guards returned with benches. "Many more Ekhat! They come!"

"It means they will send more ships," Wrot said quietly in English. "And it is right. The Melody lost one ship in the first battle, now five more. They will be back and in still greater force."

"You fight more Ekhat?" Jihan said.

There was a pause as chairs were removed, then benches positioned along the table. Caitlin took a seat on the opposite side as the Lleix gingerly maneuvered themselves onto what was for them a rather narrow target.

"Humans and Jao do not find it convenient at the present time to fight another battle in this nebula," Caitlin said. "And even we did, that would only expose the Lleix to more danger. Would it not be better for you to travel to another system where the Ekhat cannot find you? You traveled to the derelict. Surely the Lleix have ships that can transport your people."

"Most few ships," Jihan said. Its corona wilted. "Many Lleix, few few ships. Most left behind."

Caitlin glanced aside at Wrot, then folded her hands and leaned across the shiny black table. The tension in the room made Wrot's whiskers itch. He resisted the urge to rise and pace. "How many Lleix?" she said carefully.

The Lleix's black eyes gleamed. It twitched its robes to hang at a precise angle, then sat very still as though thinking hard. "Jao numbers difficult," Jihan said finally. "Jao gone long time. This one only learn your words short time ago. I think you say—one hundred thousands."

CHAPTER
28

Caitlin winced. One hundred thousand? That was a tiny fraction of the population the Lleix must have had once, when they inhabited several well-developed planets. But, in immediate terms, the number was far too large. It would take ten ships the size of the *Lexington* to transport such a population.

Still, it was welcome news that the Jao, with their customary ferocious efficiency, hadn't managed to extinguish this species altogether. And the Lleix had a breeding population that was large enough not to be in danger of dying out from genetic bottlenecks.

"So, abject and miserable slave Wrot," she murmured in English without looking at him, "what do we do now? We can't tell them that the entire human fleet consists of only one ship big enough to even start the job, and it's already on-site, crammed to the gills with a fair number of Jao as well as humans."

"Ask them about their own transport."

The glittering Lleix eyes watched her. "You say you have 'few ships,'" she said. "How many would that be?"

"Now prepare to leave," Jihan said. "One thousands go, maybe two, no more."

"One thousand ships?" she said, trying to visualize the situation. Perhaps they were all just very small, like the vessel Tully's people had found moored to the derelict.

The black eyes glittered. "One thousands Lleix."

"My god," Tully murmured in English. "Then most of them

are trapped here, and everyone knows that the Ekhat are coming back. Poor buggers."

Caitlin's head whirled. "Jihan, where are the few Lleix ships going? To other Lleix worlds?"

"No other Lleix worlds," Jihan said in its musical voice, then turned its silver head to regard Wrot. Its corona stilled. "Dead everywhere, all dead."

At the hands of the Jao. The creature left that unspoken. But upon their last meeting, the Jao had exterminated its kind down to the last elder and infant with ruthless efficiency. And from that day until now, this segment of their population must have hidden here in this nebula, knowing that at some point the Ekhat—and the Jao—would return.

It had all been a long time ago and things were very different now, due in large part to the Lleix being able to see a capacity for self-direction in the Jao they had not been able to perceive in themselves at the time. The Jao owed these people. They could not be abandoned here to die at the hands of the crazed Ekhat.

She turned to Wrot. "We have to help them," she said in English. "How much time do we have before the Ekhat sweep back through this system?"

"There is no way to be certain," the Jao said. He hesitated, apparently consulting his Jao timesense. "But it feels like not long."

She wanted to shake him until his ears rattled. Instead, she clasped her hands on the table's gleaming surface and studied her reflection. "Days?" she said finally, raising her eyes. "Weeks? Months?"

His whiskers quivered with *indecision*, not something she'd ever seen on him before. "Weeks, I think."

"We could hide them on Earth, at least until we find them a proper world of their own," she said. "A hundred thousand, that's not even a medium-sized city. North America alone has dozens of areas that might suit, depending on their climatic needs. Do you have any issues with that?"

The three Lleix sat gazing at her as though she had all the answers, as though she could make their problems, the problems of an entire beleaguered civilization, just evaporate.

Because she was Caitlin, Queen of the Universe—only she was nothing of the kind. Caitlin, Recovering Political Prisoner, was more like it! Or Caitlin, Bond Lackey!

"You must excuse me," she said in Jao, wondering how much the Lleix really understood. Jihan's grammar was awkward, its word choice basic and repetitive. How it had acquired any knowledge of Jao at all after such a long lapse in contact was totally beyond her. "I will consult my underlings on best how to assist the Lleix," she said, her face hot. "Stay in this place for now. I am arranging for better quarters."

She rose, heart pounding, and stalked out of the room, followed by Wrot and Tully. The door slid shut and then she whirled upon the pair of them, hands fisted. "This is all your fault!"

Tully backed into the wall, palms facing out as though to protect himself. "Me? I had nothing to do with any of this! You and Wrot obviously had some idea about what we were headed into out here and wouldn't give me the slightest heads-up! My people could have easily shot these characters before thinking to count arms and legs. You might have at least told me what to be on the lookout for."

"Caitlin, Queen of the Universe!" Her face was so heated, she knew her cheeks must be fiery. "That's not your fault?"

"Well, Kaln did get a little carried away with all this tall-tale stuff," he said, trying and failing not to smile.

"And, you!" She glared at Wrot. "Play along, you said!"

Green lightning flickered in the old Jao's eyes. "This was a fortuitous blunder," he said. "If they understood the reality of the situation, they would be terrified."

"And well they should be!" Her pulse was pounding. "Sooner or later, they're going to figure out the truth!"

"By then," Wrot said, "they will have learned not to fear the Jao."

Fat chance, Caitlin thought. There were still millions of humans on Earth who hadn't learned that. She herself still bore the scars from her Jao guard's beatings from not that long ago when she'd been a young political hostage.

She crossed her arms, resisting the temptation to drop into a Jao posture to make her point. "Look at the position you've put me in. They're asking *me*, Queen of the Universe, to make all their problems just disappear, only I don't have the authority to do anything of the sort! I can't promise to fight off the Ekhat when they come back, or to load up the Lleix and transport the whole lot of them to Terra. I'm not in charge here! I can't promise a single damned thing and then make good on it!"

Upon hearing "Queen of the Universe," one of the guards glanced at her, clearly startled. She glared at him. "Not a word, soldier!"

He squared his shoulders and gazed over her head at the corridor wall.

Wrot's angles went to *discomfitted-recognition-of-truth*. "If the number they've given us is correct," he said slowly, "I think transport might be arranged through the Bond's resources, as long as you can persuade your father to authorize sanctuary in North America. Even if it's only a temporary sanctuary."

Her mind whirled. She wasn't Queen of the Universe, not by a long shot, but she was a sort of princess. Her father was still President of the United States, at least until elections were once again held, and he could do that much. But would he? She remembered the poem engraved long ago on the now battered Statue of Liberty: *Give me your tired, your poor, your huddled masses yearning to breathe free.* Wonderful sentiments, sure—but even before the Jao conquest a lot of North Americans had been hostile to immigrants.

And those had been human immigrants. "Illegal aliens," they had been called. How would people now react to the prospect of taking in a hundred thousand real aliens? In a continent which the conquest and the ensuing twenty years of brutal rule by Oppuk had made much poorer?

But she knew that her father still believed in the old ideals of the republic. And there was a lot of unoccupied land in North America. Had been, even before the Jao devastated much of it. He would agree, she decided, if she got a chance to explain.

"For now, this contemplated commitment of resources is simply beyond my *oudh*," Wrot said. "And I cannot send a communication asking for clarification that could be intercepted by one or more of the kochan." His whiskers stiffened. "I must go back and consult with Preceptor Ronz in person."

"What about our Lleix guests?" Caitlin said. "Are you planning on taking them as well? If so, it's quite likely to be an even bigger shock than they've already had."

"No, I think they should remain here," Wrot said. He glanced aside at Tully. "And I think you should stay as well with Tully's company for guards. They have no function on the ship at the moment, since we had to jettison Spine C."

"But I have a number of Jao in my unit," Tully said, "Won't that freak these guys out if we all just drop in on their settlement?"

"You are their commander," Wrot said. "The Lleix will see that all the Jao answer to you. That will only reinforce the idea that my kind are now human slaves and put off the time when we must make a full explanation." He turned to Caitlin. "You can use the opportunity to continue negotiations with them, evaluate their preparations for the diaspora, and generally learn all you can about the situation, so that when we return, they will be ready to leave."

Go down to that planet with only a few jinau to back her up? Caitlin closed her eyes, seeking for calm. He was going to strand her with the Lleix who had been so brutally mistreated for such a long time that they were quite likely to look upon contact with any alien species as nothing but the direst of threats.

But she had lived in the eye of the storm raging between human and Jao for most of her life before the deposing of Oppuk and the formation of Terra's new taif two years ago. She knew better than anyone what existing in that sort of maelstrom was like. Venturing among the Lleix mostly likely would not be pleasant, but she could manage, and they deserved what help Terra Taif could provide.

"All right," she said. At least he would have to be the one to explain all this to Ed, including the part about her being left behind on a potentially hostile world. She didn't envy Wrot *that*. "When do we get started?"

"As soon as we can work out the logistics," Wrot said. "Tully, requisition enough supplies to last at least three weeks and get the assault craft prepared."

"What about Mallu and Kaln and the rest of the Krants?" Tully said. "They've been under my temporary command."

Wrot considered. "They will remain under your command for the duration of this assignment. Anyone who can deal with the human Resistance on a regular basis can handle a few obstinate Krants."

Tully looked unhappy, but didn't argue. Caitlin took a deep breath and tucked up a stray lock of hair. The Queen of the Universe should always look her best. "Okay, now we have to go in there and sell this whole idea to the Lleix."

She nodded at the guard who reached over and opened the conference room door for her. Holding her head high, she sailed back into the room, trying to exude confidence.

"Jihan," she said with a calm that she most definitely did not feel, "we have a proposal for you, one that might save all Lleix, not just two thousand."

The bright black gaze turned to her. "All Lleix?" Jihan said.

"All," Caitlin said, taking a seat across from the silver-skinned trio. "I cannot promise yet, but we will try."

Jihan spoke to the other two in the lilting Lleix language. They answered, eyes narrowed, and then all three focused upon her. "How save?" Jihan said.

"If we can work out the logistics," Caitlin said, "we will summon our own ships to transport the Lleix to safety."

"Many ships?" Jihan said. Its silver corona stood on end. "And what is lo-jiss-tix?"

"Many many ships," Caitlin said. "I'll explain logistics later. But, as I said, I cannot promise. For now, while we are trying to work out the details, this ship will take you back to your world, and I will go with you to meet the rest of the Lleix."

"Cat-lin, Queen of the Universe, goes now to Valeron?" Jihan said.

"Well, something like that," she said.

Wrot left Caitlin with the Lleix while he went up to the control deck to give Terra-Captain Dannet her new orders. One hundred thousand Lleix! The number chased itself round and round in his mind, both a wonderful and frightening revelation. The marvelously many descendants of those who had escaped the Jao's ancient brutality now translated into the same number who were, as a human would say, in harm's way. When they had all been believed extinct, the Jao could feel regret at having exterminated such a wise species, but now that the Lleix had been discovered alive, they became a responsibility, and a heavy one at that. What had been a matter of regret was now a matter of conscience.

The lift doors opened and he stepped inside, his thoughts racing. The Lleix had to be moved soon. There was no time to scout out-of-the-way worlds for a suitable new permanent home. Taking them to Terra was the best option available at the moment, unless Preceptor Ronz had a better idea. But settling them there, even for a short time, could draw the attention of the Ekhat once again. If they realized that Terra Taif had cheated them of their prey, they might well launch another major attack on Terra.

Therefore, speed was of the essence. The sooner the Lleix were removed, the less likely the diaspora was to be detected. The Ekhat *were* coming back. He felt it with every fiber of his being. Not now, or even "tomorrow," but soon.

The lift stopped and he stepped out onto the busy control deck. Lights were flashing, crewmen darting from station to station. Dannet was leaning over a console, pointing out a discrepancy to a human technician.

"Terra-Captain," he said, striding across the deck. "We have new orders."

Her eyes blazed green, but her body said only *respectful-attention*. They both knew who had *oudh* now that the battle was over, however little she might like it.

"We will achieve orbit around the fourth planet in this system for a short time," he said, "then head back to Terra with all speed possible."

PART VI:
Valeron

CHAPTER
29

Humans actually bore little resemblance to Jao, Jihan thought, as the little transport soared down through Valeron's buffeting atmosphere. They were shorter than their ancient enemy, even the oldests, and much slighter in build. Their ears were not mobile. Their skin was mostly sleekly bare like that of a Lleix, a variety of shades, none of them even close to silver. Some of them, though, possessed sparse scatterings of fur on arms, legs, and chest, and even occasionally on their prominent-nosed faces.

She was already picking up some English words, which seemed to surprise Cat-lin—no, Jihan reminded herself, the correct pronunciation was "Caitlin." Evidently humans found it much harder to learn new languages. On this short journey from the big ship, she was doing her best to decipher as many terms as possible, though, since most of the humans spoke in this English language, not Jao, unless addressing their slaves.

She gazed around the crowded cabin. Oddly enough, the Jao slaves were clad the same as the rest, in dark-blue "shirts" and "trousers" which fit rather snugly and required little in the way of draping to look their best. Jao carried the same equipment, even weapons, and performed the same tasks. To outward appearances, humans did not seem to regard them as inferior or untrustworthy. That was strange—but also boded well for the Lleix. Even in the short time since she'd met them, it was clear that, whatever else they might be, humans were far different from the savage Ekhat.

The ship landed finally with a jolt that wrung a painful throb from her wrenched arm. Jihan sniffed, twisting about in her safety harness to survey the other passengers. They did not seem alarmed, so such carelessness must be standard. She could have done far better with a Starsifter ship. Perhaps human pilots did not get much practice.

The Queen, Caitlin, rose and made her way back to the three Lliex. "You should go out first," she said. "We do not wish to frighten your people unnecessarily."

Jihan wished the queen looked more impressive. She would have difficulty convincing her people of the richness of Caitlin's resources when they had never seen the gigantic *Lexington* for themselves. Perhaps she could have the Patternmakers design traditional Lleix robes that would disguise her seeming frailty. Nothing, though, could hide her distressing lack of height.

The hatch unsealed and Jihan peered out. With a jolt, she saw that the sun was just disappearing over the mountains. It was early evening planet-side. On the ship, it had been considered morning.

A veritable sea of silvery faces watched. Just beyond, she could see the low graceless buildings of the *dochaya*. A murmur went up at the sight of her Lleix face. "There is no danger!" she called, then ducked her head to get through the low door and took up a position on the extended ramp where all could see her. "The great devils who invaded our system are dead, though more will surely come."

They were clad in the simple gray shifts of the unassigned and shifted from foot to foot, unsure of how to react to this unprecedented sight. She knew they were not used to working things out for themselves.

She turned back and motioned Lliant, with his bruised face, and weary Hadata out into the fading light. It was nearly the time of evening-meal. She could smell sourgrain roasting in the communal cooking house. Most likely, they were weary from the day's labors as well as hungry.

Caitlin eased out to stand beside them. The yellow fur on her head fluttered in the chill breeze coming down from the mountains. The human rubbed her arms with her hands, braced against the wind. "Now what?"

Jihan had been thinking about this ever since Caitlin had said they would accompany the three Lleix back to Valeron. "We request meeting of *elian* in Hall of Decision."

She gazed down at the little queen with her delicate hands and felt almost a moment of tenderness, such as usually reserved for the young and helpless of the Children's Court. Really, for one who held a great deal of authority and power, she was so tiny! "You and rest staying here. I go to Grijo, return soon."

"All right," Caitlin said and hastened back into the ship, apparently uncomfortable. Two humans emerged to take up positions just outside the hatch, weapons in hand. The unassigned stared in dumb amazement at the diminutive creatures.

"What are they?" one, bolder than the rest, whispered. "Are they Ekhat?"

"These are humans," Jihan said patiently. "They came in a great ship, bigger than any ever seen before, and defeated the Ekhat, or we three would not be standing here before you now."

Aureoles flared with interest. The murmuring grew and some even pushed forward to get a better look at the aliens.

"Go partake of evening-meal," she told them as Lliant and Hadata followed her down the ramp. "Nothing will happen here until I consult the Eldests."

And then, because this was their sole meal of the day and hunger blunted curiosity, the unassigned turned away to drift toward the cooking house and left the three human ships sitting out on the plain unattended.

"No one will disturbing you now until I return," Jihan called from the foot of the ramp. "I hoping to come back with news from the Eldests soon."

Caitlin stood in the hatch and waved her small arm, possibly a gesture of permission to depart, then Jihan set off, trailed by the other two.

She went first to the Dwellingconstructors to consult Grijo, who was currently Eldest of all the *elian*. He met them in the *elian*'s Application Room. The house was redolent with bluebean stew. Jihan realized with a start how very hungry she herself was. The humans had offered food on their great ship, but it all smelled wretched and she had been too excited to think of eating anyway.

Grijo settled his magnificent bulk on a padded bench while Lliant retreated to a corner as if ashamed, staring down at his feet. "News has preceded you," the Eldest said after a few moments of deliberation. "The Starwarders reported that a great ship of unfamiliar design is in orbit around our world."

"They are called humans," Jihan said, her eyes respectfully downcast. Her feet were filthy, she saw. She should have taken time to bathe them before coming into this august house. "They defeated five Ekhat ships with only the one of theirs!"

"And you thought it safe to bring these aliens back to our city?" His aureole rippled.

"They are the Ekhat's enemy," she said, "and they wish to help the Lleix."

"They have Jao among them," Lliant blurted.

Grijo's eyes went to the Ekhatlore.

"The Jao are their slaves," Jihan said, "as once they were slaves of the Ekhat. As long as the humans control them, they are no longer a danger to us."

"Then you were correct, little Jaolore," Grijo said, "that day up on the mountain."

She turned her head aside. It was not polite to acknowledge an Eldest's error in judgment. "Not entirely, Eldest. I believed the Jao had returned with the Ekhat to destroy us. Instead, it seems that at some point, these humans subjugated them, so that now the Jao do their bidding, not the Ekhat's."

"They are very short," Hidata said softly. "These humans."

"They are another kind," Jihan said. "I do not believe height and girth have as much meaning to them as they do to us."

Grijo considered. "We will have to meet," he said finally.

"Tonight, if at all possible," Jihan said, shocking even herself with her haste. "Though they are vanquished for now, the humans believe the Ekhat will return with even more ships. This will be Last-of-Days if the Lleix do not flee to safety."

"We are already preparing the few ships we have left," Grijo said. "You know that."

"They may be able to help, though," Jihan said, abandoning all attempts at propriety. She met his black gaze with her own, positively round-eyed with urgency. "They have many ships and are considering transporting all Lleix to safety."

"And what would they want in return for this?" Grijo said.

She looked away. "I do not know. They have never named any sort of price or trade."

"I will call the Han to the Hall of Decision tomorrow," Grijo said. "Perhaps older heads than yours can make sense of this."

"But," cried Jihan, "we should meet tonight! They are waiting and there is no time to waste! The Ekhat—"

"If you do not conduct yourself appropriately, little Eldest, no one will ever listen to you," Grijo said. "Surely, you know that."

With an effort, she bit back all the arguments she longed to make. Matters would proceed as they always did, in an orderly and precise and leisurely fashion. The Han would be called, everyone would dress properly, and then parade up the mountain. Only this time, her presence as Eldest of Jaolore would be expected.

"Go to your houses," Grijo said. "Partake of evening-meal. Bathe and prepare for tomorrow. The sun will rise soon enough and we will decide all the better for having eaten and rested."

Jihan dropped her gaze and then the three of them retreated.

Half an hour after Jihan departed, Caitlin put on a heavy coat and went back outside the ship with Tully and Nam. The red tinged light was fading with the setting sun, but enough lingered to illuminate their surroundings. This was her first chance to experience a new world and she wasn't going to waste a single minute skulking inside while they waited for Jihan to return.

The air, a bit thinner than humans liked, was dry and cold, close to freezing, and a stiff wind blasted down from the mountains to the west. The darkening sky had a greenish cast. She could see white blanketing the crests of the two tallest peaks. Evidently the Lleix were not sensitive to the chill because, from what she'd observed, they all went about quite barefoot. At any rate, the city had a pleasantly herbal scent, a bit like sage, she thought, with a hint of rosemary.

Before her, the Lleix buildings were low and squat, only a single story each, laid out in long rows and constructed of ugly gray stone, possibly mined from those nearby mountains. Waist-high posts were studded along the narrow "streets" and were now brightening with green-tinged light. She could see small leathery flyers fluttering about them as though chasing insects in the growing dusk.

"This place sure isn't much to look at," Tully muttered as the three of them walked down the assault craft's ramp. He shoved his hands into his pockets.

No, it wasn't, thought Caitlin. On the other hand, if this sort of high desert terrain and climate suited the Lleix, it would be easy to find a place for them in North America. The continent's southwest had lots of areas like this that were sparsely inhabited—or even completely uninhabited, if the Lleix could handle more severe conditions.

Taller buildings, which seemed to promise more interesting architecture, loomed in the distance. Caitlin wished they could explore, but didn't want to alarm the natives any more than necessary by setting off on their own. The Lleix must already be spooked by the arrival of five Ekhat ships in their system. Having three alien ships land right in their midst, filled with both humans and Jao, just added to the confusion.

"They've been in hiding for hundreds of years," she said. She'd filled Tully in on the history between the Jao and the Lleix on the way down from the *Lexington.* "I would imagine that design wasn't foremost on their minds. They may not even have been here very long or meant for this to be a permanent settlement." The wind gusted and she huddled into her coat. "I guess we'll learn more once Jihan arranges a meeting with their authorities."

Two figures rounded a corner, then hurried toward the assault craft. Squinting through the growing dimness, Caitlin thought she recognized Jihan, but not the other who was much slighter.

The Lleix stopped at the foot of the ramp. "Caitlin, Queen of the Universe," it said.

Really, this was going to get old very fast, Caitlin told herself. "Jihan?"

"The Han will meet next-sun," Jihan said softly, using the Jao term for tomorrow. "Nothing can be done before then."

Caitlin blinked in surprise. Alien ships land in the middle of their settlement after a huge battle in the solar system with their ancient enemies, and no one can be bothered to leave the dinner table long enough to say *hi* or even *get off my grass*? "I...see," she said, though she didn't, not at all.

"Humans come to Jaolore *elian*-house," Jihan said, its corona fluttering. "Stay through night there."

"No," Tully said in English. He had stepped closer and held his gun ready, angling to protect Caitlin. "You're better off here where we can seal the hatch. With their history, they have to be paranoid about contact with aliens. Who knows what's going on inside their heads? They might be planning to slaughter us the minute we leave the ship."

"I agree about making this our base," she said softly. "But I would like to at least see this *elian*-house. Leave the Jao here for now, but let's take a small armed company into the city and accompany Jihan for a short visit."

He shook his head, plainly not liking the idea. "You only have this creature's word that they mean you no harm," he said. "There's no telling what kind of reception we'll get."

A few Lleix emerged from one of the low buildings and walked toward the ship, their gray shifts fluttering in the stiff breeze. They looked strangely aimless. "We are here to help," Caitlin said. "I don't want to act guilty and make them think we have something to hide."

"We *do* have something to hide," Tully said, glancing back inside the ship at Kaln and Mallu, who, against his better judgment, were listening to Miller spin a highly improbable yarn about Pecos Bill. "And you darn well know it."

"Yes," Caitlin said to Jihan, "we would like to see the Jaolore *elian*-house, though we will come back here."

Tully sighed. "Burgeson, Reese, Murphy, Estrada, Fligor, fall in. Lieutenant Murphy, you're in charge here until we get back. Just sit tight." He checked the power indicator on his own rifle, then hefted it meaningfully.

More Lleix gathered as the armed party, with Caitlin maneuvered into its center, descended the ramp. The Lleix's coronas rippled like flowers waving in the wind and Caitlin thought the newcomers all looked cold, dressed only in those brief gray garments. How strange that none of them wore garments similar to Jihan's extravagantly decorated robes. Evidently their contact must hold high rank.

"Do you understand the concepts of male and female?" she asked Jihan as they drew together.

"Yes," the Lleix said, setting off down a crushed stone path, its face green-tinged from the artificial lights.

"Humans and Jao have both male and female genders," Caitlin said, hurrying to keep up with the Lleix's flowing stride. "Do Lleix have these same genders also?"

"Yes," Jihan said. "I am being female. Pyr—" She gestured at her slight companion. "—is being male. The heads of males are rounder, usually."

Pyr's corona flattened, making him seem embarrassed. He kept glancing at them, then looking away, as though their alienness was overwhelming.

Well, at least now Caitlin could stop thinking of Jihan as "it." She mulled over the information, wanting to know more about Lleix society so that her negotiations would be effective. Did gender play a part in determining who would rule? "Do males or females make the decisions for Lleix?" she asked finally as they walked.

"Eldests make decisions," Jihan said in her lyrical voice. "Male sometimes, sometimes female."

There were no stars visible overhead, though the evening sky was cloudless. Evidently, the nebula's dust and gas obscured such sights. How lonely to live here down through the centuries hiding from the Ekhat without even stars in the night sky.

More Lleix appeared in the narrow roadway, staring with their gleaming black eyes. Several approached Caitlin, four-fingered hands outstretched, speaking to her in soft fluting voices. Jihan answered sharply and they drew back, but then trailed after the humans once they'd passed.

"What do they want?" Caitlin asked, glancing back over her shoulder. Tully edged closer to her, his expression grim. None of them seemed to be armed, but still her heart raced. There were so very many. Maybe this hadn't been such a good idea after all. Should they perhaps turn back to the ship?

"Are they afraid of us?" she asked Jihan.

"Not afraid," Jihan said. "They wish—employment."

"Work?" Tully said. His brow creased and he glanced back at the following Lleix. "They want to work for us?"

"This is the *dochaya*," Jihan said, sweeping an arm toward the long rows of buildings. "Home for unassigned. They have no—" She thought for a moment as they walked, feet crunching over the crushed stone. "—no purpose, no reason for living. They want employment so they can leave."

Understanding formed. This was some kind of slum. Caitlin stopped in the roadway, surrounded by silver faces and inscrutable black eyes, all trained upon her as though she possessed the answer to the meaning of life. Five Ekhat ships had just blazed through this system, ready to extinguish these people. Then aliens had landed in the middle of their city, and all these poor wretches were worried about was a *job*?

Tully whistled in surprise, which startled the Lleix far worse than their ships had. The natives screeched, then scuttled back into the structures, coronas flattened. He stared after them. "You've got to be kidding," he said in English. "What the hell kind of place is this?"

Caitlin cleared her throat, trying to think how to proceed. "Do all Lleix feel this way?"

"No," Jihan said, "only those without an *elian*." She had held her ground, but she looked unnerved and kept glancing at Tully as though afraid he would whistle again. Pyr had ducked behind her and was staring at his feet. "Please not doing that—sound—again! Lleix find such—most alarming."

"Sorry," Tully said.

What in the blazes was an *elian*, Caitlin wondered, and why didn't these particular Lleix have one? Jihan set off again and the small party walked in silence, passing stone building after building until finally Lleix again emerged. The silvery forms shuffled together, mostly silent, jostling to get a better look at the strangers.

She could almost feel their hunger as though they yearned for—something. "Are we in danger?" she said, shivering in the cold wind. "Are they angry that we have come to Valeron?"

Jihan turned to her. "No, Caitlin, Queen of the Universe, Eldest of all Humans," she said. "They will not hurting you. They are being sad."

CHAPTER
30

"I don't think I like this place," Tully said, gripping his rifle in both hands. "Let's go back to the ship before we get ourselves into real trouble."

"We came to meet the Lleix," Caitlin said, refusing to lose her composure. "And here they are." She was a diplomat now. Ronz was counting upon her. It would not do to impute human motivations to these people. They were another kind, as alien in their mind-set as Jao were to humans. The "unassigned" had not made any moves of aggression, after all.

"Yeah, great reception, isn't it?" Tully said, craning his head, apparently scanning the crowd for weapons. "Keep walking."

Jihan's small companion, Pyr, suddenly waved his arms and called out at the pressing mob. Startled, they milled, their coronas wilting, then turned away and retreated to their ugly buildings. Pyr darted after them, still shouting.

"What is he saying?" Caitlin asked Jihan.

"He say unassigned alarming Queen of Universe," Jihan said, shortening her long graceful strides to keep pace with Caitlin. "Telling them to go away."

About what it had seemed, she thought. Perhaps the cultural referents weren't that different after all. A moment later, Pyr returned. "They not meaning frighten," he said to her in mangled Jao. "Not understanding no work here."

Another speaker of the tongue of their ancient enemies. Caitlin suppressed her surprise, though she did wonder how many there actually were. "If we did request them to work for us, how would we pay them?"

"Pay?" Jihan said. "Not knowing this word."

"What—would they expect in return for working?" Caitlin said as they passed yet another long row of the dreary gray stone buildings.

"Better food," Pyr said. "Clean garments, reason to live, perhaps nice place to sleep, all that *elian* giving."

It sounded then like an *elian* was a sort of organization, perhaps even a clan, like a Jao kochan, but Jao were born into a kochan which nurtured their development and trained them for their future occupation. No matter how badly they behaved, they were never cast out, but there seemed to be an inordinate number of Lleix here with no *elian*.

Finally they reached the edge of the depressing *dochaya*, as Jihan called it, and entered a neighborhood of ornate, much more attractive multistory wooden buildings with peaked roofs and carvings, adorned with flags. At least half, though, seemed to be unoccupied and were sadly dilapidated with gaping roofs, tumbled down fences, and peeling walls. Why didn't those in the *dochaya* move out here, Caitlin wondered, and occupy themselves with the repairs since they craved work and there was obviously room?

She didn't ask Jihan though, saving that question, and a number of others, for later. A few of the so-called "unassigned" had slipped out and were doggedly following them again, but at a discreet distance. Tully and his jinau walked in a tight formation, keeping her at the center. All the humans' lungs labored to breathe the cold, thin air as the party attempted to match Jihan and Pyr's stiff, apparently effortless pace.

Most of the sunlight had faded now. A thin rind of a moon was rising, adding its illumination to that of the light-posts lining the pathway. The houses they passed grew larger and more magnificent, all decorated with carved faces that looked nothing like the Lleix, surrounded by lavish gardens, though this was obviously the cold season and most of the vegetation lay dormant. The streets were narrow and winding, crossing a number of ornate bridges. The streams below were studded with stone weirs so that the water frothed, rushing musically.

"Is it much farther?" Caitlin asked finally, grown weary of the sights. She'd thought she was in pretty good shape, but this trek had thoroughly winded her and it was so achingly cold! Even her nose was numb. She felt a bit dizzy and very much did not want to disgrace herself.

"Jaolore *elian*-house there." Jihan pointed at a one-story building.

As they neared, Caitlin could see that it had an especially large garden and huge floor-to-ceiling windows. Dim lights glowed within. Pyr opened a door carved with scowling faces and disappeared inside. Jihan followed and Tully turned to Caitlin, putting a hand out to stop her.

His face was grim in the faint moonlight. "Let us check for trouble," he said. "You wait out here."

She nodded, too chilled to answer without her teeth chattering. This had been a boneheaded idea. Ed would certainly have chided her for being impulsive. She should have waited until tomorrow, only she had wanted so badly to see something of the Lleix city and get started with her assignment. They didn't have much time before the Ekhat would return.

Tully ducked inside with two of the five jinau, weapons ready, leaving her by the door with the remaining three. He needn't have bothered, she thought, tucking her poor frozen hands under her arms. The unassigned had dropped off several bridges ago. The humans were alone outside in the silent starless darkness. Nobody cared that they were here.

She huddled into her coat, trying to stay warm. The air felt cold enough to snow, if there had been any clouds. Her ears were freezing too, despite the scarf she tied over her head, and the thought beat through her that the Lleix went quite barefoot and bare-headed in this weather.

Jao tolerated a much greater temperature range than humans, comfortable at both higher and lower readings, but she thought if they'd brought any along tonight, even they would have been glad of their boots.

Tully reappeared. "It's all right," he said in English. "One of their elders is inside, so I think it's good that we came after all."

Grijo was waiting for Jihan in the Jaolore Application Chamber to discuss the current situation when a trio of the most astonishing creatures burst into the room. They had patches of fur on their small heads and were quick, darting here, poking into there with a most unseemly haste as though they simply could not be still.

These must be the umans. Grijo eyed them critically. They certainly were not much to look at, positively slight. He could have broken their necks with very little trouble. One of them faced him and said something unintelligible in a high little voice. The tone sounded rather demanding. Grijo's aureole quivered. He was Eldest of the Han and due respect, even from such as these.

Jihan entered and cast herself to his feet. "Forgive them, Eldest! They are of another kind and know nothing of our courtesies!"

"Obviously," he said with the dry narrowing of a single eye. "Rise, little Eldest of Jaolore. Eldests never greet one another so, no matter how grievously they last parted, and we two have much to discuss."

The three humans disappeared and Grijo could hear their rigid footwear clattering across the wooden floors. He winced at the unharmonious noise. "What do they seek?"

"Danger, I believe," young Jihan said with a rueful flutter of her aureole. "My command of Jao is far from perfect and though I have told them there is nothing to fear here among us, they wish to see for themselves."

"They value their Eldest then," Grijo said. "Quite proper. One cannot fault them for that." He settled his great bulk upon a padded bench and gestured toward Kajin who was lurking in the far doorway that led to the Duty Chamber. "While waiting for your return, I have been familiarizing myself with their growly tongue through the records. It is not as difficult as I feared."

"They all speak Jao, as well another language they call 'English,'" Jihan said. "I have been acquiring some of those words as well."

The three humans reappeared with three more, including one swaddled in layers of clothing as though it were quite young. Shortest of all of them, it advanced, head down, arms wrapped around itself as if frightfully chilled, though Grijo had found the night rather moderate for the season.

"Caitlin," Jihan said, hurrying across the room.

The creature answered the Jaolore, hanging back.

"The Queen of the Universe is cold," Jihan said to Kajin, rendering the alien's title in its own language. "Bring a brazier."

The youth disappeared, his demeanor communicating unease. Grijo did not blame him. He too found it disquieting to be in the company of these aliens. They might not be Ekhat, but Lleix experience with other species had not been positive down through the long years of flight. Many of their former trading partners had also been exterminated by the Ekhat. Those who were left feared aiding the Lleix would attract Ekhat attention and had refused them sanctuary. In the end, the Lleix had been able to depend only upon their own resources, losing colony after colony, most of their numbers dying, until the remnants fled here.

A second bench was brought and placed across from Grijo with a blazing brazier between them. Caitlin splayed her fingers—ten rather than eight—before the fire and then slowly pulled off her cumbersome outer garment. For an Eldest, she was indeed unpreposessing, with small hands and small round blue eyes. Although they could not be seen due to the clumsy-looking outerwear, her feet had to be tiny. It was hard to imagine how she managed to stay erect.

Different species would have differing protocols for rank, though, Grijo reminded himself. These humans, however strange, had defeated five Ekhat ships and they were at least willing to confer with the Lleix. Their council should be received, however this turned out.

"You had a good landing, I hope," he said, signaling to Jihan that she should translate. He had as yet too few Jao words to communicate adequately himself. That would take several more days, at least. "Why have you come in our time of great troubles?"

Caitlin straightened, conveying dignity in spite of her unimpressive bulk. "To save the Lleix," she said through Jihan.

"We have never encountered humans before, so you do not know the Lleix," he said. "Why then would you come for us?"

"We knew of the Lleix," she said, "through our association with the Jao."

His aureole stiffened. "The Jao drove us from our homeworlds," he said. "At the behest of the Ekhat, they destroyed our trade, slaughtered our children, laid waste to our cities. No more than a splinter of our former number survives hidden here. Why should you believe we would trust the Jao or anyone associated with them?"

After Jihan translated, Caitlin hesitated, seeming to consider. "What you say is true," she said finally, "of the Jao long ago. They were as you describe, but they are different now."

"Because they are human slaves," Jihan said.

Caitlin's pallid face went curiously red. "Because of themselves," she said. "They understand the great wrong they once inflicted upon the Lleix, who sought only to improve their lives. They wish to make amends."

Grijo glanced sharply at Jihan after she translated that last bit. "Are you certain you really understand these words?"

Jihan bowed her head. "Most of them."

"How can we possibly put our faith in such creatures?" Grijo said.

"I do not know, Eldest," Jihan said, "but if we do not, most of us will surely face Last-of-Days, for it is a certainty that the Ekhat will come back."

Grijo levered his bulk up, rising with all the dignity to which his many years and height entitled him. "I will go now back to the Dwellingconstructors to ponder." He glanced at the tiny human Eldest. "Escort this Caitlin to the Han tomorrow and we shall see what the assembled wisdom of the colony can make of this matter."

"Yes, Eldest," Jihan said, her voice a respectful whisper.

The humans scuttled aside to make room as Grijo strode briskly toward the door. His thoughts likewise scuttled, trying without success to make sense of this encounter. There should be a pattern, a rightness, a proper way to conduct themselves, but he could find no hint of order in the situation.

These creatures, who had somehow wrested control of the unholy Jao from the great devils themselves, wished to help the Lleix? Such a proposal with its corresponding monumental commitment of resources would not occur without a reason, one that would benefit them in some way. The Han could not possibly accept the offer without understanding what motivated it.

But, he told himself, they were aliens. Perhaps the Lleix would never be able to understand them, or at least not in time, and the Ekhat were indeed coming.

He exited the Jaolore-house and walked in perplexed silence back to his own *elian*. Above, the empty sky kept watch. What would it be like, he wondered, pausing in the middle of an especially lovely bridge, to live under stars again?

"He was huge," Caitlin said staring at the door after the elder lumbered out of the house. "I thought Jihan and the others were tall, but..."

"Yes, yes," Jihan said in English. "Grijo very tall of us all."

English? When the blazes had *that* happened? Every human in the room turned to her as though she should be able to explain. Caitlin's heart skipped a beat. There was just too much going on here to take in all at once. "Jihan," she said in Jao, trying to control her shock, "where did you learn English?"

"On ship," Jihan said still in English. "Listen very much."

Caitlin had assumed that Jihan had been studying Jao for years, learning it painstakingly in fits and starts from ancient recordings as a human would. "And how long have you been learning Jao?"

"Not keeping count," Jihan said, settling on the vacant bench and arranging the folds of her elaborate robes so that they hung just so, making herself a half-sized replica of Grijo. She switched to Jao. "You would saying twenty days maybe."

Twenty days! There were humans who had been trying to learn Jao for twenty years who did not possess as much useful vocabulary as Jihan had already picked up. Very young children might acquire language at something approaching this rate, but not adults. Very young *human* children. Obviously, she told herself, Lleix brains retained the facility after maturity much better than humans or Jao.

Caitlin and Tully glanced at one another. She could see the realization dawn in his green eyes. They would have to watch what they said—in any language—around the Lleix all the time. If they could pick up vocabulary and syntax that easily, they would all speak both Jao and English very quickly.

She sighed, suddenly unutterably weary. They should go back to the ship. She stood. The room they were in was quite striking, the wood floor polished to a high sheen, the roof supported by huge exposed rafters, a bare minimum of furniture. A woven mat lay in one corner, but no pictures hung on the walls, she noted. In fact, no decorative knickknacks of any sort. The sense of order was almost—restful.

"We will go back now," she said.

"No, no, must staying!" Jihan said in badly accented English. "Caitlin go to Han very early tomorrow. Not being late or great badness!"

Tully stepped in front of Caitlin, weapon ready, as though he thought the Lleix would try to detain her physically. "Come to the ship when it is time," he said, squaring his shoulders. "Then we will go to this—Han."

Whatever that was, Caitlin thought. How strange these people were. If Earth had been under imminent threat from the Ekhat, humans would have been working through the night to ready ships and load supplies. No one would have stayed home and dusted the furniture. And if aliens had come offering help, everyone would either have thronged to see them and hear what they had to say, or run away in stark raving terror. But only one member of the Lleix government seemed the least bit concerned about all of this, and even *he* had just gone home to bed!

The Ekhat could come back tonight or tomorrow, or it might not be for weeks, but they would come. Even she had enough experience now to know that. The Lleix had to know it too, with even more certainty, given their history, and yet still the colony slumbered.

"Let's go," she told Tully, bundling back into her coat, and the seven of them headed out into the frigid night.

Just before dawn, Jihan presented herself at the lead assault ship. Caitlin had already risen and was as ready as she could be, given the limited sanitary facilities, to go out and make interstellar history. Combing her fingers through her short blond hair, she gazed at the viewscreen with its image of the Lleix waiting outside by the ramp. Compared to the elder, Grijo, Jihan looked almost childlike.

She sighed. Wrot should be here, or Aille, or Ronz, someone with experience who had the authority to promise these people what they needed. She felt like a little girl playing at dress-up.

"All right," she said to Tully. "I'm ready."

The temperature had dropped even lower than the night before. It was so cold outside that she could see her breath. Frost rimed the rocks scattered about the ramp. Just beyond, Lleix were emerging from the squat buildings of the *dochaya*, which looked even more shabby now that she'd toured the main city and seen its handsome wooden houses.

She stood at the top of the ramp, thinking. It would be best to lay all their cards on the table, so to speak. The Jao were a major factor in this situation. They could not be left out. "Bring one of the Jao," she said. "Nam, or Mallu, perhaps."

"Not Kaln?" Tully said with an upward quirk of his lips.

Kaln, who prattled incessantly these days of Pool Buntyam,

Bab the Green Ox, Pay-cose Bill, ships that had jumped wrong and turned inside out, and Caitlin, Queen of the Universe? "No," she said, crossing her arms. "We've got enough problems as it is."

"Krant-Captain Mallu!" Tully called.

The Krant's dark bay face appeared in the hatch.

"Come with us to this Han, whatever that is," Tully said.

"Please make haste," Jihan said in Jao. The Lleix kept glancing toward the mountains. "We have far to go."

They set off trailing the Lleix. Caitlin's security escort numbered ten, including Tully and Mallu. She wasn't sure what the Lleix authorities would make of them bringing along a Jao, but the truth would come out, sooner or later. The Lleix might as well get accustomed to Jao faces from the start.

Unassigned, identifiable by their simple gray shifts, were already wandering the city, in search of a day's employment, Jihan explained.

The silver faces glanced at the little party, but did not speak. Their coronas were limp, suggesting a dispirited attitude. "How many of them will find work today?" Caitlin asked as they walked.

Jihan's own corona fluttered. "I do not know, Queen of the Universe," she said. "Not many, I think."

The Lleix's syntax seemed improved. "Did you work on your Jao last night?" she asked.

"Yes, yes," Jihan said. "It is important now to speak well between us, and as there are no records of English, I listened again to the Jao interviews, few though they are."

Good God, Caitlin thought. If they survived, Lleix could find employment wherever they went simply as translators.

They wove back through the city and she found the houses with their peaked roofs even more lovely in the gray morning light. Unlike the Jao, the Lleix had an artistic bent, carving elongated faces into the posts and beams of their homes, flying colorful flags, and weaving fanciful patterns into the fabric of their clothing. In some ways, humans might be able to understand them more easily than the Jao, who disdained such fancies.

From time to time, wheeled vehicles, open to the air and loaded with crates, crowded them off the narrow roadway. They all seemed to be headed toward the outskirts of the city. "Vehicles take supplies to the ships," Jihan explained when she saw Caitlin staring after them.

"What ships?" Caitlin asked.

"Ships to leave, to escape Ekhat," Jihan said.

When they reached the far edge of the city, they boarded a wheeled transport and sat on padded rows of seats with other high-ranking Lleix, every single one of them larger than Jihan. In some fashion here, size equalled rank, Caitlin realized, and wondered if her stature would lessen her authority in their eyes.

This vehicle, like the others, was also open so that the wind blasted through. The chassis creaked and shuddered, as though it might break down at any moment, creeping up the mountain ever so slowly. Caitlin huddled between Mallu, who did not seem to feel the chill bite, and Tully, trying not to shiver.

The other Lleix passengers glanced aside at her, eyes severely narrowed, then spent the rest of the short trip ignoring Caitlin, fussing instead with the hang of their robes as though the activity ordered their minds.

They all exited the transport halfway up a low mountain. The wind gusted, whining against the rocks. Leaden gray clouds boiled over the peaks above them and flakes of snow with a strange bluish cast pelted Caitlin's cheeks. Tully took her arm as the other Lleix fell into a column and trudged barefoot over the naked granite up toward an ornate building built into the mountain itself.

"Hall of Decision," Jihan said, bowing her head. "We must go there for much discuss."

Caitlin turned and looked back down the mountain. From here, she could see the sprawling city below with its ordered gardens, the squalid *dochaya* at the eastern edge, their own three ships, and to the south, a field of Lleix vessels, all woefully small. If they had to depend upon those to escape, she thought, their reduced numbers would threaten genetic viability. The Lleix would probably not survive as a species.

The air was so cold up here, it took her breath away. She pulled her scarf tighter, then lowered her head and joined the line of Lleix, surrounded by Mallu, Tully, and the armed jinau. Before her, the Lleix strode with their graceful flowing stride, heads up, robes arranged just so, as though they had all the time in the universe to see to this little matter of survival.

Her escort probably wasn't necessary, she thought. So far, the ethereal Lleix with their long graceful necks didn't seem to get worked up about anything, even defending themselves against certain extinction.

✳   ✳   ✳

Jihan was painfully young, compared to the other Eldests, and, of course, they all knew full well that she had broken *sensho* upon her last appearance here. That she had been at least partially correct and the Jao had indeed returned was no defense for her shocking behavior. She had branded herself graceless in their eyes. No one would heed anything she had to say, no matter how important.

Even worse, the Queen of the Universe had seen fit to bring one of the hated Jao along to the Han. The furred creature was behaving itself, for the moment, and did not appear dangerous. Perhaps Caitlin was right and these Jao were different from the barbarians who had hunted them long ago. If so, humans had done a credible job of civilizing the brutes.

Grijo had already taken his ornate seat when they appeared in the open doorway. Out of respect, Jihan made herself small, which seemed hardly necessary when she was but half his magnificent size no matter how she stood. "Esteemed Eldest," she said above the reproving whispers, "may I present the leader of the humans, whose vessel destroyed the five Ekhat ships seeking to attack our colony?"

CHAPTER
31

Head tilted back, Jihan spoke to the huge individual seated in the chair on a central dais. Her tone seemed plaintive. Caitlin hung back by the oversized doorway, shivering, fairly certain the leader was Grijo, the same elder she had met the night before. At least, the patterns on his garment seemed the same.

She tucked her gloved hands under her arms, trying in vain to keep warm, and surveyed the echoing hall. Most of the benches toward the back were empty, suggesting that the drafty building had originally been constructed to hold more attendees.

Jihan turned to Caitlin. "Tell them of humans," the Lleix said in her fluting voice. "Tell them of Jao slaves."

Caitlin glanced back at Mallu, who was waiting patiently among the jinau retinue, his body communicating simple unadorned *attentiveness*. Jao slaves, yes, she was going to have to do something about *that* and soon. The longer the lie went on, the harder it would be to rebuild trust after the facts came out.

She raised her head, standing tall and straight, but still feeling like a child among the tall Lleix, then breathed deeply of the shockingly icy air, nerving herself for this shameful skirting of the truth. "Humans learned from the Jao how once the Lleix suggested that they free themselves from their masters, the terrible Ekhat," she said, pausing to allow Jihan to translate. "This was an immense kindness for which the Lleix afterward suffered greatly at the hands of those same Jao."

Jihan related her words and the coronas of the listening assemblage stirred as though a wind had gusted through a field of flowers.

"The Jao were not ready to heed such advice when it was first offered," Caitlin said, her heart pounding. This was so damned important. They should have sent someone else! "But the Lleix's suggestion stayed with them, and finally, a very long time later, they realized the Lleix had given them wisdom. By then, though, it was too late. The Lleix were all dead, or so the Jao thought."

Grijo leaned forward, black eyes glittering, waiting for her to continue.

"Now we find the Lleix here, in danger once again from the Ekhat. To honor your ancestors, who attempted to help the Jao so long ago at great personal cost, humans may be able to offer assistance. I have sent the *Lexington*, the great ship that brought us here, back to Terra to learn what can be done."

She fell silent then and waited to see what they would make of that explanation. At least none of it was a lie.

Discussion broke out among the fancily robed Lleix. Jihan stood before Grijo in the open middle, head bowed, as the words flew back and forth, not even trying to translate. Delegate after delegate spoke, often gesturing at Caitlin and her escort. The frigid mountain wind sang through the open doors, scattering flakes of unmelting snow across the stone floor. Caitlin's feet felt like blocks of frozen granite. She'd never been so cold in her entire life.

Finally Grijo gazed at her and spoke in mangled Jao. "Why humans would helping Lleix?"

Her eyes widened and she fought to maintain her composure. Did everyone on this isolated world speak their ancient enemy's language? "Because the Jao owe the Lleix a great debt," she said carefully, "and because humans are sympathetic with those who suffer from the persecution of the Ekhat. Terra too has been attacked. We understand your peril."

None of that was a lie either, she thought, feeling shaky. Did all diplomats have to dance around the truth like this?

Finally Grijo spoke to Jihan. The Jaolore listened, then motioned to her. "You go back now," the Lleix said, her corona rippling. "Much discuss here. Last all day, more maybe."

They had to *decide* whether it would be okay if someone saved their lives? Caitlin shook her head. They were like a bunch of old firefighters squabbling over seniority and who got to hold the hose while the city burned down around their ears. "Very well," she said with a rueful shake of her head. Tully and his men fell in around her, faces grim, and they hiked back down the mountain trail to the transports.

The Han went on and on after the humans left, so Jihan did not return to the city until after the sun had set. She walked past the silent houses, watching servants scurry on errands, heads lowered, aureoles flattened. Everyone down to the least unassigned was upset. Last-of-Days had arrived. She herself did not speak with anyone until she presented herself at the humans' ship and was allowed to enter.

"What did they decide?" diminutive Caitlin asked, taking a seat on a long bench close to the outer hatch. Her fellow humans crowded in.

"Not decide yet," Jihan said, remaining on her feet. Narrow human seats were not made for Lleix proportions. "They not understand why humans wish to help."

"Why did the Lleix wish to help the Jao long ago?" Caitlin said.

"So the Jao would not kill them," Jihan said.

Caitlin exhaled a long slow breath. Her face curiously *reddened*. "Yes, there was that."

"Do not stay here," Jihan said, gesturing at the assault craft. She had been thinking about this matter all the way down the mountain. Such cramped, fusty quarters were not fit for the Human Queen of the Universe. "Come to Jaolore *elian*-house until your great ship returns."

"Thank you," Caitlin said, glancing at the one called Tully. "I—"

Tully broke out in a string of English words, talking too fast for Jihan to parse. If Caitlin came to Jaolore, though, Jihan was confident she would acquire more English very quickly.

"If I come, I would bring an escort," Caitlin said. "How many would you have room for?"

Jihan thought. She was not sure. The building she had selected had once supported a medium-sized *elian*. "Half, maybe," she said. "I have not lived in this house long and Jaolore is still small, being very new, so we have not filled it."

"Jaolore is new?" Caitlin said, canting her small head to the side as she sometimes did when perplexed.

"Long ago, there must have been a Jaolore but at some point

it died out," Jihan said. "This Jaolore formed after I realized that Jao fought with the Ekhat in this system."

"But that was not long ago," Caitlin said slowly. Her strange blue eyes blinked.

"Yes, yes, a short time." Jihan looked around at the Humans and Jao. "You come now?"

"Jihan, how old are you?" Caitlin asked, watching the Lleix closely as though the answer were important.

"I am five years out of the Children's Court," Jihan said, puzzled. Surely it was obvious to all that Jihan was woefully short?

"And when are children released from this court?" Caitlin was still studying Jihan, and her changeable face had now lost its ruddiness.

"At sixteen years," Jihan said. "Is it not so with humans and Jao?"

"Then you are only twenty-one?" Caitlin said.

"Yes," Jihan said. "I am the youngest of all the Eldests, and, even worse, I broke *sensho* when I realized the Jao had come back. No one in the Han wishes to listen to me now."

"Twenty-one!" Caitlin seemed to be distressed.

Perhaps that number had some sort of ceremonial significance for humans. Jihan waited.

"Ooomigod!" Caitlin said in English, looking aside at Tully; then she took a deep breath. "We will accept your kind offer to stay at Jaolore," she said, reverting to Jao. "And then, when there is time, there are some matters we should discuss."

"You can't tell her," Tully said as they hiked back through the elegant city, past trees painstakingly pruned into pretzel shapes and tiny sculpted waterfalls. Frost rimed the greenish light-posts lining the narrow roads and the handrails over the bridges. They trod carefully, watching their footing. "At least not yet. Wait until Ronz gets back."

Caitlin glanced ahead at Jihan, but the young Lleix was striding ahead, presumably out of earshot. Although, Tully cautioned himself, who knew how acute their hearing was?

"We have to be straight with her," Caitlin said. Her cheeks were flushed with the cold. "She's already very low ranked because of something she did when the Jao first turned up a couple of months ago. What's going to happen to her when the leadership finds out the Jao are not our slaves, but our conquerors? We'll have a full scale panic and they're going to consider it at least partially her fault for having been duped into fronting for us."

Tully indicated Nam, Mallu, and Kaln with a jerk of his chin. "We have a number of Jao along and they're not exactly raping and pillaging. By the time we have to lay our cards on the table, the Lleix won't be afraid of them anymore."

"They'll be terrified—of them and of us," she said. "And rightfully so, because we're willfully misleading them."

He couldn't think of an answer to that so they walked in silence until they passed another vacant house. "Why are so many of these places abandoned," he said, "when there are Lleix stuck out there in the *dochaya*? Couldn't they just homestead some of these houses so they'd all have a decent place to live?"

"Jihan tried to explain to me about the social set-up with the *elian*," Caitlin said as they turned down yet another narrow lane. A few flakes of snow drifted down from the leaden clouds. "It sounds like they're a bit like Jao kochan, but even more like fraternities and sororities back on Earth. At sixteen, the children are released from the Children's Court for the Festival of Choosing. They wander the city for twenty days, visiting the *elian*, trying to make a favorable impression so that they'll be invited to join."

Tully, who'd grown up in Resistance camps, had of course never attended a university, but he'd heard about snooty frat boys and their antics. He shook his head. "Sounds godawful."

"Some of them get a lot of invitations and can choose their future occupation," she said. "Some, like Jihan, get only one. At least half, though, receive none and are remanded to the *dochaya* as 'unassigned' for the rest of their lives, working in the city's common fields and factories while hoping for employment as servants in one of the *elian*."

Tully remembered the sea of silver faces surrounding the assault ship after they had landed, none of them concerned that a potful of aliens, including Jao, had just set down next to their homes, but instead desperate to simply work for them.

Hair prickled on the back of his neck. The Lleix were slumlords, the whole lot of them! "They won't let them live in those empty houses, will they?" he said.

"I guess not," she said. "How soon do you think the *Lexington* will be back?"

"Not goddamn soon enough," he said, scowling.

                    ✳   ✳   ✳

Caitlin was glad to escape the close quarters of the assault ship. It had never been intended for long-term habitation. The layout provided no privacy and the interior was, frankly, getting a bit rank. She hoped the skeleton crew left behind as guards would at least air it out before they all had to cram themselves in there again and return to the *Lexington*.

The Jaolore *elian*-house, on the other hand, was roomy and smelled pleasantly of oiled wood and herbs. She especially liked the exposed rafters overhead that created the sensation of even more space. Jihan showed them the back of the house with its many bed platforms. Evidently, the Lleix sleeping patterns were more like those of humans, with a substantial dormancy each night, rather than that of the Jao, who preferred short naps scattered around the clock. Unfortunately, though, the Lleix had never conceived of anything resembling a mattress.

According to Jihan, the Han was still considering whether they would allow the humans to assist them in fleeing this world. Really, Caitlin told herself, as she slung her small travel bag onto the low wooden platform, if this was any indication of their ability to respond to emergencies, it was a wonder they weren't extinct already.

Tully poked his head into the tiny room. "There isn't nearly enough space here for the rest of my troops," he said. "Jihan is going to help me find an abandoned house or two for the rest. Do you want to come?"

She nodded, though she was tired. That trip up the mountain had taken a lot out of her. The oxygen content of Valeron air was a shade lower than humans preferred, making her feet seem heavy. She retrieved her coat and scarf and joined him.

"Why are so many houses empty?" she asked Jihan, as they walked out of Jaolore into its winter-bare gardens. The slight male named Pyr dropped behind their small group and followed, head bowed, corona flattened.

"Before, when Lleix come to Valeron, there were many *elian*," Jihan said, her gliding pace, as always, difficult to match. "But over time, some die out, not replaced."

So they were losing their culture along with their populace, Caitlin thought as they turned the corner. Her lungs wheezed as she struggled with the thin air.

Jihan stopped before a large house. The wind was driving down off the mountains to the west and dead leaves were skittering across the frozen ground. "All abandoned houses needing cleaning and repair," the Lleix said.

"My troops can handle that," Tully said.

"No, no!" Jihan said, and entered the long fallow gardens surrounding this particular structure. She glanced at her fellow Jaolore and motioned with one arm. "Pyr will go to the *dochaya* and bring servants to do what is needed."

"Yes," Pyr said in Jao and scuttled in the direction of the grim slum.

Tully stared after the retreating figure. "But we cannot pay them."

Jihan's black eyes regarded him. "You say that word again," she said, walking up to the front doors. "We do not know it."

"To pay is to give something valuable in return for goods or services," Caitlin said, picking her way along the washed-out path to the empty house as she followed.

"Then work is 'pay,'" Jihan said. "Unassigned desire only to work—to be useful to colony."

"But how do they get food then, when they have no work?" Tully said. "Where do they acquire garments?"

"They draw what they need from the kitchens in the *dochaya*, which is supplied by the Distributionists." Jihan's corona shifted. "They give garments too. Is it not being so with humans?"

Soup kitchens for the needy, Caitlin thought. Shelters for the homeless. Humans were indeed only too familiar with the poor and indigent, especially in the early years after the Conquest when so many had been displaced. Still, this was something different. It seemed that for the Lleix, social status and custom completely overrode the economic concerns that humans would have been mostly preoccupied with. The well-off *elian* were perfectly willing to see to it that the unassigned were housed, clothed and fed. But they would not allow them any of the dignity brought by work that had recognized status.

"We have—something like that," she said, not knowing what else to say.

The vacant house's broad wooden doors were unlocked and swung open with a creak. Caitlin realized she had seen nothing like a lock anywhere in the city. Did the Lleix even have a concept of crime? "Jihan," she said carefully as Tully peered inside, rifle ready, "what happens when someone does something bad, hurts someone or takes something that is not hers?"

"Let me check the place out first." Tully disappeared within with a handful of jinau.

"Why would they do that?" Waiting just outside the doors, Jihan blinked in apparent surprise, her silver corona standing on end. "If one needs garments, one applies to the Patternmakers. If one is hungry, she goes to the Distributionists and draws food for the *elian* kitchen. If one needs a home, one joins an *elian* or sleeps in the *dochaya.*"

"But if you took something, a robe or a bowl, perhaps, what would happen?" Caitlin persisted. It was so important that she figure out these people. Once she did, she might be able to find the right words to make them understand humans and Jao as well.

"No one would wear a robe that did not belong to her," Jihan said. "It would have the wrong pattern. For all else, there is *sensho.*"

Jihan had mentioned that word earlier. "You said you had broken *sensho,*" she said.

The Lleix's entire body stilled. "Yes," their guide said softly, gazing down at the frozen ground. "No need for humans to listen to Jihan about anything. I am quite in disgrace."

"What is *sensho*?" Caitlin said, edging closer.

"*Sensho* is—right way to behave always," Jihan said. "Listen to those who are older and taller, do as they say."

For Jihan, then, who was so very young, that would be just about everyone, Caitlin thought. "How did you break *sensho*?"

Jihan hesitated so long, Caitlin thought the young Lleix would not answer. "The Starsifters said the Ekhat had returned, which they had, but I knew from my study the Jao had fought in that battle too. This they did not believe. I went to the Han when Sayr made his report and would not let the error pass."

"You pointed out that they were wrong?" Caitlin said.

"Yes, yes, it was a great discourtesy," Jihan said, hunched as if expecting a blow. "The shame of it will be on me forever."

Caitlin blinked. "But the Jao had come back. You were right!"

"It does not matter," Jihan said.

"They would rather you be polite than correct?" Caitlin was having a hard time with this.

Tully reappeared. "The place is deserted except for a few vermin that look like a cross between a blue mouse and a grasshopper," he said in English. "Come in and see what you think."

Inside, it smelled musty. Something tiny leaped away as they approached. Stools and benches, some broken, were heaped against one wall and a layer of dust blanketed everything. "This place is larger than Jaolore," Tully said, brushing off his dark-blue uniform trousers. Evidently he'd gotten down on his knees at some point. "If we can find another this big, we'll be able to house the crew of all three ships until *Lexington* returns."

"Once Pyr brings servants," Jihan said, "we will select another. Then I will check with the Han and see if they have made decision yet."

"Right," Caitlin said, then turned over a battered bench and sat down. The more she heard about the Han and the way things worked here, the more she dreaded the revelation of the reality of the situation concerning the Jao. Exactly where did telling the truth fit in with the Lleix concept of *sensho*?

That evening, once they had returned to Jaolore, Caitlin decided to level with Jihan. The truth had to come out, especially if they were going to transport these people back to Earth. The Lleix needed to know the situation before they got on the ships, not after. That would only make things worse.

She knew now that Jaolore was indeed very small, consisting of only three full-fledged members, Jihan, Pyr, and a sturdy male named Kajin. The latter spent a lot of time oiling his skin and avoided humans and Jao whenever possible, always leaving a room if any of them entered. A few white-clad permanent servants, as opposed to gray-clad unassigned, worked in the house too, but they never spoke in her presence, not even in the local dialect.

She padded through from room to room, seeking Jihan in the kitchen, the sleeping quarters, the front hall, finally finding her with Kajin in an officelike chamber with viewing machines and stacks of flat recordings. Both were seated on tall stools before screens, studying old files. Kajin gave her a smoldering look and bolted through the closest door.

Caitlin sighed. Obviously, humans were not universally popular around here. "Are you too busy to talk right now?" she asked Jihan.

"No, no," Jihan said. "I practice Jao to speak better."

She already had an amazing command of the language for someone who had only been studying it for weeks, not years. As nearly as Caitlin could tell, though, Jihan had no concept of the vast Jao vocabulary of postures.

"I have something to tell you," Caitlin said, climbing up on the stool next to Jihan and clasping her hands.

"Yes, yes?" the Lleix said, corona standing at attention.

Her heart raced. Damn Wrot and Kaln for putting her in such a position! None of this mess was her lamebrained idea. *They* should have been the ones who had to fess up and make amends, if such a bungled first contact could ever be made right.

"We have not told you the truth about the situation between the humans and the Jao," she said slowly.

Jihan's black, black eyes narrowed.

CHAPTER
32

Jihan waited. Caitlin was so short, the human made Jihan think of her last season in the Children's Court when she had been assigned to instruct the youngers. She gazed down at the round little head with some of the tenderness it was appropriate to feel for youthful creatures weak and small.

"We never conquered the Jao," Caitlin said. The words were spoken slowly with apparent reluctance. The human's tiny fingers were interlaced, one hand gripping the other. "They are not our slaves. They discovered our solar system and then conquered Terra."

Conquered? Perhaps, Jihan thought, she was not understanding the words correctly. After all, she was still learning Jao. Perplexed, she shifted her weight on the stool so that it creaked. "But you are Queen of the Universe."

"No," Caitlin said softly, "I am not." Her strangely colored eyes looked aside as though she were ashamed. "My father is a leader among the humans, but though I work for the government of Terra, I have no actual rank."

The words piled up, creating a terrible picture, if Jihan truly comprehended what Caitlin was saying. Certainly, she had no idea what the term "father" meant. Her aureole wilted against her skull and the *elian*-house seemed unnaturally hushed. A cold frisson of dread shivered through her. "I—do not understand."

"Over twenty orbital periods ago," Caitlin said, still not meeting

319

her gaze, "heavily armed Jao ships entered Terra's solar system. Humans fought a great war against them, but the Jao won."

Jihan's mind reeled. She could not breathe. "Then humans are Jao slaves?"

"No." Caitlin bowed her head. "Not slaves, but for a very long time they did rule us. It was—an unpleasant situation."

"But the Jao said this thing-that-is-not-true to me," Jihan said. "It said you are 'Queen of the Universe'—why would it do that?"

"That particular Jao suffered a head injury in the recent battle inside this star system against the Ekhat," Caitlin said. "Her behavior has been erratic ever since. I believe she genuinely thought she was being funny."

"I do not know that word—funny." Jihan's mind continued to spin. She felt utterly lost. Such a great error! How could she have ever let herself be so misled? "It is not in the records."

"No, it would not be." Caitlin appeared to think, staring down at the burnished wooden floor, tapping her booted foot. "I do not know how to explain it," she said finally. "Both Jao and humans think some situations are amusing, but usually not the same things. Whatever seems funny to the Lleix probably would not to us either."

"The Jao rule humans now?" Jihan said. A great trembling seized her, and she remembered the face of the brave Eldest who had faced the Jao so long ago and been brutally cut down. The Jao had not changed over the years into beneficent rescuers. They were simply more duplicitous than Jihan had ever realized.

"Not—exactly," Caitlin said. "We have come to an understanding which makes us equal. We work with one another now."

Another word she did not understand—"equal." This was bad. The situation was spinning out of control like a damaged ship whose controls no longer answered the helm. Jihan could not begin to think how such a crucial misunderstanding was to be explained to the Han, who could not even make up their collective minds to accept help from humans they believed to be conquerors of their old enemy. That Jao, back at the Ekhat derelict, had lied to her for its own sly reasons, and the humans, including Caitlin, had allowed it to do so.

"If the Jao who told this untruth was injured, why did you let it continue?" Jihan said, turning her head away.

"I did not want to," Caitlin said. "I thought it was a mistake, a great discourtesy, but the Lleix have long feared the Jao, with good reason. Wrot, the Jao who is senior to me, thought you would not be afraid to accept our help if we let you go on believing Jao were human slaves, at least until you knew them better."

Jihan felt her tension ease somewhat. It was true that all the Jao who had accompanied them back to Valeron had behaved well, even the crazy one with the droopy ear who had set this unfortunate situation into motion. So far she had not seen the least sign of aggression from any of them. The great ship *Lexington* could have obliterated their colony between one breath and the next, had this strange Jao-human coalition so desired. She had not the slightest doubt about that.

"I believe the only way for the Lleix to survive is to flee this world and come to Earth, at least for a while," Caitlin said. "I cannot promise this will be done until the *Lexington* returns after seeking the counsel of our rulers, both human and Jao. But if they agree with me, the Lleix must be ready to go."

And to do that, they would have to trust these aliens, who had just revealed they could not be trusted. In her distress, Jihan's arm accidently knocked a stack of recording flats to the floor. She stared down at the chaos, unable in her woeful shortness to think what to do.

Tully appropriated the second house and placed the third under the command of Lieutenant Miller. Mallu was left in charge of the jinau and Krants posted at Jaolore. Both abandoned residences were filthy, with gaping holes in the roofs and infested with several species of vermin. The creatures resembling tiny blue mouse-hoppers were particularly destructive, chewing on wood, fabric, and leather, and even a substance that reminded him of plastic, apparently able to digest everything but stone.

At dawn the next day, he set his troops to repair and clean the premises. The wind was still blasting down from the mountains and the skies were lowering gray lead. The work would both warm his soldiers up and keep them busy, and he thought their industriousness would look good to the locals too. Just sitting around, waiting for the *Lexington* to return, cleaning their guns and looking menacing, might convey the wrong message. The Jao had already torn their pants, so to speak, with these folks. No point in making the situation even worse.

The slender Jaolore, Pyr, arrived just after sunrise followed by twelve Lleix of varying heights, all wearing the gray shifts of unassigned. They bunched outside the front doors, breath frosting in the air, gazing at the dilapidated house with what Tully interpreted as something akin to hunger.

"These being servants," Pyr said in mangled Jao when Tully poked his nose out the door to see what the Lleix wanted. "Work very hard. Tell me what you wish, they do."

"Thanks, but we can take care of things ourselves," Tully said, edging beyond the door while shoving his hands into his pockets for warmth. His ears immediately went numb and he shivered. Damn, but it was cold!

"No, no, letting servants do!" Pyr seemed distressed, hopping from one foot to the other. His robe, brocaded with the figures of snarling Jao, fell open, and he hastily pulled it closed. "No let, making them most sad!"

Tully remembered the *dochaya* with its hopeless sea of silver faces. They wanted to work. Employment meant something to them, far more than it would have to a human under similar circumstances. "All right," he said. "They can at least help. We need to clean the house, get rid of the little hopper-things that are chewing the place down, repair the roof, and see what we can do about some furniture."

Pyr turned back to the waiting servants and warbled a string of apparent instructions. Without a word in answer, half of them sidled around Tully and disappeared into the house.

"Taking these now to other human house," Pyr said. "Back soon." He set off down the path to the street with that great reaching stride humans found it difficult to match. The remaining six trailed after him single-file like obedient ducklings.

Tully darted back inside, shivering, his nose already half-frozen. The chamber just beyond the entrance was large and roomy—and utterly frigid. Lleix didn't seem to have developed the concept of central heating, which wasn't a big surprise since they all went about lightly clad as well as barefoot. Upon searching the house, the jinau had found a few small braziers scattered through the various rooms, but they were empty of fuel. Even though the Lleix were going to flee this world, the old fuss-budgets that ruled this place would probably object to his troops chopping down a few of the elaborately pruned trees that studded the gardens.

The temperature would rise some, now that it was day, but from the look of those clouds, it could very well snow. He sighed. Having grown up in the Resistance camps in the Rockies, he knew only too well what it was like to be cold all the time.

The door opened and Caitlin hurried inside, followed by Sergeant Debra Fligor and Mallu. Her cheeks were pink with wind-burn, her blond hair jumbled. "How's it going?" she asked, huddling into her coat and watching as a servant swept the room.

"Not bad, if you like living inside a freezer," Tully said. "I think it's colder in here than outside!"

"I wouldn't be surprised." She looked around the debris-cluttered chamber. "Have you got anywhere we can sit and talk?"

"There's some beat-up benches in the back in what I think might have been a kitchen." He led Caitlin through a series of rooms, some littered with dried blue leaves that had blown in through the holes in the roof, others dusty and choked with the detritus of some past Lleix life.

She followed, leaving Mallu and Fligor behind. "I told Jihan last night," she said quietly, settling on one of the benches when they got to the silent kitchen area. She shrugged out of her coat and laid it across her lap.

"You told her what?" He sat across from her. She combed her wind-tossed hair with her fingers. Her clothes were rumpled and she looked tired, he thought, like she hadn't slept well in days.

"Everything," she said, "or at least as much of it as I thought she could understand."

The back of his neck prickled. "You told her about the Jao?"

She nodded.

"Jesus!" he said. "You might at least have given me some warning so I could tighten up our security! What if they'd all decided to slaughter us in our sleep after that?"

"I'm sorry," she said. "It was a judgment call and the moment seemed right. I just blurted it all out." She rubbed her eyes. "It wasn't easy, Gabe. Jihan was really shocked and the lie makes us look bad. I think the truth would have been easier to handle from the beginning."

"Caitlin, Queen of the Universe," he said. "Well, it was nice while it lasted."

"No," she said, "there was nothing 'nice' about it. I lived a lie for most of my life, masquerading as the supposedly pampered daughter of the President of the United States to those around me, when I was really a battered political hostage under constant guard. I'd hoped to have put such deception behind me forever."

"Yeah, sometimes I forget about that," he said. "Sorry."

"It's not your fault," she said. "Wrot made this decision, however it turns out, all on his own. Let's just hope we haven't completely blown our credibility with these people." She hesitated.

"There's more?" he said.

"After I explained the situation to Jihan, we stayed up late and discussed logistics for getting her people off this world." Caitlin rose and prowled the bare kitchen, opening doors, peeking into dusty cabinets filled with gnawed shreds. "You know about the *dochaya*, right?"

He grimaced. "The slum? Yeah, we got a damned good look at it when we landed. I can't say I'm impressed by their social arrangements."

"It's huge," Caitlin said. "At least half the population lives out there, maybe three quarters." Her eyes were haunted.

"That many?" He shook his head. "I hadn't realized."

"Whenever they have to flee a world," Caitlin said, "they only take the *elian*, the elite, the ones who live in these elegant houses, wear beautiful robes, and make all the decisions." She was trembling. "They always leave everyone in the *dochaya* behind."

Jihan was summoned back to the Han early that morning. Caitlin had already left the *elian*-house, which was just as well. Jihan did not want the little human present when she revealed the deception perpetrated by the humans and Jao.

She boarded the transport at the foot of the mountain and rode up into the windy heights in silence. The other Eldests also traveling to the Han spoke with one another in low measured tones, but none turned to her, and that was quite proper. She was the most youthful of all their number. What counsel could such as she provide, even if she hadn't been so graceless as to break *sensho*?

The wind blasted through the open windows. Flakes of snow pelted her face. She breathed deeply of the aromatic freshness of high altitude *lir*-trees that clung to the rocks and wondered if this Terra, of which Caitlin had spoken, possessed such lovely scents.

Then she sighed. It did not matter. Terra might be a terrible place with no beauty at all, but still the Lleix would have to go with the humans or it would be Last-of-Days. The next time the Ekhat returned, the great devils would come with ten or twenty or thirty ships. All that would be left of Valeron in their wake was ashes. Of that, she was certain.

With a rush, she suddenly realized that revealing the truth of this situation between humans and the Jao would serve no purpose. If telling would save her people, she would readily come forward and admit her grievous error, but after talking with Caitlin through the night, she saw that it would just frighten the Han into turning away from the only help they had ever been offered.

Then they would launch their few remaining rickety ships containing only a fraction of the population, leaving most behind to die when the Ekhat came. Those ships that escaped might not find another suitable world in time to establish a new colony, or indeed even manage to make the jump out of this star system. Many generations had passed since Lleix had attempted such travel. The ships might well malfunction.

And if they did find another suitable planet, they might very well be too small in numbers to form a large enough gene pool. Without intervention, the Lleix were probably doomed under any circumstances.

Her aureole stiffened, standing against the fierce mountain winds. The Lleix needed these humans, even with all their duplicity. They needed their ancient enemy, the Jao. They even needed Jihan, in all her shortness, to make them listen.

The transport halted at the curving steps carved into the naked striated gray stone. She hung back to let the others who outranked her disembark. Her mind raced as they edged off, slowly, carefully, as though the Lleix had eons to decide this matter. Then she trudged up the mountainside after them, ordering her mind as one ordered her robes, seeking the precise approach that would both follow *sensho* and gain their understanding.

Her superiors would all have to speak before she was allowed to come forward, as was their right, and she would have to sit there and listen through the long morning well into the afternoon, knowing with every breath they were wrong, that they had not seen what she had seen, did not know what she knew, that not one of them possessed the correct information upon which to base such a momentous decision.

She strode in through the great doors, crossing the old flagstones, worn with steps of many generations, laid down when they had first fled to this world. Thoughts rattled around inside her head like pebbles in a jar. How could so many venerable Eldests be wrong? Lleix society said they could not, that assembled wisdom, such as the Han represented, always achieved the right decision, however long it took. But the Lleix did not have time for pointless posturing and rehashing of one another's words, for statement and restatement of the obvious, for every single voice to be heard.

Jihan crossed the hall's open square, which was bordered on all four sides by benches, headed for Jaolore's place tucked into a corner at the very back, hidden among the shortests, then stopped, unable to make herself take another step toward proper obscurity when so very much was at stake.

Grijo looked down at her from his great carved chair in the center and the room stilled. Carefully dressed aureoles of every color fluttered. The Eldests were all waiting for her to make a graceless fool of herself again, to break *sensho*, to reinforce the poor opinions they had already formed about her.

But what did it matter? She could not be any more shamed than she already was. She looked up, surrounded on all sides by the gleaming black gaze of her betters, feeling their disdain.

Grijo blinked down at her, so grand in his immensity. "Shortest," he said in his booming voice. "Little Jaolore, take your seat. We have much to debate."

She started to obey, but then stopped. There must be words, there must! But she did not know what they were. "Eldest," she said and her voice was only a hoarse whisper. Her fingers twitched the hang of her robe a bit, adjusting that which needed no adjustment. If only she could adjust their minds so easily! "Time runs away from us. I believe that we must be ready to leave this world when the humans come back. We should be preparing the *elian*, not spending yet another day in endless discussion of the obvious. They are willing to help, as we once tried to help the Jao. Should we turn away now as the Jao did, refusing the offering of wise advice?"

The Eldests stiffened with disapproval at her brashness. More than a few looked away, exercising *oyas-to*, refusing to see the repetition of such disgraceful behavior.

Grijo's aureole rippled, but the Eldest of all of them did not turn away. "You have taken these humans and their Jao into your *elian*-house."

Jihan bowed her head, making herself even smaller. "Yes, Eldest."

"Why?"

Why, indeed? Because the humans were small and needed shelter? Because the Jao should be watched? Because she wanted to hear more of this Terra and their possible salvation from death at Ekhat hands? Because, by doing so, she had learned the frightening truth at last? There were many reasons, shading into one another, all valid, yet none that would make the Han *listen*.

She raised her head. "Because," she said, not gazing into anyone's eyes, "if they are going to save us, I wished to know the full breadth of their minds before we subjected ourselves to their judgment."

Voices whispered through the immense hall like wind through ripening grain. Aureoles rose, fell, rose again. Knowing the humans' minds—this was a new idea, hard to take in. The Eldests tried it out upon one another, saying it in their own voices so it seemed more like something they had thought for themselves.

It was all so brainless, Jihan lost patience and forgot to be ashamed of her audacity. "Unending discussion of this matter is of no benefit!" She turned, meeting the startled eyes of her superiors as they sat, spines stiff, in their carefully ranked rows, tallests in front, shortests in the rear. "In fact, endless discussion has brought us to this day, which *is* Last-of-Days, unless we take action! We can no longer afford to cower in this out-of-the-way corner of the galaxy, hoping the Ekhat will not find us. They *have* found us, twice, and *will* be back." She could feel her aureole standing on end. "I have boarded one of their ships and seen the great devils eye to eye, and I tell you that they are even more terrible than you can imagine! They will never stop coming! They will never leave us alone, no matter how far we flee! We need this alliance!"

Silence fell as all eyes turned again to her, graceless Jihan, who it seemed could not keep quiet even when propriety absolutely demanded. They weighed her, those fathomless black eyes. They took her measure and found her still so very short.

Old Sayr of the Starsifters, her former mentor, rose, levering his bulk onto his feet ponderously. The Eldests turned to him. Though he was not quite as old as Grijo, he did not lack much in being his match. "Despite her youth, Jihan is speaking truth," he said. "It is time to do things a new way. Old ways have led us here and, unaided, there is no path out. We have to give over our minds to something unexperienced. We must tell the humans yes when they return." He hesitated, gazing steadily at Jihan. "If they return in time."

"They must," she said, humbled by his generosity in considering the ideas of one so short. "It cannot all have been for nothing. We must make a new home somewhere safe."

Grijo gazed over the rows of heads as the Eldests in their gaily brocaded robes gazed numbly at one another. "Will any here say no?"

Pont of the Stonesculptors rose, her aureole flat on one side, quivering on the other. "You cannot be serious," she said. "You think that we should trust these humans with the future of our entire species?"

"What I think," Grijo said, rising, "is that any who do not wish to go with the humans should remain behind and greet the Ekhat in our stead, once we have gone. Will that please you?"

The Stonesculptor sat again, hard, as though her legs had given way.

"Young Jihan has only said what has been in my mind these past few days," Grijo said. "I have been remiss in remaining silent." He gazed pointedly down at Jihan, who was staring up at him in amazement. "It is time for us to leave this world."

CHAPTER
33

Tully lingered outside their appropriated house, watching the Lleix servants work alongside his troops, and all the while, despite the frost-ridden air, he seethed. He'd thought the Jao social set-up was bad with its high and low ranked kochan and limited personal choices, but their system didn't have a patch on this! By Caitlin's estimate, more than half the Lleix population lived in the *dochaya*, going out into the main city each day, begging to be allowed to work at the stuck-up *elian*.

Oh, they weren't left to starve, even if they couldn't find employment, but hanging out in the empty *dochaya* barracks without employment or hope of training or education was no kind of life for anyone, alien or not. They were the most thoroughly disenfranchised creatures he'd ever encountered. About the only parallel Tully could think of were the old Hindu untouchables.

Even Pyr, who, Tully learned, had only recently been accepted into Jaolore, was tarred with the disgrace of having spent time in the *dochaya*. Tully saw how the Lleix from other *elian*, who delivered supplies and furniture to the humans quartered in the abandoned buildings, snubbed him. Each encounter left the young Lleix silent and dispirited.

"Why do you let them treat you that way?" Tully asked, after a tall Lleix threw a box constructed of a plasticlike substance to the frosty earth at Pyr's feet without speaking, then stalked away.

"They know I am nothing," Pyr said. "No one would have me

until Jaolore was formed. The other *elian* are much offended that I dare look into the eyes of my betters." He gazed dolefully at Tully's feet for a moment, then turned away. "Is it not being so among humans?"

Tully noted that the slender male's Jao had improved even since last night. His syntax was almost perfect now. How were he and Jihan learning so quickly? Had the two of them stayed up into the wee hours practicing night after night, just in case they one day encountered Jao?

"No, it is not so among humans," he said, walking up and down before the house and flapping his arms to warm himself. It was still cold enough to freeze your bits off. "We believe that all are born with the same opportunities, and it is up to the individual to make of himself as much as possible. Anyone can advance if he is willing to work hard and learn."

"How can that be?" Pyr said. His small hands dithered with the box, then he hefted it to his shoulder. "Caitlin, Queen of the Universe, is your Eldest. She is having high rank, does she not?"

That again! Tully resisted the urge to find Kaln and thrash the babbling tech within an inch of her Krant life. And of course, Wrot, blast his hide, deserved a full measure of the blame for this as well. He cleared his throat, acutely uncomfortable. "I will explain about that later. For now, I promise you that Caitlin has worked hard to earn the rank she holds."

"What has work to do with rank?" Pyr blinked. "One is either aged and tall or young and short. It is well known that the young are always foolish. Only the Eldests have accumulated wisdom." He shifted the box's weight to balance it better. "I do not have understanding."

A diminutive gray-clad servant emerged to take the just deliv-ered box from Pyr. It looked far too heavy for its slight frame. Though the Lleix were on the whole quite a bit taller than most humans, this one would not have topped Caitlin. Debra Fligor appeared in the doorway and the soldier reached for the box too. "Let me take that," she said in Jao. The little servant backed off and hung its head. Its corona, a grayish-black, drooped around its face like a wilted flower.

"Much badness if you not let her do work," Pyr said. "No work, must go back to *dochaya.*"

"But—" Fligor backed off and looked confused.

"Go inside with her," Tully said, exasperated. "Oversee the unpacking. Show her where to put things. Maybe that will make her happy."

"Yes, yes, give directions!" Pyr said, his gray corona fluttering. "That will be goodness."

"But none of these servants speak Jao," Fligor said.

"You can damn well point, can't you?" Tully said in English.

Fligor flushed to the roots of her sandy hair. "Yes, sir!" The good-natured sergeant saluted, then edged aside so the servant could struggle through the entrance beneath the oversized box like an ant with a pebble.

"Besides," Tully said as Fligor followed her, "she'll probably speak both Jao and English by dusk."

"Yes, yes, all servants listen very hard," Pyr said in Jao. "Learn Jao and English soon."

Tully had no doubt that was true. These people seemed to sop up language like a sponge. He pulled his cap off and scratched his head. The Lleix were amazing in some areas, totally backwards in others. Just like humans, he thought, whose factionalism had been their downfall, and even like Jao who counted innovation and individual ambition to be of no consequence. Each of the three species had its strengths and blind spots.

Shivering, he watched servants scurry past carrying shattered benches and rickety stools and pile them in a heap at the street's edge for removal. The Lleix were missing a bet with so much willing manpower wasted. Obviously they had a work ethic. If these *dochaya* residents were all educated and then given something useful to do, instead of just sitting around and pining for status, this city would not be half-abandoned and falling to bits.

And the Lleix would not be sitting here, easy targets, waiting for the Ekhat to come back and finish them off.

Still stationed at the Jaolore *elian*-house, Mallu heard his com crackle to life. Tully's code appeared on the small screen. "Major?" he said, stepping outside into the chill air.

"Tully here," a human voice answered. "I learned from Jihan last night that the Lleix techs, called Shipservicers and Enginetuners, are busy repairing what ships the Lleix have left, but they only have a few experts."

Mallu's ears rose. He could hear several Jao squabbling inside the house. It sounded like Kaln and someone unfamiliar, probably one of the jinau. There were no pools here and they were all prickly with boredom. He rubbed a weary hand over his whiskers. "Yes?"

"I want you to take our jinau and Krant techs down to the landing field and offer assistance while we wait for the *Lexington* to return."

Something crashed inside the *eliaṅ*-house. Mallu hoped it was not valuable. "I doubt our techs could be effective without extensive instruction. Lleix concepts and design are bound to differ from our own, perhaps radically so. Also, none of their experts are likely to speak Jao and it will not help if we just get in the way."

"Perhaps," Tully said. "Perhaps not. We will not know though until we try. At any rate, it would be interesting to get a look at their technology and see if we can pick up some new ideas."

Mallu grimaced. Humans were so endlessly preoccupied with *ollnat*. What point was there in learning something new and different? Jao tech had served the kochan for a long time and they already knew how to make it operate quite well.

"Besides, Krant-Captain, the troops need something to do, especially the Jao. Soldiers just get into trouble sitting around all the time. I have put a number of them to work rehabilitating these two abandoned houses, but Jaolore does not need work and it seems to me that the techs' time would be better spent helping the Lleix get ready to flee."

Mallu's appreciation for Tully's cross-species leadership skills rose another notch. Having accepted a number of Jao into his jinau unit, the major obviously understood just how restless they would be without direction and useful occupation.

"Take the techs down to the field and see what, if anything, you can accomplish. I will send Pyr along as translator." Tully hesitated. "Just keep an eye out for trouble from the locals. Caitlin Kralik told Jihan the truth of the matter between humans and Jao last-dark, and now our young Lleix contact has gone back up to the Han. Once she tells them that Caitlin is not Queen of the Universe and the Jao are not our slaves, they are likely to come back down that mountain really angry."

Mallu started to punch the com off, then it crackled again.

"And, Krant-Captain?"

Mallu canted a single ear forward. "Yes?"

"Keep an especially close eye on Senior-Tech Kaln," Tully said. "You know how she can get."

Indeed, Mallu did. "Yes, Major Tully." The connection clicked off. Mallu stared at the small black device in his hand, his whiskers bristling in *respect*, though there was no one to see. Tully, for all that he was human, dealt with Jao amazingly well. From the beginning of this assignment he had forged association with Mallu's Krant crew under difficult circumstances. Kaln, who, despite her brilliance as a tech, had always been exceedingly difficult to manage, positively preened whenever Tully was near these days simply because the human had allowed her to tinker with the gun's loading hoist.

He had come to his decision. When this mission was over, he was going to propose that the kochan seek association with Terra Taif as Tully had suggested. Unlike the more powerful kochan, these Terrans judged individuals upon their performance, not their preexisting status. For Krant, consigned always to the backwaters of kochan politics and little regarded, it might be a way to advance.

But—this idea of working on alien ships was crazy. Most likely the aging hulks would have to be abandoned, if the Bond did decide to render the colony aid. He wished fervently the *Lexington* would come back and put an end to all this pointless waiting, but from what he could feel from the flow of the situation, it would not be today. He just hoped it would be soon.

Something, or someone, crashed again inside the *elian*-house. Mallu shook himself, longing for a swim, then headed inside to round up the techs, or at least those who had not killed each other yet.

Upon her return from the Han, Jihan found Caitlin and Tully in the Application Chamber of the second *elian*-house, overseeing its refurbishment. The Pennantmakers had evidently been consulted, most likely by Pyr, and outside a row of gaily colored flags now adorned the roof's crest. Inside, the floors had been polished, the rubbish swept out, and a line of *dochaya* servants was trooping in, bearing newly repaired benches and stools, pots and bowls. The air smelled pleasantly of red-seed oil.

The old house was quite lovely, the interior's exposed beams covered with elegantly carved *Boh*-faces. She could see how it must have looked long ago when it had been home to the

Watercrafters, who had once designed the winding streams and ornamental ponds that still gave grace to the city.

The building would be abandoned all over again if the humans took the Lleix away to safety, and then certainly destroyed when the Ekhat swept back through the system. Sadness overwhelmed her. Though this was just a colony, still this world had been home to the Lleix for many generations, harboring them for a very long time.

They would have to flee their refuge, barren of resources though it was, and who knew if they might ever find anyplace half so pleasant again? Study of the old records revealed that the Lleix had taken shelter on far less hospitable worlds than Valeron during their endless flight from the Ekhat.

"Caitlin," Jihan said, approaching the diminutive human, who was bundled into thick layers of cloth despite being indoors. The human had even pulled a fold of fabric over her head so that it looked something like a Lleix aureole. "The Han will accept the humans' offer of assistance, if they feel able to offer upon their return."

"You told them then, about the humans and the Jao?" Caitlin said.

Jihan stared at her feet, so much larger than those of a human. "No, no," she said. "I did not tell." She raised her gaze and looked into the round blue-gray eyes of the human Eldest. "If I tell, then they will not come. I see that for a certainty. Once the Lleix are safe, then we must explain." She inhaled, her mind with filled the implications of that decision and her part in such a momentous deception.

"Very well," Caitlin said, pushing back the fold of fabric. "I am sure you know far better than we do how to handle the situation. Now, we must make sure your population is ready to leave when they return."

"There is just one problem," Tully said, glancing down at Caitlin with his odd green and white eyes. He pulled up one of the refurbished benches and sat. "What about the *dochaya*?"

Jihan blinked. "When the Lleix flee a world, the *dochaya* remains behind. There is no room for unassigned."

Tully crossed one leg over the other, an awkward pose. He looked as though he might tip over. "That is not acceptable to us."

"But they are our unassigned, not yours," Jihan said. "What can it matter to humans who goes from Valeron and who does not?"

"We—" Tully began, but Caitlin put a hand on his arm and sat down beside him on the bench.

"Let us just say that it does matter to us," Caitlin said. She interlaced her fingers. "So then what can be done about this?"

Jihan bowed her head, thoughts spinning like leaves in a whirlwind. "The matter—would have to be taken before the Han," she said slowly. "There would be discussion, much discussion, perhaps even endless, of such an issue. This is part of *sensho*, the way things are always done. No one would understand why humans would believe survival of the *dochaya* to be necessary or even desirable. The *elian* bear all the culture, training, and knowledge of our kind, everything that is necessary to start again somewhere else. The *dochaya* contains only the rejected, the unnecessary, who would just consume resources without being able to give anything back at a point when we will have nothing extra."

The two humans stared at one another. Caitlin inhaled deeply. "What about Pyr? Is he unnecessary?"

"He has made himself useful when I could not wait for the Festival of Choosing and recruit properly from the season's youth," she said. "But even he has said that he will remain behind with the *dochaya* when the moment comes to leave Valeron. He does not feel worthy to travel with the *elian*."

Tully shook his head and turned away with a muffled exclamation she could not translate.

"And you would just abandon him here to die?" Caitlin said quietly.

Jihan could not understand why they were so preoccupied with the matter. "Things are as they have always been," she said. "Each time we had to flee home after home, we took with us little more than who we are. Such knowledge is all we have and we keep that inviolate. If we give up the way matters are conducted, even in the smallest measure, we will lose ourselves." Her aureole stiffened. "I do not know how to explain better."

"We will not leave the *dochaya* behind!" Tully said. One of his hands was knotted into a fist as if he wanted to strike something.

Caitlin looked into his tight face, shaking her head. "Not now, Gabe," she said in English. "Later."

"You cannot say this to the Han," Jihan said. Her fingers were fluttering with distress. She had worked too hard to let a foolish misunderstanding ruin everything now. "The Eldests argued for days before deciding to decide to accept the humans' assistance, which had few drawbacks. Demanding that they ignore *sensho* to do what has never been done will only make them turn away again."

"You broke *sensho*," Caitlin said. "Once, for a good reason. This is a good reason too. Humans value life, all life, not only the *elian*. We cannot just fly away and leave the unassigned to die."

"The shame of that day when I broke *sensho* will be upon me forever," Jihan said hoarsely, reliving the terrible moment when she had gainsaid Sayr at the Han and the assembled Eldests had looked upon her with such unmitigated contempt. She shuddered. "Such things can never be made right. Perhaps I should also remain behind and blot out my disgrace that way."

"No," Caitlin said. "No one should be left behind!"

"We must do as we have always done," Jihan said. "No matter what you say on this matter, the Eldests will not listen."

Tully's eyes glittered. "We will see," he said, then jerked to his feet.

Caitlin and Jihan watched as he stalked out of the Application Chamber into the back of the old house. The boards creaked with his every step.

"I do not understand his urgency," Jihan said, gazing after him. "Perhaps I need to watch the recordings again and further improve my grasp of your Jao language."

"That will not help," Caitlin said. "You speak Jao very well already, and, in truth, the Jao would probably agree with you about abandoning the *dochaya*. This is an entirely human matter."

Tully grabbed his coat off his bed, if the uncomfortable wooden platform could be graced by such a designation, back in the sleeping quarters. He felt like steam must be pouring out of his ears. He couldn't believe that Wrot had made them come all this way and fight five sodding Ekhat ships just to save the hides of a bunch of aliens who were fully prepared to jettison over half their population because they had lost out in a stupid teenage popularity contest!

He slipped out one of the back doors into the frosty midmorning air, unwilling to encounter Jihan again until he had calmed down. She was what she had been raised to be, what her culture had made her. It was not her fault and arguing with her would do no good. Caitlin had been right to shut him up. It was the Han and all those blasted Eldests who had control of this situation.

But—he had three ships full of assault troops, each and every one of which had a gun and knew how to use it. The Lleix obviously possessed shipboard weapons because they had fought the Ekhat in the same battle that had destroyed the Krant ships, but so far, he hadn't seen a single hand weapon in any of the *elian*-houses or openly carried in the city by a Lleix. He hadn't even seen so much as a lock on a door. That blasted code of *sensho* had such a grip on the Lleix, he doubted whether these people had any sort of police force at all.

He made up his mind. When the time came to load the ships, then he and his jinau troops would just round up the *dochaya*, too. Who cared what the Eldests wanted? They were just a bunch of hidebound old farts who couldn't see past the ends of their noses. He wasn't going to hang around begging their permission to do the right thing!

The only person he really had to convince was Wrot, and that meant he would have to get past the stubborn Jao precept that everything and everyone had to be "of use." The *dochaya* residents weren't useless, though. They were very hard-working, given the opportunity. He just had to make Wrot see that.

The bushes next to the *elian*-house rustled, then a small silver face appeared, gazing at him with narrow black eyes. The Lleix was wearing the gray shift of an unassigned. "Inside." Tully pointed back at the house. "Much work," he said, "inside."

"No, no," the Lleix said in heavily accented Jao. "Not work." It gazed at him hungrily. "Words."

It had obviously been soaking up Jao over the last few days like Pyr and Jihan. "What words?" he said.

It closed its eyes and concentrated. "We believe—that all are—born with the—same opportunities," the Lleix said in halting Jao, obviously producing the words from memory.

Footsteps padded closer and three more just like it in dress and stature appeared. "It—is up to the—individual to make of himself—as much as possible," a second unassigned said. Then a third piped up and the two finished in unison. "Anyone can—advance if he—is willing to work hard—and learn."

Tully had said that to Pyr earlier that morning, when the youth had been snubbed by one of his fellow Lleix. What an ear these people had. "Those are my words," he said slowly. "Do you understand them?"

"Pyr explain," the first one said. The four of them gazed at Tully with that same hungry expression. "We very much interested."

"I am going to the *dochaya*," Tully said. "Come with me. We will talk along the way." He shoved his hands into his pockets, shivering as the Valeron wind gusted down off the mountains.

"Let me see," he said, "if I can explain the concept of inalienable rights."

CHAPTER
34

The unassigned flocked to Tully as he passed and he spent the rest of the day in the dreadful *dochaya*. Very few could speak some Jao, though he was still amazed that any of them did. It seemed they traded the alien words among them with the fervent fascination of human children trading baseball cards.

He entered the first barracks he encountered. The interior of the low building was dim, lit only by tiny windows near the ceiling to admit the gray winter sunlight, furnished with nothing but row upon row of sleeping platforms. He sat on one, wrinkling his nose against the musty smell, and spoke to them in English until he was hoarse. They seemed to acquire language much as an infant did, needing only exposure and repetition, so he gave them as much as he could. If they were going to Earth, English would do them more good than Jao.

He talked about the probable upcoming evacuation and how all Lleix deserved to leave, not just the *elian*. He talked about human history and the theory of advancement by individual effort and hard work, not just social connections. He recited the Declaration of Independence and the Constitution, as least as much as he could remember, and made up the rest. He recounted the Revolutionary War. He had to restrain himself from depicting the valiant struggle against the Jao conquest and the tenacious resistance thereafter.

The four servants who had accompanied him from the jinau's appropriated *elian*-house sat on their haunches at his feet and stared up into his face with rapt black eyes. More and more Lleix crowded into the building until finally it was so stuffy he couldn't breathe and retreated back outside. The Lleix scrambled after him, murmuring random phrases to one another in English.

Stiff and cramped, he stretched and saw that the sun was low in the west, red-tinged, about to disappear behind the mountains and realized he had been here all day. His stomach rumbled. He was monstrously hungry and thirsty.

"I must go back," he said hoarsely to the silver faces and their dancing coronas, which were always in motion.

They stiffened in alarm. "No go!" one said and then the words were echoed throughout the ranks. "No go! Speak more English!"

He rubbed a weary hand over his face and felt stubble. In his bad mood that morning, he'd forgotten to shave. He needed a bath, even if it was only with a basin of cold water. "I have work of my own to do."

They stared at him silently then. Work was something they understood and respected.

"Come back?" a tiny Lleix said finally.

"Tomorrow," Tully said. "I will come back tomorrow. Until then, practice your English with one another. Learn all that you can."

"Learn very much best!" one of the original four said. None of them had left his side the entire day. They must be hungry and thirsty too, he thought.

The Lleix was just about his height, so was probably still quite young. "How are you called?" he said.

"This one Lim," it said.

"Are you male or female?" he asked.

The narrow black eyes blinked. Lim did not answer.

Tully sighed. Words, words, words, they all needed more words. "Tomorrow, Lim. We'll find out tomorrow."

He set off toward the *elian*-house district, huddled into his coat against the chill wind, then pulled his com out of his coat pocket. It was in the Off position. Damn. They'd probably been looking for him all day. If one of his officers had been that careless, he'd have had his ears for breakfast and he could just imagine what Yaut would have done. He keyed it on, then punched in a code. "Miller? How are things going?"

The com crackled. "Major? Thank God. We thought maybe you'd fallen down a hole somewhere."

A rabbit hole, maybe. Like Alice. This place seemed almost as bizarre as the realm of the Red Queen. "I've just been out of touch. Any problems?"

"Minor stuff," Miller said. "Nothing we couldn't handle."

"I'll be at the Jaolore *elian*-house in ten," he said. "Meet me there."

"Will do." The com crackled off.

The Lleix needed more words, he thought as he strode along in the chilly air. And soldiers loved to talk. He'd bring a handful who didn't have anything better to do with him tomorrow and station one in each of the *dochaya* barracks. Forget Jao. By the time the *Lexington* returned, he'd have the whole damn place reciting the Bill of Rights in English.

Caitlin thought Tully looked tired, but oddly exhilarated, when he finally turned up at the Jaolore *elian*-house and announced he was starving. "Where have you been all day?" she said, handing him a rations bar out of her pack. "Mallu has been trying to contact you for hours."

"I've been at the *dochaya*," he said, sinking onto a bench in the front room, then biting into the fruit and nut bar. He chewed for a moment. "What did he want?"

She frowned. "He wouldn't say. I'm not one of your jinau, so he told me it would be of no use for me to know."

"Ah, that old excuse," Tully said. "Jao always say that when they mean it's none of your business."

"If I'm Queen of the Universe," she said with a sniff, "everything is my business."

"I don't know how much longer we'll have to keep that up," he said. "The *Lexington* is bound to come back soon."

"I'm rather getting to like it," she said, though that wasn't the least bit true. "How long do you think it will take Ed to get used to calling me 'Your Highness?'"

He took another bite. "Remind me not to be there for that one."

The door opened, admitting a gust of frigid air along with Krant-Captain Mallu. Dried leaves skirled through in his wake. She suspected a storm was brewing up in the mountains. The big Jao flicked an ear at Tully in *acknowledgment-of-rank*. "*Vaish.*" I-see-you.

Tully nodded. "*Vaist,*" he said, in the superior-to-inferior mode. *You see me.* "How did the work on the Lleix ships go?"

"Surprisingly well," Mallu said. "Most of what was needed was beyond my skill, but Senior-Tech Kaln is still there, fiddling with the mechanics of their jump-drive."

"Are their ships space-worthy?" Caitlin asked.

Mallu glanced at her, plainly startled that she had inserted herself into the conversation. Silence stretched out.

"Caitlin Kralik is second only to Wrot's authority on this mission," Tully said. He stood and assumed a stiff, very military stance, shoulders braced, head high, communicating with his body in a way he was sure would make an impression upon the Jao. "You have not been present at all the planning sessions, so you may not have perceived her rank. Terra's Governor, Aille krinnu ava Terra, has every confidence in her judgement, as well as Preceptor Ronz of the Bond. You will heed her orders as you would Wrot's, Ronz's, or mine."

"Their ships?" Caitlin repeated pleasantly, as though there had been no dispute, letting her arms and upper body fall into the graceful curves of *respectful-inquiry*.

"The situation is alarming," Mallu said. His lines had now gone pretty much *neutral*, as though he didn't know what to think. "Their vessels are very old and few of them presently function. Kaln believes that most would not complete a jump, even if they could take off from this world and make it into position to try, which is doubtful."

"Then this will be their Last-of-Days," she murmured, "unless we do something."

"They have been hiding here a long time," Mallu said, "and this world is resource poor. They cannot mine the metals they need to fashion replacement parts or construct new ships."

"So they pruned their trees," she said, thinking of the vast park-like city, "and dug their winding little streams, built ornamental bridges, carved faces in their houses, decorated their clothes—and waited for the Ekhat to come and kill them."

"That pretty much sums it up," Tully said in English. "Don't forget to toss in consigning the majority of their population to a lifetime of misery in the *dochaya*. Nice picture, isn't it? They make the Jao look almost kindly, as hard as that is to imagine."

That night, the winds howled down off the mountains, shaking the *dochaya*-houses, but Lim was too excited to huddle with her fellow unassigned and sleep. The human had spent the entire day talking to them and it had not taken very long before they began to understand. First, just a word here and there in the stream of sounds, then several together, like pieces fitting together in one of the puzzles from the Children's Court before they had been cast out.

A leaving time was near. Everyone knew that. The dreadful Ekhat had hunted them down to exterminate this colony and the *elian* would flee. The *dochaya* would be left behind. They were the unwanted and that was *sensho*, the way of things.

But Tully said it did not have to be so, that the unassigned could leave too. Such a strange idea, that anyone would care what happened to the denizens of the *dochaya*. They were the dust of the city, fit only to be swept out of sight. Such startling new thoughts made her eyes stay open, when others had piled onto the platforms to slumber. It made her head go on thinking after the sky had darkened and the wind blasted and pale-blue snow sifted against the windows, piling up outside the doors. It made her—hope.

She remembered hope from the Children's Court, when she and her fellow youngers had played at being chosen by *elian*. She had always wanted to enter one of the artistic crafts, the Patternmakers, perhaps, or the Stonesculptors, even the Treebinders, just someplace where she could fashion beauty and contribute to the colony's elegant fabric of life. Instead, she had been rebuffed at every door. Her skin was too dull, her aureole unbalanced, her legs positively thin. She would not bring grace to anyone's house. She was, everyone decided, fit only for the *dochaya*.

So many doors, so many refusals. Remembering those days of trying so very hard to be appealing without success still made her chest ache. But then Pyr, who was equally unappealing in appearance, had been accepted by Jaolore. This was a new thing, escape from hopelessness. Even if Jaolore never accepted another from the *dochaya*, it had happened once and so became a part of *sensho*. It might happen again, someday.

And this funny looking human, who was really quite short and thin-shanked itself, said the unassigned should evacuate with the *elian*, that they could find safety on a faraway world called Urth, then help to build another colony under a new sun. That new colony would need beauty, she was quite sure. Maybe even they would have need of other new *elian*, like Jaolore. Even if she were not accepted by one of them, as Pyr had been, perhaps she would at least be allowed to serve.

That was more than she'd ever had. She walked up and down the rows of sleeping platforms, softly repeating her new English words: fre-dum…rites…tir-ran-ee…jus-tis.

She did not really know what they meant yet, but Tully had said they were important, that they had once changed everything for a large number of humans. That was an interesting concept. Lleix life went on always the same from world to world, generation to generation, *elian* to *elian*. They took solace in preserving the steady course of life in its every aspect, doing their best to see that nothing ever changed. Lim was eager to hear what this Tully would say tomorrow.

Tully went to the *dochaya* every day after that, leaving Lieutenant Miller and Krant-Captain Mallu to oversee the restoration of the dilapidated *elian*-houses they had appropriated. He designated Kaln in charge of the techs working on Lleix ships at the landing field and then handpicked twenty human jinau to go with him to the *dochaya*, ostensibly also to occupy themselves with repairing, but really to speak with the unassigned.

The slum residents labored alongside his troops, seemingly in awe that humans would put their hands to grunt-work in such low-class surroundings when there were unassigned available. As the days passed, the unassigned trailed after him wherever he went, always pestering for "more English, more!"

Higher ranking Lleix turned away when they came across the sight, obviously offended by his attention to those they had long ago designated unworthy. He didn't care. In his opinion, the *elian* were nothing more than a bunch of arrogant elitists who had cowered here on this barren world for generations, distracting themselves by ornamenting their city while waiting for the Ekhat to hunt them down. Insofar as he had any sympathies for the Lleix, they were bestowed entirely on the inhabitants of the *dochaya*. The *elian* could rot in hell, as far as he was concerned—or get fried by the Ekhat.

Many of the Jao under his command also thought his preoccupation with the downtrodden was nuts. In accordance with Jao values, everyone should make himself of use in whatever way benefitted the greater good. Unassigned were not useful so they did not matter.

Mallu, though, was more thoughtful. Over the centuries, Krant had experienced its own measure of social oppression from the other better-situated kochan. The Krant-captain did not fully understand what drew Tully to the Lleix slum, but he was intrigued, and several times even accompanied Tully to the *dochaya*.

Some of the more enterprising unassigned even organized English classes, which were conducted when Tully and the rest retired at night. Each morning thereafter, he was greeted with a larger audience and better English conversation than the day before. Young Lim, who turned out to be female, was particularly adept at picking up the new language, then teaching it to others. She seemed to have boundless energy.

He supposed the young female was homely in terms of what a Lleix might find attractive, but it was difficult to fathom that some *elian* hadn't perceived her mental quickness and recruited her anyway.

The subject of "Caitlin, Queen of the Universe" cropped up from time to time because those in the *dochaya* had gotten the improbable story from Pyr, but, when it did, Tully always just changed the subject. Jihan had decided it wasn't time to reveal the truth, but he was damned if he was going to perpetuate the lie. They were going to have a lot to answer for once the real situation between Jao and humans came out. He didn't see any point in heaping error upon error.

Fifteen days after they had first landed upon Valeron, the *dochaya* had been transformed. That morning, Tully noted with satisfaction, as he peered into barracks after barracks, the floors were swept clean, the windows repaired, splintered sleeping platforms mended, sanitary facilities spotless, and the formerly ubiquitous trash removed. Once his troops had begun renovations, the unassigned had joined in joyfully. If they weren't about to leave this world, he had a feeling they would be sculpting trees and digging streams next so that the *dochaya* would resemble the rest of the city.

There had only been one off-putting moment at the start of the clean-up, when a pair of his jinau, Debra Fligor and Gary Young, had broken into an off-key rendition of "Oh, Susannah!" to pass the time while they caulked windows. At the first note, the Lleix had regarded them with obvious horror, then fled the barracks, bawling in alarm.

"Jeez, Major," Gary said, staring after them, his face flushed. His dark-brown eyes blinked. "We weren't *that* off-key!"

"It's more than that," Tully said. His heart was pounding as he glanced around the barracks. It was deserted, not a single cowering Lleix left in the building. Only dust motes hung in the shafts of thin winter sunlight to mark their passage. "They must have a thing about singing." He realized then he hadn't heard anything remotely like music since landing on this world, and then he remembered the whistling incident when they'd first landed. He'd gotten a similar panicked response.

Cautioning them against further performances, he went to find Jihan and see what the problem was. Unassigned were skulking outside the barracks, their coronas flattened, their hands a-dither. They turned away and did not speak to him.

He located the Jaolore at her *elian*-house, as always poring over the old records in the back room she called the Duty Chamber. Pyr and Kajin were with her, each absorbed in a viewer. "Something strange just happened in the *dochaya*," Tully said, shrugging out of his coat. "I am hoping you can explain."

Kajin gave him a sideways look. His eyes were very narrow, which Jihan had told Tully was considered highly attractive. Tully thought it made him look sly. "It does not matter what happens in the *dochaya*," the Lleix said with a ripple of his corona. "You should not concern yourself with such." He turned back to his viewer.

"Several of my soldiers sang an old song," Tully said, "just something to pass the time, but it upset your people."

With an exclamation, Kajin jerked off his stool and backed against the wall as though Tully had threatened him. Jihan and Pyr turned and stared at Tully, their eyes gone positively wide, which was unusual for a Lleix. "Humans *sing*?" Jihan said, her voice a strained whisper.

"Yes," Tully said. "Do the Lleix not sing?"

The three Lleix glanced at one another, then Pyr bowed his head, his corona flat around his face. "Ekhat, the great devils, *they* sing," the youth said.

Kajin straightened, seeming to recall his dignity, then returned to his stool. "Before I became Jaolore," he said, "I had the great honor to be Ekhatlore. I spent my life studying the great devils. They value patterned noise above all else and destroy entire worlds in its name. Their songs are abomination!"

Tully began to get an inkling what was wrong here. "So the Lleix fear music?"

"Music belongs to the great devils who eat the universe," Kajin said. "It is their wicked creation."

"Humans create music too?" Jihan said. She seemed incredulous.

"Yes, they do, but they do not kill in its name," Tully said. "It is—a pleasure to them, a relaxation, even an art, like when the Lleix prune their trees into attractive shapes or carve faces into their houses. If you come to Earth, there will be much music."

"We find all structured noise an abomination," Jihan said. "If humans sing like the Ekhat, does that mean their minds think the same way?" She drooped, making herself small. "I am far too young to think this situation through. This needs the wisdom of Sayr or Grijo."

"No," Tully said. "Do not bother the Eldests with this right now. There is already too much upset over the impending evacuation." He paced the room, trying to decide what to do. "Let me talk the matter over with Caitlin. In the meantime, I will make sure no one else sings while we are on Valeron."

And that had been the end of it for the moment, but it was another unfortunate revelation that had to come out before all was said and done: Humans sang. They loved music and it infiltrated many aspects of their day-to-day lives. If the Lleix came to Earth, as they surely must to survive, they would encounter music over and over. Somehow they would have to learn to cope.

But for now, there could be no careless humming, no tuneless whistling, not even fingers drumming on a table. Their hosts were perhaps understandably phobic about patterned noise of any kind and they would have to respect that.

It was just surprising it hadn't already come up. He had pulled out his com to spread the prohibition, once he understood, and from that moment on, the jinau were careful.

CHAPTER
35

Kaln was once again working through the night at the Lleix space-port, if a landing field that housed so few working ships could be dignified with such a designation. Lleix tech was fascinating in theory, differing from Jao designs in significant ways, but the ships were frightfully old and hadn't been properly maintained. Not that she could blame the Lleix. If they did not have the resources to craft parts, they simply did not.

But why had they not left Valeron when that became apparent? By staying here, they must have known they were tying themselves to this world, no matter how secluded, where the Ekhat would eventually sniff them out. Their ancestors had long ago chosen to die on Valeron. Now their Last-of-Days was coming true.

She went to one small ship after another out on the frozen field and repaired what she could anyway. It was not in her nature to sit idle. Perhaps the Bond of the Ebezon would authorize help for the Lleix, and perhaps they would not. No one truly understood the ways of the Bond. They saw deeper beneath the surface of things than the kochan did. But until the *Lexington* returned, Kaln could make herself of use while learning a bit about the alien tech and it pleased her to do so.

The other Krant and jinau techs worked with her through the daylight, but humans required longer periods of dormancy than Jao, and they returned to their assigned quarters at night. Some of the Jao stayed behind, though, busying themselves, and she found herself working alongside one of her Krant shipmates.

"What do you think of these humans?" she asked Braltan, as the two of them wedged themselves into yet another engine compartment. The youth was a terniary-tech on his first voyage after being released from his natal compound. She reached for a wrench, then flattened her good ear when its span proved far too wide for its intended target.

"They talk a lot," he said, his body settling into the lines of unabashed *weariness*. He was an unusually handsome youth to have been generated by Krant, with a lighter colored nap that allowed his *vai camiti* to stand out.

She rummaged through the scanty trove of Lleix implements for a smaller tool and came up with something that was at least vaguely wrenchlike. "I did not like them at first," she said, "but now I find them interesting, or at least some of them." She held the tool up to the greenish-tinged overhead light, trying to decide if it would work. "They do not look down upon Krant like the great kochan."

"They are stub-eared aliens," Braltan said, holding what seemed to be a sort of manifold cover steady for her. "And we have conquered them. Who are they to look down upon anyone?"

"But now they have their own taif," Kaln said, "so they must be making themselves useful to other kochan, and they are clever, always creating new things as well as finding different ways to make tech work."

"*Ollnat*," Braltan said, as the cover finally came loose and they could peer into the engine workings beneath. The stench of burnt metal was strong. The youth tapped an exposed joint with the end of a wrench and it fell into two pieces. "What use is that?"

"More than you know, obviously," she said, annoyed, thinking of her improvement to the artillery hoist. It had worked so splendidly, it made her happy just to remember. She picked up the pieces and tried to fit them back together. The end of one crumbled into blackened metal shavings. "Humans are clever about other things too," she said, laying the useless pieces aside. "Caewithe Miller told me that they have whole libraries about the problem of social inequality. Some of their political units have even fought wars with one another to prevent it." She stared around the ruined engine room. "Jao almost never write about such matters, or even think about them very often."

"Humans *fight* among themselves?" Braltan stiffened, his lines gone to *outrage*. "That is shameful! Kochan never fight over status."

"Not directly," Kaln said, "but think how Krant is never sought out for trade agreements, so that our worlds remain poor and our fleet minimal. Nor are we included in councils when important decisions must be made. Narvo and Dano and Pluthrak have never turned weapons upon us, but no Krant would ever be appointed governor of a conquered world. We are considered good enough to fight the Ekhat and die, when the need arises, but not to have a place at the forefront of kochan politics."

Braltan fell quiet then, the set of his ears and jaw gone to *uncertainty*. She had given him much to think about and he was still but newly emerged.

"It is the way things are," he said finally, the tool in his hand forgotten. "The way things have always been."

"The Lleix only honor what has been done before," she said, "and see where that has brought them—to the brink of extinction."

Braltan sat back on his haunches and rubbed fretfully at his whiskers. "This will not function without replacement parts," he said, apparently changing the subject to one he could handle.

And there were no replacement parts. They both knew that. Perhaps the *Lexington* could fabricate such from the stock in its machine shops, but that would take time, even after it returned, and, with a sudden surge, Kaln felt that both the Ekhat and the *Lexington* would be back *soon*.

"Something has changed," she said softly, resisting the urge to rush outside to the landing field and stare up into the night sky. A storm had blown in from the mountains while they were working and they would see nothing but clouds and swirling pale-blue snow. "Do you feel it?"

His black eyes gazed at her, flickering with green. "I do not have a strong timesense," the youth said, "but I think there is— something."

"They are coming back," she said.

Braltan replaced the manifold cover, a useless gesture, but she noted with approval that he was a tidy worker. "Who?" he asked, his ears flicking nervously from *doubt* to *dread* and then back again.

"I do not know," she said. "We must find Major Tully and see if there has been word from the *Lexington*." Because, if it was the Ekhat, entering the star system with ten or twenty ships instead of five, they were all exposed down here, Jao, human, and Lleix, waiting for the first attack run. The three assault ships would no doubt make excellent targets.

Mallu, sprawled on one of the uncomfortable bare wood sleeping platforms, came awake suddenly as though someone had poked him. He sat up, wincing at a stab of pain from his still-healing ribs, and peered through the darkness. Outside, the wind howled, making the flags along the roof snap, and it was even colder than it had been earlier. He would have given a great deal for a decent *dehabia* blanket upon which to sleep. Had the storm woken him?

At the front of the *elian*-house, he heard a door open. Of course, the Lleix had no locks so anyone could come in at any time, but he'd posted a guard at every entrance. The Lleix were aliens with good reason to hate Jao. Though they seemed to be tolerating their presence for now, he had no intention of depending on their goodwill.

A human male poked his head into the sleeping quarters. "Krant-Captain?" he said softly.

Mallu scrubbed at his ears, then stood. What was the creature's name? Yunk? "Yes?"

The human edged into the room, holding his rifle. "Senior-Tech Kaln is here and asking to speak with you."

Yung. That was it. Private Gairy Yung. Mallu flicked his ears in *assent*, a bit of bodyspeak which humans seemed to universally understand, then maneuvered through the maze of rooms in the dark house to the vast front hall, called the Application Chamber, according to Jihan.

Kaln was pacing up and down, tracking in snow across the gleaming wooden floor, detouring the scavenged benches and stools. Her ear was pinned in *alarm*. She whirled when he came into the room. "Krant-Captain!"

He settled carefully on a bench, trying not to jar his ribs. "Senior-Tech." His mouth tasted like sand and his whole body itched. It seemed forever since he'd had a proper swim.

"Can you feel it?" Her eyes were alive with green. "They are coming!"

"Who is coming?" said a sleepy human voice from the doorway to the back of the house. It was Caitlin Kralik. Obviously the noise had woken her too.

"I do not know!" Kaln said. Her lines went to pure *agitation*. "Either the *Lexington* or the Ekhat, but something has changed and they are coming!"

"The Jao timesense," Caitlin said. She ran fingers through tousled hair that she usually kept quite orderly. Her clothing was haphazardly thrown on, her feet bare. Mallu saw how her toes curled against the cold wood.

Kaln's timesense was especially keen. Mallu's irritation seeped away. The tech might well be the first to know about the approach of an important event and that could give them an edge. He closed his eyes and felt inside his head. At first there was nothing, just the tug of weariness and a longing to return to dormancy, but then…

He stiffened. There was something, a faint turning…a change. "Wake Major Tully," he said. "And check with the assault ships. See if they can detect any contacts entering the system."

"Which is it?" Caitlin asked. "The Ekhat or the *Lexington*?" Her face had gone pale, which Mallu now understood was a sign of distress among her kind.

"I cannot say yet," he said. "But it is surely one or the other."

Roused out of a dead sleep by a guard, Tully jammed his feet into his cold, stiff boots and headed out into the howling night to join Caitlin, Mallu, and the rest of his jinau over at Jaolore. Something, evidently, was up, or at least the Jao seemed to think so.

Snow had come in from the mountains and a wild wind was driving flakes into the elegant *elian*-houses as he trudged, head down, through the precisely laid-out city. He had experienced the worst winter weather the Rocky Mountains had to offer back on Earth during his time in the Resistance camps. This storm didn't fall far short.

Nancy Burgeson, who had been on duty and taken the call, slogged along beside him. They waded through ankle-deep, curiously dry snow that didn't adhere into drifts, but blew about like sand. Tully had checked with the assault ships as soon as Burgeson had woken him, but all was quiet there. No sign of any vessels entering the system. Of course, Valeron was smack in the middle of a planetary nebula. All that scattered dust and gas threw off the readings so that you couldn't always trust the instruments.

His nose had gone numb two seconds after he'd plunged outside into the freezing wind. His fingers and hands weren't far behind. "This had better be good," he muttered, following the bend that led to Jaolore. Their footsteps crunched through the snow.

Burgeson gave him a startled glance. "Sir?"

"Never mind," he said, turning into the walkway up to the house. Lights shone through the floor-to-ceiling windows that distinguished this house from all the others he'd seen so far.

A human guard was posted at the door and reached to open it for them. "Helluva night, sir," a muffled female voice said. The figure was too bundled up for identification, swathed in several layers of scarves and coats. She saluted.

Tully returned the salute, stamped the snow off his boots, and plunged inside. "You got that right," he said over his shoulder.

Inside, benches had been placed around the airy room. It was marginally warmer. Someone'd had the sense to stoke a small Lleix brazier and it was radiating a bit of heat. Mallu looked up from his seat. "*Vaish*, Major Tully," he said with the shift in his shoulders that signified *recognition-of-authority*.

Kaln and several other unfamiliar Jao clad in Krant-maroon were standing behind Mallu, all of them evidently too restless to sit.

Jihan and Pyr were gazing into the room from a doorway, their coronas a-flutter. Caitlin had taken a seat across from Mallu and was sipping a cup of coffee that smelled inviting. Tully wondered if there was any more to be had. She had dark circles under her eyes that would no doubt be worse by morning. No one, it seemed, was getting much sleep tonight.

"You had a concern, Krant-Captain?" he said, assuming a Yautlike stance, one that he hoped would communicate something like *barely-restrained-impatience*.

The corner of Caitlin's mouth quirked and she turned away to smother a grin. She got what he was trying to do even if no one else in the room did.

"It was Kaln who felt it first," Mallu said, "but once I reached out, I felt it too, though not as strongly. She has always been one of the most sensitive of all Krant to temporal shifts and she is right. Conditions out there have changed or altered. Something—someone—is coming."

The famous Jao timesense. Infamous, as far as Tully was concerned. Somehow the buggers always knew when something would happen. Before being inducted into Aille's personal service, Tully had thought the veterans of the Conquest were making this stuff up, but he'd seen Jao anticipations of an event come true too many times now to be skeptical. The sickening zing of adrenaline spilled through his blood. "Who is it?"

Kaln regarded him with bristling whiskers and eyes gone almost pure green, a measure of her agitation. "I do not know," she said, "but their arrival is imminent."

"I checked with the assault ships before I came over here," Tully said. "They have not detected anything yet on their instruments."

"Whoever it is, they will come through the framepoint," Mallu said. "The assault ships should have their instruments trained there."

"Wake everyone up," Tully said. "Have them report to our ships on the double. If it is the Ekhat, we'll need to lift as soon as possible." Though what kind of stand they could make against an entire Ekhat fleet was beyond him. The maniacs had sent five ships on the last run and got their rears handed to them. This time, it would be more, a lot more. But he wasn't going to just sit here and wait, like the Lleix, for the inevitable.

Caitlin was staring at him, blue-gray eyes wide, hands buried in the pockets of her rose-colored sweater. He remembered his promise to Ed Kralik that he would look out for her. Well, if he failed to keep that promise, at least he wasn't going to have to explain it to her husband. If she died, he would no doubt be just as dead himself. "Get your coat!" he said, crossing the room to her. "We can't stay here!"

"But—" She glanced at Jihan and Pyr. The two Lleix were still standing in the doorway, watching with narrowed black eyes, their coronas on end. "What about the Lleix?"

"No point," he said. "If it's the Ekhat, it won't do any good to save one or two, and that's all we could manage."

"We can't fight a whole Ekhat fleet," she said, rising.

"No," he said, "we can't, but we can hide until the *Lexington* comes back."

She left the Application Chamber. He then he turned to Kaln. "What about the Lleix ships? How many can lift off right now?"

"More than twenty," the senior-tech said. "But they are all very small."

"Send word," Tully said to Jihan. "Everyone who can should fit into the space-worthy ships. Someone is coming and soon—and we cannot say for certain who it is. The Lleix should save as many of their kind as possible." But it wouldn't be any out of the *dochaya*, he thought angrily. Well, there was no remedy for that at the moment. Dammit, he needed more time!

Caitlin returned, shoes on, bundled into her coat. Tully took her arm and then they plunged outside into the storm. Snow that was more than half ice pelted their faces and they bent their heads, leaning into it. The cold bit deep.

Fligor, Burgeson, and Estrada fell in behind them. The city lay dark and quiet under the onslaught of the storm, the only illumination coming from the light-posts, and those were far too few. He kept seeing the colony blasted to ashes in his imagination, which was all too possible in the immediate future.

They turned a corner and a form approached them out of the swirling snow. "Tully!"

He thought it was Lim, though it was hard to be sure in the howling wind. "Go back to the *dochaya*," he said, raising his voice to make himself heard. "We will not have classes today."

More tall shapes appeared out of the darkness. "What is wrong?" Lim said, falling into step alongside him. "We will help."

"You can't help!" Tully said. Caitlin slipped and he steadied her. She clung to his arm. "I wish you could, but there is nothing you can do."

Lim didn't argue further, but neither did she go back to the slum barracks. She and her three companions trailed after them instead all the way to the assault ships.

He hustled Caitlin inside the open hatch of their ship. Fligor, Estrada, and Burgeson followed, all swearing under their breath. Behind them, three lines of jinau were jogging toward the ships from the *elian*-houses, equipment bundled on their backs.

Lieutenant Miller was there to meet them. She pointed toward something over Tully's shoulder. "Major? What do you want to do about those Lleix?"

Beating snow off his hat, Tully glanced outside into the skirling storm. The wind had eased for a moment so that he could make out the four Lleix standing barefoot in the snow, gazing hungrily at the passing jinau.

What did the Lleix want? Tully hadn't the faintest idea, unless it was what everyone in the *dochaya* wanted—work to give meaning to life. But there was no work for them on the assault ship. He wasn't even sure what useful action the jinau could take if the

Ekhat were about to burst through the framepoint into this star system. The best they might accomplish was to hide and witness the end of this species.

But the ship had a bit of extra room and in the end it would make no difference if Lim and her fellow unassigned died on Valeron or out in space with them. He ducked back out into the stinging cold again. "All right!" he said, motioning to them. "Come aboard!"

The four Lleix walked inside with that oddly graceful step he'd come to know, then Tully ordered the ramp retracted while the humans and Jao strapped in. As they had found on the way here with Jihan, Lliant, and Hadata, Lleix posterior proportions were not meant for seats that would accommodate Jao or humans. The four had to sit on their haunches, braced against the bulkhead.

Caitlin gave the latecomers a troubled look before she took her own seat. Snow was melting in her hair. "They could wind up being the last of their kind," she whispered to Tully as he slid in beside her.

He nodded grimly, then snapped on his harness and leaned his head back. "They've had a raw deal their whole lives," he said, "kicked out of the Children's Court only to be refused a place at any of the *elian*." He glanced at the four, who had been his most eager and apt students. Their black eyes took in their new surroundings, but, as nearly as he could tell, they were not afraid. Tully turned back around. "Just this once, they should get to dictate their own fate."

The craft's engines revved and the small ship quivered like a racehorse in the starting gate. "Here we go," he muttered, closing his eyes and bracing himself. He'd always hated launches.

"Major!"

Tully's eyes flew open. Dalgetty, the assault craft's pilot, was lurching down the center aisle toward him. Tully stiffened. "Jesus, Kristal. Aren't you supposed to be flying this crate?"

"We've got a reading on the scope!" Dalgetty's young face was flushed. Her fingers dug into the seat back.

Caitlin made a soft exclamation. She turned to Tully.

He unbuckled his harness, his heart racing. "The Ekhat?"

"I—" The pilot stared at him. "Sir, you need to come forward and see for yourself."

PART VII:
The Return

CHAPTER
36

Tully jerked out of his seat and followed the pilot back to the cockpit. John Hardy, sitting copilot on this run, was hunched over the radar scope, wearing headphones, his dark eyes staring. "Lordamighty!" he said, shaking his head.

"*What* in the name of hell is it?" Tully said, dropping into Dalgetty's seat.

"Not the Ekhat, sir," Hardy said. "The configuration is way off anything they've ever fielded, but—"

"But—what?" He resisted the urge to shake him.

"There's so many of them," he said. "None of the readings match the *Lexington* either. I haven't a clue who—or what—it is."

"Readings, as in more than one?" A fourth player in this already crowded drama? Tully shook his head. Very freaking improbable. Lack of sleep dragged at his wits as though he had massive jet lag. He studied the dark-green screen as more bright contacts emerged from of the star's photosphere. They were large, but didn't resemble the spindly collection of tinker toys of an Ekhat vessel, and certainly none came close to the size of the *Lexington*. Plasma sheared off the still-vague shapes as the intruders headed outbound from the star.

The ground shook as, over at the colony's landing field, Lleix ships took off, one after the other. "Are we go for launch, Major?" Caewithe Miller asked from the cockpit's doorway.

They should launch, Tully thought, drumming his fingers on the

359

armrest, no matter who it was. Whatever the developing situation, they were just sitting ducks down here. "Is there any chatter on the audio channels?" he said, punching in vector assessments on several of the largest targets.

"No," Hardy said. "So far it's—" He broke off, one hand to his headphones. "Wait!"

Tully's calculations came back with the figures. The ships, all of them, were coming about, accelerating toward Valeron.

Hardy pulled off his headphones and passed them to Tully. "Major, it's—for you," he said. His eyes were crinkled with delight.

Tully held one earpiece up to his head. "—port," a Jao voice was saying. "This is Preceptor Ronz of the Bond of Ebezon. Major Tully, report."

He jammed the headphones on and keyed the mike open. "Major Gabriel Tully here," he said. "Welcome to Valeron."

"Rendezvous with the *Lexington* as soon as we have shed the plasma envelope, Major," Ronz said. "We have a lot to discuss."

"Yes, sir!" Tully said. On the screen, he saw it now, a huge blip, massive enough this time to be the *Lexington* herself. "I'll be damned," he said softly, then pulled off the headphones and passed them back to Hardy.

"They're ours, sir?" Miller said.

"It would seem so," Tully said. They'd brought a whole fleet! The screen was filled with blips, more ships than Earth had seen at one time since the Conquest over twenty years ago, and he'd been just a kid then. He hadn't seen them personally. He rubbed his face, feeling beard stubble. Maybe a hot shower, something unknown to the Lleix, was in his immediate future. He felt way too grungy to report to anyone. "This is going to be interesting, Lieutenant."

"Is that 'interesting,' like in a good movie, sir? Or 'interesting' like in the Chinese curse?"

He grinned at her. "Why not both?"

Ed Kralik paced the busy bridge of the *Lexington*, stopping every so often to check the markers on the screen. The three jinau assault ships were still on course for a rendezvous.

Caitlin had to be all right, he told himself for the hundredth time. No casualties had been reported, But then they might not transmit such terrible news over the radio, he told himself for the hundredth time also, preferring to deliver it in person.

Terra-Captain Dannet gave him a sour look every time he passed her station. Her posture seemed all prickly curves and lines that probably communicated something rude like *get-out-of-my-face!* Ed had a limited bodyspeak vocabulary, at least compared to that of his wife. But if he studied the Terra-captain for a moment, he could have probably been able to make out the central elements of her posture.

That would have meant, though, that he gave a damn what Dannet thought—which he most decidedly did not, at the moment. By all reports, she was a talented officer and had certainly proved herself useful in the best Jao tradition. But he was in no mood to be friendly to any Narvo-striped face.

The problem was that, to a Jao, showing more than a passing concern to a mate outside the breeding pool was considered poor taste. But he wasn't a goddamn Jao. He was a healthy human male who missed his wife after she'd been whisked off to a dangerous corner of the galaxy on the inscrutable whim of the Bond.

At least all the secrecy made more sense after Preceptor Ronz finally had filled him in. The Lleix represented a shameful chapter in the Jao's past. Ronz hadn't wanted to dredge up old sins unless it were necessary, which now apparently it was. Despite being hunted for centuries by the Ekhat, thousands of Lleix had survived here, hidden in this planetary nebula. That was nothing short of amazing.

"Docking with the lead assault craft in ten minutes," a helm officer announced. Human, obviously. A Jao would never bother with chopping up time into segments, then counting them. Every Jao on this ship knew when the docking would take place without anyone having to say.

Ed headed for the lift. No doubt Ronz and Aille were already down in the hanger bay, having felt the moment of arrival near. The doors closed and he watched the deck indicator flash as the lift dropped with a precipitous speed that left his stomach somewhere back around the bridge.

He exited on the hangar deck, then jogged to the observation/control room with its broad windows looking down upon the deck below. The cavernous bay had already been depressurized. The warning lights were flashing and the doors had retracted so that the deck was open to space. Outside the *Lexington*, Ed could see the characteristic swirls of red and blue, heralding the dust and gas that curled through the region, rendering instruments less than reliable.

Preceptor Ronz waited beside the officer on duty, a Jao clad in Terra Taif's blue, discussing the ships' approach. Aille krinnu ava Terra, current governor of Earth, turned to Ed as he entered. The governor's ears were flat-out *eager*. Even Ed could tell that much.

Aille's fraghta, Yaut, hovered behind his shoulder, still as bull-necked and ugly as ever. He gave Ed a dour look, but then he looked at everyone like that, even Aille. Ed couldn't imagine the Jao veteran in a lighthearted mood.

"There is no sign the Ekhat have yet returned, General Kralik," Aille said. "And it does not feel as though they will be here soon. Still, there is need for haste. Flow can alter as conditions change rapidly." His body assumed the angles of something like *introspection*, though, the governor being born of Pluthrak, Ed was sure it was nothing that simplistic. The Pluthrak were famous for notoriously difficult tripartite stances and it amused them to show off.

The first assault craft drifted through the huge doorway, firing station-keeping jets as the *Lexington*'s artificial gravity field asserted itself. The vessel eased into a cradle, then shut down as the next vessel appeared. When all three had settled, the bay doors rolled closed again so that the deck could repressurize.

He wanted to ask how long it would take, but knew the Jao officer would have just stared at him. It took as long as it took. Jao knew how long that was without asking. Timeblind humans just had to wait.

Finally the warning lights went green and the three ships' hatches popped open. Ed dashed through the access hatch and down the steps before Aille, Ronz, and Yaut, as was thankfully proper according to Jao protocol, craning his head for a glimpse of his wife's blond hair.

"Ed!"

He descended the last few steps with a jump, then spotted Caitlin. Her slim figure darted through a crowd of jinau, both human and Jao, then around Tully and four oddly pyramidal silver-skinned creatures to throw herself in his arms. He buried his face in her hair, holding her so tightly that her feet dangled above the deck. She smelled of wood smoke and herbs. Two arms, two legs, one head. Everything seemed to be in place. She felt warm and pliant and wonderful. "Are you all right?" he said a moment later when the tightness in his chest eased and he could breathe again.

"Hey, I'm better than all right," she said, then kissed him with a ferocity that promised a far more tantalizing reunion—later. "I'm the Queen of the Universe, or haven't you heard?"

"Um, no." He blinked down at her. Had she hit her head? Maybe she wasn't so completely all right after all.

She laughed and towed him by the arm toward the silver-skinned aliens, who were huddled next to the assault craft, staring around the huge shuttle bay. "Ed," she said, stopping before the closest. "This is Lim."

The creature, who topped his own five-foot, ten-inch height, was clad only in a simple rough-spun gray shift that had gone ragged around the hem. The Lleix had a long graceful neck and dished silver face with understated features, a mere suggestion of a nose, a lipless mouth, and narrow glittering black eyes. A strange fleshy crown ran over the top of its head from right jaw to left and wavered constantly as though blowing in a breeze. Its legs were sturdy as tree trunks, its hips wide, then the torso tapered up to its shoulders.

"Pleasure to meet you, Ed," the Lleix said in quite good English, its voice oddly musical. "How's it hanging?"

"They learned their English from Tully and his jinau," Caitlin said, when she could stop laughing at the startled look on Ed's face. "I'm afraid a lot of it is highly colloquial."

"How did it learn that much English—of any sort—in such a short time?" Ed asked, slipping her arm through his. "The *Lexington* only left you here a few weeks ago."

"Fifteen days, to be exact." She glanced back at the crowd of jinau off-loading from the assault ships. "That's a long time when you think that the Ekhat might pop back through the framepoint at any moment."

His face tightened. She could tell he was still angry about her being left on Valeron. "Wrot only did what was necessary and you know it," she said softly, glancing over his shoulder to see who was close. Jao had hearing like cats. "I've been making myself of use as we all must."

"I know that," he said. His gray eyes had gone steely. "I just don't have to like it."

"As for the language lessons," she said, "they're almost superfluous. The Lleix sop up vocabulary like a sponge soaks up water. Their brains work very differently from ours in that regard. If you speak a language around them, they *will* learn it, whether you want them to or not. A few of them already spoke some Jao when we first made contact."

His eyebrows rose. "Jao?"

"They have ancient recordings," she said, "from back when they tried to convince the Jao to turn against the Ekhat. That, apparently, was enough for at least a grounding in Jao."

"Caitlin!"

She looked up and saw Tully waving at her from across the bay. "Yes?"

"We're meeting up in a conference room on Deck Forty-Two," he called.

"Come on," she said, then laced her fingers through Ed's. It felt so good to have him close again, almost like when they had first found each other. She inhaled the scent of his aftershave and associated memories burst through her head, some of them most certainly not for public view. She grinned. "We have to save the Lleix so we can have some alone-time."

He nodded, suddenly all soldier again and not just her husband. He inhaled, the lines of his body gone starkly military. "We're organizing an evacuation," he said.

"Then they will let the Lleix come to Earth?" Relief surged through her. She'd wanted to believe all along that the Jao would reach out to the Lleix, but the reality was they were aliens and frequently did things, or left things undone, in a manner that baffled humans.

"For now," he said. "Ronz decided, which means the Bond decided that we're going to evacuate the Lleix, whether they agree or not. That's why I'm here. We've brought along enough jinau troops to get the job done, even if we have to kill some Lleix in the process. Better to sacrifice a few of them than an entire species. No one is promising what will happen about them living on Earth, though, in the long run."

"When last we spoke to their ruling body, the Han," she said, "they agreed to accept our help if we offered." She gazed at the four *dochaya* Lleix who were shadowing Tully like puppies. "They are a good people, I think, all things considered. They have their own quirks and odd values, of course, some of which I don't like at all. But their culture is incredibly ancient and they're well worth saving."

He tucked her arm through his as they headed for the lift. "If it wasn't for the *Lexington*, they would already be dead," she said as the doors opened and they stepped inside, alone for the moment. "Did you hear the particulars of the battle? The *Lexington* took out five Ekhat ships! Terra-Captain Dannet was amazing! I wish you could have seen it!"

"I'd very much prefer that *you* hadn't," he said, and then his arms were around her again as the lift raced upwards. She pressed her face to his broad comforting shoulder and drank in his warmth, letting him hold her until all too quickly they'd reached their destination.

It was a strange meeting, Preceptor Ronz thought, as Caitlin and Ed Kralik, faces oddly flushed, joined them in the conference room. Four Lleix were present at the wooden table, along with Wrot and a number of other high-ranking Jao, eight Bond representatives, and an assortment of humans, including Gabe Tully and Rob Wiley, who had both once been steadfast members of Terra's Resistance. The moment's flow raced so that it was all happening just too fast. He tightened his timesense to slow it down.

This was a crucial nexus. He could not allow himself to experience it in headlong haste. Mistakes simply could not be made this time as they had been so long ago at the last official meeting of the Jao and the Lleix.

"Are these their leaders?" he asked, as several crewmen hurried in carrying benches for the silver-skinned aliens.

Caitlin looked at Tully, then folded her hands on the gleaming wood. "No," she said. "The Eldests of the *elian* decide policy for the Lleix. When your ships jumped into the system, we did not know if they were ours or the Ekhat's. As a safety precaution, we loaded up the three assault ships. The *elian* launched what Lleix ships still functioned as well, and I'm sure the Eldests boarded them. By now they must have examined the instrument readings and know the Ekhat haven't come back—yet. Once the excitement of your arrival settles down, we'll request a meeting with their ruling body, the Han, to present our proposal."

"Then who are these?" Ronz said.

The four Lleix bowed their heads.

"They are workers from a disadvantaged sector of the colony called the *dochaya*," Tully said. His green eyes gazed boldly at Ronz. "Like the Jao, they desire only to be of use."

There was something prickly in the human's manner, something that Ronz couldn't quite pick up—affront, perhaps, or even anger?

"There is need of workers on your world?" one of their guests said in lilting English. Its fleshy corona fluttered. "We would serve to our best ability."

It spoke English? In spite of himself, Ronz was startled. The creature had a heavy accent, but its inflection was accurate. When he'd first come to Terra, it had taken more than a hundred successive nights of language imprinting before he'd become that fluent. How in the name of All-That-Swam had a Lleix acquired command of an alien language in only fifteen days?

The Jao present were watching him closely for a reaction. Stillness, he counseled himself. Calm. He must preserve Bond neutrality. He could not allow his body to give his thoughts away.

"I'm sure there will be work on Terra for all who desire it," Caitlin said, leaning forward on the table. Her angles had gone to *suppressed-discomfort* and she did not look at Ronz.

"Caitlin, Queen of the Universe, is kind," the Lleix said in its fluting voice.

Ronz molded his lines into classic *neutrality*. "About that," he said to the Lleix, every whisker, every line and angle, and both ears, exquisitely *neutral*, as though he were only speaking of tomorrow's meal or the mending of a bit of harness. "The moment has come to explain."

"Preceptor!" Caitlin came to her feet. "The Han, after days, endless days, in fact, of discussion, decided to accept *human* assistance." Her body had gone to *desperate-to-intercede*. "Can I speak to you in private?"

Silence filled the conference room as all looked to the Preceptor. Then he rose and followed her, along with Tully, out into the corridor.

"Preceptor, you don't know how hard it was to get them to agree to accept the offer of assistance from humans," Caitlin said as the door whisked shut. "If they find out we lied and the Jao are not our slaves, they'll have to talk it to death for months before they can decide again, and even then they very well may refuse."

"They cannot refuse," he said, "else they will all die."

"Even our primary contact, Jihan, agreed to keep this quiet once we were straight with her," Tully said. "Nobody likes it, but I figure we're stuck with the story for now."

"I understand why it was done and that indeed its fabrication is not your fault," Ronz said. "But this matter cannot be allowed to continue. What has happened thus far—especially given that it was initiated by Krant, not a human—can be explained well enough. But if we allow it to go on, the damage to Terra Taif's reputation among the kochan will become enormous. That is far more important now that the tactical concerns of how best to maneuver the Lleix."

"These four have no power to decide anything for the Lleix," Caitlin said. "But if you reveal the truth to them now, they will tell the whole *dochaya* upon their return. The details will spread throughout the colony within hours."

"So be it," Ronz said. "Flow signals that the time to reveal the deception is now. We must tell the truth and then make ourselves of use by transporting the Lleix away from this exposed position, even if they then believe they do not wish to go." He let his words sink in. "If we must force them, then we will. I have brought sufficient troops and firepower to handle the situation, should that be necessary."

"Let me try to convince the Han first," Caitlin said. Her hands were knotted together, a purely human gesture of distress. "I'll get Jihan to help. We'll make them understand."

Tully looked obstinate, shoulders hunched, body stiff, but then he often looked that way. "And you?" Ronz said, turning to the blond human.

"Hell, I never liked all this stupid storytelling anyway," Tully said. "Let the cards fall as they may."

An interesting colloquialism, praising the power of luck, in which Jao did not believe, a quintessentially human notion. "Very well." Ronz swept an arm toward the door, indicating the two, as was proper according to their lesser rank, should precede him back into the conference room.

Once inside, they took their seats, both folding their hands upon the broad table. *Question* was in the angle of Aille krinnu ava Terra's ears, but they all waited, Jao and Human and Lleix.

Still. Ronz did not speak until his body was perfectly, gloriously still so it would not betray his inner misgivings about this precarious situation. "Caitlin is not Queen of the Universe," he said to the Lleix.

The four long necks turned so that the inscrutable narrow black eyes were fixed upon his face. Their bodies had gone motionless enough even to do credit to a member of the Bond itself.

"Caitlin Stockwell Kralik does hold high rank among her kind," Ronz said, "but Jao are not, and never have been, human slaves. When my species first came to Terra, we conquered them, and then for a time were their rulers."

The Lleix seemed hardly to be breathing. Even their odd head-coronas had stopped moving.

"Do you understand this word—conquer?" Ronz said.

"Yes," one of them said. "It means to overcome in battle."

"We did not mean to deceive you," Wrot said, his scarred ears frankly *abashed*, "but the Lleix feared the Jao with good reason. When your representatives initially misunderstood the nature of the relationship between our two species, it seemed easier to let you believe that Jao were under human control, at least until you knew them better."

Finally one of the four turned to Tully and Caitlin. "Does this mean there is no work where we are going?"

"No," Caitlin said, her eyes suddenly bright with that peculiar human tendency to shed moisture when under emotional stress. "This means the Lleix will come on our ships to Terra where there will be much work for everyone."

The four Lleix gazed at one another. Their coronas fluttered, almost in unison, then the same one spoke again. "Then that," it said, "will be a goodness."

Recruited by Hadata, Jihan piloted one of the Starwarders' ailing craft out into the system as alien ships emerged one after the other through the framepoint. After the first few had cleared the star's photosphere enough to be analyzed, Hadata concluded from their design that they most likely did not belong to the Ekhat.

Which meant, logically, this huge fleet must have been sent by the humans. But why so many ships, Jihan wondered, as her hands flew over the little Starwarder craft's controls, unless they meant to fight the Lleix after all?

And even that did not make sense. The *Lexington*'s armaments could easily have destroyed the colony if the humans had so wished. But then they were aliens. Much of what they thought and did would likely make no sense to Lleix and they had already revealed themselves, at least to her, to be exceptionally duplicitous. Jaolore was a failure. The three of them had never understood their ancient enemy's mind. She just hoped the Jao did not turn out to be as insane as the Ekhat themselves.

After Hadata ordered her to assume a high orbit where they could monitor the emerging alien fleet, Jihan tuned the radio to the same frequency as the three assault craft that Tully had commanded and broadcast a call for him. It took much time, but finally she received an answer.

"Major Tully here," she heard in English.

"Tully, this is Jihan of Jaolore," she said. "What are these strange ships? Have they come to destroy the Lleix after all?"

The radio crackled. "No," the human said, "these are human and Jao ships, well, mostly Jao, come to transport the Lleix to safety."

And the Jao were not human slaves, but the *elian* did not know that. "When we arrive on Terra, will you tell the Han about the true relationship between Humans and Jao?" she said, keeping her voice low, though she did not think Hadata had picked up much, if any, English yet.

Tully hesitated. "We will tell them now, before we leave the system," he said. "As soon as a meeting of the Han can be arranged."

CHAPTER
37

Jihan's mind whirled after the conversation with Tully. As disagreeable as preservation of the untruth had been, revealing the deception now seemed the worst possible decision. The Han would not trust either the humans or the Jao. And most certainly they would refuse to leave Valeron under their protection.

Fear coursed through her, bitter and dark. She had played a part in this, a terrible part. It was her fault as much as theirs. They were aliens. It was understandable that their actions would not benefit the Lleix, but she should have known better. Her aureole throbbed with dismay and she did not know which way to turn. The Starsifters had been right to send her away. She was woefully short, but she had let herself forget that for a brief span of time. When Caitlin had revealed the truth, Jihan should have laid this problem at the large and capable feet of her elders and let them decide, rather than taking that right upon her inadequate self.

In a daze, she relayed the humans' wish to speak at the Han to Hadata and then requested permission to pilot the Starwarder ship back to the landing field at the edge of the colony. It was a difficult approach and for a while she lost herself in the complex calculations. The rest of the Lleix ships were coming in, too, most of their pilots short on experience so that they crowded all the best approach vectors.

Once safely down, she disembarked, pushing past the rest of the crew in her distress. Though all of them were taller, they edged back out of her way. Outside the ship, the early morning was crisp with the promise of more snow, though the air stank with the unharmonious exhaust of burnt fuel. She looked around, seeing the crews of the other ships as they swarmed out, then promptly fell to servicing their vessels. This time they did not have to flee the Ekhat, but that day was almost here. All ships had to be ready to launch now at any moment. The Lleix could not afford to be caught unprepared.

Although she knew she should stay to help with the Starwarder ship, she instead padded over the nearest bridge, seeking solitude so that she could force her brain to think. She passed servants and youngsters who were coming to the landing field, as well as elders, but acknowledged none of them.

Leaving behind the unnerving racket of landing ships and shouting voices, she found herself outside an abandoned house elegantly decorated with *Boh*. She traced the carvings with her fingers. The ancient faces gazed past her, their eyes enigmatic, looking somewhere else as they had for so long, not-seeing the Lleix here in their exile.

In the west, the mountains stood under leaden clouds, angular and gray against the gradually brightening dawn. To the east lay the plains, clear gray-green sky, the *dochaya* and the landing field. She was mired in the middle, caught between two extremes, the Jao and the Ekhat, and did not know what to do.

The Eldests had agreed to leave with the humans if they offered, but they would never go with the Jao once they understood the truth of the matter, not even to escape the great devils who ate the Universe. The Jao had presented untruth most grievously. The humans had supported them in the deception and then she herself had kept silent when she knew better. Jao might well be every bit as savage as the ancient recordings indicated. She had been a fool to trust them.

Finally, exhausted and hungry, she trudged home to Jaolore, speaking to no one she passed. Inside the *elian*-house, Kajin and Pyr had already risen for the day. A simple meal was cooking in the kitchens so that the air was fragrant with sourgrain porridge, but she found the pair already in the Duty Chamber, examining the old records, industriously attempting to learn more about these duplicitous creatures. All was as it should be and yet nothing was right.

"Set aside your studies for now," she said, then returned to the kitchens to sag onto a bench before the cooking unit. There, she stared at the rising steam from the pot, finding herself too weary and agitated to even think of eating.

The two Jaolore followed her. "I have reason," she said, "to think that the archives have little more of relevance to teach us about the Jao. The records are simply too old and out of date. Matters have changed. Things are not as we thought. Jaolore would do better to study the living Jao who walk among us."

Pyr only bowed his head, but Kajin's elegant black gaze regarded her shrewdly. "You have learned something about the Jao," he said with a flick of his fingers, "something that disturbs you."

"Yes." She could not look at him, but instead studied the ceiling with its lovely exposed beams. They had been anointed with red-seed oil day after day by diligent servants down through the generations until they gleamed. Such care had been taken in the construction of this house, and then in its maintenance. Now they must either abandon it or die beneath its broad rafters when the Ekhat returned. She felt so miserably inadequate. It was Last-of-Days on this world either way.

"The humans and the Jao have sent many ships," she said. "Enough to transport our entire population. They wish us to flee before the Ekhat return."

Kajin blinked, plainly not understanding her agitation. "That is what the Han previously discussed."

"Yes." She returned her eyes to the overhead beams, though she could feel both of her Jaolore staring at her.

"Eldest, that is a good thing," Pyr said finally, "is it not? The Ekhat have found us. We cannot stay here and survive."

"After today, the Han will not agree," she said.

Kajin's aureole fluttered. "But the Han already decided to accept human assistance."

"That," she said, "was before." Her robe gaped open and she was too frazzled to care. Indeed, she was so exhausted, she did not know if she would ever be able to rise from this bench again. Tully had decided that it was time for the truth, though, so truth was going to be told. She might as well begin telling it here. Everyone would know soon enough, once the humans and the Jao spoke to the Han. She would not shame her *elian* further by withholding the information.

Kajin's eyes glittered. "Before what?"

She tried to speak, but the terrible words would not come.

Pyr edged closer. "You are tired, Eldest." He ladled steaming sourgrain into a bowl and held it out. "You must eat and then rest."

She waved the well-meaning youth aside. "That was before they knew the truth," she said.

"And what exactly is there to know?" Kajin said, catching the implications when Pyr clearly did not.

But then, she thought, Kajin had spent many seasons studying the duplicitous Ekhat. His mind was far more prepared for this devious situation than hers.

"I will tell you," she said. The two pairs of eyes followed as she rose on shaky legs and headed for the Application Chamber, the most appropriate setting for such a discussion. "Both of you," she added, in case the overly reticent Pyr thought to exclude himself. "What I say can go no further than this *elian* for now, but I think soon, perhaps even by tonight, everyone in the colony will know these things."

She took the Eldest's seat in the Application Chamber, letting Kajin and Pyr arrange themselves before her by seniority. They were a small *elian*, but they would do things properly.

"A great untruth was given to us after the battle," she said, though the words were leaden upon her tongue. "Jao are not and never have been human slaves. Instead, some time ago, Jao traveled to Terra, homeworld of humans, and conquered them."

Pyr's startled gaze never left her face, though Kajin stared over her head. She went on. "The human, Caitlin, is not Queen of the Universe."

After the human ship returned to Valeron, Lim and her three companions hastened to the *dochaya*. Tully wanted to go with them, but given the possible repercussions when the Lleix learned the truth, knew he had to stay with his unit.

Fortunately, Caitlin had returned with the assault ships. Ed hadn't been at all happy about that, but Ronz was calling the shots and he thought having Caitlin on the scene might be a help.

"You go with them, Caitlin," Tully said. "You too, Lieutenant Miller."

Caewithe's eyes widened. "And, ah...Do what, exactly? Sir?"

He smiled crookedly. "Damfino. But you both know the situation.

Just do what you can. Nothing else, at least we'll know what happened."

He turned his head. "I'll detail a squad to accompany you."

Caitlin shook her head. "I'd recommend against that, Gabe. Look, as oppressive as their setup is, from our point of view, we've never seen any indication at all that the Lleix are prone to violence."

"She's right, sir," said Miller. "Makes no sense to me, personally. Where I come from, any boss conducted himself the way these *elian* do, the least you'd have is a walkout. But, there it is. The point being, sir, that I think we're perfectly safe—and dragging along a squad is more likely to cause trouble than prevent it."

Tully had read Miller's personnel file, since she was one of his subordinates. "Where you come from is San Francisco, Miller." Even a quarter of a century after the Conquest, the city was famous for being the most liberal city in the continent. "What—"

"Stereotypes, stereotypes," she said, clucking her tongue. "I don't come from Nob Hill, sir. Or Haight-Ashbury. My family are dockworkers. Have been for at least three generations." She and Caitlin began putting on their outerwear, preparing for the trek back through the cold. "We don't take kindly to management, you might say."

She gave him a sly smile. "Except for military management, of course. Most of us do a term of service, too."

As they slogged toward the *dochaya*, Caitlin thought about Miller's remarks. They'd been offhand, of course. More in the way of wisecracks than any serious suggestion.

Still…

"Do you really think the Lleix in the *dochaya* could organize a union, Caewithe?"

The young lieutenant's shrug was barely visible under her heavy outerwear. "Probably not, ma'am. I don't know if I think the differences between humans and aliens are genetic or cultural, or most likely a combination of both. What I do know is that changing their attitudes is awfully damn hard. I mean, look at how often we still clash with Jao—and how often the underlying reason is simply because we're misunderstanding each other. And we've been dealing with them for a generation."

They slogged on further. By now, the figures of the four Lleix they were following were barely visible in the distance. "Here's what I do know," Miller continued. "Major Tully has been talking to these *dochaya* people about our notions of equality and justice since the minute he got wind of what was happening to them. And even though they're incredibly capable when it comes to learning languages, and listened carefully to everything he said, I think the words still don't really mean a thing to them. Or whatever they do mean to them, they're not what we mean by the terms."

Caitlin was sure she was right. Human social arrangements and customs—trade unions being just one of many—were the product of centuries of history. Even if you assumed there were no genetic differences between humans and Lleix when it came to determining their social customs, it was unlikely that the Lleix would adopt human customs so quickly. Even underdog Lleix, much less a hidebound and ossified elite like the *elian*.

Jihan might—but Caitlin had already come to the conclusion that Jihan was an exceptional individual. She was certainly exceptional for a member of an *elian*.

Still…

When Caitlin Kralik and Caewithe Miller returned to the assault craft, they were both smiling widely.

"She's a genius, sir," Caewithe reported.

"I already knew that," said Tully. He waved down Caitlin's sputter of protest. "What'd she do? Organize them into a union?"

Miller shook her head, as she began removing the bulky outerwear. "Not exactly. I really don't think the word would mean much to them, even if they'd learn to pronounce it right inside of twenty minutes. Any more than—meaning no offense, sir—words like 'justice' and 'equality.'"

"She's right, Gabe," said Caitlin, struggling with her own outerwear. "The notion of a 'trade union' presupposes exactly what these people don't have, which is a preexisting notion that all Lleix share some sort of equal rights. We got that in our own history from a host of influences, including the Enlightenment, the Reformation and—when you get right down to it—some of the basic premises of the world's great religions."

Tully waited patiently. Once Caitlin kicked into her Professor Kinsey mode, she'd insist on beating around the bush for a while. Not as long as Kinsey himself would, of course.

Seeing the expression on his face, she smiled. "Some things really can't be explained in sound bites, Gabe. But I'll make it short. What I decided I *might* be able to do was persuade the *dochaya* people that the work they do of organizing themselves every day into a labor force ready, willing and able to provide the *elian* with whatever assistance they need is *itself* a specific skill." Her smiled widened into something very close to a grin. "In other words, I proposed a new *elian*. I suggested they call it the Workorganizers."

She hooked a thumb at Miller. "When they looked dubious, I told them that we humans had such an *elian*, and that she'd once belonged to it."

Caewithe shrugged. "I did, too, sorta. I'd get work as a casual laborer whenever I needed some money. I didn't formally belong to the union, but the dispatcher didn't care. Not with a brother, an uncle and two cousins in the same local."

Tully had never worked on the docks himself, but he knew people who had and understood the setup. Longshoremen didn't work for any specific stevedoring company. They all got work out of the union-run hiring hall, to which the companies applied whenever they needed laborers.

"In other words, you convinced them that the *dochaya* oughta be a hiring hall—and because a hiring hall is under the control of the workers instead of management, it amounts to its own kind of business. And so it damn well oughta be allowed to join the local Chamber of Commerce."

He started chuckling. "God, girl, on Earth you'd get laughed out of court. And I'm not sure who'd be laughing harder—the chambers of commerce or the union movement."

She and Miller were chuckling too. "Probably—but we're not on Earth. Once the *dochaya* people were told that the idea had of-fi-cial human approval, that was good enough." She stopped chuckling and gave Tully a nod that was almost deep enough to be called a bow. "All that stuff you said to them wasn't really a waste of time, Gabe. I think it laid enough of a groundwork to make them receptive."

By now, she and Miller had removed their outerwear. Caewithe began storing it away in the locker next to the hatch. "I think what's more important, probably, is that the *dochaya* folks have figured out that there's a new sheriff in town."

Tully had come to the same conclusion himself. "Yeah—but I'm not the sheriff, any more. Never was, really, just the deputy. And now Sheriff Ronz has arrived. Who's also known as a Preceptor of the Bond of Ebezon—and the Jao don't recognize trade unions any more than the Lleix do. So what's *he* going to think?"

Caitlin and Caewithe looked at each other. Then Miller smiled coolly and said, "Oh, I figure Mrs. Kralik can sweet-talk him into it."

Tully's smile matched hers. "Yup, so do I. So hop to it, Mrs. Kralik."

"Why me?" complained Caitlin.

"Haven't you figured it out yet, Caitlin? Like it or not, you're the human race's premier diplomat when it comes to dealing with Bug Eyed Aliens. Bemmies, for short."

"Neither the Jao *nor* the Lleix are 'bug-eyed,' Major Tully," Caitlin said reprovingly.

"See?" Tully said to Miller. "She's already being diplomatic."

Ronz was somewhat skeptical. But...

Caitlin Kralik's skills as a negotiator were a matter of record. And while the Preceptor doubted that Caitlin's maneuver would work for very long, it really didn't have to. Just long enough to get the Lleix aboard the ships and transported to Terra.

Ronz was prepared to use force if necessary to accomplish that, after all. So why not try Caitlin's scheme first? If it didn't work, Ronz could always fall back on the use of soldiers.

He'd brought human jinau for that. Using Jao troops, given the history, would have almost certainly guaranteed that the Lleix would resist bitterly.

"Very well, Caitlin. We'll try it." He turned away from the comm station to consider the commander of those jinau troops.

Who was, of course, Caitlin's very capable husband.

"And what do you think, General?" he asked.

"My wife is smart about these things, sir."

"Yes, I know."

Ronz turned away and began pondering that truth. Time he did so, he thought. If her scheme worked, as had her scheme to solve the human-Jao conflict by forming a new taif...

Once might be chance. Twice, no.

CHAPTER
38

Grijo departed the Dwellingconstructors' *elian*-house for the Hall of Decision as soon as the humans requested the meeting. The wind was fierce that morning up on the mountain, running hard before an incoming storm, and the deep chill cleared his head. That day, for the first time in his long life, he had traveled out into the solar system on one of the Lleix's increasingly few ships. Now, his feet had hardly touched the ground of home again before the aliens were clamoring to speak before the Han. It was a disquieting request. Supposedly all matters between their species had already been settled.

Everything was disarrayed. No one was behaving as she or he ought. In the Children's Courts, younglings were not being taught. The *elian* had put aside their crafts and services to instead prepare for abandoning this world. Some of the unassigned still sought employment, but most had fallen into unmitigated sloth, lounging about in the *dochaya* to whisper among themselves.

Was this what it was like each time the Lleix fled a colony world just ahead of the Ekhat? If so, it was a wonder his kind had not simply lain down and surrendered their lives. The constant physical and emotional turmoil exhausted his old mind.

After exiting the transport, he trudged up the stony path, step by careful step, and found the Hall's immense doors thrown open in readiness. Both of the resident Hallkeepers waited at the entrance, making themselves respectfully small as Grijo passed. His bones felt brittle and his aureole could barely stir. This day, with all its attendant problems, had fallen to him. If the crisis had waited just a few more seasons, he would have been safely dead and the weight of all this would have been someone else's to bear.

He settled his bulk into the ornate seat with its traditional discomfort and then watched as the rest of the colony's Eldests filed in after him and arrayed themselves in orderly ranked rows, the most aged closest to him, comparative youths in the back.

Finally, Jihan entered with several humans and two Jao. The young Jaolore crossed the hall to stand at the foot of his raised chair and gaze up at him.

Was she going to misbehave yet again? "Take your seat, little Eldest," he said. His hands gripped the carved armrests of the chair, seeking for a comfortable position when he well knew there was not one.

"I will stand with these," the Jaolore said, sweeping an arm back toward the aliens. "I deserve nothing more."

That did not sound promising. "What have you done or left undone, littlest," he said, "to say such a thing?"

Jihan's aureole stilled. Her eyes glittered. "I stood aside and said nothing when untruth was presented to the Han," she said. "Only hear what these have to say and then you will know."

The slightest of the four, the one called "Caitlin," a tiny human with golden fluff on her head, stepped forward and spoke. Jihan translated.

"Eldest-of-All," the human said, huddling into her heavy outer garment as though she found the day's pleasant chill oppressive, "a mistake has been made, one which we regret. When Jihan, Lliant, and Hadata were rescued from the Ekhat ship, one of our Jao crew told them an untruth." The creature gazed around at the assembly. "She said that Jao were human slaves. This is not true and indeed has never been true."

Grijo blinked. All around him, aureoles stiffened. Murmurs of shock ran through the assembled Eldests. A deep dread suffused him.

"The Jao who said this thing thought she was being *funny*," the human said. "I do not think she ever considered that her words would actually be believed."

Jihan had rendered the human word without translating it. "What is this term *funny*?" Grijo said.

"I do not know, Eldest," Jihan said, bowing her head. "I have learned a great deal of English in the time the humans have been among us, but I have not grasped that particular word."

Grijo studied the two Jao who had accompanied this small human. They did not seem to feel the chill as deeply, though they did wear foot covers and swathe themselves in blue cloth. "If the Jao did not think we would believe," he said, trying to make his startled brain think, "then why did she say this untrue thing?"

"Humans and Jao find the construction of humorous tales relaxing," Caitlin said. "It is a form of recreation. To explain further now would take too long, and we must make haste. As we discussed before, we have brought ships to transport your people to Terra. We need to make plans with you to evacuate the colony."

Grijo sat back, considering. Throughout the great hall, Eldests craned their heads for a better look and murmured to one another. Fear dried his eyes so that they ached, made his old hands tremble. They were not safe after all. This breach of an already fragile trust was yet another sorrow heaped upon their many past sorrows. It seemed to be their fate. The Lleix found nothing but obstruction and loss whichever way they turned. The *Boh* had indeed deserted them.

He leaned back in the seat as though he could distance himself from this unwelcome news. "Did the Jao compel you to let them tell this untruth?"

"No," the lithe little creature said through Jihan's translation. "But we knew the Lleix feared the Jao with good reason. When the untruth was presented, it seemed a way our three species could become acquainted without the Lleix worrying that the Jao would attack as they did so long ago."

"They drove us from our homes over and over again," Grijo said. "They rained death down upon the *elian* and most of what we once were is now lost. Because of the Jao, we are but a sliver of our former selves."

"They did all of those things," the human said, "but that was long ago under the direction of the Ekhat and no one present here today took part in the atrocities. Now, as you can see, they have committed a huge amount of time and resources to transport the Lleix to safety and in some measure atone for what their ancestors did."

"Present the truth," Grijo said. His mind was spinning with contradictions. "Now, in this sacred place, all of it." They must know the worst before they could decide what to do.

Caitlin bowed her head, seeming to compose herself, then told a startling tale, translated by Jihan, of the Jao coming to Terra and using their mighty ships to conquer an already divided blue and green world. It was a terrible war, she said, involving many ships and lasting several orbital cycles. Much of Terra's roads, factories, domestic habitations, and agricultural concerns were destroyed before humans yielded. Even then, she said, some pockets of resistance continued fighting whenever they had the opportunity. In the time that followed, it was never more than an uneasy conquest until the Ekhat attacked Terra itself, forcing Jao and human to learn to fight together.

"Now, we have taif status among them," Caitlin said. "We are considered equals by the Jao kochan."

Again, Jihan did not translate several of the alien terms. Grijo assumed the young Jaolore did not understand them.

The human gripped her small hands together in what seemed a gesture of strain or distress. "They recognize human culture as having strengths of its own, which when combined with those of the Jao, make us stronger together than either would be struggling against the Ekhat alone."

The strange tale chased itself round and round inside Grijo's old head. The Eldests shifted in their orderly rows, gazing up at him, waiting for him with all his accumulated experience to make sense of this bizarre situation. "They conquered your world and not even that long ago," he said finally. "The havoc they created sounds much like the savage persecution of our people. You would have us believe they have changed, but I see no reason why we should trust that they will not destroy the Lleix yet again."

"They regret what they long ago did to the Lleix," Caitlin said. "You must trust in their good will and let us evacuate your population to Terra, or once the Ekhat return, they will certainly murder you—"

The Starsifter Eldest, Sayr, rose from his bench. "They gave untruth at the moment of first meeting when the truth would have better served," he said, aureole rippling. "This apparent rescue is most likely also untruth. They mean to either enslave or do away with us at their own leisure, trusting that we will walk aboard their ships calmly and lend our own wills to our destruction."

"It is all untruth!" Alln of Ekhatlore cried, also jerking up from his bench. "By this, they prove themselves as duplicitous as ever

were the Ekhat! Better that we should take our own ships and
seek sanctuary as we have always done. Then the Jao will not
know where we have gone. Otherwise, we put ourselves at their
nonexistent mercy."

One after the other Eldests rose, speaking their objections,
presenting their only too logical fears. Patternmakers, Wordthreaders, Waterdirectors, Groundtillers, all spoke eloquently against
the offered assistance. The human gazed about the echoing hall
with her round little eyes, then retreated to the doorway with her
human and Jao companions, dwarfed by the building's vastness.

Some of the Eldests had remained seated, though, and left their
voices silent, Grijo noticed. Not very many, but some of them
were notable—including Childtenders and Weaponsmakers, who
were very important *elian.*

He turned to Caitlin. "Most of the *elian,* as you can see, are
against accepting this offer." His sonorous voice carried enough
even in this immense space to quiet the others. "Please take your
ships and go while we make preparations to do as we must."

"You will all die," Caitlin said, once Jihan had translated. "If
we leave, as you request, we abandon your people and culture
to their deaths."

"It may well be Last-of-Days," Grijo said, "but we have thought
that before and survived."

The wind gusted, howling around the hall. Then another one
of the humans spoke, in its high fluting little voice. Oddly, it was
accompanied by a Lleix clad in the gray shift of an unassigned.

"This is Tully," the young unassigned female said, planting her
legs in a bold stance. "He says—you speak of the colony leaving.
What of the *dochaya*?"

Grijo blinked. The question had no meaning. All through the
great hall, aureoles flattened in confusion.

The one named Tully spoke again and the unassigned translated.
"What will happen to the *dochaya* when the Lleix flee this world?"

"What always happens," Grijo said. "There is not room in our
ships for all to leave. Even the *elian* will have to select among
their membership for passage, each sending only a representative to carry on their skills and crafts. Unassigned have no such
knowledge. Those of the *dochaya* must remain behind."

The Tully human spoke again, very briefly. The translation came
immediately. "He says that is completely unacceptable."

CHAPTER
39

Tully gazed into the vast hall filled with the silvery Eldests, all clad in their elaborately brocaded robes, sitting in orderly rows, calmly considering whether or not they would allow the Jao to save them or just go off to die on their own. Late morning light slanted down from broad open windows that lined the walls just below the vaulted ceiling and it was so cold, he could see the white plume of his breath.

Ed Kralik had come with them, and Caitlin had been giving him a quiet translation throughout. Judging from the sourness of Ed's expression, things weren't going smoothly. Well, Tully could have predicted that. The Jao had a bad history with these folks. That damned tall tale Kaln constructed had eased things at first, but was now making everything worse.

At least fifty unassigned crowded in around the doors, having followed him along with Miller, Mallu and Kaln up the winding mountain path. They'd had to come on foot the whole freaking way because all the available transports had already gone up the mountain.

"You cannot abandon those in the *dochaya* to their deaths without their consent," he said to the Lleix leadership, trusting Lim to translate.

Her voice rang out through the hall. The Eldests jerked around to stare at him, apparently in shock at being so rudely addressed. Then Lim spoke for herself and her fellow unassigned. "We will go with the humans and Jao to Terra," she said, pausing every

383

few words to translate for Tully, "even if the *elian* would rather push their faces into the snow and pretend that they have better choices from which to choose. We of the *dochaya* do not plan to remain here and die!"

"Graceless creature, you know that you are not permitted to speak in this sacred place!" Old Grijo lurched to his feet.

"We have been permitted nothing except labor, food, and sleep!" Lim cried, "yet we are your children, the same as any ever accepted into an *elian*!"

"You are not the same!" an immense Lleix elder boomed. "You were turned away at the Festival of Choosing, quite rightly refused, because you have been judged by those with knowledge to be without sufficient value. And such behavior as this proves that judgment correct!"

Caitlin saw Lim's fleshy corona tremble, but the unassigned darted into the hall to confront the elder, even though he towered over her. "Humans have an *elian* for such as we." She pointed back at Caewithe Miller. "That one belonged to it at one time, before she joined their soldier *elian*."

"What is this nonsense?" demanded one of the huge elders. "How can unassigned belong to an elian? You do no work."

Lim wasn't giving an inch. "That is nonsense. We do whatever work is needed for the other *elian*. That is a task of its own, which we organize—not you! So we should be an *elian* also."

Several of the elders started to speak but little Lim's voice was loud enough to rise over them. "We have accepted the name the human Caitlin proposed for us. We are the Workorganizers. And we insist we have the same rights as all other *elian*."

The booming voices of huge elders finally rode her down. For a while, the hall rocked with terms like "nonsense" and "preposterous" and "outrageous."

But Lim fought out from under it. "And it doesn't matter, anyway!" she shrilled. "Accept us, or don't." She pointed at Tully. "He accepts us, and he commands the human and Jao soldiers on this world. And he has spoken with the commander of the fleet"—she didn't mention that the commander was Jao; no mean diplomat herself, it seemed—"and the commander says we will be given passage to Terra. So we are leaving—whether you say we can or not. It doesn't matter!"

A lifetime of misery gave the next sentence a tone that was harsher and more bitter than even the wind. "You no longer command here. You have hardly any ships, even for yourselves. So stay here and die. No unassigned will mourn you, be sure of that."

She turned and left the hall, the other unassigned following. Had she been human or Jao, Caitlin would have said she "stalked off." But that phrase just couldn't be applied to the graceful gliding walk that the Lleix always seemed to use, no matter how mad they might be.

After Caitlin gave Tully a quick explanation of what had happened, he looked around at the elders gathered in the hall. Truth be told, he had no use for them either. "What she said. Die and be damned."

He left then, following Lim and the people of the *dochaya*. To hell with it. He was no diplomat. If the pigheaded *elian* elders could be persuaded not to commit suicide, Caitlin would have to do it.

Tully looked down the mountain trail and saw a long line of silvery forms that stretched all the way back to the city. I'll be damned, he thought. The whole blasted *dochaya* had apparently decided to come up to the hall. But now, as Lim and the ones around her moved down the line toward the city, Tully could see the unassigned starting to turn around and go back. The word was obviously spreading.

That was probably a good thing for the elders, he thought, if there was any parallel at all between the Lleix and humans. The big crowd of unassigned would have easily been able to storm into the hall and physically overpower the elders. As enormous as they were, the *elian* leaders were almost all very old as well.

I wonder what the Lleix term for "lynch mob" is? he wondered, quite cheerfully.

Ed Kralik put an arm around Caitlin's shoulders and pulled her close. "I can signal *Lexington* and bring down the jinau to round them up," he said. "The Lleix have weapons on their ships, but so far I haven't seen any sign of handguns. I doubt there would be much hand-to-hand resistance."

"They need to come of their own free will," Caitlin said, "not as prisoners. That would be a terrible start, especially given their past history with the Jao. It would be years before they'd ever come close to trusting us again."

The Eldests were still arguing, more softly now, though they clearly were not even close to running out of steam. They had a such a civilized, fastidious way of disagreeing with each other— like old ladies squabbling in a sewing circle. Caitlin wanted to personally shake the teeth out of every single one of them.

Jihan was watching the proceedings with narrowed black eyes. Her body was very still. Finally, she strode up to Grijo's immense chair, tilted her head back so that she could look straight up at him, and spoke in a clear, ringing voice. All other conversation died.

"Jaolore will go to Terra also. We will join the unassi—the new Workorganizers *elian*."

Jihan tried to say more then, but the chamber filled with another uproar, much louder than before, the agitated voices rolling like a great wave. Jihan waited it out, gazing steadily at the elders. Then she spoke again.

"I belong to a new *elian*," she said, "so maybe that is why it is being given to me to think so many new thoughts. And, as most of you know, because there was much work for Jaolore and I could not wait for the Festival of Choosing, I accepted one from the *dochaya*. Rather than being unworthy for such elevation, I find Pyr talented and hardworking, industrious beyond understanding."

She gazed around the hall. "I have to order him to stop working and take care of his nutritional needs. I have to demand that he sleep at least a short time each night. My former *elian*, the Starsifters, were competent and focused, doing their duty for the colony without fail, but no one there, including me, had that kind of dedication." Her corona flared with determination. "I believe the *dochaya* harbors many such individuals and we have been forcing them to live in quiet desperation when they could have been giving their talents to the colony and enriching us all. When the *dochaya* goes to Terra, they will need to understand the Jao. I will take Jaolore and go with them to see what they build there."

"You would choose the *dochaya* over the combined wisdom of the colony's Eldests?" Grijo rose, his body stiff.

"I choose life over a so-called graceful death," Jihan said. "I choose the chance to think new things and experience a world that welcomes us. I choose to avoid Last-of-Days."

"You are breaking *sensho* again, child, even more grievously than before," an elder said, rising from a bench in the front. His robes were embroidered with starbursts and planets. "Have your errors these past days taught you nothing?"

Jihan started to shrink under his scrutiny, then raised her head. "What you forget, Eldest, is that I was right when I broke *sensho*. The Jao *had* returned. The information I possessed was crucial to understanding our situation. *Sensho* is useless when it causes us to turn away from the truth."

"Truth," Grijo said, seizing control again. "Which we were not given by these creatures, these Jao and humans."

"Because they feared it would lead to this," Jihan said. "Pointless, endless bickering while the Ekhat prepare to kill us all. And look at yourselves! Think how you have spent your time this day, invaluable, irreplaceable moments, when we could have been saving ourselves. Instead, they are just slipping away so that each can stand and make themselves heard, saying the same thing over and over! The Jao and humans were right to mislead us. I only wish they had kept the truth to themselves until we had reached Terra—but they were too honorable to do that."

Jihan turned to glare at Caitlin. "I weary of honor—on both sides!" she said. "Honor will not bake our bluebread, plant our fields, or raise our children! It will not mend our ships or fabricate new parts! It will not fight off the Ehkat!"

Grijo sat, slowly, as though his legs simply would not hold him for another breath. Caitlin gazed at the silvery Lleix faces, oriented as one upon Jihan like flowers tracking the sun. What were they thinking?

Then, in one of the foremost rows, a sturdy male topped by a dark pewter corona rose. "Weaponsmakers will go to Terra also," he said stolidly. "I am not certain how I feel about the unassigned claiming themselves to be a new *elian*. But I agree with the Eldest of Jaolore on all the rest. She is right, little as she may be. She is right now, as she has been right all along."

Weaponsmakers, Caitlin thought. That didn't bode well for the rest who would have to fight future battles on their own. Murmurs rippled through the crowd as the Lleix officials processed the information.

Grijo started to speak, but then from the middle rows, an aged female Eldest rose. Her robe was decorated with vivid scenes of Lleix youth, seemingly at play. She gathered her garment's folds before she spoke so that the fabric draped perfectly. Her corona stilled. "Childtenders will also go to Terra," she said.

Mouth agape, Grijo visibly wilted in his great seat. "Mahnt, you cannot mean that," he said. "If Childtenders go, then—"

"We take the Children's Court with us," she said, her posture very straight.

And the children were the colony's future, Caitlin thought. Jihan had done it. She'd put the ultimate squeeze on the other *elian*. They couldn't go off on their own without their children. What would be the point? Within a generation, their precious *elian*—so many of which had been lost already, over the long centuries of exile—would all start to die off.

Except the ones on Terra. The new ones, being raised and created by the unassigned with whatever help they could get from the Childtenders and the Weaponsmakers.

And then another stone came down from the wall. And this, perhaps the biggest stone of all. Grijo bowed his massive head. Outside, the wind gusted, blowing snow in through the open windows so that it sifted against their faces. "Dwellingconstructors will go, too, then," he said after a long pause. "We cannot leave our youth without shelter."

After that, a cascade of Eldests rose to make the same commitment, most reluctantly, though Caitlin thought that at least some of them were secretly relieved not to have to face the Ekhat without allies.

In the end, they didn't achieve complete participation. Some of the most hidebound *elian* remained firm in their refusal, including two called Stonesculptors and Distributionists. Why those particular *elian* were holding out, Caitlin hadn't the faintest idea, but their crafts didn't sound essential. Most likely, the new Lleix colony could do without them. She was pretty sure some of the *dochaya* unassigned had some idea how to fill in the missing services, anyway. They'd spent their lives working as servants in all those snobbish *elian*-houses. They'd certainly know far more about the crafts and services than any of their so-called "betters" suspected.

"What about the holdouts?" Caitlin asked Ed as the Eldests headed for the transports parked down the mountain a ways.

She and her husband were standing with Tully, Miller and Lim not far from the hall. Mallu and Kaln were with them also. "Do we force them to come with us anyway?"

"Ronz will have to make that decision. Hold on a sec, hon." Ed brought up his communicator and spoke into it briefly. Then, waited while Ronz was summoned. Eldest after Eldest passed the little group, none looking at them. Their bare feet shuffled through the drifting snow as though they were too upset to pick them up and walk properly.

When the Preceptor was listening on the command ship, Kralik gave a quick summary of the situation.

"Do not use force," Ronz said. "Most of the Lleix have now agreed to come to Terra. If we use force against those still recalcitrant, it will most likely cause the others to change their minds again."

"Yes, sir. That's my opinion also."

"We will provide coordinates to Terra," the Preceptor said, "then allow them to take as many of the functioning Lleix ships as they require and go off on their own, if that is what they wish. Perhaps they will reconsider before it is too late. Their numbers will be too few to maintain genetic viability even if they do locate a suitable planet before their ships give out." After a brief pause, he added: "And to be realistic, it will probably make our task easier if we leave behind those who are most strongly opposed to us."

"They're dooming themselves for their stupid pride," Caitlin said, as she watched the Lleix exodus. "I guess there's nothing we can do."

"Pride is important to Lleix," Jihan said, coming up beside Caitlin. "It means one is always correct and does things properly, that she can hold herself tall in her own *elian*, before her elders as well as the Han."

"You mean it's important to the *elian*," Tully said. He rubbed his ears, which were going numb in the frigid wind rushing in through the doors. "I can't see as how anyone has ever allowed the unassigned anything in which they could take pride."

"We will take pride," Lim said, "when we go to Terra. We will learn *sensho* and conduct ourselves as properly as anyone else."

Grijo and another Eldest stopped before Jihan, gazing at her in what Tully interpreted as a reproachful air. "I thought better of you, littlest," Grijo said, then headed out into the driving wind. The sun shone outside, but clouds were coming in.

The other Eldest only turned his silver face away and followed.

The humans, Jao, Jihan and Lim followed them down the icy path. Jihan was silent. Finally, the Lleix turned to Tully and Caitlin. "I have behaved badly again this day," she said, as they reached the turn led to the transport staging area.

"You saved your people by making them see what they had to do," Caitlin said. Her cheeks were red from the bitter wind. "You were very brave to stand up to them like that."

Jihan stared mutely out into the vast drop-off of the mountain side, her eyes gone very narrow. Brown flying creatures no bigger than a silver dollar wheeled overhead in the wind. "You do not understand," she said. "Lleix value *sensho* more than being accepted into an *elian*, more than graceful service, more even than breathing, but somehow I always have no choice but to break it." Her corona drooped. "I may have saved them, but they will never forgive my crude behavior. Perhaps I have more in common with the *dochaya* than I thought."

"Don't sell yourself short," Tully said. "From what I've seen, there's a lot of raw energy and untapped talent in the *dochaya*. I think those folks are going to do some amazing things once they get to Terra."

"But I am short," Jihan said. "Can you not see that for yourself?" She rippled her fingers at him, a gesture which probably had significance, though he had no idea what. It would take years to truly know these people, he thought, and some corners of their minds would most likely always be inaccessible to human understanding. Probably Jihan was right. They would never forgive her, though her words had saved them.

The colony spent the next three days in frantic preparations to abandon Valeron. Jihan had relatively little to do since her *elian* had existed for only a short time and they possessed nothing to pack beyond two viewers and a few crates of records. So Ronz, who seemed to be the equivalent of a Jao Eldest, appointed her his representative. Her job was to go to each of the *elian* and see what they needed, if anything, from the humans and Jao, to be ready to go, and then to make a schedule, assigning them a departure time.

Many of the Eldests refused to receive her, when she called at their *elian*-houses, but the youngers in residence cooperated and things got done in an orderly enough fashion.

Records, both written and recorded, would be taken, of course, and enough food for the journey to Terra, which would not be terribly long, according to Tully. They would need a few viewers for the records, though more could be constructed later. Seeds of their favorite foodstuffs, patterns for machinery, layouts for building houses—the list went on and on. Just when Jihan thought she had covered everything necessary to start their new lives, someone would point out an essential she had missed.

The unassigned evacuated to the Jao ships first. They had nothing to transport other than themselves. The *dochaya* housed little else. She toured the empty buildings afterward to be certain nothing was left behind. They were dreadful, dark and empty, barren and graceless. And Pyr had spent years here, she thought. That was what *sensho* had required, but how could it have been right?

Then she orchestrated the *elian*, transporting them in the same order of seniority which ordered their seating in the Han. By that standard, Jaolore would be last, which was proper.

The remaining holdouts, eleven *elian* in all, remained indoors as they prepared, steadfastly not-seeing this thing which mightily displeased them. She gave them the pick of what was left in the city after those going to Terra were ready, stores and foodstuffs, garments and tools. She'd had historical records copied for them and left the flats outside their doors when they would not accept them from her hand.

Tully predicted the hold-outs would not survive more than a few generations with such reduced numbers, but she hoped he was wrong. He was human. He did not know the strength of her kind. Many times, the Lleix had faced Last-of-Days and then found afterwards that they had lived through the crisis yet again. They were tougher than even they knew themselves. This splinter group might just surprise them all.

On the final morning, she made one last sweep through the abandoned city, making certain no one was left behind and revisiting one last time the elegantly sculpted trees, ornamental bridges, artfully placed light-posts, wandering streams, and mute *Boh* faces peering down from the rafters of every *elian*-house. For all the generations they had sheltered on Valeron, the *Boh* had never been with them. Would their gods finally look upon the Lleix again when they reached Terra, or would they always remain something wonderful left behind long ago on another of their headlong flights from the terrible Ekhat?

The reticent *elian*, the Stonecrafters, Distributionists, and all the rest, had taken the old Lleix ships and taken off two days ago in search of a new colony world. She had gone down to the landing field and watched, aching for the dangerous journey they were undertaking with no aid and little chance of success.

Now, pale-blue snow sifted down from a leaden sky and the wind swirled it against the vacant houses. She inhaled the sweet cold scent. The Lleix had known many homes down through the generations, but she had only lived here. Was there snow on Terra? She had forgotten to ask.

Pyr and Kajin waited for her as she crossed the final bridge to the landing field. Both were dusted with snowflakes and stood outside the small ship, ignoring one another as always. She had sent them ahead to load Jaolore's records along with their precious viewers.

All the other Terra-bound *elian*, as well as the *dochaya*, had already boarded the fleet of ships in orbit around Valeron. They were the most junior and last.

"Eldest!" Pyr rushed forward to greet her, his usually dull gray skin positively glowing. He looked almost presentable. "Tully says it is time to go! The other ships have already made the jump to Terra. Only the huge one, *Lex-in-tun*, is still in the system."

It was time, past time, most likely. They were just fortunate the Ekhat hadn't already come back. "Yes," she said. "I have finished checking. The city is indeed empty now."

Together, the three walked up the ramp into what the humans called an "assault craft." Swathed in heavy clothes against the chill, Caitlin stood just inside with a male of her species. His name was Edkraalek and he seemed oddly possessive of her, always touching Caitlin's hand or shoulder, never more than an arm's length away. "Welcome aboard, Jaolore," the little human said.

"I have been thinking about that," Jihan said, ducking through the undersized door into the crew's preparatory bustle, "and I believe we should not call ourselves Jaolore any longer."

Kajin's elegant eyes narrowed with angry suspicion. "Are we going to cast away even our name then and lose ourselves in the *dochaya*?"

"No," she said as a Jao crewman squeezed past to take a seat and strap in. "There will be no more *dochaya* once we reach Terra. The unassigned plan to form their own *elian*." She gazed around at the busy cabin, the humans and the Jao readying the ship for launch, working together without apparent concern for their many obvious differences.

Pyr watched her closely.

"Our knowledge of the Jao will be critical, but there is so much more to learn. We must understand humans and Terra and the history of the Jao from the time we last knew them until now, the events which transformed them into allies who reached out to assist us." She settled on the floor and braced her back against the bulkhead. "We need a wider, more inclusive—"

"Terralore!" Pyr exclaimed.

The designation fit. She tried it out in her mind, seeing if it would stretch to include everything needed. "Yes, youngest," she said, "I think you are right."

Kajin, as always, glowered.

PART VIII:
Terra

CHAPTER
40

Just after the last craft from Valeron docked with the *Lexington*, the command crew reported a contact deep in the local star's blazing photosphere. Terra-Captain Dannet was prowling the command deck, where she belonged at this critical point in the evacuation. To her irritation, the Preceptor, Ronz, and Terra's governor, Aille krinnu ava Terra, had come up and were now poking about where they were most decidedly not wanted. The governor, a former Pluthrak, was quite the pilot himself, evidently, and felt free to pry into every detail of *Lexington*'s operation.

Her whiskers bristled. The new sensor contact was unlikely to be one of their ships. The rest of the Jao fleet had already jumped back to Terra, conducting their portion of the Lleix population to safety. It had to be the Ekhat. Dannet imported the stats to her own screen and studied them.

Lacking their own assignments, Ronz and Aille crossed the bridge to examine the readings over a crewman's shoulder. Dannet remained at her station, ears lowered in thought. She had felt flow quicken a short time ago, but had erroneously thought it only indicated the return of all remaining crew from Valeron and their own immanent departure from the system.

"Multiple contacts now, Terra-Captain!" her sensor tech reported. She was a human female, quite competent at her task. "Ten, no, make that thirteen!"

Arriving vessels were vulnerable at this stage before they could break free of the photosphere, and Dannet was not averse to another fight. The last, when she had defeated five Ekhat ships in a single engagement, had increased her status in Terra Taif immensely.

And the *Lexington* was designed for exactly this situation. Dannet wouldn't have to improvise as she had before. Her shoulders assumed the sweet lines of *anticipated-success.*

The doors opened and the scarred old veteran Wrot krinnu ava Terra came onto the command deck. "All secure—" he began, then saw Ronz and Aille huddled over a screen, ears *intent.* "Preceptor?"

"Enemy contacts," Ronz said without looking up. "The Ekhat are returning."

Dannet rose, unable to sit still, her body angled into *readiness-to-be-of use.* Flow raced and she tightened her perception so that she experienced the moment more sedately. "Permission to engage?" she said. "We will rarely if ever get an opportunity as good as this to use *Lexington* to maximum effect. I am confident our kinetic weapons can destroy several of those ships with little risk to ourselves while the Ekhat are still submerged in the photosphere. And we can make our own escape before they can regroup."

Ronz turned and met her gaze. His eyes flickered only a faint green like lightning from a faraway storm, while she knew her own must be blazing with eagerness. His body was exquisitely neutral, betraying not a single hint of his thoughts.

The normal sounds of the command deck continued around all around them, clicking and whirring and the excited murmurs of the crew, but the Preceptor remained silent.

"No," he said finally. "It is indeed tempting, but we have a responsibility to the Lleix we have taken onboard. We have an ancient matter of conscience to resolve." He turned back to the screen. "Besides, the universe produces a seemingly inexhaustible supply of Ekhat. *Lexington* will see more than enough action before its usefulness is completed."

Dannet was disappointed, but...it was a sensible choice on the Preceptor's part, she supposed. She adjusted her body-harness, which had gotten a bit twisted in her excitement, then sank back into her seat and studied the oversized navigation viewscreen. "Navigator Sten," she said. "Are our return framepoint coordinates calculated?"

"Yes, Terra-Captain," the Jao officer said, his angles gone to *swift-readiness.* "Shall I lock them in?"

The Ekhat contacts strengthened, but the enemy ships would not clear the photosphere in time to detect the *Lexington*. For a wild moment, she was tempted to withhold the order to jump away from the dust and haze of this benighted system just long enough to ensure they would be forced to engage, but then her strict Narvo training reasserted itself. Such a circumvention of the Preceptor's order would be dishonorable, reflecting badly upon Terra Taif as well as those who had once schooled her for this position of trust. As always, the honor of one was the honor of all.

This would have been an excellent opportunity for honing the crew's battle skills, but as the Preceptor had pointed out, there would always be more Ekhat. That was the one great truth of the universe as far as she could tell. No matter how many battles she fought, the Jao would not see the end of the Ekhat in her lifetime.

She flicked an ear at Sten. "Jump when ready, Navigator. This ship is returning to Terra."

Caitlin looked around the room on the ship that served Preceptor Ronz as an admiral's stateroom. She was pretty sure it had originally been a storeroom for kitchen supplies. It had the appearance of being a chamber that had been hastily refitted when Ronz decided to accompany the *Lexington* back to NGC 7293.

On the plus side, it was certainly big enough to serve as an admiral's headquarters. There was plenty of room for staff meetings, such as the one that was about to get underway. On the minus side, it was far removed from the command deck. But that was probably an advantage, looked at from the standpoint of the ship's captain. Kept the admiral from being underfoot all the time.

Ronz made the little hawking sound that served Jao as an equivalent for a human clearing his throat.

"I believe we are all here, so let's begin. I think a good place to start would be with Major Tully's proposal."

"I do not mean to offend, Preceptor," said Wrot. "But the issue of association between Terra Taif and Krant is not actually a matter for the Bond's concern."

Caitlin couldn't stop herself from wincing a little. Wrot was right, true. But couldn't he have made *some* effort to say it diplomatically?

Fortunately, the Preceptor was not given to being easily offended. "Normally, that would be true," he said, in a very mild tone. "But this situation is more complicated."

"Why?" Wrot asked, as bluntly as ever.

"Because I think, to borrow a human phrase, that we are in position here to kill two birds with one stone. Possibly even three."

Before Wrot could say anything, Aille spoke up. "Please continue, Preceptor. I am interested in hearing your opinion."

So much for that, Caitlin thought. Technically, since he was not one of the elders of the Jao portion of Terra Taif, Aille's views didn't carry much weight when it came to purely kochan matters like determining association with another kochan. But the Jao were just as subject as humans—and Lleix, for that matter—to the imperatives of practical reality. Aille was not only the governor of Terra, he was the single central figure in the new taif. Wrot might chafe privately at the youngster's presumption, but he wasn't going to make a public issue out of it.

"The first bird to be slain is the question of association between Terra and Krant," Ronz said. He gave Wrot the same little dip of the head. "Into which, as my former agent points out with his usual delicacy and tact, I have no business sticking my snout. To paraphrase another human expression."

Wrot looked slightly abashed. Only slightly, though.

"But there is the second bird. I believe Terra Taif should adopt a new institution. More precisely, adopt an institution which will be very familiar to its human members, if not to its Jao. I speak of what humans would call a 'diplomatic corps.'"

Wrot and Aille stared at him. They both looked so dumbfounded that Caitlin had to suppress a laugh.

"Diplomacy," as such, was no stranger to the Jao. But diplomatic relations were simply part and parcel of kochan business, handled by the clan elders like all other kochan matters. The idea that you would separate out the process and assign the work to a specialized unit was simply bizarre, from a Jao viewpoint.

Aille recovered quickly, of course. "Please explain the need for such, Preceptor."

"Consider the business with the Lleix. And then contemplate the fact that the galaxy contains many sapient species. Some of whom we have already encountered, most of whom we have not."

"Except for humans and Lleix, though," Wrot said, "they are all extremely primitive."

Ronz placed his hands on the big round table that served all of them as a conference table. "True. But why is that? Perhaps it is because we have only encountered species in this region of the galaxy—which is the same region infested by the Ekhat."

Wrot was obviously puzzled. "Naturally. Here is where we have concerns to deal with. Why would we go elsewhere?"

His attitude was pretty typical. Exploration for the sake of exploration was a variety of *ollnat,* you could say. An impractical enterprise which would hold little interest for the Jao.

Ronz didn't answer the question directly. "Consider the corollary. The Ekhat rigorously search out any sapient species in order to enslave them or destroy them. But there is no way to search for sapience as such. What they are actually seeking are the byproducts of technological advancement, not so?"

"Yes," said Aille. "And I understand your point. Because of the Ekhat, there is a selective pressure against technologically advanced intelligent species in this portion of our galactic arm. But that might not be so, in some other region where the Ekhat have not gone yet."

"Exactly. And from observing what has happened with the Lleix, it occurs to me that we are possibly missing an opportunity. Who is to say there are not other species as advanced as humans or Lleix—or even we Jao ourselves? And if so, could they not make powerful allies in our war against the Ekhat?"

Wrot was still looking confused. "But no kochan would devote resources to such an uncertain enterprise. Perhaps the Bond...?"

The Preceptor shook his head, one of the few human gestures which had been adopted by many Jao. "That would be unwise, I think. The function of the Bond is to mediate between the kochan. Were we to begin acting on behalf of all kochan, that would inevitably stir up antagonism."

"True," said Aille. "But if one of the kochan were to begin such an effort—better still, a new taif—"

"Better still," Ronz interrupted, "a new taif in association with a little known and poorly regarded kochan, like Krant."

Aille leaned back in his chair. So did Wrot.

So did Caitlin and Ed, for that matter. And Tully actually whistled. Softly, thank God.

Caitlin's mind was racing ahead. A diplomatic expedition of the sort Ronz was proposing would be dismissed by all the great kochan as the silliness you might expect from a new and bizarre taif like Terra. And as for the Krant... Who cared what Krant did?

It was quite possible, of course, that such an expedition would be a failure. The rarity of technologically-advanced species might be one of the stark realities of the universe, and not just a function of Ekhat genocide. But if so, no real harm was done. No harm at all, actually, from a human standpoint. The Jao might consider exploration for its own sake to be a pointless waste of resources, but humans had a much greater interest in abstract knowledge. And, at least in the long run, there was plenty of evidence that the human attitude was more practical than the Jao.

But if the expedition was *not* a failure... If it did, in fact, come across potential allies in the war against the Ekhat...

Whichever kochan—or taif—led the way in the process would come out of it with its power and influence greatly enhanced. She glanced at Ronz. And so would the Bond, of course. Since, the Preceptor's protestations notwithstanding, Caitlin had no doubt at all that the Bond would be closely allied to the project, in fact if not formally.

Tully was the first to raise the obvious problem. "But why would Krant agree? They are poor as it is, hardly in position to devote resources to such a project."

Aille's body posture, even seated, was practically exuding enthusiasm. "Not if we provide the resources." He leaned forward. "We all know how effective Terra's shipbuilding industry can be, if we throw our full efforts into it. We need to build a big fleet of *Lexington*-class warships in any event, since the Ekhat are sure to launch another attack on Terra. Why not give two of them to the Krant—with the proviso that one of the ships is to be used for such a diplomatic mission? Krant could provide much of the crew."

"Sure could," said Tully. "Mallu could be the ship-captain—and who better than Kaln for an engineering officer?"

Ed spoke up, for the first time. "You'd need a lot more than a single ship, though, even a ship the size of the *Lexington*."

Ronz looked at him. "Why, General Kralik?"

"Consider the logistics involved. The region of space known to you already is huge—and now you propose to explore beyond it? Whichever direction you choose to go, up or down the galactic arm, you will be operating very far from Terra. It is simply not practical to think that such an effort—a sustained effort, at any rate—could be maintained without establishing a forward base. A very large and substantial forward base."

There was something a bit odd about the cant of the Preceptor's ears, Caitlin noticed. As if Ronz was amused by something but trying to keep from showing it.

"Indeed, I think you are right," said Ronz. "It would have to be a military base, of course. With a sizeable number of troops, the resources to carry out major ship repairs—"

"We would need more than one ship," Aille interjected. "At least two the size of *Lexington*, I think, possibly three or four. And a number of smaller ships better suited for exploration."

"It'd be a good idea to have at least a couple of big assault ships, too," Ed added. "You never know what you might run into—and just being able to blow something up isn't always the best alternative."

"Quite true," said Ronz. The hint of humor in his ears was more pronounced, now. "A force like that would require a general in command, I think."

Caitlin glanced at Ed. He was looking suspiciously good-humored himself, as if a scheme of his was shaping up nicely. What was going on?

"Who would we select to be in charge of such a mission?" Wrot asked.

"I should think the choice is obvious." The Preceptor pointed at Caitlin. "Her, of course."

Wrot stared at her. Caitlin thought she was probably cross-eyed, since she was trying to stare at herself too.

Was Ronz joking? For Pete's sake, she was in her mid-twenties! Not to mention being human instead of Jao.

"Excellent choice," said Aille abruptly. "I will support the proposal when we return to Terra."

"But—I'm—"

"I will release you from my service," the governor added. "If that would be necessary."

"Oh, I think not," said Ronz. "Probably a bad idea, in fact. Most Jao, even those belonging to Terra Taif, will be skeptical of a human being placed in charge of such a mission. But if the human is a well-known member of your service, Aille..."

"He's right," said Caitlin. She felt vaguely—and perhaps oddly—relieved. As much as the notion of being part of a high-born Jao's personal service had once struck her as rather demeaning, she no longer felt that way about it. Not, at least, given that the Jao in question was Aille.

Beyond that...

The proposal itself would be a tremendous challenge. Opportunity, too. There was a big part of her that wanted to seize it with both hands. But there was another part of her, that very personal and very emotional part that involved being married to Ed, that was not happy at all. She'd hated being separated from Ed even during this recent expedition to a relatively nearby planetary nebula. The idea of being parted for...months, certainly, and quite possibly years, when you were talking about exploring a whole galactic arm...

Her mouth moved into a little round shape. "Oh." No wonder Ronz had been amused—and Ed had looked like he was scheming.

"I imagine you would volunteer to be in command of the forward base, General Kralik?" Ronz's ears were no longer trying to hide his humor.

"Oh, sure," said Ed.

Ronz then turned to Tully. "The expedition would require a unit such as yours, I think. Would you be willing to volunteer?"

Tully hesitated, which was unlike him. But then he jerked his head. "Yeah, sure. I mean, yes, Preceptor."

"Excellent. It remains only to persuade Terra Taif when we return." But Ronz didn't seem too concerned about that. No reason to be, really, with Aille so strongly in support.

"And the Krant," Tully added. But he didn't seem too concerned, either. Caitlin hoped he was right.

"*Two* ships?" Mallu asked, sounding a bit shaky. "Both *Lexingtons*?"

"*Lexington*-class," Tully corrected. That was a little pointless, though. The Jao didn't have the habit of naming ships in the first place, so they weren't likely to make fine human distinctions between a class of vessels and the specific ship after which the class was named.

"You understand," Caitlin said, "that part of the bargain is that one of the ships must be devoted to our enterprise. The other, Krant may do with as it wishes."

"Yes, I understand. But...*two* ships? Both *Lexingtons*? You are certain of this?"

"Absolutely dead sure positive," Tully replied. "Assuming Terra Taif agrees, of course, after we get back. Aille and Wrot can't really make the decision on their own."

Mallu and his two subordinate officers stared at him, for a moment. Then Kaln said, "But you don't expect…"

"It would be very surprising if Terra Taif did not support their decision," Caitlin said firmly. "Not impossible, of course."

That seemed to bring Mallu up short, a bit. "Yes, naturally. And—of course—you must also understand that I cannot commit Krant to this project. The kochan would have to agree."

Kaln came as close to spluttering as Caitlin had ever seen a Jao come. "Don't be silly, Krant-Captain! There is not a chance—no chance at all—that the kochan will not agree. Two *Lexingtons*? They would agree to almost anything for that! They will certainly agree to associate with Terra Taif—very closely, too." Her body posture was a Krant-crude version of *cheerful-anticipation*. "They will even agree to the Terran insistence that the two ships have to be named, according to silly human custom."

"Huh?" said Tully.

"I will not be disturbed," Kaln said. "Given that the names will be *Pool Buntyam* and *Bab the Green Ox*."

EPILOGUE

The Eldest

Their hosts designated the Lleix's new home Call-ah-ra-doh. Jihan didn't have the name's sounds quite right yet, but she was close. She had finally mastered the slippery word "human" with its tricky "hwah" sound on the wondrous journey to Terra, with a bit of coaching from Tully, and was finally closing in on the exact pronunciation of "Caitlin." That name's sound combinations were particularly elusive but the little human assured Jihan that she was doing very well.

"We'll have to study your language for years before we achieve anywhere close to your mastery of English," the once alleged Queen of the Universe said.

Een-glish, Jihan thought, not Enn-glish. The Lleix were determined to speak the new language properly and do their benefactors honor. She had considered making the study of English part of Terralore's function, but then decided it would be taking on too much. Instead, she suggested the function to Lim, who promptly formed her own English-study *elian* on the ship before they even landed on Terra.

More new *elian* had come into being over the course of the following days, popping up with precipitous haste. All of them had been organized by unassigned from the *dochaya*, and Jihan suspected many of them would not last. But that would be no tragedy. If some of the newly organized *elian* fell apart, she was quite confident others, more urgently needed, would arise to take their place.

And then, after they'd arrived in Call-ah-ra-doh, there had been the unexpected defection by more than a few members of the traditional *elian* to the new ones created by the unassigned. Grijo, Sayr, and most of the Eldests were quite disturbed by the shake-up. They were calling a meeting of the Han to discuss it, but privately Jihan thought the trend was healthy.

Why should one have to work all her life in a craft that did not please her or labor with disagreeable individuals? She knew far better than anyone that adherence to *sensho* was not always productive. So far, Kajin had gone back to Ekhatlore and she'd accepted one of the deserters, a female from Treebinders, into Terralore, along with twenty-three former unassigned who were all ecstatic to have a place.

The one great certainty was that, on this world, there would be no *dochaya* as it had been on Valeron. Since arriving here, Jihan had discovered that Tully's hostility toward that Lleix custom was widely shared on Terra. By humans, if not Jao. Within three days of their landing, in fact, a number of humans had showed up in the quarters of the unassigned. Sent there by Tully, it seemed, or at least on his suggestion.

They called themselves "union organizers." A peculiar group, most of whose speech seemed close to gibberish. Still, they were treated very respectfully. By now, all members of the *dochaya* were partial to humans.

The established *elian* were not so friendly, of course. But not even they would go so far as to be openly hostile to their human hosts. Partly, because they really had little choice. The survival of the Lleix was now completely dependent on the humans and Jao, and everyone knew it.

But, partly, it was because the Jao and humans seemed sensitive enough to keep the Jao very far removed from the Lleix. Occasionally, a Jao would be seen visiting the area. But almost all of the contact the Lleix had with Terrans was with the indigenous species. Which suited all of them quite well, of course—except for Jihan herself. As the eldest of Jaolore, she wanted to have extensive contact with the Jao, even though they still frightened her.

There was so much to think about, so much new information and ways of living to absorb. On the journey, Jihan had used the time to learn about the structure of the Jao kochan. Preceptor Ronz had explained that each group maintained many functions:

choosing mates, generating, raising, and educating children, building space-going ships and houses, even making cloth for capes and trousers and raising food. In a sense, each Jao kochan resembled a tiny Lleix colony, complete in and of itself.

Ronz had been very friendly and helpful, in fact. So had the younger one named Aille. This, despite the fact that they both occupied very prestigious places in their own society. As time passed, it was becoming obvious to Jihan that the long centuries since the Jao had almost exterminated the Lleix had produced a profound change in both species—and perhaps even more so among the Jao. It was difficult to see the blindly murderous being who had so casually struck down the Wordthreader Eldest so long ago, in the sophisticated and subtle persons of Preceptor Ronz and Governor Aille.

Even Grijo and the other *elian* elders, she thought, were slowly coming to that understanding.

She looked around, enjoying the vista. The wind was rushing down from the mountains, producing a pleasant briskness. The day was clear and the sky so achingly blue that she had difficulty looking up into the brightness after the chronic gray-green atmosphere of Valeron. Jao-style "quantum crystal" shelters were being poured with humans working alongside the Lleix immigrants. The glimmering blue structures were beautiful once they hardened, but very strange inside without a single corner or right angle. They would suffice as shelters for the moment, certainly. But if the Lleix were to stay for any time on Terra they would want to build proper wooden homes. That was quite feasible, the Dwellingconstructors told her. Terra had many fine woods to work with, it seemed.

Jihan's gaze left that sight and wandered to the snow-topped mountains that filled the western horizon. The range was much taller and more rugged than the peaks left behind on Valeron. She longed to explore.

"We selected this region because its climate and geology are similar to what you had back on Valeron," Caitlin said, coming up behind her. "Even before the Conquest, it was sparsely populated with only a few farms and cattle ranches. But almost no one has lived out here since. It gets really cold in the winter and snows a lot. After the Jao came, no one maintained the roads anymore. Fuel and lack of electricity became a problem. Survivors moved to the cities."

Jihan had been glad to see snow on the distant mountains and was even gladder to hear now that it would snow down here. "Will it snow soon?" she asked, longing for that familiar sweet crisp scent.

"Perhaps," Caitlin said. "In fact, even probably. It's early October, and winter comes early at this elevation. I'll check the long-range weather forecast for you."

She left on an errand, then, and Jihan went back to her study of their new planet. This place was not a permanent solution to the Lleix's lack of a home, but the Terran version of a Han had voted to give them sanctuary until a suitable world of their own could be located. Ronz had suggested they might even be able to return to one of the worlds from which they had long ago first fled. The Jao elder had pointed out that it was unlikely the Ekhat would think to look for them there again after all this time.

The ancient names of those abandoned planets were only legend now: Sankil, Thrase, Gisht, and Remaht. The coordinates had been lost on their migrations long ago. Might one or more of those worlds still exist, lying fallow, waiting for their former residents to return? And if the Lleix could locate them, would the *Boh* be there, ready to watch over the Lleix again? The possibility was exciting, and in the meantime, they had these glorious green and gold hills as well as snow-covered mountains to explore.

Two former unassigned dashed past her, arguing energetically about their new *elian*, whatever it was. There were many new *elian* emerging out of the Workorganizers, these days. The people of the former *dochaya* had decided that one of their new *elian*'s duties was to create other new *elian* where needed.

It was a claim that few of the established *elian* recognized, but that hardly mattered any more. Most of the old *elian* were mired in dull and sullen resentment. Not all, though. In addition to Terralore, two of the most important established *elian*—Childtenders, who had been the largest until Workorganizers was formed, and Weaponsmakers—were adjusting well to the changes. They were on good terms with the huge new *elian,* and were cooperating with it.

The Childtenders had always been sensitive to the plight of those of their former charges relegated to the *dochaya*. As for the Weaponsmakers...

For them, this new situation was a blessing. Terra-Taif had

decided to design one of the new *Lexington*-class ships for a largely Lleix crew. So the Weaponsmakers had a lot of work again, along with new skills to learn. They were taking in many new members from the unassigned. A small host, in fact. By long custom, Weaponsmakers would provide most of the crew when the ship was built.

Jihan was keeping a record of these new *elian* as they came into being, so she followed them out of the invigorating wind into their shelter.

"What is the designation and purpose of your *elian*?" she asked.

The smaller of the two, a young male, had a bronze aureole and silver skin of a shade far lighter than most. He stared at his feet. The other, an older male, met her gaze, then looked away, making himself respectfully small. "We are the *Boh*-Finders, Eldest," he said.

"On this world—Terra?" She could not keep the surprise from her voice, though she tried most diligently to support all the new *elian*.

"No, Eldest," the smaller said. He looked up into her face and his black eyes sparkled with plans. His young body radiated eagerness and he simply could not be still. "We will go to Sankil someday, or Thrase, or even Remaht, and find them there."

It was a long-range plan, but worthy of effort and study. All Lleix had dreamed down through the generations that someday the *Boh* would once again look upon their lost children and enfold them in their beneficent sacred attention. "Then," she said carefully, "you will need a viewer to examine all the old records and learn as much as you can."

Their aureoles crumpled. Unassigned possessed nothing beyond themselves and had all come away from Valeron with only their shifts. They would not know how to operate a viewer even if one did come their way. Servants, such as they had been, cooked and scrubbed, fetched and carried, labored in the fields, cleaned waterways, streets, and houses. They were not allowed to operate valuable devices.

"Terralore has two such machines," Jihan said. "We will reassign one of them to the *Boh*-Finders and allow our Pyr some time off from his *elian* duties to instruct your members in its use."

They would need many more viewers, she realized. Unfortunately, the *elian* which traditionally handled that work had been one of the eleven which had refused to make the voyage to Terra. She would have to speak with the Workorganizers to see about forming a new *elian* which could manage the task.

"You would do that," the older said, his aureole now rippling with emotion, "for such as we, for mere—"

"For a new *elian* with a great purpose," she said. "For that wondrous day when you do find the *Boh* and we can all finally go home."

The Ship-Captain

Dannet was too surprised to speak, for a moment. And when she did finally manage to utter a word, she immediately felt like a fumble-witted crecheling.

"Me?"

Dumbfounded, she stared at the small human female, Caitlin Kralik. She had apparently once had a different birth name—"family name," they called it, after that peculiar human institution that seemed to substitute poorly for a proper clan. But when Caitlin married her husband—they usually only mated in pairs—she'd taken his family name for her own. That custom also struck Dannet as peculiar, but so did much else about humans.

She looked then to the husband in question, Ed Kralik. He was one of the top commanders of Terra's jinau troops. A very capable commander, by all accounts including those of Jao.

He nodded his head, seeming to be amused. "As she says, Terra-Captain. You, indeed."

Dannet now looked to the two Jao in the room: Wrot, who was one of the new taif's Jao elders, and the much younger former Pluthrak who was the planet's governor. Wrot said nothing and neither did Aille. But the postures of both of them indicated their agreement, Aille's in that damnably sophisticated Pluthrak manner that anyone Narvo-born like Dannet found simultaneously engaging and irritating.

Her wits returned in sufficient force to muster a two-word sentence. "Why me?"

Caitlin's eyebrows went up. Dannet had learned enough of the primitive and overly plastic human methods of body language to know that facial gesture was the rough human equivalent of *surprise.* That was itself a very rough posture, of course, which was usually combined with another for less coarse effect. But perhaps there were subtleties in that eyebrow-raising expression that Dannet did not recognize yet.

Yet. The qualifier came easily, these days. As time passed, Dannet had come to realize that the Bond's instinct had been a good one, here on Terra. Humans were indeed far more advanced and subtle than she had ever imagined when she first arrived. She still didn't like them much, aside from a few individuals, but she no longer felt much in the way of derision, either.

As it happened, she had already come to the conclusion that Caitlin Kralik and her husband were two of the humans whom she did like. So she was not entirely surprised at Caitlin's next words.

"Why would we not choose you, Terra-Captain?" was her counter-question. "You performed superbly in the expedition to NGC 7293. And you are already familiar with most of the central figures who will be involved in the explora—ah, Operation Sagittarius. Myself, Major Tully—Colonel Tully, now—and the Krants. The only real question is how well you will handle the duties of commanding a fleet instead of a single ship." She gave Dannet a wide smile. "But none of us have any real doubts on that matter. If for no other reason, because we are quite certain that Narvo would have selected you very carefully—and with eventual fleet command in mind."

Subtle, indeed. Dannet had assumed that almost all humans would still react to anything Narvo with nothing but antagonism. Neither she nor the Narvo kochan leaders had expected that hostility would abate in less than a generation. But it seemed that was not true, at least for some of them—and those, very highly placed and influential.

Dannet nodded stiffly, doing her best to mimic that human gesture. That had the advantage of lowering her head, so she could disguise her momentary amusement. Quite obviously, Caitlin had intended to use the human term "exploration," before realizing that to most Jao its use would seem frivolous. So she'd substituted the ponderous alternative "Operation Sagittarius."

Dannet lifted her head back up. And was careful not to let anything in her body posture betray the fact that she herself was one of those few Jao who thought exploration for its own sake was well worth the effort and resources.

Aille spoke next. "You understand that Caitlin will have *oudh*, when it comes to the basic mission? I am certain she will consult with you closely, as will General Kralik, but any final decisions will be hers. Your authority is over the fleet and naval matters."

Dannet nodded again. Despite the powerful naval forces that were to be committed to the expedition—no fewer than three *Lexington*-class vessels, along with a large number of smaller ships—the purpose of the project was not primarily military. And besides...

She really did approve of the human Caitlin. She foresaw no major problems.

But all she said was, "Yes, Governor."

The Captain

Glumly, Tully stared into his beer. Now that the initial excitement of deciding on the exploratory expedition—no, they were calling it something pompous and stupid; "Operation Riders of the Purple Sage" or something like that—was over, the darker realities were setting in.

Yeah, fine, he'd been promoted to colonel and he'd be in command of an entire regiment and he even got along fairly well with Ed Kralik, who'd be in overall command of the ground forces attached to the expedition. But Tully also knew damn good and well that Kralik had stiff notions concerning the military proprieties.

True, the expedition was going to have a strong scientific component, as well. Maybe some of those scientists would be female, reasonably young—colonel or not, Tully was still shy of thirty—and not too hard to look at.

And willing to overlook the fact that Tully didn't have a high school diploma, much less a college degree. Just a don't-look-too-close Resistance version of a GED.

Yeah, sure. A blue-collar lady astrophysicist or astronomer. Not impossible, no. Just about as likely, Tully figured, as snow in August.

In Florida.

He looked up, and his dark mood got darker. Speak of the devil, and his minion is sure to sashay up. His very off-limits minion.

But he let none of it show. Without quite looking at her, he waved his hand and said: "Have a seat, Lieutenant Miller. Can I buy you a beer?"

"Yes, thank you," she said, sitting across from him in the corner booth in the officers club. "But it's Captain Miller, now. I just got promoted."

She pointed to the insignia on her cap. Now that he looked directly, Tully saw that there were two bars instead of one.

"Congratulations, Caewithe. I'll be sorry to see you go, though. I don't have an opening for a captain in my regiment. Which unit is Kralik assigning you to?"

Miller shook her head. "I'm not under Kralik's command at all. Not Ed Kralik, that is. The powers-that-be decided that Caitlin Kralik needed a special unit of her own. Call it an expanded bodyguard—that's how we apes would look at it—or call it her own personal service, the way the Jao would look at it. Either way, I'm going to be a captain in charge of a platoon-sized force that really ought to have a lieutenant in command except Caitlin told me privately she likes working with me and figures I'll be more in the way of a civilian adviser than a soldier. Assuming nobody tries to kill her, anyway, at which point my formal gorilla status kicks back in."

She gave Tully a big smile. The sort of big smile that a first-grade teacher bestows on one of her brighter students, when she expects him to solve a problem all on his own.

Tully's mind was racing. *Special unit. Answers directly to Caitlin Kralik. Not connected to the regular military force at all. Not even indirectly part of my chain of command.*

Hot diggedy damn. Well…

"I guess this a stupid question, Captain, but…" Tully waved over one of the waitresses. "Ah…what sort of an education did you pick up along the way?"

By now, Miller had taken off her cap and the waitress had arrived. "I'll have what he's having," she told her. Then, gave Tully the same sort of smile that a first-grade teacher gives one of her brighter students when the stout lad is struggling with the problem but making forward progress. "About what you'd expect. Northern California got hit pretty hard during the Conquest, and, like I said, my family were dockworkers."

She shrugged, using the gesture to get out of her jacket at the same time. "One year in community college, that was it."

The heavy jacket was well suited for Colorado coming into winter but did absolutely nothing for her figure. Tully thought the change was splendid. The answer was even better.

"Well, then. I was wondering, Captain—ah, Caewithe—what you are doing Friday night?"

She bestowed on him the same smile that first-grade teachers bestow on one of their brighter students when the plucky lad finally gets the answer right.

"What a coincidence. As it happens, Colonel Tully—Gabe, rather—I'm at loose ends this coming Friday night."

The smile widened, and lost any trace of the schoolteacher.

"I'm at loose ends Saturday morning, too," she said. "As it happens."

Tully took a long swallow of his beer. By the time he finished, her beer had arrived. He held up his glass in a little salute.

"Here's to Operation Riders of the Purple Sage."

She clinked glasses with him, chuckling. "It's Operation Sagittarius, Gabe. They named it after the galactic arm we're in, not a Zane Grey western."

"And a good thing, too," he said. "A galactic arm is way bigger than Texas. Which way are we going, have they decided yet?"

"Inward, Caitlin tells me. The brains figure there's more chance of finding intelligent life that way, at least until we start getting too close to the center."

Tully summoned up his knowledge of astronomy. It was fairly rudimentary, but some things are pretty basic, too. "We're about two-thirds out on the arm, if I remember right."

She nodded. "Yes, you are. Which means this is likely to be a long expedition."

That was a devil's minion type smile, if Tully had ever seen one.

"I'm at loose ends Sunday and Monday, too," Caewithe added. "As it happens."

GLOSSARY

Jao terms

ata: Suffix indicating a group formed for instructional purposes.

az: Jao measurement, slightly longer than a yard.

azet: Jao measurement, about three fourths of a mile.

bau: A short carved baton, usually but not always made of wood, issued by a kochan to those of its members it considers fit for high command. The bau serves as an emblem of military achievement, with carvings added to match the bau-holder's accomplishments.

bauta: An individual who has retired from service honorably and has chosen to relinquish his automatic kochan ties.

bodyspeech: Postures, used to communicate emotions.

bodystyle: Individual kochan's style in bodyspeech.

dehabia: Traditional soft, thick blankets used for lounging.

dry-foot: Dry-footed, as in incapable of swimming; insult.

early-light: The period between dawn and early morning.

emerged: Officially released from one's childhood (as in natal pool).

first-mate: First sexual partner in one's marriage group.

first-light: Dawn.

formal movement: Codified postures, taught to young Jao.

fraghta: An older and experienced batman/valet/advisor/bodyguard assigned to young Jao of high kochan status.

framepoint: A stargate, the means for interstellar transit.

hai tau: Life-in-motion.

heartward: Right.

jinau: Sepoy troops recruited from conquered species.

jints: Huge, lumbering land animals native to Mannat Kar, one of the Krant homeworlds, notable for their awkwardness.

kochan: Jao clan. The term is used also to refer to "root clans" or "great kochan."

kochanata: Instructional group taught in the kochan.

kochanau: The leader of the clan, at any given time, chosen by the elders. The office is neither hereditary nor permanent, although some kochanau retain it for long periods of time.

kroudh: Outlawed, officially severed from one's clan.

last-sun: Yesterday.

late-dark: Midnight or after.

late-light: Afternoon.

lurret: A large herbivore found on Hadiru, a Dano world. Specifically, an old rogue male, notorious for its belligerence and unstable temperament.

mank: Sea creature that inhabits Mannat Kar, about the size of a manatee, very strong swimmer, not aggressive.

medician: Combination of doctor and medical technician.

mirrat: Small finned swimmers on Jithra's homeworld.

namth camiti: To be of highest ranking in an emergent generation, sometimes referred as "of the clearest water." Loosely equivalent, in human terms, to graduating first in the class from a military academy.

natal compound: Where one was born.

Naukra: Assembly of all the kochan called to deal with a specific issue.

next-sun: Tomorrow.

ollnat: Conceiving of things-that-never-were, or what-might-be, lies, imagination, creativity, etc. It is a quality mostly lacking in Jao, except in a frivolous manner.

oudh: In charge, having official authority in a situation.

pool-sib: Children born during the same season of mating so that they are raised together: they may or may not be born of the same parents; the relationship is equally close, either way.

sant jin: A formal question requiring a formal answer.

smoothface: An insult, implying no incised bars of rank or experience; roughly equivalent to such humans expressions as "wet behind the ears" or "greenhorn."

stub-ears: An insult.

tak: Woody substance burned for its aromatic scent.

taif: A kochan-in-formation, affiliated to and under the protection and guidance of a kochan.

timeblind: Having no innate sense of time as the Jao do.

timesense: Innate ability to judge the passage of time and sense when something will happen.

vai camiti: The characteristic facial pattern by which one may often recognize a Jao's kochan; faint vai camiti are considered undesirable, a mark of homeliness.

vaim: Traditional Jao greeting between two who are approximately equal in status. Can also be used as a compliment by a higher status Jao to a lower. The literal translation is "We see each other."

vaish: Traditional Jao greeting of inferior to superior. The literal translation is "I see you."

vaist: Traditional Jao greeting of superior to inferior. The literal translation is "You see me."

vithrik: Duty, what one owes to others, the necessity of making one's self of use.

what-is: Reality.

what-might-be: Something imagined.

windward: Left.

wrem-fa: A technique of instruction through body-learning in which nothing is explained, laid down in the brain too deep for conscious understanding. Also, in a broader sense, used to refer to life experience.

Lleix terms

Boh: Ancient guardian spirits, left behind during the exodus.

Children's Court: Home for youth before they are released for the Festival of Choosing that takes place in their fifteenth year; if they are not chosen, they must live thereafter in the *dochaya*.

dochaya: Unskilled laborers' living area at the far edge of the city, a slum.

elian: Social and occupational grouping; similar to a human caste, except members are selected, not born into it.

Han: Meeting of all the most senior elders of the *elian*.

Last-of-Days: Long foretold time when the Ekhat will finally exterminate the Lleix.

newest: Term of low age-rank.

oyas-to: Shunning, not-seeing, disciplinary mode for being disharmonious and flaunting social order.

sensho: The correct manner of behavior which includes order in the Han and *elian* according to age-rank.

shortest: Term of low age-rank.

unassigned: Those without an *elian* who must live in the dochaya.

vahl: Black cosmetic stick with which to emphasize the upswept lines of the eye.

APPENDIX A:
THE EKHAT

The Ekhat are an ancient species which began spreading though the galaxy millions of years ago, an expansion which reached its peak before the onset of what human geologists call the Pleistocene Age on Earth. That final period of expansion is called by the Ekhat themselves, depending on which of the factions is speaking, either the *Melodious Epoch*, the *Discordance*, or by a phrase which is difficult to translate but might loosely be called the *Absent Orchestration of Right Harmony.*

Three of the four major Ekhat factions, whatever their other differences—the Melody and both factions of the Harmony—agree that this period was what humans would call a "golden age," although the Harmony is sharply critical of some of its features. A fourth faction, the Interdict, considers it to have been an unmitigated disaster. The golden age ended in a disaster usually known as the Collapse. (See below for details.)

The era which preceded this golden age is unclear. Even the location of their original home planet is no longer known to the Ekhat. They spread slowly throughout the galactic arm by use of sub-light-speed vessels, and in the course of that expansion began to differentiate into a number of subspecies, some of which became distinct species, unable to crossbreed with other Ekhat lines.

The Ekhat today are a genus, not a species, and some human scholars even think it would be more accurate to characterize them as a family. They are widespread throughout the galactic arm, but are not very numerous on any particular planet. That is partly because they are a slow-breeding species, and partly because they are still recovering from the devastations of the Collapse.

The golden age began when Ekhat scientists discovered the principles behind the Frame Network, a method used to circumvent the lightspeed barrier. By then, they were already widely dispersed and the Frame Network enabled them to reunite their disparate branches into a single entity. Whether that entity was purely cultural and economic, or involved political unification, is a matter of sharp debate. This is, in fact, one of the main issues in dispute among the factions of the Ekhat in the modern era.

It is unclear how long this golden age lasted. The lack of clarity is primarily with the beginnings of the era. There is much greater agreement about its end: approximately two million years ago, the entire Frame Network disintegrated in what is usually known as the Collapse (although the Interdict faction calls it the Rectification or the Purging).

The collapse of the Network was quite clearly accompanied by (and probably caused by) a massive civil war which erupted among the Ekhat and quickly engulfed their entire region of galactic space. By the end, Ekhat civilization was in ruins and most Ekhat had perished. There was an enormous amount of collateral damage, including the extinction of many other intelligent species.

Slowly and painfully, in the time which followed, three different Ekhat centers were able to rebuild themselves and begin to reconstruct the Network. Two of them did so for the purpose of restoring the Ekhat to their former position (although one of them proposes doing so along radically different lines) and another wishes to prevent it.

The factions can be roughly depicted in the following manner:

THE MELODY

The Melody can be considered the "orthodox" faction. It believes the "golden age" was truly golden, an era during which the different strains of the Ekhat were working together toward the ultimate goal of merging and becoming a species which would be "divine" in its nature.

The Ekhat notion of "divinity" is difficult for humans to grasp, and can sometimes be more clearly expressed in quasi-musical rather than religious terminology. Each branch of the Ekhat contributes to the slowly emerging "supreme work of art" which is the "destiny" of the Ekhat. No faction of the Ekhat seems to have anything close to the human notion of "God." The closest parallel in human philosophy is probably Hegel's notion of God-in-self-creation, except that the Ekhat see themselves, not some outside deity, as what Hegel would call the Subject.

The Melody advocates a pluralistic approach to Ekhat advancement. They are insistent that no single branch of the Ekhat is superior to any other, and that the "emergence of divinity" (or "unfolding of the perfect melody") will require the input of all Ekhat. In this sense, they are supremely tolerant of all the distinctions and differences within the genus.

But, while they tolerate differences, they do not tolerate exclusion or isolation. Since, according to them, the talents of all Ekhat will be needed for "divine emergence," no Ekhat can withhold themselves from the developing "Melody." In this, they are a bit like the old Roman or Mongol emperors: you can believe whatever you want, but you must submit to Melody rule and you must subscribe (formally, at least) to the Melodic creed. In short, they are uncompromising "imperialists."

On the other hand, the Melody is utterly hostile—genocidal, in fact—toward any intelligent species which cannot trace its lineage back to the Ekhat. All non-Ekhat species are an obstacle to the Ekhat's "divine emergence," considered by them to be static or noise impeding the "perfect melody." The Melody envisions a universe in which the transformed Ekhat are all that remains.

Scholars suspect the Melody's eventual goal is to exterminate all non-Ekhat life of any kind. The Melody believes the Ekhat were well on their way toward "divine emergence" when the sudden and unexpected treason of a faction which they call (translating roughly) the *Cowardly Retreat* or the *Deaf Lesion* launched a vicious campaign of sabotage which brought down the Network and collapsed Ekhat civilization across the galactic arm.

Human scholars believe that the *Cowardly Retreat* is essentially identical with the faction known in the modern era as the Interdict. What can be determined of current Melodic policy seems to substantiate that belief—the Melody is utterly hostile to the Interdict and will slaughter them on sight.

THE HARMONY

The Harmony arose after the collapse of the Network and can be considered the "revisionist" wing of the Ekhat. They believe the civil war which produced the great collapse was due to the anarchic and disorderly nature of Ekhat civilization which led up to it, an era they do not consider to be a "golden age" so much as a "bronze age." (Keep in mind that these are very rough human approximations of mental concepts which, in the case of the Ekhat, are difficult for other intelligent species to analyze.)

In the view of the Harmony, all Ekhat are not equal. Basing themselves on what they believe is a true genetic picture of Ekhat evolution, the Harmony ranks different branches of the Ekhat genus (or family) on different levels. All Ekhat have a place in the new "Harmony," but, to use a human analogy, some get to be first violinists and others belong in the back beating on kettle drums.

The Harmony ranks different Ekhat branches according to how closely they fit the original Ekhat stock. The closer, the better; the farther apart, the more inferior. Not surprisingly, they consider the Ekhat branch which inhabited the planet where the Harmony first began spreading as the "true Ekhat." In fact, they seem to believe that theirs is the home planet of the Ekhat (which no one else does, and the claim is apparently very threadbare).

The Harmony advocates a genetically determined hierarchy, in which all Ekhat will have a place, but in which (for most of them) that place will be subordinate.

To complicate things further, the Harmony is split by an internal division of its own. The *True Harmony* believes the rankings of the Ekhat species are permanent and fixed. The *Complete Harmony* believes all Ekhat, no matter how lowly their genetic status at the moment, can eventually be uplifted into "complete Ekhat-dom."

This division, whose ideology is murky from the outside, does have a major impact on the external policies of the different wings of the Harmony. The True Harmony shares the basic attitude of the Melody toward non-Ekhat intelligent species: they are destined for extermination. The Complete Harmony, on the other hand, believes that non-Ekhat species have a place in the universe. The process of uplifting all Ekhat will require replacing the "sub-Ekhat" strains with other intelligent species to, in essence, do the scut work. The flip side of "improving" all Ekhat is to subjugate and enslave all non-Ekhat.

It was this wing of the Harmony which uplifted the Jao into full sentience.

THE INTERDICT

Of all the Ekhat factions, the Interdict is probably the hardest to understand. The closest equivalent in human terms would be something like "fundamentalist, Luddite reactionary fanatics."

The core belief of the Interdict is that the Network was always an abomination. Some human scholars think that the origins of the creed were scientific—i.e., that some Ekhat scientists became convinced the Network was placing a strain on the fabric of spacetime which threatened the universe itself (or at least the portion of the galaxy where it had spread).

Whatever their scientific origins might have been, the Interdict, as it developed during the long years after the Collapse, became something far more in the nature of a mystical cult. From what can be gleaned from their extremely murky writings, the Interdict seems to believe the speed-of-light barrier is "divine" in nature and any attempt to circumvent it is "unholy."

It seems most likely that the Melody's charge against the Interdict is correct: it was they, or at least their ideological predecessors, who launched the civil war which destroyed the Network. In fact, that seems to have been the purpose of the war in the first place.

What is definitely established in the historical record is that it was the Interdict which freed the Jao. Not, of course, because of any concern over the Jao themselves, but simply to strike a blow at the Complete Harmony. It was they, as well, who provided the Jao with the initial technology to obtain control of a portion of the Network and begin to create their own stellar empire.

The fact that they did so—and still, in an off-and-on and unpredictable way, maintain a certain quasi-"alliance" with the Jao—underscores the bizarre nature of the Interdict creed. The Jao, after all, are also maintaining and even extending the Network. Yet the Interdict seems not to object.

One theory is that whatever scientific underpinnings originally lay beneath Interdict ideology have long since been lost. What has come to replace the notion that the Network itself threatens the universe is a more mystical notion that the Network is "unclean." The danger is spiritual, in other words, not physical.

One contradiction this situation presents is that in order to destroy the Network, the Interdict must use it themselves. Indeed, in many areas of the galaxy, it is they who are rebuilding the old framepoints and extending new ones. Apparently, Interdict adherents go through some sort of purification rite which allows them to do so. As always, the precise tenets of the Ekhat creed are at least murky if not quite unfathomable to non-Ekhat.

APPENDIX B:
INTERSTELLAR TRAVEL

The method of supra-light travel used by all intelligent species is usually called, by the Jao, the "Frame Network." The method involves warping spacetime using extremely powerful generators positioned in at least three widely spaced locations in the stellar neighborhood. (Three will work, but is risky; four is better; five is ideal; more than five is redundant.) These "framepoints" must be at least three light-years apart, but are not effective if the distance between any two extends much more than eleven light-years.

Existing framepoints allow ships to cross the stellar distances between them in what is effectively an instantaneous transition. There is theoretical debate over whether the transition is "really" instantaneous. But from the subjective standpoint of any human or other intelligent species, the travel is instantaneous. The dispute is whether or not it actually requires a few nanoseconds.

In essence, two framepoints working together are creating what can be called an artificial wormhole. New territory, where there does not exist a framepoint, can be reached in one of two ways. One way is to use sub-light exploratory ships. Once arrived at a suitable location for a new framepoint, the ship (or multiship expedition) can begin to create the new framepoint, which can then begin to participate in extending the entire Frame Network.

Of course, this method of extending the Frame is very slow. The other method is to use existing FP generators to create what is called a "Point Locus."

Triangulating (more often: quadri-angulating or quint-angulating) their power, these framepoint generators can create a temporary Point Locus at a distance. For a certain period of time, ships can travel to the Point Locus from any one of the FP generators which created it.

This is the normal method used for invasion fleets, since it is impossible to invade a framepoint held by an enemy. (They just "turn off" their end of the Network and the invaders vanish, no one knows exactly where.) Invaders from the outside can triangulate on an enemy solar system, create a point locus which is independent of the enemy's side of the Network, and send an invasion fleet that way.

The expense and risk involved are considerable, however. Point loci tend to be unstable over any extended period of time, so the window of opportunity for an invasion is limited. To use an historical analogy, each invasion is like a major amphibious assault during World War II. If a large enough beachhead is not secured quickly, the invasion will face disaster by being stranded and overrun. Moreover, because of the impossibility of matching loci in open space, the point locus must always be created within the photosphere of a star. In essence, the star itself serves the participating frame generators as a common target. But that obviously presents its own set of dangers.

How unstable and temporary a point locus proves to be varies according to a wide range of factors. These include: the number of FP generators used, distance, and a multitude of more subtle factors involving a lot of specific features of the galactic neighborhood—dust cloud densities, nearby novas or neutron stars, etc. Creating a point locus is as much an art as a science, as well as being extremely expensive, and is never something to be undertaken lightly.